KINCAID'S BATTERY

"If any one alive," he cried, "knows any cause why this thing should not be"

KINCAID'S BATTERY

BY

GEORGE W. CABLE

ILLUSTRATED BY

ALONZO KIMBALL

CHARLES SCRIBNER'S SONS
NEW YORK :: :: :: :: :: 1908

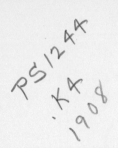

𝕿o
E. C. S. **C.**

CONTENTS

Contents

Contents

Contents

ILLUSTRATIONS

Kincaid's Battery

I

CARROLLTON GARDENS

FOR the scene of this narrative please take into mind a wide quarter-circle of country, such as any of the pretty women we are to know in it might have covered on the map with her half-opened fan.

Let its northernmost corner be Vicksburg, the famous, on the Mississippi. Let the easternmost be Mobile, and let the most southerly and by far the most important, that pivotal corner of the fan from which all its folds radiate and where the whole pictured thing opens and shuts, be New Orleans. Then let the grave moment that gently ushers us in be a long-ago afternoon in the Louisiana Delta.

Throughout that land of water and sky the willow clumps dotting the bosom of every sea-marsh and fringing every rush-rimmed lake were yellow and green in the full flush of a new year, the war year, 'Sixty-one.

Though rife with warm sunlight, the moist air gave distance and poetic charm to the nearest and humblest things. At the edges of the great timbered swamps thickets of young winter-bare cypresses were budding yet more vividly than the willows, while in the depths of those overflowed forests, near and far down their lofty gray colonnades, the dwarfed swamp-maple drooped the winged fruit of its limp bush in pink and flame-yellow and rose-red masses until it touched its own image in the still flood.

That which is now only the "sixth district" of greater New Orleans was then the small separate town of Carrollton. There the vast Mississippi, leaving the sugar and rice fields of St. Charles and St. John Baptist parishes and still seeking the Gulf of Mexico, turns from east to south before it sweeps northward and southeast again to give to the Creole capital its graceful surname of the "Crescent City." Mile-wide, brimful, head-on and boiling and writhing twenty fathoms deep, you could easily have seen, that afternoon, why its turfed levee had to be eighteen feet high and broad in proportion. So swollen was the flood that from any deck of a steamboat touching there one might have looked down upon the whole fair still suburb.

Widely it hovered in its nest of rose gardens, orange groves, avenues of water-oaks, and towering moss-draped pecans. A few hundred yards from the levee a slender railway, coming from the city, with a highway on either side, led into its station-house; but mainly the eye would have dwelt on that which filled the interval between the nearer high road and the levee—the "Carrollton Gardens."

At a corner of these grounds closest to the railway station stood a quiet hotel from whose eastern veranda it was but a step to the centre of a sunny shell-paved court where two fountains danced and tinkled to each other. Along its farther bound ran a vine-clad fence where a row of small tables dumbly invited the flushed

2

visitor to be inwardly cooled. By a narrow gate in this fence, near its townward end, a shelled walk lured on into a musky air of verdurous alleys that led and misled, crossed, doubled, and mazed among flowering shrubs from bower to bower. Out of sight in there the loiterer came at startling moments face to face with banks of splendid bloom in ravishing negligée—Diana disrobed, as it were, while that untiring sensation-hunter, the mocking-bird, leaped and sang and clapped his wings in a riot of scandalous mirth.

In the ground-floor dining-room of that unanimated hotel sat an old gentleman named Brodnax, once of the regular army, a retired veteran of the Mexican war, and very consciously possessed of large means. He sat quite alone, in fine dress thirty years out of fashion, finishing a late lunch and reading a newspaper; a trim, hale man not to be called old in his own hearing. He had read everything intended for news or entertainment and was now wandering in the desert of the advertising columns, with his mind nine miles away, at the other end of New Orleans.

Although not that person whom numerous men of his acquaintance had begun affectionately to handicap with the perilous nickname of "the ladies' man," he was thinking of no less than five ladies; two of one name and three of another. Flora Valcour and her French grandmother (as well as her brother of nineteen, already agog to be off in the war) had but lately come to New Orleans, from Mobile. On a hilly border of that smaller Creole city stood the home they had left, too isolated, with war threatening, for women to occupy alone. Mrs. Callender was the young widow

3

of this old bachelor's life-long friend, the noted judge of
that name, then some two years deceased. Constance
and Anna were her step-daughters, the latter (if you
would believe him) a counterpart of her long-lost,
beautiful mother, whose rejection of the soldier's suit,
when he was a mere lieutenant, was the well-known
cause of his singleness. These Callender ladies,
prompted by him and with a sweet modesty of quietness, had just armed a new field battery with its six
splendid brass guns, and it was around these three
Callenders that his ponderings now hung; especially
around Anna and in reference to his much overprized
property and two nephews: Adolphe Irby, for whom
he had obtained the command of this battery, which he
was to see him drill this afternoon, and Hilary Kincaid,
who had himself cast the guns and who was to help the
senior cousin conduct these evolutions.

The lone reader's glance loitered down a long row of
slim paragraphs, each beginning with the same wee
picture of a steamboat whether it proclaimed the
Grand Duke or the *Louis d'Or*, the *Ingomar* bound for
the "Lower Coast," or the *Natchez* for "Vicksburg
and the Bends." Shifting the page, he read of the
Swiss Bell-Ringers as back again "after a six years'
absence," and at the next item really knew what he
read. It was of John Owens' appearance, every night,
as *Caleb Plummer* in "Dot," "performance to begin at
seven o'clock." Was it there Adolphe would this
evening take his party, of which the dazzling Flora
would be one and Anna, he hoped, another? He had
proposed this party to Adolphe, agreeing to bear its
whole cost if the nephew would manage to include in

Carrollton Gardens

it Anna and Hilary. And Irby had duly reported complete success and drawn on him, but the old soldier still told his doubts to the newspaper.

"Adolphe has habits," he meditated, "but success is not one of them."

Up and down a perpendicular procession on the page he every now and then mentally returned the salute of the one little musketeer of the same height as the steamboat's chimneys, whether the Attention he challenged was that of the Continentals, the Louisiana Grays, Orleans Cadets, Crescent Blues or some other body of blithe invincibles. Yet his thought was still of Anna. When Adolphe, last year, had courted her, and the hopeful uncle had tried non-intervention, she had declined him—"and oh, how wisely!" For then back to his native city came Kincaid after years away at a Northern military school and one year across the ocean, and the moment the uncle saw him he was glad Adolphe had failed. But now if she was going to find Hilary as light-headed and cloying as Adolphe was thick-headed and sour, or if she must see Hilary go soft on the slim Mobile girl—whom Adolphe was already so torpidly enamored of—"H-m-m-m!"

Two young men who had tied their horses behind the hotel crossed the white court toward the garden. They also were in civil dress, yet wore an air that goes only with military training. The taller was Hilary Kincaid, the other his old-time, Northern-born-and-bred school chum, Fred Greenleaf. Kincaid, coming home, had found him in New Orleans, on duty at Jackson Barracks, and for some weeks they had enjoyed cronying. Now they had been a day or two

apart and had chanced to meet again at this spot.
Kincaid, it seems, had been looking at a point hard by
with a view to its fortification. Their manner was
frankly masterful though they spoke in guarded tones.

"No," said Kincaid, "you come with me to this
drill. Nobody'll take offence."

"Nor will you ever teach your cousin to handle a
battery," replied Greenleaf, with a sedate smile.

"Well, he knows things we'll never learn. Come
with me, Fred, else I can't see you till theatre's out—
if I go there with her—and you say——"

"Yes, I want you to go with her," murmured Greenleaf, so solemnly that Kincaid laughed outright.

"But, after the show, of course," said the laugher,
"you and I'll ride, eh?" and then warily, "You've
taken your initials off all your stuff? . . . Yes, and
Jerry's got your ticket. He'll go down with your
things, check them all and start off on the ticket himself. Then, as soon as you——"

"But will they allow a slave to do so?"

"With my pass, yes; 'Let my black man, Jerry——'"
The garden took the pair into its depths a moment
too soon for the old soldier to see them as he came out
upon the side veranda with a cloud on his brow that
showed he had heard his nephew's laugh.

Carriage Company

II

CARRIAGE COMPANY

BAREHEADED the uncle crossed the fountained court, sat down at a table and read again. In the veranda a negro, his own slave, hired to this hotel, held up an elegant military cap, struck an inquiring attitude, and called softly, "Gen'al?"

"Bring it with the coffee."

But the negro instantly brought it without the coffee and placed it on the table with a delicate flourish, shuffled a step back and bowed low:

"Coffee black, Gen'al, o' co'se?"

"Black as your grandmother."

The servant tittered: "Yas, suh, so whah it flop up-siden de cup it leave a lemon-yalleh sta-ain."

He capered away, leaving the General to the little steamboats and to a blessed ignorance of times to be when at "Vicksburg and the Bends" this same waiter would bring his coffee made of corn-meal bran and muddy water, with which to wash down scant snacks of mule meat. The listless eye still roamed the arid page as the slave returned with the fragrant pot and cup, but now the sitter laid it by, lighted a cigar and mused:—

In this impending war the South would win, of course —oh, God is just! But this muser could only expect to fall at the front. Then his large estate, all lands and slaves, five hundred souls—who would inherit that and hold it together? Held together it must be! Any partition of it would break no end of sacredly humble

7

household and family ties and work spiritual havoc incalculable. There must be but one heir. Who? Hilary's mother had been in heaven these many years, the mother of Adolphe eighteen months; months quite enough to show the lone brother how vast a loss is the absence of the right mistress from such very human interests as those of a great plantation. Not only must there be but one heir, but he *must have the right wife*.

The schemer sipped. So it was Anna for Hilary if he could bring it about. So, too, it must be Hilary for his adjutant-general, to keep him near enough to teach him the management of the fortune coming to him if he, Hilary, would only treat his kind uncle's wishes— reasonably. With the cup half lifted he harkened. From a hidden walk and bower close on the garden side of this vine-mantled fence sounded footsteps and voices:

"But, Fred! where on earth did she get—let's sit in here—get that rich, belated, gradual smile?"

A memory thrilled the listening General. "From her mother," thought he, and listened on.

"It's like," continued his nephew— "I'll tell you what it's like. It's like— Now, let me alone! You see, one has to *learn* her beauty—by degrees. You know, there *is* a sort of beauty that flashes on you at first sight, like—like the blaze of a ball-room. I was just now thinking of a striking instance——"

"From Mobile? You always are."

"No such thing! Say, Fred, I'll tell you what Miss Anna's smile is like. It's as if you were trying—say in a telescope—for a focus, and at last all at once it comes and—there's your star!"

Carriage Company

The Northerner softly assented.

"Fred! Fancy Flora Valcour with that smile!"

"No! Hilary Kincaid, I think you were born to believe in every feminine creature God ever made. No wonder they nickname you as they do. Now, some girls are quite too feminine for me."

In his own smoke the General's eyes opened aggressively. But hark! His nephew spoke again:

"Fred, if you knew all that girl has done for that boy and that grandmother— It may sound like an overstatement, but you must have observed——"

"That she's a sort of overstatement herself?"

"Go to grass! *Your* young lady's not even an understatement; she's only a profound pause. See here! what time is it? I prom——"

On the uncle's side of the fence a quick step brought a newcomer, a Creole of maybe twenty-nine years, member of his new staff, in bright uniform:

"Ah, Général, yo' moze ob-edient! Never less al-lone then when al-lone? 'T is the way with myseff——"

He seemed not unrefined, though of almost too mettlesome an eye; in length of leg showing just the lack, in girth of waist just the excess, to imply a better dignity on horseback and to allow a proud tailor to prove how much art can overcome. Out on the road a liveried black coachman had halted an open carriage, in which this soldier had arrived with two ladies. Now these bowed delightedly from it to the General, while Kincaid and his friend stood close hid and listened agape, equally amused and dismayed.

"How are you, Mandeville?" said the General. "I am not nearly as much alone as I seem, sir!"

9

A voice just beyond the green-veiled fence cast a light on this reply and brought a flush to the Creole's very brows. "Alas! Greenleaf," it cried, "we search in vain! He is not here! We are even more alone than we seem! Ah! where is that peerless chevalier, my beloved, accomplished, blameless, sagacious, just, valiant and amiable uncle? Come let us press on. Let not the fair sex find him first and snatch him from us forever!"

The General's scorn showed only in his eyes as they met the blaze of Mandeville's. "You were about to remark—?" he began, but rose and started toward the carriage.

There not many minutes later you might have seen the four men amicably gathered and vying in clever speeches to pretty Mrs. Callender and her yet fairer though less scintillant step-daughter Anna.

III

THE GENERAL'S CHOICE

ANNA CALLENDER. In the midst of the gay skirmish and while she yielded Greenleaf her chief attention, Hilary observed her anew.

What he thought he saw was a golden-brown profusion of hair with a peculiar richness in its platted coils, an unconsciously faultless poise of head, and, equally unconscious, a dreamy softness of sweeping lashes. As she laughed with the General her student noted further what seemed to him a rare silkiness in the tresses, a vapory lightness in the short strands that played over

Anna

the outlines of temple and forehead, and the unstudied daintiness with which they gathered into the merest mist of a short curl before her exquisite ear.

But when now she spoke with him these charms became forgettable as he discovered, or fancied he did, in her self-oblivious eyes, a depth of thought and feeling not in the orbs alone but also in the brows and lids, and between upper and under lashes as he glimpsed them in profile while she turned to Mandeville. And now, unless his own insight misled him, he observed how unlike those eyes, and yet how subtly mated with them, was her mouth; the delicate rising curve of the upper lip, and the floral tenderness with which it so faintly overhung the nether, wherefrom it seemed ever about to part yet parted only when she spoke or smiled.

"A child's mouth and a woman's eyes," he mused.

When her smiles came the mouth remained as young as before, yet suddenly, as truly as the eyes, showed—showed him at least—steadfastness of purpose, while the eyes, where fully half the smile was, still unwittingly revealed their depths of truth.

"Poor Fred!" he pondered as the General and Mandeville entered the carriage and it turned away.

A mile or two from Carrollton down the river and toward the city lay the old unfenced fields where Hilary had agreed with Irby to help him manœuvre his very new command. Along the inland edge of this plain the railway and the common road still ran side by side, but the river veered a mile off. So Mandeville pointed out to the two ladies as they, he, and the General drove up to the spot with Kincaid and Greenleaf as outriders. The chosen ground was a level stretch of wild turf

maybe a thousand yards in breadth, sparsely dotted
with shoulder-high acacias. No military body was yet
here, and the carriage halted at the first good view
point.

Mrs. Callender, the only member of her family who
was of Northern birth and rearing, was a small slim
woman whose smile came whenever she spoke and
whose dainty nose went all to merry wrinkles whenever
she smiled. It did so now, in the shelter of her diminu-
tive sunshade opened flat against its jointed handle to
fend off the strong afternoon beams, while she explained
to Greenleaf—dismounted beside the wheels with Mandeville—that Constance, Anna's elder sister, would
arrive by and by with Flora Valcour. "Connie," she
said, had been left behind in the clutches of the dressmaker!

"Flora," she continued, crinkling her nose ever so
kind-heartedly at Greenleaf, "is Lieutenant Mandeville's cousin, you know. Didn't he tell you something
back yonder in Carrollton?"

Greenleaf smiled an admission and her happy eyes
closed to mere chinks. What had been told was that
Constance had yesterday accepted Mandeville.

"Yes," jovially put in the lucky man, "I have di-
vulge' him that, and he seem' almoze as glad as the
young lady herseff!"

Even to this the sweet widow's misplaced wrinkles
faintly replied, while Greenleaf asked, "Does the
Lieutenant's good fortune account for the —'clutches
of the dressmaker'?"

It did. The Lieutenant hourly expecting to be ordered
to the front, this wedding, like so many others, would

The General's Choice

be at the earliest day possible. "A great concession," the lady said, turning her piquant wrinkles this time upon Mandeville. But just here the General engrossed attention. His voice had warmed sentimentally and his kindled eye was passing back and forth between Anna seated by him and Hilary close at hand in the saddle. He waved wide:

"This all-pervading haze and perfume, dew and dream," he was saying, "is what makes this the Lalla Rookh's land it is!" He smiled at himself and confessed that Carrollton Gardens always went to his head. "Anna, did you ever hear your mother sing—

"'There's a bower of roses—'?"

She lighted up to say yes, but the light was all he needed to be lured on through a whole stanza, and a tender sight—Ocean silvering to brown-haired Cynthia—were the two, as he so innocently strove to recreate out of his own lost youth, for her and his nephew, this atmosphere of poetry.

"'To sit in the roses and hear the bird's song!'"

he suavely ended—"I used to make Hilary sing that for me when he was a boy."

"Doesn't he sing it yet?" asked Mrs. Callender.

"My God, madame, since I found him addicted to comic songs I've never asked him!"

Kincaid led the laugh and the talk became lively. Anna was merrily accused by Miranda (Mrs. Callender) of sharing the General's abhorrence of facetious song. First she pleaded guilty and then reversed her plea with an absurd tangle of laughing provisos delightful even to herself. At the same time the General withdrew from his nephew all imputation of a frivolous mind, though the nephew avowed himself nonsensical from birth and destined to die so. It was a merry moment, so merry that Kincaid's bare mention of Mandeville as Mandy made even the General smile and every one else laugh. The Creole, to whom any mention of himself, (whether it called for gratitude or for pistols and coffee,) was always welcome, laughed longest. If he was Mandy, he hurried to rejoin, the absent Constance "muz be Candy—ha, ha, ha!" And when Anna said Miranda should always thenceforth be Randy, and Mrs. Callender said Anna ought to be Andy, and the very General was seduced into suggesting that then Hilary would be Handy, and when every one read in every one's eye, the old man's included, that Brodnax would naturally be Brandy, the Creole bent and wept with mirth, counting all that fine wit exclusively his.

"But, no!" he suddenly said, "Hilary he would be Dandy, bic-ause he's call' the ladies' man!"

"No, sir!" cried the General. "Hil—" He turned upon his nephew, but finding him engaged with Anna, faced round to his chum: "For Heaven's sake, Greenleaf, does he allow——?"

"He can't help it now," laughed his friend, "he's tagged it on himself by one of his songs."

"Oh, by Jove, Hilary, it serves you right for singing them!"

Hilary laughed to the skies, the rest echoing.

"A ladies' man!" the uncle scoffed on. "Of all things on God's earth!" But there he broke into lordly mirth: "Don't you believe *that* of him, ladies,

The General's Choice

at any rate.   If only for my sake, Anna, don't you *ever* believe a breath of it!"

The ladies laughed again, but now Kincaid found them a distraction.   Following his glance cityward they espied a broad dust-cloud floating off toward the river. He turned to Anna and softly cried, "Here come your guns, trying to beat the train!"

The ladies stood up to see.   An unseen locomotive whistled for a brief stop.   The dust-cloud drew nearer. The engine whistled to start again, and they could hear its bell and quickening puff.   But the dust-cloud came on and on, and all at once the whole six-gun battery— six horses to each piece and six to each caisson—captain, buglers, guidon, lieutenants, sergeants and drivers in the saddle, cannoneers on the chests—swept at full trot, thumping, swaying, and rebounding, up the highway and off it, and, forming sections, swung out upon the field in double column, while the roaring train rolled by it and slowed up to the little frame box of Buerthe's Station with passengers cheering from every window.

The Callenders' carriage horses were greatly taxed in their nerves, yet they kept their discretion.   Kept it even when now the battery flashed from column into line and bore down upon them, the train meanwhile whooping on toward Carrollton.   And what an elated flock of brightly dressed citizens and citizenesses had alighted from the cars—many of them on the moment's impulse—to see these dear lads, with their romantically acquired battery, train for the holiday task of scaring the dastard foe back to their frozen homes!   How we loved the moment's impulse those days!

15

What a gay show! And among the very prettiest and most fetchingly arrayed newcomers you would quickly have noticed three with whom this carriage group exchanged signals. Kincaid spurred off to meet them while Greenleaf and Mandeville helped Anna and Miranda to the ground. "There's Constance," said the General.

"Yes," Mrs. Callender replied, "and Flora and Charlie Valcour!" as if that were the gleefulest good luck of all.

IV

MANŒUVRES.

CAPTAIN IRBY, strong, shapely, well clad, auburn-haired, left his halted command and came into the carriage group, while from the train approached his cousin and the lithe and picturesque Miss Valcour.

The tallish girl always looked her best beside some manly form of unusual stature, and because that form now was Hilary's Irby was aggrieved. All their days his cousin had been getting into his light, and this realization still shaded his brow as Kincaid yielded Flora to him and returned to Anna to talk of things too light for record.

Not so light were the thoughts Anna kept unuttered. Here again, she reflected, was he who (according to Greenleaf) had declined to command her guns in order to let Irby have them. Why? In kindness to his cousin, or in mild dislike of a woman's battery? If intuition was worth while, this man was soon to be a captain somewher:. Here was that rare find for which even maid-

ens' eyes were alert those days—a born leader. No
ladies' man this—"of all things on God's earth!" A
men's man! And yet—nay, *therefore*—a man for some
unparagoned woman some day to yield her heart and
life to, and to have for her very own, herself his con-
summate adornment. She cast a glance at Flora.

But her next was to him as they talked on. How
nearly black was the waving abundance of his hair.
How placid his brow, above eyes whose long lashes
would have made them meltingly tender had they not
been so large with mirth: "A boy's eyes," thought she
while he remembered what he had just called hers. She
noted his mouth, how gently firm: "A man's mouth!"

Charlie Valcour broke in between them: "Is there
not going to be any drill, after all?"

"Tell Captain Irby you can't wait any longer," replied Kincaid with a mock frown and gave Anna yet
gayer attention a minute more. Then he walked beside his cousin toward the command, his horse close at
his back. The group, by pairs, chose view points.
Only Miss Valcour stayed in the carriage with the General, bent on effecting a change in his mind. In Mobile
Flora had been easily first in any social set to which she
condescended. In New Orleans, brought into the
Callenders' circles by her cousin Mandeville, she had
found herself quietly ranked second to Anna, and Anna
now yet more pointedly outshining her through the
brazen splendor of this patriotic gift of guns. For this
reason and others yet to appear she had planned a
strategy and begun a campaign, one of whose earliest
manœuvres must be to get Irby, not Kincaid, made
their uncle's adjutant-general, and therefore to persuade

the uncle that to give Kincaid the battery would endear him to Anna and so crown with victory the old man's perfectly obvious plan.

Greenleaf left his horse tied and walked apart with Anna. This, he murmured, was the last time they would be together for years.

"Yes," she replied with a disheartening composure, although from under the parasol with which he shaded her she met his eyes so kindly that his heart beat quicker. But before he could speak on she looked away to his fretting horse and then across to the battery, where a growing laugh was running through the whole undisciplined command. "What is it about?" she playfully inquired, but then saw. In response to the neigh of Greenleaf's steed Hilary's had paused an instant and turned his head, but now followed on again, while the laughter ended in the clapping of a hundred hands; for Kincaid's horse had the bridle free on his neck and was following his master as a dog follows. Irby scowled, the General set his jaws, and Hilary took his horse's bridle and led him on.

"That's what *I* want to do every time I look at him!" called Charlie to his sister.

"Then look the other way!" carolled back the slender beauty. To whom Anna smiled across in her belated way, and wondered if the impulse to follow Hilary Kincaid ever came to women.

But now out yonder the two cousins were in the saddle, Irby's sabre was out, and soon the manœuvres were fully under way. Flora, at the General's side, missed nothing of them, yet her nimble eye kept her well aware that across here in this open seclusion the desperate Greenleaf's words to Anna were rarely explanatory of the drill.

"And now," proclaimed Mandeville, "you'll see them form into line fazed to the rear!" And Flora, seeing and applauding, saw also Anna turn to her suitor a glance, half pity for him, half pleading for his pity.

"I say unless—" Greenleaf persisted——

"There is no 'unless.' There can't ever be any."

"But may I not at least say——?"

"I'd so much rather you would not," she begged.

"At present, you mean?"

"Or in the future," said Anna, and, having done perfectly thus far, spoiled all by declaring she would "never marry!" Her gaze rested far across the field on the quietly clad figure of Kincaid riding to and fro and pointing hither and yon to his gold-laced cousin. Off here on the left she heard Mandeville announcing:

"Now they'll form batt'rie to the front by throwing caisson' to the rear—look—look! . . . Ah, ha! was not that a prettie?"

Pretty it was declared to be on all sides. Flora called it "a beautiful." Part of her charm was a Creole accent much too dainty for print. Anna and Greenleaf and the other couples regathered about the carriage, and Miss Valcour from her high seat smiled her enthusiasm down among them, exalting theirs. And now as a new movement of the battery followed, and now another, her glow heightened, and she called musically to Constance, Mrs. Callender and Anna, by turns, to behold and admire. For one telling moment she was, and felt herself, the focus of her group, the centre of its living picture. Out afield yet another manœuvre was on, and while Anna and her suitor stood close below her helplessly becalmed each by each, Flora rose to her feet and caught a great breath of delight. Her gaze was on the glittering mass of men, horses, and brazen guns that came thundering across the plain in double column—Irby at its head, Kincaid alone on the flank—and sweeping right and left deployed into battery to the front with cannoneers springing to their posts for action.

"Pretties' of all!" she cried, and stood, a gentle air stirring her light draperies, until the boys at the empty guns were red-browed and short of breath in their fierce pretence of loading and firing. Suddenly the guns were limbered up and went bounding over the field, caissons in front. And now pieces passed their caissons, and now they were in line, then in double column, and presently were gleaming in battery again, faced to the rear. And now at command the tired lads dropped to the ground to rest, or sauntered from one lounging squad to another, to chat and chaff and puff cigarettes. Kincaid and Irby lent their horses to Mandeville and Charlie, who rode to the battery while the lenders joined the ladies.

Once more Hilary yielded Flora and sought Anna; but with kinder thought for Flora Anna pressed herself upon Irby, to the open chagrin of his uncle. So Kincaid cheerfully paired with Flora. But thus both he and Anna unwittingly put the finishing touch upon that change of heart in the General which Flora, by every subtlety of indirection, this hour and more in the carriage, had been bringing about.

Hilary?—Yes, Uncle?

A query: With Kincaid and Irby the chief figures in their social arena and Hilary so palpably his cousin's better in looks, in bearing, talents, and character, is it not strange that Flora, having conquest for her ruling passion, should strive so to relate Anna to Hilary as to give her, Anna, every advantage for the higher prize? Maybe it is, but she liked strangeness—and a stiff game.

V

HILARY?—YES, UNCLE?

SECOND half as well as first, the drill was ended. The low acacias and great live-oaks were casting their longest shadows. The great plain rested from the trample and whirl of hoofs, guns, and simulated battle. A whiff of dust showed where the battery ambled town-ward among roadside gardens, the Callender carriage spinning by it to hurry its three ladies and Mandeville far away to the city's lower end. At the column's head rode Irby in good spirits, having got large solace of Flora's society since we last saw her paired with Kin-caid. Now beside the tiny railway station Hilary was with her once more as she and Charlie awaited the train from town. Out afield were left only General Brodnax and Greenleaf, dismounted between the Northerner's horse and Hilary's. Now Kincaid came across the turf.

"Greenleaf," said the old soldier, "why does Hilary forever walk as though he were bringing the best joke of the season? Can't you make him quit it?"

The nephew joined them: "Uncle, if you'd like to borrow my horse I can go by train."

That *was* a joke. "H-m-m! I see! No, Greenleaf's going by train. Would you like to ride with me?"

"Well, eh—ha! Why, uncle, I—why, of course, if Fred really—" They mounted and went.

"Hilary?"

"Yes, uncle?"

"How is it now? Like my girl any better?"

"Why—yes! Oh, she's fine! And yet I——"

"You must say? What must you say?"

"Nothing much; only that she's not the kind to seem like the owner of a field battery. My goodness! uncle, if she had half Miss Flora's tang——"

"She hasn't the least need of it! She's the quiet kind, sir, that fools who love 'tang' overlook!"

"Yes," laughed Hilary, "she's quiet; quiet as a fortification by moonlight! Poor Fred! I wish——"

"Well, thank God you wish in vain! That's just been settled. I asked him—oh, don't look surprised at *me*. Good Lord! hadn't I the right to know?"

The two rode some way in silence. "I wish," mused the nephew aloud, "it could be as he wants it."

The uncle's smile was satirical: "Did you ever, my boy, wish anything could be as *I* want it?"

"Now, uncle, there's a big difference——"

"DAMN THE DIFFERENCE! I'm going to try you. I'm going to make Adolphe my adjutant-general. Then if you hanker for this battery as it hankers for you——"

"Mary, Queen of Scots!" rejoiced Hilary. "That'll suit us both to the bone! And if it suits you too——"

"Well it doesn't! You know I've never wanted Adolphe about me. But you've got me all snarled up, the whole kit of you. What's more, I don't want him for my heir nor any girl with 'tang' for mistress of my lands and people. Hilary, I swear! if you've got the sand to want Anna and she's got the grace to take you, then, adjutant-general or not, I'll leave you my whole fortune! Well, what amuses you now?"

"Why, uncle, all the cotton in New Orleans couldn't tempt me to marry the girl I wouldn't take dry so without a continental cent."

"But your own present poverty might hold you back even from the girl you wanted, mightn't it?"

"No!" laughed the nephew, "nothing would!"

"Good God! Well, if you'll want Anna I'll make it easy for you to ask for her. If not, I'll make it as hard as I can for you to get any one else."

Still Hilary laughed: "H-oh, uncle, if I loved any girl, I'd rather have her without your estate than with it." Suddenly he sobered and glowed: "I wish you'd leave it to Adolphe! He's a heap-sight better business man than I. Besides, being older, he feels he has the better right to it. You know you always counted on leaving it to him."

The General looked black: "You actually decline the gift?"

"No. No, I don't. I want to please you. But of my own free choice I wouldn't have it. I'm no abolitionist, but I don't want that kind of property. I don't want the life that has to go with it. I know other sorts that are so much better. I'm not thinking only of the moral responsibility——"

"By ——! sir, I am!"

"I know you are, and I honor you for it."

23

"Bah! . . . Hilary, I—I'm much obliged to you for your company, but——"

"You've had enough," laughed the good-natured young man. "Good-evening, sir." He took a cross-street.

"Good-evening, my boy." The tone was so kind that Hilary cast a look back. But the General's eyes were straight before him.

Greenleaf accompanied the Valcours to their door. Charlie, who disliked him, and whose admiration for his own sister was privately cynical, had left them to themselves in the train. There, wholly undetected by the very man who had said some women were too feminine and she was one, she had played her sex against his with an energy veiled only by its intellectual nimbleness and its utterly dispassionate design. Charlie detected achievement in her voice as she twittered good-by to the departing soldier from their street door.

VI

MESSRS. SMELLEMOUT AND KETCHEM

NIGHT came, all stars. The old St. Charles Theatre filled to overflowing with the city's best, the hours melted away while Maggie Mitchell played *Fanchon*, and now, in the bright gas-light of the narrow thorough-fare, here were Adolphe and Hilary helping their three ladies into a carriage. All about them the feasted audience was pouring forth into the mild February night.

The smallest of the three women was aged. That

Messrs. Smellemout and Ketchem

the other two were young and beautiful we know already. At eighteen the old lady, the Bohemian-glass one, had been one of those royalist refugees of the French Revolution whose butterfly endeavors to colonize in Alabama and become bees make so pathetic a chapter in history. When one knew that, he could hardly resent her being heavily enamelled. Irby pressed into the coach after the three and shut the door, Kincaid uncovered, and the carriage sped off.

Hilary turned, glanced easily over the heads of the throng, and espied Greenleaf beckoning with a slender cane. Together they crossed the way and entered the office of a public stable.

"Our nags again," said Kincaid to one of a seated group, and passed into a room beyond. Thence he re-issued with his dress modified for the saddle, and the two friends awaited their mounts under an arch. "Dost perceive, Frederic," said the facetious Hilary, "yon modestly arrayed pair of palpable gents hieing hitherward yet pretending not to descry us? They be detectives. Oh—eh—gentlemen!"

The strangers halted inquiringly and then came forward. The hair of one was black, of the other gray. Hilary brightened upon them: "I was just telling my friend who you are. You know me, don't you?" A challenging glint came into his eye.

But the gray man showed a twinkle to match it: "Why—by sight—yes—what there is of you."

Hilary smiled again: "I saw you this morning in the office of the Committee of Public Safety, where I was giving my word that this friend of mine should leave the city within twenty-four hours." He introduced him: "Lieutenant Greenleaf, gentleman, United States Army. Fred, these are Messrs. Smellemout and Ketchem, a leading firm in the bottling business."

Greenleaf and the firm expressed their pleasure. "We hang out at the corner of Poet and Good-Children Streets," said the black-haired man, but made his eyes big to imply that this was romance.

Greenleaf lifted his brows: "Streets named for yourselves, I judge."

"Aye. Poet for each, Good-Children for both."

Kincaid laughed out. "The Lieutenant and I," he said as he moved toward their approaching horses, "live on Love street exactly half-way between Piety and Desire." His eyes widened, too. Suddenly he stepped between Greenleaf and the others: "See here, let's begin to tell the truth! You know Kincaid's Foundry? It was my father's——"

"And his father's before him," said the gray man.

"And I've come home to go into this war," Hilary went on.

"And just at present," said Gray, "you're casting shot and shell and now and then a cannon; good for you! You want to give us your guarantee——?"

"That my friend and I will be together every moment till he leaves to-morrow morning on the Jackson Railroad, bound for the North without a stop."

"To go into this war on the other side!"

"Why, of course!" said the smiling Kincaid. "Now, that's all, isn't it? I fear we're keeping you."

"Oh, no." The gray man's crow's-feet deepened playfully. "If you think you need us we'll stick by you all night."

By Starlight

"No," laughed Kincaid, "there's no call for you to be so sticky as all that." The horsemen mounted.

"Better us than the Patriots' League," said the younger detective to Hilary as Greenleaf moved off. "They've got your friend down in their Send-'em-to-hell book and are after him now. That's how come we to be——"

"I perceive," replied Hilary, and smiled in meditation. "Why—thank you, both!"

"Oh, you go right along, Mr. Kincaid. We'll be at the depot to-morrow ourselves, and to-night we'll see that they don't touch neither one of you."

Hilary's smile grew: "Why—thank you again! That will make it more comfortable for them. Good-night."

The two friends rode to a corner, turned into Poydras Street, crossed Magazine and Tchoupitoulas and presently, out from among the echoing fronts of unlighted warehouses, issued upon the wide, white Levee.

VII

BY STARLIGHT

"Wait," murmured Greenleaf, as they halted to view the scene. From their far right came the vast, brimming river, turbid, swift, silent, its billows every now and then rising and looking back as if they fled from implacable pursuers; sweeping by long, slumbering ranks of ships and steamboats; swinging in majestic breadth around the bend a mile or more below; and at the city's end, still beyond, gliding into mystic oblivion. Overhead swarmed the stars and across the flood came faintly the breath of orange-groves, sea-marshes and prairies.

Greenleaf faced across the wide bend at his left. In that quarter, quite hidden in live-oaks and magnolias, as both well knew, were the low, red towers of Jackson Barracks. But it was not for them the evicted young soldier claimed this last gaze. It was for a large dwelling hard by them, a fine old plantation house with wide verandas, though it also was shut from view, in its ancient grove.

"Fred," said Hilary, "didn't she tell you why?"

"No," replied the lover when they had turned away and were moving up the harbor front, "except that it is n't because I'm for the Union."

Hilary's eyes went wide: "That's wonderful, old man! But I don't believe she likes a soldier of any sort. If I were a woman I'd be doggoned if I'd ever marry a soldier!"

"Yet the man who gets her," said Greenleaf, "ought to be a soldier in every drop of his blood. You don't know her yet; but you soon will, and I'm glad."

"Now, why so? I can't ever please her enough to be pleased with her. I'm too confounded frivolous! I love nonsense, doggon it, for its own sake! I love to get out under a sky like this and just reel and whoop in the pure joy of standing on a world that's whirling round!"

"But you do please her. She's told me so."

"Don't you believe her! I don't. I can't. I tell you, Fred, I could never trust a girl that forever looks so trustworthy! S'pose I should fall in love with her! Would you—begrudge her to me?"

By Starlight

"I bequeath her to you."

"Ah! you know I haven't the ghost of a chance! She's not for po' little Hil'ry. I never did like small women, anyhow!"

"My boy! If ever you like this one she'll no more seem small than the open sea."

"I suppose," mused Hilary, "that's what makes it all the harder to let go. If a girl has a soul so petty that she can sit and hear you through to the last word your heart can bleed, you can turn away from her with some comfort of resentment, as if you still had a remnant of your own stature."

"Precisely!" said the lover. "But when she's too large-hearted to let you speak, and yet answers your unspoken word, once for all, with a compassion so modest that it seems as if it were you having compassion on her, she's harder to give up than——"

"Doggon her, Fred, I wouldn't give her up!"

"Ah, this war, Hilary! I may never see her again. There's just one man in this world whom——"

"Oh, get out!"

"I mean what I say. To you I leave her."

"Ha, ha! No, you don't! It's only to her you leave me. Old boy, promise me! If you ever come back and she's still in the ring, you'll go for her again no matter who else is bidding, your humble servant not excepted."

"Why—yes—I—I promise that. Now, will you promise me?"

"What! let myself——?"

"Yes."

"Ho-o, not by a jug-full! If ever I feel her harpoon

in me I'll fight like a whale! But I promise you this, and warn you, too: That when it comes to that, a whole platoon of Fred Greenleafs between her and me won't make a pinch of difference."

To that Greenleaf agreed, and the subject was changed. With shipping ever on their left and cotton-yards and warehouses for tobacco and for salt on their right their horses' feet clinked leisurely over the cobble pavements, between thousands of cotton-bales headed upon the unsheltered wharves and only fewer thousands on the narrow sidewalks.

So passed the better part of an hour before they were made aware, by unmistakable odors, that they were nearing the Stock-Landing. There, while they were yet just a trifle too far away to catch its echoes, had occurred an incident—a fracas, in fact—some of whose results belong with this narrative to its end. While they amble toward the spot let us reconnoitre it. Happily it has long been wiped out, this blot on the city's scutcheon. Its half-dozen streets were unspeakable mud, its air was stenches, its buildings were incredibly foul slaughter-houses and shedded pens of swine, sheep, beeves, cows, calves, and mustang ponies. The plank footways were enclosed by stout rails to guard against the chargings of long-horned cattle chased through the thoroughfares by lasso-whirling "bull-drivers" as wild as they. In the middle of the river-front was a ferry, whence Louisiana Avenue, broad, treeless, grassy, and thinly lined with slaughter-houses, led across the plain. Down this untidy plaisance a grimy little street-car, every half-hour, jogged out to the Carrollton railway and returned. This street and the water-front were lighted—twilighted

By Starlight

—with lard-oil lamps; the rest of the place was dark. At each of the two corners facing the ferry was a "coffee-house"—dram-shop, that is to say.

Messrs. Sam Gibbs and Maxime Lafontaine were president and vice-president of that Patriots' League against whose machinations our two young men had been warned by the detectives in St. Charles Street. They had just now arrived at the Stock-Landing. Naturally, on so important an occasion they were far from sober; yet on reaching the spot they had lost no time in levying on a Gascon butcher for a bucket of tar and a pillow of feathers, on an Italian luggerman for a hurried supper of raw oysters, and on the keeper of one of the "coffee-houses" for drinks for the four.

"Us four and no more!" sang the gleeful Gibbs; right number to manage a delicate case. The four glasses emptied, he had explained that all charges must be collected, of course, from the alien gentleman for whom the plumage and fixative were destined. Hence a loud war of words, which the barkeeper had almost smoothed out when the light-hearted Gibbs suddenly decreed that the four should sing, march, pat and "cut the pigeon-wing" to the new song (given nightly by Christy's Minstrels) entitled "Dixie's Land."

Hot threats recurring, Gascony had turned to go, Maxime had headed him off, Italy's hand had started into his flannel shirt, and "bing! bang! pop!" rang Gibbs's repeater and one of Maxime's little derringers— shot off from inside his sack-coat pocket. A whirlwind of epithets filled the place. Out into the stinking dark leaped Naples and Gascony, and after them darted their whooping assailants. The shutters of both barrooms clapped to, over the way a pair of bull-drivers rushed to their mustangs, there was a patter of hoofs there and of boots here and all inner lights vanished. A watchman's rattle buzzed remotely. Then silence reigned.

Now Sam and Maxime, deeming the incident closed, were walking up the levee road beyond the stock-pens, in the new and more sympathetic company of the two mounted bull-drivers, to whose love of patriotic adventure they had appealed successfully. A few yards beyond a roadside pool backed by willow bushes they set down tar-bucket and pillow, and under a low, vast live-oak bough turned and waited. A gibbous moon had set, and presently a fog rolled down the river, blotting out landscape and stars and making even these willows dim and unreal. Ideal conditions! Now if their guest of honor, with or without his friend, would but stop at this pool to wash the Stock-Landing muck from his horse's shins—but even luck has its limits.

Nevertheless, that is what occurred. A hum of voices—a tread of hoofs—and the very man hoped for —he and Hilary Kincaid—recognized by their voices— dismounted at the pool's margin. Sam and Maxime stole forward.

One Killed

VIII

ONE KILLED

THE newcomers' talk, as they crouched busily over their horses' feet, was on random themes: Dan Rice, John Owens, Adelina and Carlotta Patti, the comparative merits of Victor's and Moreau's restaur'—hah! Greenleaf snatched up his light cane, sprang erect, and gazed close into the mild eyes of Maxime. Gibbs's more wanton regard had no such encounter; Hilary gave him a mere upward glance while his hands continued their task.

"Good-evening," remarked Gibbs.

"Good-morning," chirped Hilary, and scrubbed on. "Do you happen to be Mr. Samuel Gibbs?—Don't stop, Fred, Maxime won't object to your working on."

"Yes, he will!" swore Gibbs, "and so will I!"

Still Hilary scrubbed: "Why so, Mr. Gibbs?"

"Bic-ause," put in Maxime, "he's got to go back through the same mud he came!"

"Why, then," laughed Hilary, "I may as well knock off, too," and began to wash his hands.

"No," growled Gibbs, "you'll ride on; we're not here for you."

"You can't have either of us without the other, Mr. Gibbs," playfully remarked Kincaid. The bull-drivers loomed out of the fog. Hilary leisurely rose and moved to draw a handkerchief.

"None o' that!" cried Gibbs, whipping his repeater into Kincaid's face. Yet the handkerchief came forth, its owner smiling playfully and drying his fingers while

33

Mr. Gibbs went on blasphemously to declare himself
"no chicken."

"Oh, no," laughed Hilary, "none of us is quite that.
But did you ever really study—*boxing?*" At the last
word Gibbs reeled under a blow in the face; his revolver, going off harmlessly, was snatched from him,
Maxime's derringer missed also, and Gibbs swayed,
bleeding and sightless, from Hilary's blows with the
butt of the revolver. Presently down he lurched in-
sensible, Hilary going half-way with him but recovering
and turning to the aid of his friend. Maxime tore loose
from his opponent, beseeching the bull-drivers to attack, but beseeching in vain. Squawking and chatter-
ing like parrot and monkey, they spurred forward,
whirled back, gathered lassos, cursed frantically as
Sam fell, sped off into the fog, spurred back again, and
now reined their ponies to their haunches, while Kincaid halted Maxime with Gibbs's revolver, and Greenleaf sprang to the bits of his own and Hilary's terrified
horses. For two other men, the Gascon and the
Italian, had glided into the scene from the willows, and
the Gascon was showing Greenleaf two big knives, one
of which he fiercely begged him to accept.

"Take it, Fred!" cried Hilary while he advanced on
the defiantly retreating Maxime; but as he spoke a
new cry of the drovers turned his glance another way.
Gibbs had risen to his knees unaware that the Italian,
with yet another knife, was close behind him. At a
bound Hilary arrested the lifted blade and hurled its
wielder aside, who in the next breath seemed to spring
past him head first, fell prone across the prostrate
Gibbs, turned face upward, and slid on and away

One Killed

—lassoed. Both bull-drivers clattered off up the road.

"Hang to the nags, Fred!" cried Hilary, and let Maxime leap to Gibbs's side, but seized the Gascon as with murderous intent he sprang after him. It took Kincaid's strength to hold him, and Gibbs and his partner would have edged away, but—"Stand!" called Hilary, and they stood, Gibbs weak and dazed, yet still spouting curses. The Gascon begged in vain to be allowed to follow the bull-drivers.

"Stay here!" said Hilary in French, and the butcher tarried. Hilary passed the revolver to his friend, mounted and dashed up the highway.

The Gascon stayed with a lively purpose which the enfeebled Gibbs was the first to see. "Stand back, you hell-hound!" cried the latter, and with fresh oaths bade Greenleaf "keep him off!"

Maxime put Gibbs on Greenleaf's horse (as bidden), and was about to lead him, when Kincaid galloped back.

"Fred," exclaimed Hilary, "they've killed the poor chap." He wheeled. "Come, all hands," he continued, and to Greenleaf added as they went, "He's lying up here in the road with——"

Greenleaf picked up something. "Humph!" said Hilary, receiving it, "knives by the great gross. He must have used this trying to cut the lasso; the one he had back yonder flew into the pond." He reined in: "Here's where they—Why, Fred—why, I'll swear! They've come back and—Stop! there was a skiff"—he moved to the levee and peered over—"It's gone!"

The case was plain, and while from Greenleaf's

saddle Gibbs broke into frantic revilings of the fugitives for deserting him and Maxime to sink their dead in the mid-current of the fog-bound river, Kincaid and his friend held soft counsel. Evidently the drovers had turned their horses loose, knowing they would go to their stable. No despatch to stop Greenleaf could be sent by anyone up the railroad till the Committee of Public Safety had authorized it, so Hilary would drop them a line out of his pocket note-book, and by daybreak these prisoners could go free.

"Mr. Gibbs"—he said as he wrote—"I have the sprout of a notion that you and Mr. Lafontaine would be an ornament to a field-battery I'm about to take command of. I'd like to talk with you about that presently." He tore out the page he had written and beckoned the Gascon aside:

"*Mon ami*"—he showed a roll of "city money" and continued in French—"do you want to make a hundred dollars—fifty now and fifty when you bring me an answer to this?"

The man nodded and took the missive.

The old "Jackson Railroad" avoided Carrollton and touched the river for a moment only, a short way beyond, at a small bunch of flimsy clapboard houses called Kennerville. Here was the first stop of its early morning outbound train, and here a dozen or so passengers always poked their heads out of the windows. This morning they saw an oldish black man step off, doff his hat delightedly to two young men waiting at the platform's edge, pass them a ticket, and move across to a pair of saddled horses. The smaller of the pair stepped upon the last coach, but kept his companion's hand till the train had again started.

"Good-by, Tony," cried the one left behind.

"Good-by, Jake," called the other, and waved. His friend watched the train vanish into the forest. Then, as his horse was brought, he mounted and moved back toward the city.

Presently the negro, on the other horse, came up almost abreast of him. "Mahs' Hil'ry?" he ventured.

"Well, uncle Jerry?"

"Dat's a pow'ful good-lookin' suit o' clo'es what L'tenant Greenfeel got awn."

"Jerry! you cut me to the heart!"

The negro tittered: "Oh, as to dat, I don't 'spute but yone is betteh."

The master heaved a comforted sigh. The servant tittered again, but suddenly again was grave. "I on'y wish to Gawd," he slowly said, "dat de next time you an' him meet——"

"Well—next time we meet—what then?"

"Dat you bofe be in de same sawt o' clo'es like you got on now."

IX

HER HARPOON STRIKES

THE home of the Callenders was an old Creole colonial plantation-house, large, square, strong, of two stories over a stoutly piered basement, and surrounded by two broad verandas, one at each story, beneath a great hip roof gracefully upheld on Doric columns. It bore that air of uncostly refinement which is one of the

most pleasing outward features of the aloof civilization
to which it, though not the Callenders, belonged.

Inside, its aspect was exceptional. There the inornate
beauty of its finish, the quiet abundance of its delicate
woodwork, and the high spaciousness and continuity of
its rooms for entertainment won admiration and fame.
A worthy setting, it was called, for the gentle manners
with which the Callenders made it alluring.

They, of course, had not built it. The late Judge
had acquired it from the descendants of a planter of
indigo and coffee who in the oldest Creole days had
here made his home and lived his life as thoroughly in
the ancient baronial spirit as if the Mississippi had been
the mediæval Rhine. Only its perfect repair was the
Judge's touch, a touch so modestly true as to give it a
charm of age and story which the youth and beauty of
the Callender ladies only enhanced, enhancing it the
more through their lack of a male protector—because
of which they were always going to move into town, but
never moved.

Here, some nine or ten days after Greenleaf's flight,
Hilary Kincaid, in uniform at last, was one of two
evening visitors, the other being Mandeville. In the
meantime our lover of nonsense had received a "hard
jolt." So he admitted in a letter to his friend,
boasting, however, that it was unattended by any
"internal injury." In the circuit of a single week,
happening to be thrown daily and busily into "her"
society, "the harpoon had struck."

He chose the phrase as an honest yet delicate reminder of the compact made when last the two chums
had ridden together.

Her Harpoon Strikes

All three of the Callenders were in the evening group, and the five talked about an illumination of the city, set for the following night. In the business centre the front of every building was already being hung with fittings from sidewalk to cornice. So was to be celebrated the glorious fact (Constance and Mandeville's adjective) that in the previous month Louisiana had seized all the forts and lighthouses in her borders and withdrawn from the federal union by a solemn ordinance signed in tears. This great lighting up, said Hilary, was to be the smile of fortitude after the tears. Over the city hall now floated daily the new flag of the state, with the colors of its stripes——

"Reverted to those of old Spain," murmured Anna, mainly to herself yet somewhat to Hilary. Judge Callender had died a Whig, and politics interested the merest girls those days.

Even at the piano, where Anna played and Hilary hovered, in pauses between this of Mozart and that of Mendelssohn, there was much for her to ask and him to tell about; for instance, the new "Confederate States," a bare fortnight old! Would Virginia come into them? Eventually, yes.

"Oh, yes, yes, yes!" cried Constance, overhearing. (Whatever did not begin with oh, those times, began with ah.)

"And *must* war follow?" The question was Anna's again, and Hilary sat down closer to answer confidentially:

"Yes, the war was already a fact."

"And might not the Abolitionists send their ships and soldiers against New Orleans?"

39

"Yes, the case was supposable."

"And might not Jackson's battlefield of 1815, in close view from these windows, become a new one?"

To avoid confessing that old battlefields have that tendency the Captain rose and took up a guitar; but when he would have laid it on her knee she pushed it away and asked the song of him; asked with something intimate in her smiling undertone that thrilled him, yet on the next instant seemed pure dream stuff. The others broke in and Constance begged a song of the new patriotism; but Miranda, the pretty stepmother, spoke rather for something a thousand miles and months away from the troubles and heroics of the hour; and when Anna seconded this motion by one fugitive glance worth all their beseechings Hilary, as he stood, gayly threw open his smart jacket lest his brass buttons mar the instrument, and sang with a sudden fervor that startled and delighted all the group:

"Drink to me only with thine eyes."

In the midst of which Constance lifted a knowing look across to Miranda, and Miranda sent it back.

There was never an evening that did not have to end, and at last the gentlemen began to make a show of leaving. But then came a lively chat, all standing in a bunch. To-morrow's procession, the visitors said, would form in Canal Street, move up St. Charles, return down Camp Street into Canal, pass through it into Rampart, take the Bayou Road and march to a grand review away out in the new camp of instruction at the Creole Race-Course. Intermediately, from a certain Canal Street balcony, Flora would present the flag!

the gorgeous golden, silken, satin battle standard which the Callenders and others had helped her to make. So —good-night—good-night.

The last parting was with Mandeville, at the levee-road gate, just below which he lived in what, during the indigo-planter's life, had been the overseer's cottage. At a fine stride our artillerist started townward, his horse being stabled near by in that direction. But presently he halted, harkened after the Creole's receding step, thought long, softly called himself names, and then did a small thing which, although it resulted in nothing tragic at the time, marked a turning point in his life. He leapt the grove fence, returned to the shadows of the garden, and silently made his way to its eastern, down-river side. Already the dwelling's lower lights were going out while none yet shone above, and he paused in deep shade far enough away to see, over its upper veranda's edge, the tops of its chamber windows.

X

SYLVIA SIGHS

THE house was of brick. So being, in a land where most dwellings are of wood, it had gathered beauty from time and dignity from tried strength, and with satisfying grace joined itself to its grounds, whose abundance and variety of flowering, broad-leaved evergreens lent, in turn, a poetic authenticity to its Greek columns and to the Roman arches of its doors and windows. Especially in these mild, fragrant, blue nights was this charm potent, and the fair home seemed to its hidden beholder forever set apart from the discords and distresses of a turbulent world. And now an upper window brightened, its sash went up, and at the veranda's balustrade Anna stood outlined against the inner glow.

She may have intended but one look at the stars, but they and the spiced air were enchanting, and in confidence that no earthly eye was on her she tarried, gazing out to the farthest gleam of the river where it swung southward round the English Turn.

Down in the garden a mirthful ecstasy ran through all the blood of her culprit observer and he drank to her only with his eyes. Against the window's brightness her dark outline showed true, and every smallest strand of her hair that played along the contours of brow and head changed his merriment to reverence and bade his heart recognize how infinitely distant from his was her thought. Hilary Kincaid! can you read no better than that?

Her thought was of him. Her mind's eye saw him on his homeward ride. It marked the erectness of his frame, the gayety of his mien, the dance of his locks. By her inner ear she heard his horse's tread passing up the narrow round-stone pavements of the Creole Quarter, presently to echo in old St. Peter Street under the windows of Pontalba Row—one of which was Flora's. Would it ring straight on, or would it pause between that window and the orange and myrtle shades of Jackson Square? Constance had said that day to Miranda—for this star-gazer to overhear—that she did not believe Kincaid loved Flora, and the hearer had longed to ask her why, but knew she could not tell.

Sylvia Sighs

Why is a man's word. "They're as helpless without it," the muser recalled having very lately written on a secret page, "as women are before it. And yet a girl can be very hungry, at times, for a why. They say he's as brave as a lion—why is he never brave to me?"

So futilely ended the strain on the remembered page, but while his unsuspected gaze abode on her lifted eyes her thought prolonged the note: "If he meant love to-night, why did he not stand to his meaning when I laughed it away? Was that for his friend's sake, or is he only not brave enough to make one wild guess at me? Ah, I bless Heaven he's the kind that cannot! And still—oh, Hilary Kincaid, if you were the girl and I the man! I shouldn't be on *my* way home; I'd be down in this garden—" She slowly withdrew.

Hilary, stepping back to keep her in sight, was suddenly aware of the family coachman close at his side. Together they moved warily a few steps farther.

"You mus' escuse me, Cap'n," the negro amiably whispered. "You all right, o' co'se! Yit dese days, wid no white gen'leman apputtainin' onto de place——"

"Old man!" panted Hilary, "you've saved my life!"

"Oh, my Lawd, no! Cap'n, I——"

"Yes, you have! I was just going into fits! Now step in and fetch me out here—" He shaped his arms fantastically and twiddled his fingers.

Bending with noiseless laughter the negro nodded and went.

Just within her window, Anna, still in reverie, sat down at a slender desk, unlocked a drawer, then a second one inside it, and drew forth—no mere secret

43

page but—a whole diary! "To Anna, from Miranda, Christmas, 1860." Slowly she took up a pen, as gradually laid it by again, and opposite various dates let her eyes rest on—not this, though it was still true:

"The more we see of Flora, the more we like her."

Nor this: "Heard a great, but awful, sermon on the duty of resisting Northern oppression."

But this: "Connie thinks he 'inclines' to me. Ho! all he's ever said has been for his far-away friend. I wish he *would* incline, or else go ten times as far away! Only not to the war—God forbid! Ah, me, how I long for his inclining! And while I long he laughs, and the more he laughs the more I long, for I never, never so doted on any one's laugh. Oh, shame! to love before——"

What sound was that below? No mocking-bird note, no south wind in the foliage, but the kiss of fingers on strings! Warily it stole in at the window, while softly as an acacia the diary closed its leaves. The bent head stirred not, but a thrill answered through the hearer's frame as a second cadence ventured up and in and a voice followed it in song. Tremblingly the book slid into the drawer, inner and outer lock clicked whisperingly, and gliding to a door she harkened for any step of the household, while she drank the strains, her bosom heaving with equal alarm and rapture.

If any song is good which serves a lover's ends we need claim no more for the one that rose to Anna on the odors of the garden and drove her about the room, darting, clinging, fluttering, returning, like her own terrified bird above her in its cage.

Sylvia Sighs

When Sylvia sighs
And veils the worshipped wonder
Of her blue eyes
Their sacred curtains under,
Naught can so nigh please me as my tender anguish.
Only grief can ease me while those lashes languish.
Woe best beguiles;
Mirth, wait thou other whiles;
Thou shalt borrow all my sorrow
When Sylvia smiles.

But what a strange effect! Could this be that Anna Callender who "would no more ever again seem small than the ocean?" Is this that maiden of the "belated, gradual smile" whom the singer himself so lately named "a profound pause?" Your eyes, fair girl, could hardly be more dilated if they saw riot, fire, or shipwreck. Nor now could your brow show more exaltation responsive to angels singing in the sun; nor now your frame show more affright though soldiers were breaking in your door. Anna, Anna! your fingers are clenched in your palms, and in your heart one frenzy implores the singer to forbear, while another bids him sing on though the heavens fall. Anna Callender! do you not know this? You have dropped into a chair, you grip the corners of your desk. Now you are up again, trembling and putting out your lights. And now you seek to relight them, but cannot remember the place or direction of anything, and when you have found out what you were looking for, do not know how much time has flown, except that the song is still in its first stanza. Are you aware that your groping hand has seized and rumpled into its palm a long strand of slender ribbon lately unwound from your throat?

Kincaid's Battery

A coy tap sounds on her door and she glides to it. "Who—who?" But in spite of her it opens to the bearer of a lamp, her sister Constance.

"Who—who—?" she mocks in soft glee. "That's the question! 'Who is Sylvia?'"

"Don't try to come in! I—I—the floor is all strewn with matches!"

The sister's mirth vanishes: "Why, Nan! what *is* the matter?"

"Do-on't whisper so loud! He's right out there!"

"But, dearie! it's nothing but a serenade."

"It's an outrage, Con! How did he ever know—how did he dare to know—this was my window? Oh, put out that lamp or he'll think I lighted it—No! no! don't put it out, he'll think I did that, too!"

"Why, Nan! you never in your life——"

"Now, Connie, that isn't fair! I won't stay with you!" The speaker fled. Constance put out the light.

A few steps down and across a hall a soft sound broke, and Anna stood in Miranda's doorway wearing her most self-contained smile: "Dearie!" she quietly said, "isn't it *too* ridiculous!"

Miranda crinkled a smile so rife with love and insight that Anna's eyes suddenly ran full and she glided to her knees by the seated one and into her arms, murmuring, "You ought both of you to be ashamed of yourselves! You're totally mistaken!"

Presently, back in the dusk of her own room, an audible breathing betrayed her return, and Constance endeavoured to slip out, but Anna clung: "You sha'n't go! You sha'—" Yet the fugitive easily got away.

Down among the roses a stanza had just ended.

In Column of Platoons

Anna tiptoed out half across the dim veranda, tossed her crumpled ribbon over the rail, flitted back, bent an ear, and knew by a brief hush of the strings that the token had drifted home.

The die was cast. From brow and heart fled all perturbation and once more into her eyes came their wonted serenity—with a tinge of exultation—while the strings sounded again, and again rose the song:

> When Sylvia smiles
> Her eyes to mine inclining,
> Like azure isles
> In seas of lovelight shining,
> With a merry madness find I endless pleasure—
> Till she sighs—then sadness is my only treasure.
> Woe best beguiles;
> Mirth, wait thou other whiles,
> Thou shalt borrow all my sorrow
> When Sylvia smiles.

XI

IN COLUMN OF PLATOONS

LOVE'S war was declared. From hour to hour of that night and the next morning, in bed, at board, dressing for the thronged city, spinning with Constance and Miranda up Love Street across Piety and Desire and on into the town's centre, Anna, outwardly all peace, planned that war's defensive strategy. Splendidly maidenly it should be, harrowingly arduous to the proud invader, and long drawn out. Constance should see what a man can be put through. But oh, but oh, if, after all, the invasion should not come!

Kincaid's Battery

In those days New Orleans paved her favorite streets, when she paved them at all, with big blocks of granite two feet by one. They came from the North as ballast in those innumerable wide-armed ships whose cloud of masts and cordage inspiringly darkened the sky of that far-winding river-front where we lately saw Hilary Kincaid and Fred Greenleaf ride. Beginning at the great steamboat landing, half a mile of Canal Street had such a pavement on either side of its broad grassy "neutral ground." So had the main streets that led from it at right angles. Long afterward, even as late as when the Nineteenth Century died, some of those streets were at the funeral, clad in those same old pavements, worn as smooth and ragged as a gentleman-beggar's coat. St. Charles Street was one. Another was the old Rue Royale, its squat ground-floor domiciles drooping their mossy eaves half across the pinched sidewalks and confusedly trying to alternate and align themselves with tall brick houses and shops whose ample two- and three-story balconies were upheld, balustraded, and overhung by slender garlandries of iron openwork as graceful and feminine as a lace mantilla. With here and there the flag of a foreign consul hanging out and down, such is the attire the old street was vain of in that golden time when a large square sign on every telegraph pole bade you get your shirts at S. N. Moody's, corner of Canal and Royal Streets.

At this corner, on the day after the serenade, there was a dense, waiting crowd. On the other corner of Royal, where the show-windows of Hyde & Goodrich blazed with diamonds, and their loftily nested gold pelican forever fed her young from her bleeding breast,

In Column of Platoons

stood an equal throng. Across Canal Street, where St.
Charles opens narrowly southward, were similar masses,
and midway between the four corners the rising circles of
stone steps about the high bronze figure of Henry Clay
were hidden by men and boys packed as close as they
could sit or stand. A great procession had gone up-
town and would by and by return. Near and far ban-
ners and pennons rose and fell on the luxurious air, and
the ranks and ranks of broad and narrow balconies
were so many gardens of dames and girls, parasols, and
diaphanous gowns. Near the front of the lowest Hyde
& Goodrich balcony, close by the gilded pelican, sat
the Callenders, all gladness, holding mute dialogues
with Flora and Madame Valcour here on the balcony of
Moody's corner. It was the birthday of Washington.

Not of him, however, did Flora and her grandmother
softly converse in Spanish amid the surrounding babel
of English and French. Their theme was our battery
drill of some ten days before, a subject urged upon
Flora by the mosquito-like probings of Madame's
musically whined queries. Better to be bled of almost
any information by the antique little dame than to
have her light on it some other way, as she had an
amazing knack of doing. Her *acted* part of things
Flora kept untold; but grandma's spirit of divination
could unfailingly supply that, and her pencilled brows,
stiff as they were, could tell the narrator she had done
so.

Thus now, Flora gave no hint of the beautiful skill
and quick success with which, on her homeward railway trip with Greenleaf that evening, she had bettered
his impressions of her. By no more than a gentle play

of light and shade in her smile and an undulating
melody of voice—without a word that touched the
wound itself, but with a timid glow of compassionate
admiration—she had soothed the torture of a heart
whose last hope Anna had that same hour put to
death.

"But before he took the train with you," murmured
the mosquito to the butterfly, "when he said the General
was going to take Irby upon his staff and give the
battery to Kincaid, what did you talk of?"

"Talk of? Charlie. He said I ought to make
Charlie join the battery."

"Ah? For what? To secure Kincaid's protection
of your dear little brother's health—character—morals
—eh?"

"Yes, 'twas so he put it," replied Flora, while the
old lady's eyebrows visibly cried:

"You sly bird! will you impute *all* your own words
to that Yankee, and his to yourself?"

Which is just what Flora continued to do as the
grandma tinkled: "And you said—what?"

"I said if I couldn't keep him at home I ought to
get him into the cavalry. You know, dear, in the infantry the marches are so cruel, the camps so——"

"But in the artillery," piped the small dame, "they
ride, eh?" (It was a trap she was setting, but in vain
was the net spread.)

"No," said the serene girl, "they, too, go afoot.
Often they must help the horses drag the guns through
the mire. Only on parade they ride, or when rushing
to and fro in battle, whips cracking, horses plunging,
the hills smoking and shaking!" The rare creature

sparkled frankly, seeing the battery whirling into action
with its standard on the wind—this very flag she expected presently to bestow.

"And with Kincaid at the head!" softly cried the
antique.

The girl put on a fondness which suddenly became a
withering droop of the eyes: "Don't mince your smile
so, grannie dear, I can hear the paint crack."

The wee relic flashed, yet instantly was bland again:
"You were about to say, however, that in the artillery——?"

"The risks are the deadliest of all."

"Ah, yes!" sang the mosquito, "and for a sister to
push her boy brother into a battery under such a commander would be too much like murder!"

The maiden felt the same start as when Greenleaf
had ventured almost those words. "Yes," she beamingly rejoined, "that's what I told the Lieutenant."

"With a blush?"

"No," carelessly said the slender beauty, and exchanged happy signals with the Callenders.

"You tricksy wretch!" muttered the grandmother to
herself. For though Charlie was in the battery by his
own choice, Hilary would have kept him out had not
the sister begged to have him let in.

Suddenly there was a glad stoppage of all by-play in
the swarming streets. Down St. Charles from LaFayette
Square came the shock of saluting artillery, and up
Royal from Jackson Square rolled back antiphonal
thunders.

"Grandma!" softly cried Flora, as if sharing the general elation, but had begun again to tell of Greenleaf,

when from far over in Camp Street her subtle ear caught a faint stray sigh of saxhorns.

"Well? well? about the Yankee—?" urged Madame.

"Oh, a trifle! He was to go that night, and thinking he might some day return in very different fashion and we be glad to make use of him, I—" The speaker's lithe form straightened and her gaze went off to the left. "Here they come!" she said, and out where Camp Street emerges, a glint of steel, a gleam of brass, a swarming of the people that way, and again a shimmer of brass and steel, affirmed her word that the long, plumed, bristling column had got back to the arms of its darling Canal Street.

"Yes," cried many, "they're turning this way!"

"Well?—Well?" insisted the old lady amid the rising din. "And so you—you?"

"Be more careful," murmured the girl. "I told him that our convictions—about this war—yours and mine —not Charlie's—*are the same as his.*"

A charming sight she was, even in that moment of public enthusiasm and spectacle, holding the wondering stare of her companion with a gayety that seemed ready to break into laughter. The dainty Madame went limp, and in words as slow and soft as her smile, sighed, "You are a genius!"

"No, only the last thing you would suspect—a good housekeeper. I have put him up in sugar."

The distant martial strains became more coherent. In remote balconies handkerchiefs fluttered wildly, and under nearer and nearer ones the people began to pack closer and choose their footing along the curb. Presently from the approaching column came who but

In Column of Platoons

Hilary Kincaid, galloping easily over the slippery pavements. Anna saw his eyes sweep the bank of human flowers (with its occasional male caterpillar) on Moody's balcony and light upon Flora. He lifted his képi and halted. One could read his soft questions.

"All right? All ready? Where are the others?— Ah!" He sent an eager salutation to the Callenders, and two joyfully bowed, but Anna gave no sign. With great dignity her gaze was bent beyond him on the nearing host, and when Constance plucked her arm she tardily looked three wrong ways.

The rider could not wait. The police were pressing back the jubilant masses, swarms of ladies on the rear forms were standing up, and Flora, still seated, had leaned down beamingly and was using every resource of voice and fan to send him some word through the tumult of plaudits and drums. He spurred close. In a favoring hush—drum-corps inviting the band—she bent low and with an arch air of bafflement tried once more, but an outburst of brazen harmonies tore her speech to threads. Suddenly—

"Ever of thee I'm fondly dreaming—"

pealed the cornets, pumped the trombones, whipping it out, cracking it off, with a rigor of rhythm to shame all peace-time languishments—

"Thy gentle voice my spirit can cheer.
Thou art the star—"

What could the balconies do but wave more joyously than ever? The streets hurrahed! The head of the procession was here! The lone horseman reined back, wheeled, cast another vain glance toward Anna, and

53

with an alarming rataplan of slipping and recovering hoofs sped down the column.

But what new rapture was this? Some glorious luck had altered the route, and the whole business swung right into this old rue Royale! Now, now the merry clamor and rush of the crowd righting itself! And behold! this blazing staff and its commanding general —general of division! He first, and then all they, bowed to Flora and her grandmother, bowed to the Callenders, and were bowed to in return. A mounted escort followed. And now—yea, verily! General Brodnax and his staff of brigade! Wave, Valcours, wave Callenders! Irby's bow to Flora was majestic, and hers to him as gracious as the smell of flowers in the air. And here was Mandeville, most glittering in all the glitter. Flora beamed on him as well, Anna bowed with a gay fondness, Miranda's dainty nose crimped itself, and Constance, with a blitheness even more vivid, wished all these balconies could know that Captain—he *was* Lieutenant, but that was away back last week—Captain Etienne Aristide Rofignac de Mandeville was *hers*, whom, after their marriage, now *so* near at hand, she was going always to call Steve!

XII

MANDEVILLE BLEEDS

Two overflowing brigades! In the van came red-capped artillery. Not the new battery, though happily known to Flora and the Callenders; the Washington Artillery. Illustrious command! platoons and platoons

Mandeville Bleeds

of the flower of the Crescent City's youth and worth!
They, too, that day received their battle-flag. They
have the shot-torn rags of it yet.

Ah, the clanging horns again, and oh, the thundering
drums! Another uniform, on a mass of infantry, another band at its head braying another lover's song
reduced to a military tramp, swing, and clangor—

> "I'd offer thee this hand of mine
> If I could love thee less—"

Every soldier seemed to have become a swain.
Hilary and Anna had lately sung this wail together,
but not to its end, she had called it "so ungenuine."
How rakishly now it came ripping out. "My fortune is
too hard for thee," it declared, "'twould chill thy dearest
joy. I'd rather weep to see thee free," and ended with
"destroy"; but it had the swagger of a bowling-alley.

All the old organizations, some dating back to '12–
'15, had lately grown to amazing numbers, while many
new ones had been so perfectly uniformed, armed,
accoutred and drilled six nights a week that the ladies,
in their unmilitary innocence, could not tell the new
from the old. Except in two cases: Even Anna
was aware that the "Continentals," in tasseled top-
boots, were of earlier times, although they had changed
their buff knee-breeches and three-cornered hats for a
smart uniform of blue and gray; while these red-and-
blue-flannel Zouaves, drawing swarms of boys as dray-
loads of sugar-hogsheads drew flies, were as modern as
1861 itself. But oh, ah, one *knew* so many young men!
It was wave, bow, smile and bow, smile and wave, till
the whole frame was gloriously weary.

Kincaid's Battery

Near Anna prattled a Creole girl of sixteen with
whom she now and then enjoyed a word or so: Victorine Lafontaine, daughter of our friend Maxime.

"Louisiana Foot-Rifles—ah! but their true name,"
she protested, "are the Chasseurs-à-Pied! 'Twas to
them my papa billong' biffo' he join' hisseff on the
batt'rie of Captain Kincaid, and there he's now a cor-
poreal!"

What jaunty fellows they were! and as their faultless
ranks came close, their glad, buskined feet beating as
perfect music for the roaring drums as the drums beat
for them, Anna, in fond ardor, bent low over the rail
and waved, exhorting Miranda and Constance to wave
with her. So marched the chasseurs by, but the wide
applause persisted as yet other hosts, with deafening
music and perfect step and with bayonets back-slanted
like the porcupine's, came on and on, and passed and
passed, ignoring in grand self-restraint their very loves
who leaned from the banquettes' edges and from balustraded heights and laughed and boasted and worshipped.

Finally artillery again! every man in it loved by
some one—or dozen—in these glad throngs. Clap!
call! wave! Oh, gallant sight! These do not enter
Royal Street. They keep Canal, obliquing to that
side of the way farthest from the balconies——

"To make room," cries Victorine, "to form line
pritty soon off horses, in front those cannon'."

At the head rides Kincaid. Then, each in his place,
lieutenants, sergeants, drivers, the six-horse teams lean-
ing on the firm traces, the big wheels clucking, the long
Napoleons shining like gold, and the cannoneers—oh,

Mandeville Bleeds

God bless the lads!—planted on limbers and caissons, with arms tight folded and backs as plumb as the meridian. Now three of the pieces, half the battery, have gone by and——

"Well, well, if there isn't Sam Gibbs, sergeant of a gun! It is, I tell you, it is! Sam Gibbs, made over new, as sure as a certain monosyllable! and what could be surer, for Sam Gibbs?"

So laugh the sidewalks; but society, overhead, cares not for a made-over Gibbs while round about him are sixty or seventy young heroes who need no making over. Anna, Anna! what a brave and happy half-and-half of Creoles and "Americans" do your moist eyes beam down upon: here a Canonge and there an Ogden —a Zacherie—a Fontennette—Willie Geddes—Tom Norton—a Fusilier! Nat Frellsen—a Tramontana—a Grandissime!—and a Grandissime again! Percy Chilton—a Dudley—Arthur Puig y Puig—a De Armas— MacKnight—Violett—Avendano—Rob Rareshide— Guy Palfrey—a Morse, a Bien, a Fuentes—a Grand-issme once more! Aleck Moise—Ralph Fenner—Ned Ferry!—and lo! a Raoul Innerarity, image of his grand-father's portrait—and a Jules St. Ange! a Converse— Jack Eustis—two Frowenfelds! a Mossy! a Hennen— Bartie Sloo—McVey, McStea, a De Lavillebuevre—a Thorndyke-Smith and a Grandissime again!

And ah! see yonder young cannoneer half-way between these two balconies and the statue beyond; that foppish boy with his hair in a hundred curls and his eyes wild with wayward ardor! "Ah, Charlie Val-cour!" thinks Anna; "oh, your poor sister!" while the eyes of Victorine take him in secretly and her voice is still for a whole minute. Hark! From the head of the column is wafted back a bugle-note, and everything stands.

Now the trim lads relax, the balcony dames in the rear rows sit down, there are nods and becks and wafted whispers to a Calder and an Avery, to tall Numa Dolhonde and short Eugene Chopin, to George Wood and Dick Penn and Fenner and Bouligny and Pilcher and L'Hommedieu; and Charlie sends up bows and smiles, and wipes the beautiful brow he so openly and wilfully loves best on earth. Anna smiles back, but Constance bids her look at Maxime, Victorine's father, whom neither his long white moustaches nor weight of years nor the lawless past revealed in his daring eyes can rob of his youth. So Anna looks, and when she turns again to Charlie she finds him sending a glance rife with conquest—not his first—up to Victorine, who, without meeting it, replies—as she has done to each one before it—with a dreamy smile into vacancy, and a faint narrowing of her almond eyes.

Captain Kincaid comes ambling back, and right here in the throat of Royal Street faces the command. The matter is explained to Madame Valcour by a stranger:

"Now at the captain's word all the cannoneers will spring down, leaving only guns, teams and drivers at their back, and line up facing us. The captain will dismount and ascend to the balcony, and there he and the young lady, whoever she is—" He waits, hoping Madame will say who the young lady is, but Madame only smiles for him to proceed— "The captain and she will confront each other, she will present the colors, he, replying, will receive them, and—ah, after all!"

Mandeville Bleeds

The thing had been done without their seeing it, and there stood the whole magnificent double line. Captain Kincaid dismounted and had just turned from his horse when there galloped up Royal Street from the vanished procession—Mandeville. Slipping and clattering, he reined up and saluted: "How soon can Kincaid's Battery be completely ready to go into camp?"

"Now, if necessary."

"It will receive orders to move at seven to-morrow morning!" The Creole's fervor amuses the rabble, and when Hilary smiles his earnestness waxes to a frown. Kincaid replies lightly and the rider bends the rein to wheel away, but the slippery stones have their victim at last. The horse's feet spread and scrabble, his haunches go low. Constance snatches both Anna's hands. Ah! by good luck the beast is up again! Yet again the hoofs slip, the rider reels, and Charlie and a comrade dart out to catch him, but he recovers. Then the horse makes another plunge and goes clear down with a slam and a slide that hurl his master to the very sidewalk and make a hundred pale women cry out.

Constance and her two companions bend wildly from the balustrade, a sight for a painter. Across the way Flora, holding back her grandmother, silently leans out, another picture. In the ranks near Charlie a disarray continues even after Kincaid has got the battered Mandeville again into the saddle, and while Mandeville is rejecting sympathy with a begrimed yet haughty smile.

"Keep back, ladies!" pleads Madame's late informant, holding off two or three bodily. "Ladies, sit down! Will you please to keep back!" Flora still leans out. Some one is melodiously calling:

"Captain Kincaid!" It is Mrs. Callender. "Captain!" she repeats.

He smiles up and at last meets Anna's eyes. Flora sees their glances—angels ascending and descending—and a wee loop of ribbon that peeps from his tightly buttoned breast. Otherwise another sight, elsewhere, could not have escaped her, though it still escapes many.

"Poor boy!" it causes two women behind her to exclaim, "poor boy!" but Flora pays no heed, for Hilary is speaking to the Callenders.

"Nothing broken but his watch," he gayly comforts them as to Mandeville.

"He's bleeding!" moans Constance, very white. But Kincaid softly explains in his hollowed hands:

"Only his nose!"

The nose's owner casts no upward look. Not his to accept pity, even from a fiancée. His handkerchief dampened "to wibe the faze," two bits of wet paper "to plug the noztril',"—he could allow no more!

"First blood of the war!" said Hilary.

"Yez! But"—the flashing warrior tapped his sword —"nod the last!" and was off at a gallop, while Kincaid turned hurriedly to find that Charlie, struck by the floundering horse, had twice fainted away.

In the balconies the press grew dangerous. An urchin intercepted Kincaid to show him the Callenders, who, with distressed eyes, pointed him to their carriage hurrying across Canal Street.

"For Charlie and Flora!" called Anna. They could

not stir "themselves" for the crush; but yonder, on Moody's side, the same kind citizen noticed before had taken matters in hand:

"Keep back, ladies! Make room! Let these two ladies out!" He squeezed through the pack, holding aloft the furled colors, which all this time had been lying at Flora's feet. Her anxious eyes were on them at every second step as she pressed after him with the grandmother dangling from her elbow.

The open carriage spun round the battery's right and up its front to where a knot of comrades hid the prostrate Charlie; the surgeon, Kincaid, and Flora crouching at his side, the citizen from the balcony still protecting grandmamma, and the gilded eagle of the un-presented standard hovering over all. With tender ease Hilary lifted the sufferer and laid him on the carriage's front seat, the surgeon passed Madame in and sat next to her, but to Kincaid Flora exclaimed with a glow of heroic distress:

"Let me go later—with Anna!" Her eyes over-flowed—she bit her lip—"I must present the flag!"

A note of applause started, a protest hushed it, and the overbending Callenders and the distracted Victorine heard Hilary admiringly say:

"Come! Go! You belong with your brother!"

He pressed her in. For an instant she stood while the carriage turned, a hand outstretched toward the standard, saying to Hilary something that was drowned by huzzas; then despairingly she sank into her seat and was gone down Royal Street.

"Attention!" called a lieutenant, and the ranks were in order. To the holder of the flag Hilary pointed out

Anna, lingered for a word with his subaltern, and then followed the standard to the Callenders' balcony.

XIII

THINGS ANNA COULD NOT WRITE

"CHARLIE has two ribs broken, but is doing well," ran a page of the diary; "so well that Flora and Madame—who bears fatigue wonderfully—let Captain Irby take them, in the evening, to see the illumination. For the thunderstorm, which sent us whirling home at midday, was followed by a clear evening sky and an air just not too cool to be fragrant.

"I cannot write. My thoughts jostle one another out of all shape, like the women in that last crush after the flag-presentation. I begged not to have to take Flora's place from her. It was like snatching jewels off her. I felt like a robber! But in truth until I had the flag actually in my hand I thought we were only being asked to take care of it for a later day. The storm had begun to threaten. Some one was trying to say to me—'off to camp and then to the front,' and—'must have the flag now,' and still I said, 'No, oh, no!' But before I could get any one to add a syllable there was the Captain himself with the three men of the color guard behind him, the middle one Victorine's father. I don't know how I began, but only that I went on and on in some wild way till I heard the applause all about and beneath me, and he took the colors from me, and the first gust of the storm puffed them half· open—gorgeously—and the

Things Anna Could Not Write

battery hurrahed. And then came his part. He—I cannot write it."

Why not, the diary never explained, but what occurred was this:

"Ladies and gentlemen and comrades in arms!" began Hilary and threw a superb look all round, but the instant he brought it back to Anna, it quailed, and he caught his breath. Then he nerved up again. To help his courage and her own she forced herself to gaze straight into his eyes, but reading the affright in hers he stood dumb and turned red.

He began again: "Ladies and gentlemen and comrades in arms!" and pulled his moustache, and smote and rubbed his brow, and suddenly drove his hand into an inside pocket and snatched out a slip of paper. But what should come trailing out with it but a long loop of ribbon! As he pushed it back he dropped the paper, which another whiff of wind flirted straight over his head, sent it circling and soaring clear above Moody's store and dropped it down upon the roof. And there gazed Anna and all that multitude, utterly blank, until the martyr himself burst into a laugh. Then a thousand laughs pealed as one, and he stood smiling and stroking back his hair, till his men began to cry, "song! song!"

Upon that he raised the flag high in one hand, let it balloon to the wind, made a sign of refusal, and all at once poured out a flood of speech—pledges to Anna and her fellow-needlewomen—charges to his men—hopes for the cherished cause—words so natural and unadorned, so practical and soldier-like, and yet so swift, that not a breath was drawn till he had ended. But then what a shout!

Kincaid's Battery

It was over in a moment. The great black cloud that had been swelling up from the south gave its first flash and crash, and everybody started pell-mell for home. The speaker stood just long enough for a last bow to Anna while the guard went before him with the colors. Then he hurried below and had the whole battery trotting down Canal Street and rounding back on its farther side, with the beautiful standard fluttering to the storm, before the Callenders could leave the balcony.

Canal Street that evening was a veritable fairyland. When, growing tired of their carriage, the Callenders and Mandeville walked, and Kincaid unexpectedly joined them, fairyland was the only name he could find for it, and Anna, in response, could find none at all. Mallard's, Zimmerman's, Clark's, Levois's, Laroussini's, Moody's, Hyde & Goodrich's, and even old Piffet's were all aglow. One cannot recount half. Every hotel, every club-house, all the theatres, all the consul's offices in Royal and Carondelet streets, the banks everywhere, Odd Fellows' Hall—with the Continentals giving their annual ball in it—and so forth and so on! How the heart was exalted!

But when the heart is that way it is easy to say things prematurely, and right there in Canal Street Hilary spoke of love. Not personally, only at large; although when Anna restively said no woman should ever give her heart where she could not give a boundless and unshakable trust, his eyes showed a noble misery while he exclaimed:

"Oh, but there are women of whom no man can ever deserve that!" There his manner was all at once so

Things Anna Could Not Write

personal that she dared not be silent, but fell to generalizing, with many a stammer, that a woman ought to be very slow to give her trust if, once giving it, she would not rather die than doubt.

"Do you believe there are such women?" he asked.

"I know there are," she said, her eyes lifted to his, but the next instant was so panic-smitten and shamed that she ran into a lamp-post. And when he called that his fault her denial was affirmative in its feebleness, and with the others she presently resumed the carriage and said good-night.

"Flippantly!" thought the one left alone on the crowded sidewalk.

Yet—"It is I who am going to have the hardest of it," said the diary a short hour after. "I've always thought that when the right one came I'd never give in the faintest bit till I had put him to every test and task and delay I could invent. And now I can't invent one! His face *quenches* doubt, and if he keeps on this way— Ah, Flora! *is* he anything to you? Every time he speaks my heart sees you. I see you now! And somehow— since Charlie's mishap—more yours than his if——"

For a full minute the pen hovered over the waiting page, then gradually left it and sank to rest on its silver rack.

XIV

FLORA TAPS GRANDMA'S CHEEK

MEANWHILE, from a cluster of society folk sipping
ices at "Vincent's" balcony tables, corner of Carondelet Street (where men made the most money), and
Canal (where women spent the most), Flora and her
grandmother, in Irby's care, made their way down to
the street.

Kincaid, once more on horseback with General
Brodnax, saw them emerge beside his cousin's hired
carriage, and would have hurried to them, if only to
inquire after the injured boy; but the General gave
what he was saying a detaining energy. It was of
erecting certain defences behind Mobile; of the scarcity
of military engineers; and of his having, to higher
authority, named Hilary for the task. The Captain
could easily leave the battery in camp for a day or two,
take the Mobile boat— He ceased an instant and
scowled, as Hilary bowed across the way.

There was a tender raillery in the beam with which
Flora held the young man's eye a second, and as she
turned away there was accusation in the faint toss and
flicker of the deep lace that curtained her hat. Both
her companions saw it, but Irby she filled with an instant inebriation by one look, the kindest she had ever
given him.

"Both barrels!" said the old lady to herself.

As Irby reached the carriage door Flora's touch
arrested him. It was as light as a leaf, but it thrilled
him like wine—whose thrill he well knew.

Flora Taps Grandma's Cheek

"I've lost one of my gloves," she said.

He looked about her feet.

"You mus' have drop' it on the stair," said grand-mamma, discerning the stratagem, and glad to aid it.

Problem in tactics: To hunt the glove all the way up to the balcony and return before Hilary, if he was coming, could reach Flora's side. Irby set his teeth—he loathed problems—and sprang up the steps.

"No use," chanted Madame with enjoyment; "the other one is not coming."

But Flora remained benign while the old lady drew a little mocking sigh. "Ah," said the latter, "if the General would only stop changing his mind about his two nephews, what a lot of hard work that would save you!"

"It isn't hard!" cried Flora; so radiantly that passing strangers brightened back, "I love it!"

"It!" mocked the grandmother as the girl passed her into the carriage. "It!"

"You poor tired old thing!" sighed the compassion-ate beauty. "Never mind, dear; how the General may choose no longer gives me any anxiety."

"Oh, you lie!"

"No," softly laughed the girl, "not exactly. Don't collapse, love, you'll get your share of the loot yet. My choice shall fit the General's as this glove (drawing on the one Irby was still away in search of) fits this hand."

Madame smiled her contempt: "Nevertheless you will risk *all* just to show Anna——"

Flora made a gesture of delight but harkened on——

"That she cannot have her Captain till——"

"Till I'm sure I don't want him!" sang the girl.

"Which will never be!" came the quiet response.

The maiden flushed: "On the contrary, my dear, I was just going to say, you will please begin *at once* to be more civil to *our* Captain—Irby."

Madame gazed: "My God!"

"Ho!" said Flora, "I'd rather somebody else's." She cheerily smoothed the bonnet-bows under the old lady's chin: Now, *chère*, you know the assets are all you care for—even if with them you have to take a nincompoop for a grandson."

She was laughing merrily when Irby reappeared in the crowd, motioning that he had found nothing. Her gloved hands raised in fond apology, and Hilary's absence, appeased him, and he entered the vehicle.

So to Jackson Square, where it was good-by to Irby and the carriage, and Age and Beauty climbed their staircase together. "To-morrow's Saturday," gayly sighed the girl. "I've a good mind to lie abed till noon, counting up the week's successes."

"Especially to-day's," smirked weary Age.

"Ho-o-oh!" laughed the maiden, "you and to-day be——." The rest was whispered close, with a one-fingered tap on the painted cheek. In the gloom of the upper landing she paused to murmur, "hear this: Two things I have achieved this week worth all to-day's bad luck ten times over—you don't believe me?"

"No, you pretty creature; you would have told me sooner, if only for vanity."

"I swear to you it is true!" whispered the lithe boaster, with a gleeful quiver from head to foot. "Listen! First—purely, of course, for love of Anna—I

Flora Taps Grandma's Cheek

have conspired with the General to marry her to Kincaid. And, second, also purely for love of her, I have conspired with Irby to keep her and Kincaid forever and a day apart!"

She tapped both the aged cheeks at once: "I hate to share anything so delicious with you, but I must, because——"

"Ah-h! because, as usual——"

"Yes! yes, you sweet old pelican! because you are to turn the crank! But it's all for love of Anna. Ah, there's no inspiration like exasperation!"

"Except destitution!" said the grandmother.

They came before Charlie with arms about each other and openly enjoyed his only comment—a scornful rounding of his eyes.

In the Callender house, as the stair clock sounded the smallest hour of the night, Miranda, seeing the chink under Anna's door to be still luminous, stole to the spot, gently rapped, and winning no response warily let herself in.

From the diary on her desk Anna lifted her cheek, looked up, reclosed her lids, smiled and reopened them. Miranda took the blushing face between her palms, and with quizzing eyes—and nose—inquired:

"Is there any reason under heaven why Anna Callender shouldn't go to bed and have glad dreams?"

"None that I know of," said Anna.

XV

THE LONG MONTH OF MARCH

Ole mahs' love' wine, ole mis' love' silk,
    De piggies, dey loves buttehmilk,
An' eveh sence dis worl' began,
    De ladies loves de ladies' man.
I loves to sing a song to de ladies!
I loves to dance along o' de ladies!
Whilse eveh I can breave aw see aw stan'
    I's bound to be a ladies' man.

So sang Captain Hilary Kincaid at the Mandeville-
Callender wedding feast, where his uncle Brodnax,
with nearly every one we know, was present. Hilary
had just been second groomsman, with Flora for his
"file leader," as he said, meaning second bridesmaid.
He sat next her at table, with Anna farthest away.

Hardly fortunate was some one who, conversing
with the new Miss Callender, said the charm of Kincaid's singing was that the song came from "the entire
man." She replied that just now it really seemed so!
In a sense both comments were true, and yet never in
the singer's life had so much of "the entire man" refused to sing. All that night of the illumination he had
not closed his eyes, except in anguish for having tried
to make love on the same day when—and to the same
Anna Callender before whom—he had drawn upon
himself the roaring laugh of the crowded street; or in
a sort of remorse for letting himself become the rival
of a banished friend who, though warned that a whole
platoon of him would make no difference, suddenly

seemed to plead a prohibitory difference to one's inmost sense of honor.

At dawn he had risen resolved to make good his boast and "fight like a whale." Under orders of his own seeking he had left the battery the moment its tents were up and had taken boat for Mobile. Whence he had returned only just in time to stand beside Flora Valcour, preceded by a relative of the bridegroom paired with Anna.

Yet here at the feast none was merrier than Kincaid, who, charmingly egged on by Flora, kept those about him in gales of mirth, and even let himself be "cajoled" (to use his own term) into singing this song whose title had become his nickname. Through it all Anna smiled and laughed with the rest and clapped for each begged-for stanza. Yet all the time she said in her heart, "He is singing it at me!"

> De squir'l he love' de hick'ry tree,
> De clover love' de bummle-bee,
> De flies, dey loves mullasses, an'—
> De ladies loves de ladies' man.
> I loves to be de beau o' de ladies!
> I loves to shake a toe wid de ladies!
> Whilse eveh I'm alive, on wateh aw lan',
> I's bound to be a ladies' man.

The General, seeing no reason why Hilary should not pay Anna at least the attentions he very properly paid his "file leader," endured the song with a smile, but took revenge when he toasted the bride:

"In your prayers to-night, my dear Constance, just thank God your husband is, at any rate, without the sense of humor— Stop, my friends! Let me finish!"

Kincaid's Battery

A storm of laughter was falling upon Mandeville, but the stubborn General succeeded after all in diverting it to Hilary, to whom in solemn mirth he pointed as— "*that* flirtatious devotee of giddiness, without a fault big enough to make him interesting!" ["Hoh!"— "Hoh!"—from men and maidens who could easily have named huge ones.] Silent Anna knew at least two or three; was it not a fault a hundred times too grave to be uninteresting, for a big artillerist to take a little frightened lassie as cruelly at her word as he was doing right here and now?

Interesting to her it was that his levity still remained unsubmerged, failing him only in a final instant: Their hands had clasped in leave-taking and her eyes were lifted to his, when some plea with which "the entire man" seemed overcharged to the very lips was suddenly, subtly, and not this time by disconcertion, but by self-mastery, withheld. Irby put in a stiff good-by, and as he withdrew, Hilary echoed only the same threadbare word more brightly, and was gone; saying to himself as he looked back from the garden's outmost bound:

"She's *cold;* that's what's the matter with Anna; cold and cruel!"

Tedious was the month of March. Mandeville devise' himself a splandid joke on that, to the effect that soon enough there would be months of tedieuse marches—ha, ha, ha!—and contribute' it to the news-pape'. Yet the tedium persisted. Always something about to occur, nothing ever occurring. Another vast parade, it is true, some two days after the marriage, to welcome from Texas that aged general (friend of the Callenders) who after long suspense to both sides

The Long Month of March

had at last joined the South, and was to take command at New Orleans. Also, consequent upon the bursting of a gun that day in Kincaid's Battery, the funeral procession of poor, handsome, devil-may-care Félix de Gruy; saxhorns moaning and wailing, drums muttering from their muffled heads, Anna's ensign furled in black, captain and lieutenants on foot, brows inclined, sabres reversed, and the "Stars and Bars," new flag of the Confederacy, draping the slow caisson that bore him past the Callenders' gates in majesty so strange for the gay boy.

Such happenings, of course; but nothing that ever brought those things for which one, wakening in the night, lay and prayed while forced by the songster's rapture to "listen to the mocking-bird."

While the Judge lived the Callenders had been used to the company of men by the weight of whose energies and counsel the clock of public affairs ran and kept time; senators, bishops, bank presidents, great lawyers, leading physicians; a Dr. Sevier, for one. Some of these still enjoyed their hospitality, and of late in the old house life had recovered much of its high charm and breadth of outlook. Yet March was tedious.

For in March nearly all notables felt bound to be up at Montgomery helping to rock the Confederacy's cradle. Whence came back sad stories of the incapacity, negligence, and bickerings of misplaced men. It was "almost as bad as at Washington." Friends still in the city were tremendously busy; yet real business—Commerce—with scarce a moan of complaint, lay heaving out her dying breath. Busy at everything but business, these friends, with others daily arriving in command of rustic volunteers, kept society tremendously gay, by gaslight; and courage and fortitude and love of country and trust in God and scorn of the foe went clad in rainbow colors; but at the height of all manner of revels some pessimist was sure to explain to Anna why the war must be long, of awful cost, and with a just fighting chance to win.

"Then why do we not turn about right here?"

"Too late now."

Such reply gave an inward start, it seemed so fitted to her own irrevealable case. But it was made to many besides her, and women came home from dinings or from operas and balls for the aid of this or that new distress of military need, and went up into the dark and knelt in all their jewels and wept long. In March the poor, everywhere, began to be out of work, and recruiting to be lively among them too, because for thousands of them it was soldier's pay or no bread. Among the troops from the country death had begun to reap great harvests ere a gun was fired, and in all the camps lovers nightly sang their lugubrious "Lorena," feeling that "a hundred months had passed" before they had really dragged through one. March was so tedious, and lovers are such poor arithmeticians. Wherever Hilary Kincaid went, showing these how to cast cannon (that would not burst), those where to build fortifications, and some how to make unsickly camps, that song was begged of him in the last hour before sleep; last song but one, the very last being always—that least liked by Anna.

Tedious to Kincaid's Battery were his absences on so many errands. Behind a big earthwork of their

The Long Month of March

own construction down on the river's edge of the old battle ground, close beyond the Callenders', they lay camped in pretty white tents that seemed to Anna, at her window, no bigger than visiting-cards. Rarely did she look that way but the fellows were drilling, their brass pieces and their officers' drawn sabres glinting back the sun, horses and men as furiously diligent as big and little ants, and sometimes, of an afternoon, their red and yellow silk and satin standard unfurled—theirs and hers. Of evenings small bunches of the boys would call to chat and be sung to; to threaten to desert if not soon sent to the front; and to blame all delays on colonels and brigadiers "known" by them to be officially jealous of— They gave only the tedious nickname.

"Why belittle him with that?" queried Miranda, winning Anna's silent gratitude.

"It doesn't belittle *him*," cried Charlie. "That's the joke. It makes *him* loom larger!"

Others had other explanations: Their guns were "ladies' guns!" Were the guns the foremost cause? Some qualified: "Foremost, yes; fundamental, no. Rather the fact that never was a woman cited in male gossip but instantly he was her champion; or that no woman ever brought a grievance to any camp where he might be but she wanted to appeal it to him.

Anna "thought the name was all from the song."

"Oh, fully as much from his hundred and one other songs! Had he never sung to her—

"I'd offer thee this hand of mine——"?

Frankly, it was agreed, he did most laughably love

75

ladies' company; that he could always find it, as a horse can find water; that although no evening in their society could be so gay or so long that he would not be certain to work harder next day than any one else, no day could be so cruelly toilsome that he could not spend half the next night dancing with the girls; and lastly, that with perfect evenness and a boyish modesty he treated them all alike.

Anna laughed with the rest, but remembered three separate balls to which, though counted on, he had not come, she uninformed that military exigencies had at the last moment curtly waved him off, and he unaware that these exigencies had been created by Irby under inspiration from the daintiest and least self-assertive tactician in or about New Orleans.

XVI

CONSTANCE TRIES TO HELP

ONE day, in Canal Street, Kincaid met "Smellemout and Ketchem." It was pleasant to talk with men of such tranquil speech. He proposed a glass of wine, but just then they were "strictly temperance." They alluded familiarly to his and Greenleaf's midnight adventure. The two bull-drivers, they said, were still unapprehended.

Dropping to trifles they mentioned a knife, a rather glittering gewgaw, which, as evidence, ought——

"Oh, that one!" said Hilary. "Yes, I have it, mud, glass jewels and all. No," he laughed, "I can keep it quite as safely as you can."

Constance Tries to Help

So they passed to a larger matter. "For, really, as to Gibbs and Lafontaine——"

"You can't have them either," interrupted their Captain, setting the words to a tune. Then only less melodiously—"No, sir-ee! Why, gentlemen, they weren't trying to kill the poor devil, he was trying to kill them, tell your Committee of Public Safety. And tell them times are changed. You can *take* Sam and Maxime, of course, *if* you can take the whole battery; we're not doing a retail business. By the by—did you know?—'twas Sam's gun broke the city's record, last week, for rapid firing! Funny, isn't it!—Excuse me, I must speak to those ladies."

The ladies, never prettier, were Mrs. Callender and Constance. They were just reëntering, from a shop, their open carriage. In amiable reproach they called him a stranger, yet with bewitching resignation accepted and helped out his lame explanations.

"You look—" began Constance—but "careworn" was a risky term and she stopped. He suggested "weather-beaten," and the ladies laughed.

"Yes," they said, "even they were overtasked with patriotic activities, and Anna had almost made herself ill. Nevertheless if he would call he should see her too. Oh, no, not to-day; no, not to-morrow; but—well—the day after." (Miss Valcour passed so close as to hear the appointment, but her greeting smile failed to draw their attention.) "And oh, then you must tell us all about that fearful adventure in which you saved Lieutenant Greenleaf's life! Ah, we've heard, just heard, *in a letter.*" The horses danced with impatience. "We shall expect you!"

As they drove into Royal Street with Constance rapturously pressing Miranda's hand the latter tried vainly to exchange bows with a third beauty and a second captain, but these were busy meeting each other in bright surprise and espied the carriage only when it had passed.

Might the two not walk together a step or so? With pleasure. They were Flora and Irby. Presently—

"Do you know," she asked, "where your cousin proposes to be day after to-morrow evening—in case you should want to communicate with him?"

He did not. She told him.

XVII

"OH, CONNIE, DEAR——NOTHING——GO ON"

THE third evening came. On all the borders of dear Dixie more tents than ever whitened sea-shores and mountain valleys, more sentinels paced to and fro in starlight or rain, more fifers and trumpeters woke the echoes with strains to enliven fortitude, more great guns frowned silently at each other over more parapets, and more thousands of lovers reclined about camp fires with their hearts and fancies at home, where mothers and maidens prayed in every waking moment for God's mercy to keep the brave truants; and with remembrance of these things Anna strove to belittle her own distress while about the library lamp she and Miranda seemed each to be reading a book, and Constance the newspaper sent from Charleston by Mandeville.

"Oh, Connie, Dear—Nothing—Go On"

Out in the mellow night a bird sang from the tip-top of a late-blooming orange tree, and inside, away inside, inside and through and through the poor girl's heart, the "years"—which really were nothing but the mantel clock's quarter-hours—"crept slowly by."

At length she laid her book aside, softly kissed each seated companion, and ascended to her room and window. There she stood long without sound or motion, her eyes beyond the stars, her head pressed wearily against the window frame. Then the lids closed while her lips formed soft words:

"Oh, God, he is not coming!" Stillness again. And then— "Oh, let me believe yet that only Thy hand keeps him away! Is it to save him for some one fairer and better? God, I ask but to know! I'm a rebel, but not against Thee, dear Lord. I know it's a sin for me to suffer this way; Thou dost not *owe* me happiness; I owe it Thee. Oh, God, am I clamoring for my week's wages before I've earned an hour's pay? Yet oh! yet oh!"—the head rocked heavily on its support—"if only—if only——"

She started—listened! A gate opened—shut. She sprang to her glass and then from it. In soft haste she needlessly closed the window and drew its shade and curtains. She bathed her eyelids and delicately dried them. At the mirror again she laid deft touches on brow and crown, harkening between for any messenger's step, and presently, without reason, began to set the room more exquisitely to rights. Now she faced the door and stood attentive, and now she took up a small volume and sat down by her lamp.

A tap: Constance entered, beaming only too tenderly.

"It was better, wasn't it," she asked, hovering, "to come than to send?"

"Why, of course, dear; it always is."

A meditative silence followed. Then Anna languidly inquired, "Who is it?"

"Nobody but Charlie."

The inquirer brightened: "And why isn't Charlie as good as any one?"

"He is, to-night," replied the elder beauty, "except —the one exception."

"Oh, Connie"—a slight flush came as the seated girl smilingly drew her sister's hands down to her bosom— "there isn't any one exception, and there's not going to be any. Now, that smile is downright mean of you!"

The offender atoned with a kiss on the brow.

"Why do you say," asked its recipient, "'as good as any one, *to-night*'?"

"Because," was the soft reply, "to-night he comes from—the other—to explain why the other couldn't come."

"Why!"—the flush came back stronger—"why, Connie! why, that's positively silly—ha, ha, ha!"

"I don't see how, Nan."

"My dear Con! Isn't his absence equally and perfectly innocent whether he couldn't come or wouldn't come? But an explanation sent!—by courier!—to— to shorten—ah, ha, ha!—to shorten our agony! Why, Con, wouldn't you have thought better of him than that? H-oh, me! What a man's 'bound to be' I suppose he's bound to be. What is the precious explanation?"

With melting eyes Constance shook her head. "You

don't deserve to hear it," she replied. Her tears came: "My little sister, I'm on the man's side in this affair!"

"That's not good of you," murmured Anna.

"I don't claim to be good. But there's one thing, Nan Callender, I never did; I never chained up my lover to see if he'd stay chained. When Steve——"

"Oh-h! Oh-h!" panted Anna, "you're too cruel! Hilary Kincaid wears no chain of mine!"

"Oh, yes, he does! He's broken away, but he's broken away, chain and all, to starve and perish, as one look into his face would show you!"

"He doesn't show his face. He sends——"

"An explanation. Yes. Which first you scorn and then consent to hear."

"Don't scorn me, Connie. What's the explanation?"

"It's this: he's been sent back to those Mobile fortifications—received the order barely in time to catch the boat by going instantly. Nan, the Valcours' house is found to stand right on their proposed line, and he's gone to decide whether the line may be changed or the house must be demolished."

Anna rose, twined an arm in her sister's and with her paced the chamber. "How perfectly terrible!" she murmured, their steps ceasing and her eyes remote in meditation. "Poor Flora! Oh, the poor old lady! And oh, oh, poor Flora!— But, Con! The line will be changed! He—you know what the boys call him!"

"Yes, but there's the trouble. He's no one lady's man. Like Steve, he's so absolutely fair——"

"Connie, I tell you it's a strange line he won't change for Flora Valcour!"

"Now, Nan Callender! The line will go where it

ought to go. By the by, Charlie says neither Flora nor her grandmother knows the house is in danger. Of course, if it is harmed, the harm will be paid for."

"Oh, paid for!"

"Why, Nan, I'm as sorry for them as you. But *I* don't forget to be sorry for Hilary Kincaid too."

"Connie"—walk resumed, speaker's eyes on the floor—"if you'd only see that to me he's merely very interesting—entertaining—nothing more whatever—I'd like to say just a word about him."

"Say on, precious."

"Well—did you ever see a man so fond of men?"

"Oh, of course he is, or men wouldn't be so fond of him."

"*I* think he's fonder of men than of women!"

Constance smiled: "Do you?"

"And I think," persisted Anna, "the reason some women find him so agreeable is that our collective society is all he asks of us, or ever will ask."

"Nan Callender, look me in the eye! You can't! My little sister, you've got a lot more sense than I have, and you know it, but I can tell you one thing. When Steve and I——"

"Oh, Connie, dear—nothing—go on."

"I won't! Except to say some lovers take love easy and some—can't. I must go back to Charlie. I know, Nan, it's those who love hardest that take love hardest, and I suppose it's born in Hilary Kincaid, and it's born in you, to fight it as you'd fight fire. But, oh, in these strange times, don't do it! Don't do it. You're going to have trouble a-plenty without."

The pair, moving to the door with hands on each

other's shoulders, exchanged a melting gaze. "Trouble a-plenty," softly asked Anna, "why do you—— ?"

"Oh, why, why, why!" cried the other, with a sudden gleam of tears. "I wish you and Miranda had never learned that word."

XVIII

FLORA TELLS THE TRUTH!

You ask how the Valcour ladies, living outwardly so like the most of us who are neither scamps nor saints, could live by moral standards so different from those we have always thought essential to serenity of brow, sweetness of bloom or blitheness of companionship, and yet could live so prettily—remain so winsome and unscarred.

Well, neither of them had ever morally *fallen* enough even to fret the brow. It is the fall that disfigures. They had lived up to inherited principles (such as they were), and one of the minor of these was, to adapt their contours to whatever they impinged upon.

We covet solidity of character, but Flora and Madame were essentially fluid. They never let themselves clash with any one, and their private rufflings of each other had only a happy effect of aerating their depths, and left them as mirror-smooth and thoroughly one as the bosom of a garden lake after the ripples have died behind two jostling swans. To the Callenders society was a delightful and sufficient end. To the Valcours it was a means to all kinds of ends, as truly as commerce or the industries, and yet they were

so fragrantly likable that to call them accomplices
seems outrageous—clogs the pen. Yes, they were
actors, but you never saw that. They never stepped
out of their parts, and they had this virtue, if it is one:
that behind all their rôles they were staunchly for each
other in every pinch. When Kincaid had been away a
few days this second time, these two called at the Callender house.

To none was this house more interesting than to
Flora. In her adroit mind she accused it of harboring
ancient secrets in its architecture, shrewd hiding-places
in its walls. Now as she stood in the panelled drawing-
rooms awaiting its inmates, she pointed out to her
seated companion that this was what her long-dead
grandsire might have made their own home, behind
Mobile, had he spent half on its walls what he had
spent in them on wine, cards, and——"

"Ah!" chanted the old lady, with a fierce glint and
a mock-persuasive smile, "add the crowning word, the
capsheaf. You have the stamina to do it."

"Women," said the girl of stamina beamingly, and
went floating about, peering and tapping for hollow
places. At one tap her eye, all to itself, danced; but
on the instant Anna, uninformed of their presence, and
entering with a vase of fresh roses, stood elated. Praise
of the flowers hid all confusion, and Flora, with laughing
caresses and a droll hardihood which Anna always enjoyed, declared she would gladly steal roses, garden, house
and all. Anna withdrew, promising instant return.

"Flora dear!" queried the grandmother in French,
"why did you tell her the truth? For once you must
have been disconcerted!"

Flora Tells the Truth!

The sparkling girl laughed: "Why, isn't that—with due modifications—just what we're here for?"

Madame suddenly looked older, but quickly brightened again as Flora spoke on: "Don't you believe the truth is, now and then, the most effective lie? I've sometimes inferred you did."

The old lady rather enjoyed the gibe: "My dear, I can trust you never to give any one an overdose of it. Yet take care, you gave it a bit too pure just now. Don't ever risk it so on that fool Constance, she has the intuitive insight of a small child—the kind you lost so early."

The two exchanged a brief admiring glance. "Oh, I'm all right with Constance," was the reply. "I'm cousin to 'Steve'!"

There the girl's gayety waned. The pair were at this moment in desperate need of money. Mandeville was one of the old coffee-planter's descendants. Had fate been less vile, thought Flora, this house might have been his, and so hers in the happy event of his demise. But now, in such case, to Constance, as his widow, would be left even the leavings, the overseer's cottage; which was one more convenient reason for detesting— not him, nor Constance—that would be to waste good ammunition; but——

"Still thinking of dear Anna?" asked the dame.

The maiden nodded: "Grandma"—a meditative pause—"I love Anna. Anna's the only being on earth I can perfectly trust."

"Ahem!" was the soft rejoinder, and the two smilingly held each other's gaze for the larger part of a minute. Then one by one came in the ladies of the house, and it was kiss and chirrup and kiss again.

"*Cousin* Constance—ah, ha, ha!—*cousin* Flora!"

The five talked of the wedding. Just to think! 'Twas barely a month ago, they said.

Yet how much had occurred, pursued Miranda, and how many things hoped and longed for had not occurred, and how time had dragged! At those words Flora saw Anna's glance steal over to Miranda. But Miranda did not observe, and the five chatted on. How terrifying, at still noon of the last Sabbath— everybody in church—had been that explosion of the powder-mill across the river. The whole business blown to dust. Nothing but the bare ground left. Happily no workmen there. No, not even a watchman, though the city was well known to be full of the enemy's "minions" (Flora's term). Amazing negligence, all agreed. Yet only of a piece—said Constance—etc.

And how sad to find there was a victim, after all, when poor, threadbare old Doctor Visionary, inventor of the machine-gun and a new kind of powder, began to be missed by his landlady, there being, in Captain Kincaid's absence, no one else to miss him. Yes, it was the Captain who had got him a corner to work in at the powder-mill. So much the worse for both. Now plans, models, formulæ, and inventor were gone in that one flash and roar that shook the whole city and stopped all talk of Captain Kincaid's promotion as an earthquake stops a clock.

"Well," cried Constance to Flora, who had grown silent, "the battery will love him all the more!"

"And so will we all!" said Madame, also to Flora;

and Flora, throwing off a look of pain, explained to
Anna, "He is so good to my brother!"

"Naturally," quizzed Miranda, with her merriest
wrinkles. Flora sparkled, made a pretty face at her
and forced a change of theme; gave Anna's roses new
praise, and said she had been telling grandma of the
swarms of them in the rear garden. So the old lady,
whom she had told no such thing, let Constance and
Miranda conduct her there. But Flora softly detained
Anna, and the moment they were alone seized both her
hands. Whereat through all Anna's frame ran despair,
crying, "He has asked her! He has asked her!"

XIX

FLORA ROMANCES

"Dearest," warily exclaimed the Creole beauty,
with a sudden excess of her pretty accent, "I am in
a situation perfectly dreadful!"

Anna drew her to a sofa, seeing pictures of her and
Hilary together, and tortured with a belief in their exquisite fitness to be so. "Can I help you, dear?" she
asked, though the question echoed mockingly within
her.

"Ah, no, except with advice," said Flora, "only with
advice!"

"Ho-o-oh! if I were worthy to advise you it wouldn't
flatter me so to be asked."

"But I muz' ask. 'Tis only with you that I know
my secret will be—to everybody—and forever—at the
bed of the ocean. You can anyhow promise me that."

"Yes, I can anyhow promise you that."

"Then," said Flora, "let me speak whiles—" She dropped her face into her hands, lifted it again and stared into her listener's eyes so piteously that through Anna ran another cry—"He has not asked! No girl alive could look so if he had asked her!"

Flora seemed to nerve herself: "Anna, every dollar we had, every picayune we could raise, grandma and I, even on our Mobile house and our few best jewels, is—is——"

"Oh, what—what? Not lost? Not—not stolen?"

"Blown up! Blown up with that poor old man in the powder-mill!"

"Flora, Flora!" was all Anna, in the shame of her rebuked conjectures, could cry, and all she might have cried had she known the very truth: That every dollar, picayune, and other resource had disappeared *gradually* in the grist-mill of daily need and indulgence, and never one of them been near the powder-mill, the poor old man or any of his devices.

"His theories were so convincing," sighed Flora.

"And you felt so pitiful for him," prompted Anna.

"Grandma did; and I was so ambitious to do some great patriotic service—like yours, you Callenders, in giving those cannon'!—and——"

"Oh, but you went too far!"

"Ah, if we had only gone no farther!"

"You went farther? How could you?"

"Grandma did. You know, dear, how suddenly Captain Kincaid had to leave for Mobile—by night?"

"Yes," murmured Anna, with great emphasis in her private mind.

Flora Romances

"Well, jus' at the las' he gave Charlie a small bag of gold, hundreds of dollars, for—for—*me to keep for him till his return.* Anna! I was offended."

"Oh, but surely he meant no——"

"Ah, my dear, did I ever give him the very least right to pick me out in that manner? No. Except in that one pretty way he has with all of us—and which you know so well——"

An uncourageous faint smile seemed the safest response.

"Yes," said Flora, "you know it. And I had never allowed myself——"

With eyes down the two girls sat silent. Then the further word came absently, "I refused to touch his money," and there was another stillness.

"Dear," slowly said Anna, "I don't believe it was his. It would not have been in gold. Some men of the battery were here last evening— You know the Abolition school-mistress who was sent North that day?"

"Yes, I know, 'twas hers."

"Well, dear, if she could entrust it to him——"

"Ah! *she* had a sort of right, being, as the whole battery knows, in love with him"—the beauty swept a finger across her perfect brows—"up to there! For that I don't know is he to blame. If a girl has no more sense——"

"No," murmured Anna as the cruel shaft went through her. "What did Charlie do with the money?"

Flora tossed a despairing hand: "Gave it to grandma! And poor innocent grandma lent it to the old gentleman! 'Twas to do wonders for the powder and gun, and be return' in three days. But the next——"

"I see," sighed Anna, "I see!"

"Yes, next day 'twas Sunday, and whiles I was *kneeling in the church* the powder, the gun, the old man and the money— Oh, Anna, what shall I do?"

"My dear, I will tell you," began Anna, but the seeker of advice was not quite ready for it.

"We have a few paltry things, of course," she spoke on, "but barely would they pay half. They would neither save our honor, neither leave us anything for rent or bread! Our house, to be sure, is worth more than we have borrowed on it, but in the meantime——"

"In the meantime, dear, you shall—" But still Flora persisted:

"Any day, any hour, Captain Kincaid may return. Oh, if 'twere anybody in this worl' but him! For, Anna, I must take all the blame—all!" The face went again into the hands.

"My dear, you shall take none. You shall hand him every dollar, every picayune, on sight."

"Ah, how is that possible? Oh, no, no, no. Use your money? Never, never, never!"

"It isn't money, Flora. And no one shall ever know. I've got some old family jewellery——"

"Family— Oh, sweet, for shame!"

"No shame whatever. There's a great lot of it— kinds that will never be worn again. Let me—" The speaker rose.

"No, no, no! No, Anna, no! For Heaven's sake——"

"Just a piece or two," insisted Anna. "Barely enough to borrow the amount." She backed away, Flora clinging to her fingers and faltering:

Flora Romances

"No, blessed angel, you must not! No, I will not wait. I'll—I'll——"

But Anna kissed the clinging hands and vanished.

A high elation bore her quite to her room and remained with her until she had unlocked the mass of old jewels and knelt before them. But then all at once it left her. She laid her folded hands upon them, bent her brow to the hands, then lifted brow and weeping eyes and whispered to Heaven for mercy.

"Oh"—a name she could not speak even there went through her heart in two big throbs—"if only we had never met! I never set so much as a smile to snare you, you who have snared me. Can Connie be right? Have you felt my thraldom, and are you trying to throw me off? Then I must help you do it. Though I covet your love more than life I will not tether it. Oh, it's because I so covet that I will not tether it! With the last gem from my own throat will I rather help you go free if you want to go. God of mercy, what else can I do!"

In grave exultancy Flora moved up and down the drawing-room enjoying her tread on its rich carpet. She would have liked to flit back to the side of yonder great chimney breast, the spot where she had been surprised while sounding the panel work, but this was no time for postponable risks. She halted to regale her critical eye on the goodly needlework of a folding-screen whose joints, she noticed, could not be peered through, and in a pretty, bird-like way stole a glance behind it. Nothing there. She stepped to a front window and stood toying with the perfect round of her silken belt. How slimly neat it was. Yet beneath the

draperies it so trimly confined lay hid, in a few notes of
"city money," the proceeds of the gold she had just
reported blown into thin air with the old inventor—
who had never seen a glimmer of it. Not quite the full
amount was there; it had been sadly nibbled. But
now by dear Anna's goodness (ahem!) the shortage
could be restored, the entire hundreds handed back to
Captain Kincaid, and a snug sum be retained "for
rent and bread." Yet after all—as long as good stories
came easy—why hand anything back—to anybody—
even to—him?

He! In her heart desire and odium beat strangely
together. Fine as martial music he was, yet gallingly
out of her rhythm, above her key. Liked her much,
too. Yes, for charms she had; any fool could be liked
that way. What she craved was to be liked for charms
she had not, graces she scorned; and because she could
not be sure how much of that sort she was winning she
tingled with heat against him—and against Anna—
Anna giver of guns—who *had the money* to give guns—
till her bosom rose and fell. But suddenly her musing
ceased, her eyes shone.

A mounted officer galloped into the driveway, a
private soldier followed, and the private was her brother.
Now they came close. The leader dismounted, passed
his rein to Charlie and sprang up the veranda steps.
Flora shrank softly from the window and at the same
moment Anna reëntered gayly, showing a glitter of
values twice all expectation:

"If these are not enough—" She halted with lips
apart. Flora had made sign toward the front door,
and now with a moan of fond protest covered the

gem-laden hand in both her palms and pushed it from
her.

"Take them back," she whispered, yet held it fast,
"'tis too late! There—the door-bell! 'Tis Hilary
Kincaid! All is too late, take them back!"

"Take them, you!" as vehemently whispered Anna.
"You must take them! You must, you shall!"

Flora had half started to fly, but while she hung upon
Anna's words she let her palms slip under the bestowing hand and the treasure slide into her own fingers.

"Too late, too late! And oh, I can never, never use
them any'ow!" She sprang noiselessly aside. To a
maid who came down the hall Anna quietly motioned
to show the newcomer into an opposite room, but Flora
saw that the sign was misinterpreted: "She didn't
understan'! Anna, she's going to bring him!" Before
the words were done the speaker's lithe form was gliding
down the room toward the door by which the other ladies
had gone out, but as she reached it she turned with a
hand-toss as of some despairing afterthought and
flitted back.

Out in the hall the front door opened and closed and
a sabre clinked: "Is Miss Callender at home?"

Before the question was half put its unsuspected
hearers had recovered a faultless poise. Beside a
table that bore her roses she whom the inquirer sought
stood retouching them and reflecting a faint excess of
their tint, while Flora, in a grave joy of the theatrical,
equal to her companion's distress of it, floated from
view behind the silken screen.

XX

THE FIGHT FOR THE STANDARD

His red képi in hand and with all the stalwart brisk-
ness of the flag-presentation's day and hour Hilary
Kincaid stepped into the room and halted, as large-
eyed as on that earlier occasion, and even more startled,
before the small figure of Anna.

Yet not the very same Hilary Kincaid. So said her
heart the instant glance met glance. The tarnish of
hard use was on all his trappings; like sea-marshes on
fire he was reddened and browned; about him hung
palpably the sunshine and air of sands and waves, and
all the stress and swing of wide designs; and on brow
and cheek were new lines that looked old. From every
point of his aspect the truth rushed home to her livelier, deadlier than ever hitherto, that there was War,
and that he and she were already parts of it.

But the change was more than this. A second and
quieter look, the hand-grasp lingering, showed something deeper; something that wove and tangled itself
through and about all designs, toils, and vigils, and
suddenly looking out of his eyes like a starved captive,
cried, "you—you—" and prophesied that, whether
they would or not, this war was to be his and hers together. A responding thrill must have run from her
fingers into his and belied the unaccountable restraint
of her welcome, for a joy shone from him which it took
her ignoring smile and her hand's withdrawal to
quench.

"Miss Anna——"

The Fight for the Standard

They sat down. His earlier boyishness came again somewhat, but only somewhat, as he dropped his elbows to his knees, looking now into his cap and now into her face. A glance behind her had assured Anna that there was no shadow on the screen, behind which sat Flora on the carpet, at graceful ease listening while she eagerly appraised the jewels in her hands and lap.

"Miss Anna," said the soldier again, "I've come— I've come to tell you something. It's mighty hard to tell. It's harder than I thought it would be. For, honestly, Miss Anna, you—from the first time I ever saw you, you—you— Were you going to speak?"

Behind the screen Flora smiled malignly while Anna said, "No, I—I was only—no, not at all; go on."

"Yes, Miss Anna, from the first time I——"

"When did you get back from Mobile?" asked Anna seeing he must be headed off.

"From Mobile? Just now, almost. You don't sup——"

"Oh! I hope"—she must head him off again—"I hope you bring good news?" There was risk in the question, but where was there safety? At her back the concealed listener waited keenly for the reply.

"Yes," said Hilary, "news the very best and hardly an hour old. Didn't you hear the battery cheering? That's what I've come to tell you. Though it's hard to tell, for I——"

"It's from Mobile, you say?"

"No, I can tell you the Mobile news first, but it's bad. Miss Flora's home——"

Anna gave a start and with a hand half upthrown said quietly, "Don't tell me. No, please, don't, I don't

95

want to hear it. I can't explain, but I—I—" Tears wet her lashes, and her hands strove with each other. "I don't like bad news. You should have taken it straight to Flora. Oh, I wish you'd do that now, won't you—please?"

Behind the screen the hidden one stiffened where she crouched with fierce brow and fixed eyes.

Kincaid spoke: "Would you have me pass you by with my good news to go first to her with the bad?"

"Oh, Captain Kincaid, yes, yes! Do it yet. Go, do it now. And tell her the good news too!"

"Tell her the good first and then stab her with the bad?"

"Oh, tell her the bad first. Do her that honor. She has earned it. She'll bear the worst like the heroine she is—the heroine and patriot. She's bearing it so now!"

"What! she knows already?"

In her hiding Flora's intent face faintly smiled a malevolence that would have startled even the grandam who still killed time out among the roses with her juniors.

"Yes," replied Anna, "she knows already."

"Knows! Miss Anna—that her home is in ashes?"

Anna gave a wilder start: "Oh, no-o-oh! Oh, yes— oh, no—oh, yes, yes! Oh, Captain Kincaid, how could you? Oh, monstrous, monstrous!" She made all possible commotion to hide any sound that might betray Flora, who had sprung to her feet, panting.

"But, but, Miss Anna!" protested Hilary. "Why, Miss Anna——"

"Oh, Captain Kincaid, how could you?"

The Fight for the Standard

"Why, you don't for a moment imagine——?"

"Oh, it's done, it's done! Go, tell her. Go at once, Captain Kincaid. Please go at once, won't you? . . . Please!"

He had risen amazed. Whence such sudden horror, in this fair girl, of a thing known by her already before he came? And what was this beside? Horror in the voice yet love beaming from the eyes? He was torn with perplexity. "I'll go, of course," he said as if in a dream. "Of course I'll go at once, but—why—if Miss Flora already—?" Then suddenly he recovered himself in the way Anna knew so well. "Miss Anna" —he gestured with his cap, his eyes kindling with a strange mixture of worship and drollery though his brow grew darker—"I'm gone now!"

"In mercy, please go!"

"I'm gone, Miss Anna, I'm truly gone. I always am when I'm with you. Fred said it would be so. You scare the nonsense out of me, and when that goes I go —the bubble bursts! Miss Anna—oh, hear me—it's my last chance—I'll vanish in a moment. The fellows tell me I always know just what to say to any lady or to anything a lady says; but, on my soul, I don't think I've ever once known what to say to you or to anything you've ever said to me, and I don't know now, except that I must and will tell you——"

"That you did not order the torch set! Oh, say that!"

"No one ordered it. It was a senseless mistake. Some private soldiers who knew that my lines of survey passed through the house——"

"Ah-h! ah-h!"

Kincaid's Battery

"Miss Anna, what would you have? Such is war! Many's the Southern home must go down under the fire of—of Kincaid's Battery, Miss Anna, before this war is over, else we might as well bring you back your flag and guns. Shall we? We can't now, they're ordered to the front. There! I've got it out! That's my good news. Bad enough for mothers and sisters. Bad for the sister of Charlie Valcour. Good for you. So good and bad in one for me, and so hard to tell and say no more! Don't you know why?"

"Oh, I've no right to know—and you've no right— oh, indeed, you mustn't. It would be so unfair—to you. I can't tell you why, but it—it would be!"

"And it wouldn't be of——?"

"Any use? No, no!"

Torturing mystery! that with such words of doom she should yet blush piteously, beam passionately.

"Good-by, then. I go. But I go—under your flag, don't I? Under your flag! captain of your guns!"

"Ah—one word—wait! Oh, Captain Kincaid, right is right! Not half those guns are mine. That flag is not mine."

There was no quick reply. From her concealment Flora, sinking noiselessly again to the carpet, harkened without avail. The soldier—so newly and poignantly hurt that twice when he took breath he failed to speak —gazed on the disclaiming girl until for very distress she broke the silence: "I—you—every flag of our cause—wherever our brave soldiers——"

"Oh, but Kincaid's Battery!—and *that* flag, Anna Callender! The flag you gave us! That sacred banner starts for Virginia to-morrow—goes into the war,

The Fight for the Standard

it and your guns, with only this poor beggar and his boys to win it honor and glory. Will you deny us —who had it from your hands—your leave to call it yours? Oh, no, no! To me—to me you will not!"

For reply there came a light in Anna's face that shone into his heart and was meant so to shine, yet her dissent was prompt: "I must. I must. Oh, Capt— Captain Kincaid, I love that flag too well to let it go misnamed. It's the flag of all of us who made it, us hundred girls——"

"Hundred—yes, yes, true. But how? This very morning I chanced upon your secret—through little Victorine—that every stitch in all that flag's embroideries is yours."

"Yet, Captain Kincaid, it is the flag of all those hundred girls; and if to any one marching under it it is to be the flag of any one of us singly, that one can only be —you know!"

Majestically in her hiding-place the one implied lowered and lifted her head in frigid scorn and awaited the commander's answer.

"True again," he said, "true. Let the flag of my hundred boys be to all and each the flag of a hundred girls. Yet will it be also the flag of his heart's one choice —sister, wife, or sweetheart—to every man marching, fighting, or dying under it—and more are going to die under it than are ever coming back. To me, oh, to me, let it be yours. My tasks have spared me no time to earn of you what would be dearer than life, and all one with duty and honor. May I touch your hand? Oh, just to say good-by. But if ever I return—no, have no

fear, I'll not say it now. Only—only—" he lifted the
hand to his lips—"good-by. God's smile be on you in
all that is to come."

"Good-by," came her answering murmur.

"And the flag?" he exclaimed. "The flag?" By
the clink of his sabre Flora knew he was backing away.
"Tell me—me alone—the word to perish with me if I
perish—that to me as if alone"—the clinking came
nearer again—"to me and for me and with your bless-
ing"—again the sound drew away—"the flag—the
flag I must court death under—is yours."

Silence. From out in the hall the lover sent back a
last beseeching look, but no sound reached the hiding
of the tense listener whose own heart's beating threatened to reveal her; no sound to say that now Anna
had distressfully shaken her head, or that now her
tears ran down, or that now in a mingled pain and
rapture of confession she nodded—nodded! and yet im-
ploringly waved him away.

It was easy to hear the door open and close. Faintly
on this other hand the voices of the ladies returning
from the garden foreran them. The soldier's tread
was on the outer stair. Now theirs was in the rear
veranda. With it tinkled their laughter. Out yonder
hoofs galloped.

The hidden one stole forth. A book on a table was
totally engaging the eyes of her hostess and at the instant grandma reëntered laden with roses. Now all
five were in, and Anna, pouring out words with every
motion, and curiously eyed by Constance, took the
flowers to give them a handier form, while Flora rallied
her kinswoman on wasting their friends' morning these

busy times, and no one inquired, and no one told, who had been here that now had vanished.

XXI

CONSTANCE CROSS-EXAMINES

It was like turning to the light the several facets of one of those old-fashioned jewels Flora was privately bearing away, to see the five beauties part company: "Good-by, good-by," kiss, kiss—ah, the sad waste of it!—kiss left, kiss right, "good-by."

As the Callenders came in again from the veranda, their theme was Flora. "Yet who," asked Constance, "ever heard her utter a moral sentiment?"

"Oh, her beauty does that," rejoined the kindly Miranda. "As Captain Kincaid said that evening he——"

"Yes, I know. He said he would pass her into heaven on her face, and I think it was a very strange thing for him to say!"

"Why?" daringly asked Miranda—and ran from the room.

The hater of whys turned upon her sister: "Nan, what's the matter? . . . Oh, now, yes, there is. What made you start when Miranda mentioned— Yes, you did. You're excited, you know you are. When we came in from the garden you and Flora were both——"

"Now, Connie——"

"Pshaw, Nan, I know he's been here, it's in your face. Who was with him; Charlie?"

"Yes. They just dropped in to say good-by. The battery's ordered to Virginia. Virginia hasn't seceded yet, but he feels sure she will before they can get there, and so do I. Don't you? If Kentucky and Maryland would only——"

"Now, Nan, just hush. When does he go?"

"To-morrow. But as to us"—the girl shrugged prettily while caressing her roses—"he's gone now."

"How did he talk?"

"Oh—quite as usual." The head bent low into the flowers. "In the one pretty way he has with all of us, you know."

Constance would not speak until their eyes met again. Then she asked, "Did Charlie and Flora give him any chance—to express himself?"

"Oh, Con, don't be foolish. He didn't want any. He as much as said so!"

"Ye-es," drawled the bride incredulously, "but——"

"Oh, he really did not, Con. He talked of nothing but the battery flag and how, because I'd presented it, they would forever and ever and ever and ever——" She waved her hands sarcastically.

"Nan, behave. Come here." The pair took the sofa. "How did he look and act when he first came in? Before you froze him stiff?"

"I didn't freeze him." The quiet, hurt denial was tremulous. "Wood doesn't freeze." The mouth drooped satirically: "You know well enough that the man who says his tasks have spared him no time to—to——"

"Nan, honest! Did *you* give him a fair chance—the kind I gave Steve?"

Constance Cross-Examines

"Oh, Con! He had all the chance any man ever got, or will get, from me."

The sister sighed: "Nan Callender, you are the *poorest* fisherman——"

"I'm not! I'm none! And if I were one"—the disclaimant glistened with mirth—"I couldn't be as poor a one as he is; he's afraid of his own bait." She began to laugh but had to force back her tears: "I didn't mean that! He's never had any bait—for me, nor wanted any. Neither he nor I ever— Really, Con, *you* are the only one who's made any mistake as to either of us! You seem to think——"

"Oh, dearie, I don't think at all, I just know. I know he's furiously in love with you—— Yes, furiously; but that he's determined to be fair to Fred Greenleaf——"

"Oh!"—a yet wickeder smile.

"Yes, and that he feels poor. You know that if the General——"

The hearer lifted and dropped both arms: "Oh!— to be continued!"

"Well, I know, too, that he doesn't believe, anyhow, in soldiers marrying. I've never told you, sweet, but— if I hadn't cried so hard—Steve would have challenged Hilary Kincaid for what he said on that subject the night we were married!"

Anna straightened, flashed, and then dropped again as she asked, "Is that all you know?"

"No, I know what counts for more than all the rest; I know you're a terror to him."

Remotely in the terror's sad eyes glimmered a smile that was more than half satisfaction. "You might as well call him a coward," she murmured.

"Not at all. *You* know you've been a terror to every suitor you've ever had—except Fred Greenleaf; he's the only one you couldn't keep frightened out of his wits. Now this time I know it's only because you're—you're bothered! You don't know how you're going to feel——"

"Now, Con——"

"And you *don't* want to mislead him, and you're just bothered to death! It was the same way with me."

"It wasn't!" silently said Anna's lips, her face averted. Suddenly she turned and clutched her sister's hands: "Oh, Con, while we talk trifles Flora's home lies in ashes! . . . Yes, he told me so just now."

"Didn't he tell her too?"

"Why, no, Connie, he—he couldn't very well. It—it would have been almost indelicate, wouldn't it? But he's gone now to tell her."

"He needn't," said Constance. "She knows it now. The moment I came in here I saw, through all her lightness, she'd got some heavy news. She must have overheard him, Nan."

"Connie, I—I believe she did!"

"Well, that's all right. What are you blushing for?"

"Blushing! Every time I get a little warm——" The speaker rose to go, but the sister kept her hand:

"Keep fresh for this evening, honey. He'll be back."

"No, he won't. He doesn't propose to if he could and he couldn't if he did. To get the battery off to-morrow——"

"It won't get off to-morrow, nor the next day, nor the next. You know how it always is. When Steve——"

"Oh, I don't know anything," said Anna, pulling

free and moving off. "But you, oh, you know it all, you and Steve!"

But the elder beauty was right. The battery did not go for more than a fortnight, and Hilary came again that evening. Sitting together alone, he and Anna talked about their inner selves—that good old sign! and when she gave him a chance he told her what Greenleaf had said about her and the ocean. Also he confided to her his envy of small-statured people, and told how it hurt him to go about showing the bigness of his body and hiding the pettiness of his soul. And he came the next evening and the next, and the next, and the next, and the next.

XXII

SAME STORY SLIGHTLY WARPED

NOT literally. That evening, yes, an end of it, but not the very next four, did Kincaid spend with Anna. It merely looked so to Flora Valcour.

Even on that first day, after his too prompt forenoon gallop from Callender House to the Valcour apartment had, of course, only insured his finding Flora not at home, all its evening except the very end was passed with her, Flora, in her open balcony overlooking the old Place d'Armes. His head ringing with a swarm of things still to be done and ordered done, he had purposed to remain only long enough to tell his dire news manfully, accept without insistent debate whatever odium it might entail, and decently leave its gentle recipients to their grief and dismay. What steps they should take to secure compensation it were far better they should discuss with Adolphe, who would be here to aid them when he, Kincaid, would be in far Virginia. The only other imperative matter was that of the young schoolma'am's gold, which must be left in bank. Awkward business, to have to ask for it in scrambling haste at such a moment.

But on a starlit balcony with two such ladies as the Valcours, to do one's errands, such errands, in scrambling haste proved not even a military possibility. Their greeting inquiries had to be answered:

"Yes, Charlie was well. He would be along soon, with fresh messages from division headquarters. The battery was at last—Pardon? . . . Yes, the Callenders were well—he supposed! He had seen only Miss Anna, and her only for so brief an instant——"

No, Madame Valcour had merely cleared her throat. "That climate is hard on those throat'."

He had seen Miss Anna, he resumed, "for so brief an instant—on an errand—that he had not made civil inquiry after the others, but had left good-by for them about as a news-carrier wads and throws in the morning paper!"

It was so pretty, the silvery way the questioning pair laughed to each other—at his simile, if that was the genuine source of their amusement—that he let himself laugh with them.

"But how?" they further asked. "He had left good-by? Good-day, yes! But for what good-by when juz' returning?"

"Ah, because here to them, also, it must be good-by, and be as brief as there! The battery—he had sent word to them at sunrise, but had just learned that his messenger had missed them—the battery was at last ordered"—etc.

"*Mon Dieu!*" gasped the old lady as if this was too cruelly sudden, and, "Oh, my brother! Oh, Captain Kincaid!" beautifully sighed Flora, from whom the grandmother had heard the news hours before.

Yet, "Of course *any* time 'twould have to be sudden," they had presently so recovered as to say, and Flora, for both, spoke on in accents of loveliest renunciation. She easily got the promise she craved, that no ill should come to Charlie which a commander's care could avert.

The loss of their Mobile home, which also Madame had perfectly known since morning, was broken to them with less infelicity, though they would talk cheerily of the house as something which no evil ever would or could befall, until suddenly the girl said, "Grandma, dearest, that night air is not so pretty good for your rheum; we better pass inside," and the old lady, insistently unselfish, moved a step within, leaving the other two on the balcony. There, when the blow came at last, Flora's melodious grievings were soon over, and her sweet reasonableness, her tender exculpation not alone of this dear friend but even of the silly fellows who had done the deed, and her queenly, patriotic self-obliteration, were more admirable than can be described. Were, as one may say, good literature. The grateful soldier felt shamed to find, most unaccountably, that Anna's positively cruel reception of the same news somehow suited him better. It was nearer his own size, he said to himself.

At any rate the foremost need now, on every account, was to be gone. But as he rose Flora reminded him of "those few hundred gold?" Goodness! he had clean forgotten the thing. He apologized for the liberty taken in leaving it with her, but— "Oh!" she prettily interrupted, "when I was made so proud!"

Well, now he would relieve her and take it at once to a bank cashier who had consented to receive it at his house this very night. She assured him its custody had given her no anxiety, for she had promptly passed it over to another! He was privately amazed:

"Oh—o-oh—oh, yes, certainly. That was right! To whom had she——?"

She did not say. "Yes," she continued, "she had at once thought it ought to be with some one who could easily replace it if, by any strange mishap—flood, fire, robbery—it should get lost. To do which would to her be impossible if at Mobile her house—" she tossed out her hands and dropped them pathetically. "But I little thought, Captain Kincaid—" she began a heart-broken gesture——

"Now, Miss Flora!" the soldier laughingly broke out, "if it's lost it's lost and no one but me shall lose a cent for it!"

"Ah, that," cried the girl, with tears in her voice; "'tis impossible! 'Twould kill her, that mortification, as well as me, for you to be the loser!"

"Loser! mortification!" laughed Hilary. "And what should I do with *my* mortification if I should let you, or her, be the loser? Who is she, Miss Flora? If I minded the thing, you understand, I shouldn't ask."

Flora shrank as with pain: "Ah, you must not!

Same Story Slightly Warped

And you must not guess, for you will surely guess wrong!" Nevertheless she saw with joy that he had guessed Anna, yet she suffered chagrin to see also that the guess made him glad. "And this you must make me the promise; that you never, never will let anybody know you have discover' that, eh?"

"Oh, I promise."

"And you must let her pay it me back—that money— and me pay it you. 'Twill be easy, only she mus' have time to get the money, and without needing to tell anybody for why, and for why in gold. Alas! I could have kept that a secret had it not have been you are to go to-morrow morning"

"Oh, rest easy," said the cheerful soldier, "mum's the word. But, Miss Flora, tell me this: How on earth did she lose it?"

"Captain Kincaid, by the goodness of the heart!"

"But how did it go; was it——?"

"Blown up! Blown up with that poor old man in the powder-mill! Ah, what do we know about money, Captain Kincaid, we silly women? That poor, inno-cent child, she lent it to the old gentleman. His theories they were so convincing, and she, she was so ambitious to do a great patriotic service. 'Twas to make wonders for the powder and gun, and to be return' in three days. But that next day 'twas Sunday, and whiles I was *kneeling in the church* the powder, the gun, the old man and the money——"

Hilary gestured facetiously for the narrator: "That's how millions have got to go in this business, and this driblet—why, I might have lent it, myself, if I'd been here! No, I'm the only loser, and——"

"Ah, Captain Kincaid, no, no! I implore you, no! —and for her sake! Oh, what are those few hundred for her to lose, if so she can only wipe that mistake? No, they shall be in the charge of that cashier before you're at Virginia, and that shall be my first news written to my brother—though he'll not comprehend except that he is to tell it you."

So it was arranged and agreed. As again he moved to go she won a new pledge of unending secrecy, and Charlie came with a document. Beside the parlor lamp, where, with one tiny foot covertly unslippered for the easement of angry corns, Madame sat embroidering, Kincaid broke the seal and read. He forced a scowl, but through it glimmered a joy in which Flora discerned again the thought of Anna. "Charlie," he said as a smile broke through, "prepare yourself."

"Now, Captain, if those old imbeciles——"

The commander's smile broadened: "Our battery, ladies and gentlemen, can't go for a week."

All laughed but Charlie. He swore at the top of his voice and threw himself from the room.

When his Captain had followed, Flora, standing and smiling, drew from her bosom a small, well-filled jewel-bag, balanced it on her uplifted palm and, rising to her toes, sang, "At last, at last, *grâce au ciel*, money is easy!"

"Yet at the same time my gifted granddaughter," remarked the old lady, in her native tongue and intent on her embroidery, "is uneasy, eh?"

Flora ignored the comment. She laid a second palm on the upraised booty, made one whole revolution, her soft crinoline ballooning and subsiding with a seductive

swish as she paused: "And you shall share these bless-
ings, grannie, love, although of the assets themselves"
—she returned the bag to its sanctuary and smoothed
the waist where the paper proceeds of the schoolmistress's gold still hid—"you shall never handle a
dime." She sparkled airily.

"No?" said Madame, still moving the needle and
still in French. "Nevertheless, morning and evening
together, our winnings are—how much?"

"Ours?" melodiously asked the smiling girl, "they
are not ours, they are mine. And they are—at the
least"—she dropped to her senior's footstool and spoke
caressingly low—"a clean thousand! Is not that sweet
enough music to the ear of a venerable"—she whispered—"cormorant?" She sparkled anew.

"I am sorry," came the mild reply, "you are in such
torture you have to call me names. But it is, of course,
entirely concerning—the house—ahem!"

Flora rose, walked to a window, and, as she gazed
out across the old plaza, said measuredly in a hard
voice: "Never mind! Never mind her—or him either.
I will take care of the two of them!"

A low laugh tinkled from the ancestress: "Ha, ha!
you thought the fool would be scandalized, and instead
he is only the more enamored."

The girl flinched but kept her face to the window:
"*He* is not the fool."

"No? We can hardly tell, when we are—in love."

Flora wheeled and flared, but caught herself, musingly crossed the room, returned half-way, and with
frank design resumed the stool warily vacated by the
unslippered foot; whose owner was mincing on, just

enough fluttered to play defiance while shifting her attack—

"Home, sweet home! For our ravished one you will, I suppose, permit his beloved country to pay—in its new paper money at 'most any discount—and call it square, eh?" Half the bitterness of her tone was in its sweetness.

In a sudden white heat the granddaughter clutched one aged knee with both hands: "Wait! If I don't get seven times all it was ever worth, the Yankees shall!" Then with an odd gladness in her eyes she added, "And *she* shall pay her share!"

"You mean—his?" asked the absorbed embroiderer. But on her last word she stiffened upward with a low cry of agony, shut her eyes and swung her head as if about to faint. Flora had risen.

"Oh-h-h!" the girl softly laughed, "was that your foot?"

XXIII

"SOLDIERS!"

WITH what innocent openness did we do everything in '61! "Children and fools" could not tell the truth any faster or farther than did our newspapers—*Picayune, Delta, True Delta, Crescent, L'Abeille,* and *L'Estafette du Sud.* After every military review the exact number in line and the name of every command and commander were hurried into print. When at last we began to cast siege guns, the very first one was defiantly proclaimed to all the Confederacy's enemies: an eight-inch Dahlgren, we would have them to know. Kincaid and his foundry were given full credit, and the defence named where the "iron monster" was to go, if not the very embrasure designated into which you must fire to dismount it.

The ladies, God bless them, were always free to pass the guard on the city side of that small camp and earthwork, where with the ladies' guns "the ladies' man" had worn the grass off all the plain and the zest of novelty out of all his nicknamers, daily hammering—he and his only less merciful lieutenants—at their everlasting drill.

Such ladies! Why shouldn't they pass? Was it not safe for the cause and just as safe for them? Was not every maid and matron of them in the "Ladies' Society of the Confederate Army"—whereof Miss Callender was a secretary and Miss Valcour one of the treasurers? And had not the fellows there, owing to an influence or two in the camp itself and another or two just outside it, all become, in a strong, fine sense and high degree, ladies' men? It was good for them spiritually, and good for their field artillery evolutions, to be watched by maidenly and matronly eyes. Quite as good was it, too, for their occasional heavy-gun practice with two or three huge, new-cast, big-breeched "hell-hounds," as Charlie and others called them, whose tapering black snouts lay out on the parapet's superior slope, fondled by the soft Gulf winds that came up the river, and snuffing them for the taint of the enemy.

One afternoon when field-gun manœuvres were at a close, Kincaid spoke from the saddle. Facing him stood his entire command, "in order in the line," their six shining pieces and dark caissons and their twice six

six-horse teams stretching back in six statuesque rows,
each of the three lieutenants—Bartleson, Villeneuve,
Tracy—in the front line, midway between his two guns;
the artificers just six yards out on the left, and guidon
and buglers just six on the right. At the commander's
back was the levee. Only now it had been empty of
spectators, and he was seizing this advantage.

"Soldiers!" It was his first attempt since the flag
presentation, and it looked as though he would falter,
but he hardened his brow: "Some days ago you were
told not to expect marching orders for a week. Well
the week's up and we're told to wait another. Now
that makes me every bit as mad as it makes you! I
feel as restless as any man in this battery, and I told the
commanding general to-day that you're the worst dis-
contented lot I've yet seen, and that I was proud of you
for it. That's all I said to him. But! if there's a man
here who doesn't yet know the difference between a
soldierly discontent and unsoldierly *grumbling* I want
him to GO! Kincaid's Battery is not for him. Let
him transfer to infantry or cavalry. Oh, I know it's
only that you want to be in the very first fight, and
that's all right! But what we can't get we don't
grumble for in Kincaid's Battery!"

He paused. With his inspired eyes on the splendid
array, visions of its awful destiny only exalted him.
Yet signs which he dared not heed lest he be confounded told him that every eye so fixed on his was
aware of some droll distraction. He must speak on.

"My boys! as sure as this war begins it's going to
last. There 'll be lots of killing and dying, and I warn
you now, your share'll be a double one. So, then, no

indecent haste. Artillery can't fight every day. Cavalry can—in its small way, but you may have to wait months and months to get into a regular hell on earth. All the same you'll get there!—soon enough—times enough. Don't you know why, when we have to be recruited—to fill up the shot holes—they'll go by the cavalry to the infantry, and pick the best men there, and *promote* them to your ranks? It's because of how you've got to fight when your turn comes; like devils, to hold up, for all you may know, the butt end of the whole day's bloody business. That's why—and because of how you may have to wait, *un-com-plain-ing*, in rotting idleness for the next tea party."

Again he ceased. What *was* the matter? There sat his matchless hundred, still and straight as stone Egyptians, welcoming his every word; yet some influence not his was having effect and, strangest of all, was enhancing his.

"One more word," he said. "You're sick of the drill-ground. Well, the man that's spoiling for a fight and yet has no belly for drill—he—oh, he belongs to the cavalry by birth! We *love* these guns. We're mighty dogg— we're extremely proud of them. Through thick and thin, through fire and carnage and agony, remembering where we got them, we propose to *keep* them; and some proud day, when the trouble's all over, say two years hence, and those of us who are spared come home, we propose to come with these same guns unstained by the touch of a foe's hand, a virgin battery still. Well, only two things can win that: infernal fighting and perpetual toil. So, as you love honor and your country's cause, wait. Wait in self-respectful patience. Wait and work, and you shall be at the front—the foremost front!—the very first day and hour my best licks can get you there. That's all."

Bartleson advanced from the line: "By section!" he called, "right wheel——"

"Section," repeated each chief of section, "right wheel——"

"March!" commanded Bartleson.

"March," echoed the chiefs, and the battery broke into column. "Forward! Guide right!" chanted Bartleson, and all moved off save Kincaid.

He turned his horse, and lo! on the grassy crest of the earthwork, pictured out against the eastern pink and blue, their summer gauzes filled with the light of the declining sun, were half a dozen smiling ladies attended by two or three officers of cavalry, and among them Flora, Constance, and Miranda.

Anna? Only when he had dismounted did his eager eye find her, where she had climbed and seated herself on a siege gun and was letting a cavalier show her how hard it would be for a hostile ship, even a swift steamer, to pass, up-stream, this crater of destruction, and *ergo* how impossible for a fleet—every ship a terror to its fellows the moment it was hurt—to run the gauntlet of Forts Jackson and St. Philip on a far worse stretch of raging current some eighty miles farther down the river.

Not for disbelief of the demonstration, but because of a general laugh around a tilt of words between Kincaid and the cavalry fellows, Anna lighted down and faced about, to find him, for the third time in five days, at close range. With much form he drew nearer, a bright assurance in his eyes, a sort of boyish yes, for a moment, but the next moment gone as it met in hers a womanly no.

"You little artist," thought Flora.

XXIV

A PARKED BATTERY CAN RAISE A DUST

Down in the camp the battery was forming into park; a pretty movement. The ladies watched it, the cavalrymen explaining. Now it was done. The command broke ranks, and now its lieutenants joined the fair company and drank its eulogies—grimly, as one takes a dram.

Back among the tents and mess fires—

"Fellows!" said the boys, in knots, "yonder's how he puts in his 'best licks' for us!" But their wanton gaze was also fond as it followed the procession of parasols and sword-belts, muslins and gold lace that sauntered down along the levee's crest in couples, Hilary and Anna leading.

Flora, as they went, felt a most unusual helplessness to avert a course of things running counter to her designs. It is true that, having pledged herself to the old General to seek a certain issue and to Irby to prevent it, she might, whichever way the matter drifted, gather some advantage if she could contrive to claim credit for the trend; an *if* which she felt amply able to take care of. To keep two men fooled was no great feat, nor even to beguile her grandmother, whose gadfly insistence centred ever on the Brodnax fortune as their only true objective; but so to control things as not to fool herself at last—that was the pinch. It pinched more than it would could she have heard how poorly at this moment the lover and lass were getting on—as such. Her subtle interferences—a mere word yesterday, another the day before—were having more success than she imagined, not realizing how much they were aided by that frantic untamableness to love's yoke, which, in Hilary only less than in Anna, qualified every word and motion.

Early in the talk of these two Hilary had mentioned his speech just made, presently asking with bright abruptness how Anna liked it and, while Anna was getting her smile ready for a safe reply, had added that he never could have made it at all had he dreamed she was looking on. "Now if she asks why," he thought to himself in alarm, "I've got to blurt it out!"

But she failed to ask; only confessed herself unfit to judge anybody's English.

"English! oh, pass the English!" he said, he "knew how bad that was." What he wanted her criticism on was—"its matter—its spirit—whichever it was, matter or spirit!" How comical that sounded! They took pains that their laugh should be noticed behind them. Flora observed both the laugh and the painstaking.

"Matter or spirit," said Anna more gravely, "I can't criticise it. I can't even praise it—oh! but that's only be—because I haven't—the courage!"

The lover's reply was low and full of meaning: "Would you praise it if you had the courage?"

She could have answered trivially, but something within bade her not. "Yes," she murmured, "I would." It was an awful venture, made unpreparedly, and her eyes, trying to withstand his, dropped. Yet they rallied splendidly—"They've got to!" said something within her—and, "I could," she blushingly qualified, "but—I could criticise it too!"

His heart warmed at her defiant smile. "I'd rather have that honor than a bag of gold!" he said, and saw his slip too late. Gold! Into Anna's remembrance flashed the infatuation of the poor little schoolmistress, loomed Flora's loss and distress and rolled a smoke of less definite things for which this man was going unpunished while she, herself, stood in deadly peril of losing her heart to him.

"Oh, Captain Kincaid!" Like artillery wheeling into action came her inconsequent criticism, her eyes braving him at last, as bright as his guns, though flashing only tears. "It was right enough for you to extol those young soldiers' willingness to serve their country *when called*. But, oh, how *could* you commend their *chafing* for battle and slaughter?"

"Ah, Miss Anna, you——"

"Oh, when you know that the sooner they go the sooner comes the heartache and heartbreak for the hundreds of women they so light-heartedly leave behind them! I looked from Charlie to Flora——"

"You should have looked to Victorine. She wants the boy to go and her dad to go with him."

"Poor thoughtless child!"

"Why, Miss Anna, if I were a woman, and any man —with war coming on—could *endure* to hang back at home for love of me, I should feel——"

"Captain Kincaid! What we womenkind may feel

is not to the point. It's how the men themselves feel toward the women who love them."

"They ought," replied the soldier, and his low voice thrilled like a sounding-board, "to love the women—out of every fibre of their being."

"Ah!" murmured the critic, as who should say, "checkmate!"

"And yet—" persisted this self-sung "ladies' man"—

"Yet what?" she softly challenged. (Would he stand by his speech, or his song?)

"Why, honestly, Miss Anna, I think a man can love a woman—even his heart's perfect choice—too much. I know he can!"

The small lady gave the blunderer a grave, brief, now-you-*have*-done-it glance and looked down. "Well, I know," she measuredly said, "that a man who can *tell* a woman that, isn't capable of loving her half enough." She turned to go back, with a quickness which, I avow, was beautifully and tenderly different from irritation, yet which caused her petticoat's frail embroidery to catch on one of his spurs and cling till the whole laughing bevy had gathered round to jest over Flora's disentanglement of it.

"But really, Nan, you know," said Constance that evening in their home, "you used to believe that yourself! The day Steve left you said almost exact——"

"Con—? Ah, Con! I think the *sister* who could remind a *sister* of that—!" The sufferer went slowly up to her room, where half an hour later she was found by Miranda drying her bathed eyes at a mirror and instantly pretending that her care was for any other part of her face instead.

"Singular," she remarked, "what a dust that battery can raise!"

XXV

"HE MUST WAIT," SAYS ANNA

ABOUT the middle of the first week in April—when the men left in the stores of Common, Gravier, Poydras, or Tchoupitoulas street could do nothing but buy the same goods back and forth in speculation, loathed by all who did not do it, or whittle their chairs on the shedded sidewalks and swap and swallow flaming rumors and imprecate the universal inaction and mismanagement—there embarked for Pensacola——

"What? Kincaid's Bat——?"

"No-o, the Zouaves! Infantry! when the one only sane thing to do," cried every cannoneer of Camp Callender—in its white lanes or on three-hours' leave at home on Bayou Road or Coliseum Square or Elysian Fields or Prytania street—"the one sane thing to do," insisted the growingly profane lads to their elders, and assented the secretly pained elders to them, "the one thing that, if only for shame's sake, ought to have been done long ago, was to *knock* Fort Pickens to HELL with SHELL!" Sadly often they added the tritest three-monosyllabled expletive known to red-hot English.

Charlie—mm-mm! how he could rip it out! Sam Gibbs, our veritable Sam, sergeant of the boy's gun, "Roaring Betsy," privately remarked to the Captain what a blank-blank shame it was, not for its trivial self, of course, but in view of the corruptions to which it opened the way. And the blithe commander, in the seclusion of his tent, standing over the lad and holding him tenderly by both pretty ears, preached to him of his sister and grandmother until with mute rage the youngster burned as red as his jacket facings; and then of the Callenders—"who gave us our guns, and one of whom is the godmother of our flag, Charlie"— until the tears filled Charlie's eyes, and he said:

"I'll try, Captain, but it's—oh, it's no use! If anything could make me swear *worse*"—he smiled despairingly—"it would be the hope of being hauled up again for another talk like this!"

One Sunday, three days after the going of the Zouaves, while out in Jackson Square "Roaring Betsy" sang a solo of harrowing thunder-claps, the Callenders and Valcours, under the cathedral's roof, saw consecrated in its sacred nave the splendid standard of the Chasseurs-à-Pied.

Armed guards, keeping the rabble out, passed the ladies in before the procession had appeared in the old Rue Condé. But now here it came, its music swelling, the crowd—shabbier than last month and more vacant of face—parting before it. Carrying their sabres, but on foot and without their pieces, heading the column as escort of honor, lo, Kincaid's Battery; rearmost the Chasseurs, masses and masses of them; and in between, a silver crucifix lifted high above a body of acolytes in white lace over purple, ranks of black-gowned priests, a succession of cloth-of-gold ecclesiastics, and in their midst the mitred archbishop.

"He Must Wait," Says Anna

But the battery! What a change since last February! Every man as spruce as ever, but with an added air of tested capability that inspired all beholders. Only their German musicians still seemed fresh from the mint, and oh! in what unlucky taste, considering the ecclesiastics, the song they brayed forth in jaunty staccato.

"They're offering us that hand of theirs again," murmured Anna to Constance, standing in a side pew; but suddenly the strain ceased, she heard Hilary's voice of command turning the column, and presently, through a lane made by his men, the Chasseurs marched in to the nave, packed densely and halted. Then in close order the battery itself followed and stood. Now the loud commands were in here. Strange it was to hear them ring through the holy place (French to the Chasseurs, English to the battery), and the crashing musket-butts smite the paved floor as one weapon, to the flash of a hundred sabres.

So said to itself the diary on the afternoon of the next day, and there hurriedly left off. Not because of a dull rumble reaching the writer's ear from the Lake, where Kincaid and his lieutenants were testing new-siege-guns, for that was what she was at this desk and window to hear; but because of the L. S. C. A., about to meet in the drawing-room below and be met by a friend of the family, a famed pulpit orator and greater potentate, in many eyes, than even the Catholic archbishop.

He came, and later, in the battery camp with the Callenders, Valcours, and Victorine, the soldiers clamoring for a speech, ran them wild reminding them with what unique honor and peculiar responsibility they were the champions of their six splendid guns. In a jostling crowd, yet with a fine decorum, they brought out their standard and—not to be outdone by any Chasseurs under the sky—obliged Anna to stand beside its sergeant, Maxime, and with him hold it while the man of God invoked Heaven to bless it and bless all who should follow it afield or pray for it at home. So dazed was she that only at the "amen" did she perceive how perfectly the tables had been turned on her. For only then did she discover that Hilary Kincaid had joined the throng exactly in time to see the whole tableau.

Every officer of the camp called that evening, to say graceful things, Kincaid last. As he was leaving he wanted to come to the same old point, but she would not let him. Oh! how could she, a scant six hours after such a *bid* from herself? He ought to have seen she couldn't—and wouldn't! But he never saw anything— of that sort. Ladies' man indeed! He couldn't read a girl's mind even when she wanted it read. He went away looking so haggard—and yet so tender—and still so determined—she could not sleep for hours. Nevertheless——

"I can't help his looks, Con, he's got to wait! I owe that to all womanhood! He's got to practise to me what he preaches to his men. Why, Connie, if *I'm* willing to wait, why shouldn't he be? Why——?"

Constance fled.

Next day, dining with Doctor Sevier, said the Doctor, "That chap's working himself to death, Anna," and gave his fair guest such a stern white look that she had to answer flippantly.

"He Must Wait," Says Anna

She and Hilary were paired at table and talked of Flora, he telling how good a friend to her Flora was. The topic was easier, between them, than at any other time since the loss of the gold. Always before, she had felt him thinking of that loss and trying to guess something about her; but now she did not, for on Sunday, in the cathedral, Flora had told her at last, ever so gratefully and circumstantially, that she had repaid the Captain everything! yes, the same day on which she had first told Anna of the loss; and there was nothing now left to do but for her to reimburse Anna the moment she could.

Hilary spoke of Adolphe's devotion to Flora—hoped he would win. Told with great amusement how really well his cousin had done with her government claim— sold it to his Uncle Brodnax! And Flora—how picturesque everything she did!—had put—? yes, they both knew the secret—had put the proceeds into one of those beautiful towboats that were being fitted up as privateers! Hilary laughed with delight. Yes, it was for that sort of thing the boys were so fond of her. But when Anna avowed a frank envy he laughed with a peculiar tenderness that thrilled both him and her, and murmured:

"The dove might as well envy the mocking-bird."

"If I were a dove I certainly should," she said.

"Well, you are, and you shouldn't!" said he.

All of which Flora caught; if not the words, so truly the spirit that the words were no matter.

"Just as we were starting home," soliloquized, that night, our diary, "the newsboys came crying all around, that General Beauregard had opened fire on Fort Sum-

125

ter, and the war has begun. Poor Constance! it's little she'll sleep to-night."

XXVI

SWIFT GOING, DOWN STREAM

STRANGELY slow travelled news in '61. After thirty hours' bombardment Fort Sumter had fallen before any person in New Orleans was sure the attack had been made. When five days later a yet more stupendous though quieter thing occurred, the tidings reached Kincaid's Battery only on the afternoon of the next one in fair time to be read at the close of dress parade. But then what shoutings! The wondering Callenders were just starting for a drive up-town. At the grove gate their horses were frightened out of all propriety by an opening peal, down in the camp, from "Roaring Betsy." And listen!

The black driver drew in. From Jackson Square came distant thunders and across the great bend of the river they could see the white puff of each discharge. What *could* it mean?

"Oh, Nan, the Abolitionists must have sued for peace!" exclaimed the sister.

"No-no!" cried Miranda. "Hark!"

Behind them the battery band had begun—

"O, carry me back to old Vir——"

"Virginia!" sang the three. "Virginia is out! Oh, Virginia is out!" They clapped their mitted hands and squeezed each other's and laughed with tears and told the coachman and said it over and over.

Swift Going, Down Stream

In Canal Street lo! it was true. Across the Neutral Ground they saw a strange sight; General Brodnax bareheaded! bareheaded yet in splendid uniform, riding quietly through the crowd in a brilliantly mounted group that included Irby and Kincaid, while everybody told everybody, with admiring laughter, how the old Virginian, dining at the St. Charles Hotel, had sallied into the street cheering, whooping, and weeping, thrown his beautiful cap into the air, jumped on it as it fell, and kicked it before him up to one corner and down again to the other. Now he and his cavalcade came round the Clay statue and passed the carriage saluting. What glory was in their eyes! How could our trio help but wave or the crowd hold back its cheers!

Up at Odd Fellows' Hall a large company was organizing a great military fair. There the Callenders were awaited by Flora and Madame, thither they came, and there reappeared the General and his train. There, too, things had been so admirably cut and dried that in a few minutes the workers were sorted and busy all over the hall like classes in a Sunday-school.

The Callenders, Valcours, and Victorine were a committee by themselves and could meet at Callender House. So when Kincaid and Irby introduced a naval lieutenant whose amazingly swift despatch-boat was bound on a short errand a bend or so below English Turn, it was agreed with him in a twinkling—a few twinklings, mainly Miranda's—to dismiss horses, take the trip, and on the return be set ashore at Camp Callender by early moonlight.

They went aboard at the head of Canal Street. The river was at a fair stage, yet how few craft were at either long landing, "upper" or "lower," where so lately there had been scant room for their crowding prows. How few drays and floats came and went on the white, shell-paved levees! How little freight was to be seen except what lay vainly begging for export—sugar, molasses, rice; not even much cotton; it had gone to the yards and presses. That natty regiment, the Orleans Guards, was drilling (in French, superbly) on the smooth, empty ground where both to Anna's and to Flora's silent notice all the up-river food-stuffs—corn, bacon, pork, meal, flour—were so staringly absent, while down in yonder streets their lack was beginning to be felt by a hundred and twenty-five thousand consumers.

Backing out into mid-stream brought them near an anchored steamer lately razeed and now being fitted for a cloud of canvas on three lofty masts instead of the two small sticks she had been content with while she brought plantains, guava jelly, coffee, and cigars from Havana. The *Sumter* she was to be, and was designed to deliver some of the many agile counter-thrusts we should have to make against that "blockade" for which the Yankee frigates were already hovering off Ship Island. So said the Lieutenant, but Constance explained to him (Captain Mandeville having explained to her) what a farce that blockade was going to be.

How good were these long breaths of air off the sea marshes, enlivened by the speed of the craft! But how unpopulous the harbor! What a crowd of steamboats were laid up along the "Algiers" shore, and of Morgan's Texas steamers, that huddled, with boilers cold, under Slaughter-House Point, while all the dry-docks stood empty. How bare the ship wharves; hardly a score of vessels along the miles of city front. About as many more, the lieutenant said, were at the river's mouth waiting to put to sea, but the towboats were all up here being turned into gunboats or awaiting letters of marque and reprisal in order to nab those very ships the moment they should reach good salt water. Constance and Miranda tingled to tell him of their brave Flora's investment, but dared not, it was such a secret!

On a quarter of the deck where they stood alone, what a striking pair were Flora and Irby as side by side they faced the ruffling air, softly discussing matters alien to the gliding scene and giving it only a dissimulative show of attention. Now with her parasol he pointed to the sunlight in the tree tops of a river grove where it gilded the windows of the Ursulines' Convent.

"Hum!" playfully murmured Kincaid to Anna, "he motions as naturally as if that was what they were talking about."

"It's a lovely picture," argued Anna.

"Miss Anna, when a fellow's trying to read the book of his fate he doesn't care for the pictures."

"How do you know that's what he's doing?"

"He's always doing it!" laughed Hilary.

The word was truer than he meant. The Irby-value of things was all that ever seriously engaged the ever serious cousin. Just now his eyes had left the shore, where Flora's lingered, and he was speaking of Kincaid. "I see," he said, "what you think: that although no one of these things—uncle Brodnax's nonsense,

Greenleaf's claims, Hilary's own preaching against—against, eh——"

"Making brides to-day and widows to-morrow?"

"Yes, that while none of these is large enough in his view to stop him by itself, yet combined they——"

"All working together they do it," said the girl. Really she had no such belief, but Irby's poor wits were so nearly useless to her that she found amusement in misleading them.

"Hilary tells me they do," he replied, "but the more he says it the less I believe him. Miss Flora, the fate of all my uncle holds dear is hanging by a thread, a spider's web, a young girl's freak! If ever she gives him a certain turn of the hand, the right glance of her eye, he'll be at her feet and every hope I cherish——"

"Captain Irby," Flora softly asked with her tinge of accent, "is not this the third time?"

"Yes, if you mean again that——"

"That Anna, she is my dear, dear frien'! The fate of nothing, of nobody, not even of me—or of—you—" she let that pronoun catch in her throat—"can make me to do anything—oh! or even to wish anything—not the very, very best for her!"

"Yet I thought it was our understanding——"

"Captain: There is bitwin us no understanding excep'"—the voice grew tender—"that there is no understanding bitwin us." But she let her eyes so meltingly avow the very partnership her words denied, that Irby felt himself the richest, in understandings, of all men alive.

"What is that they are looking?" asked his idol, watching Anna and Hilary. The old battle ground had

Hard Going, Up Stream

been passed. Anna, gazing back toward its townward edge, was shading her eyes from the burnished water, and Hilary was helping her make out the earthwork from behind which peered the tents of Kincaid's Battery while beyond both crouched low against the bright west the trees and roof of Callender House—as straight in line from here, Flora took note, as any shot or shell might ever fly.

XXVII

HARD GOING, UP STREAM

Very pleasant it was to stand thus on the tremulous deck of the swiftest craft in the whole Confederate service. Pleasant to see on either hand the flat landscape with all its signs of safety and plenty; its orange groves, its greening fields of young sugar-cane, its pillared and magnolia-shaded plantation houses, its white lines of slave cabins in rows of banana trees, and its wide wet plains swarming with wild birds; pleasant to see it swing slowly, majestically back and melt into a skyline as low and level as the ocean's.

Anna and Kincaid went inside to see the upper and more shining portions of the boat's beautiful machinery. No one had yet made rods, cranks, and gauge-dials sing anthems; but she knew it was Hilary and an artisan or two in his foundry whose audacity in the remaking of these gliding, plunging, turning, vanishing, and returning members had given them their fine new speed-making power, and as he stood at her side and pointed from part to part they took on a living charm that was reflected into him. Pleasant it was, also, to hear two or three droll tales about his battery boys; the personal traits, propensities, and soldierly value of many named by name, and the composite character and temper that distinguished the battery as a command; this specific quality of each particular organic unit, fighting body, among their troops being as needful for commanders to know as what to count on in the individual man. So explained the artillerist while the pair idled back to the open deck. With hidden vividness Anna liked the topic. Had not she a right, the right of a silent partner? A secret joy of the bond settled on her like dew on the marshes, as she stood at his side.

Hilary loved the theme. The lives of those boys were in his hands; at times to be hoarded, at times to be spent, in sudden awful junctures to be furiously squandered. He did not say this, but the thought was in both of them and drew them closer, though neither moved. The boat rounded to, her engines stopped, an officer came aboard from a skiff, and now she was under way again and speeding up stream on her return, but Hilary and Anna barely knew it. He began to talk of the boys' sweethearts. Of many of their tender affairs he was confidentially informed. Yes, to be frank, he confessed he had prompted some fellows to let their hearts lead them, and to pitch in and win while——

"Oh! certainly!" murmured Anna in compassion, "some of them."

"Yes," said their captain, "but they are chaps—like Charlie—whose hearts won't keep unless they're salted down and barrelled, and I give the advice not in the sweethearts' interest but——"

Hard Going. Up Stream

"Why not? Why shouldn't a——" The word hung back.

"A lover?"

"Yes. Why shouldn't he confess himself in *her* interest? That needn't pledge her."

"Oh! do you think that would be fair?"

"Perfectly!"

"Well, now—take an actual case. Do you think the mere fact that Adolphe truly and stick-to-it-ively loves Miss Flora gives her a right to know it?"

"I do, and to know it a long, long time before he can have any right to know whether——"

"Hum! while he goes where glory waits him——?"

"Yes."

"And lets time——?"

"Yes."

"And absence and distance and rumor try his unsupported constancy?"

"Yes."

With tight lips the soldier drew breath. "You know my uncle expects now to be sent to Virginia at once?"

"Yes."

"Adolphe, of course, goes with him."

"Yes."

"Yet you think—the great principle of so-much-for-so-much to the contrary notwithstanding—he really owes it to her to——"

Anna moved a step forward. She was thinking what a sweet babe she was, thus to accept the surface of things. How did she know that this laughing, light-spoken gallant, seemingly so open and artless—oh! more infantile than her very self!—was not deep and complex? Or that it was not *he* and Flora on whose case she was being lured to speculate? The boat, of whose large breathings and pulsings she became growingly aware, offered no reply. Presently from the right shore, off before them, came a strain of band music out of Camp Callender.

"Anna."

"What hosts of stars!" said she. "How hoveringly they follow us."

The lover waited. The ship seemed to breathe deeper—to glide faster. He spoke again: "May I tell you a secret?"

"Doesn't the boat appear to you to tremble more than ever?" was the sole response.

"Yes, she's running up-stream. So am I. Anna, we're off this time—sure shot—with the General—to Virginia. The boys don't know it yet, but—listen."

Over in the unseen camp the strain was once more—

"I'd offer thee this hand of mine—"

"We're turning in to be landed, are we not?" asked Anna as the stars began to wheel.

"Yes. Do you really believe, Anna, that that song is not the true word for a true lover and true soldier, like Adolphe, for instance—to say to himself, of course, not to *her?*"

"Oh, Captain Kincaid, what does it matter?"

"Worlds to me. Anna, if I should turn that song into a solemn avowal—to you——"

"Please don't!—Oh, I mean—I don't mean—I—I mean——"

"Ah, I know your meaning. But if I love you, profoundly, abidingly, consumingly—as I do, Anna Callender, as I do!—and am glad to pledge my soul to you knowing perfectly that you have nothing to confess to me——"

"Oh, don't, Captain Kincaid, don't! You are not fair to me. You make me appear—oh—we were speaking only of your cousin's special case. I don't want your confession. I'm not ready for—for anybody's! You mustn't make it! You—you——"

"It's made, Anna Callender, and it makes me fair to you at last."

"Oh-h-h!"

"I know that matters little to you——"

"Oh, but you're farther from fair than ever, Captain Kincaid; you got my word for one thing and have used it for another!" She turned and they tardily followed their friends, bound for the gangway. A torch-basket of pine-knots blazing under the bow covered flood and land with crimson light and inky shadows. The engines had stopped. The boat swept the shore. A single stage-plank lay thrust half out from her forward quarter. A sailor stood on its free end with a coil of small line. The crouching earthwork and its fierce guns glided toward them. Knots of idle cannoneers stood along its crest. A few came down to the water's edge, to whom Anna and Hilary, still paired alone, were a compelling sight. They lifted their smart red caps. Charlie ventured a query: "It's true, Captain, isn't it, that Virginia's out?"

"I've not seen her," was the solemn reply, and his comrades tittered.

"Yes!" called Constance and Miranda, "she's out!"

"Miss Anna," murmured Hilary with a meekness it would have avenged Charlie to hear, "I've only given you the right you claim for every woman."

"Oh, Captain Kincaid, I didn't say every woman! I took particular—I—I mean I——"

"If it's any one's right it's yours."

"I don't want it!—I mean—I mean——"

"You mean, do you not? that I've no right to say what can only distress you."

"Do *you* think you have?—Oh, Lieutenant, it's been a perfectly lovely trip! I don't know when the stars have seemed so bright!"

"They're not like us dull men, Miss Callender," was the sailor's unlucky reply, "they can rise to any occasion a lady can make."

"Ladies don't *make* occasions, Lieutenant."

"Oh, don't they!" laughed the sea-dog to Hilary. But duty called. "No, no, Miss Val—! Don't try that plank alone! Captain Kincaid, will you give—? That's right, sir. . . . Now, Captain Irby, you and Miss Callender—steady!"

Seventh and last went the frail old lady, led by Kincaid. She would have none other. She kept his arm with definite design while all seven waved the departing vessel good-by. Then for the walk to the house she shared Irby with Anna and gave Flora to Hilary, with Miranda and Constance in front outmanœuvred by a sleight of hand so fleeting and affable that even you or I would not have seen it.

The Cup of Tantalus

XXVIII

THE CUP OF TANTALUS

QUEER world. Can you be sure the next pair you meet walking together of a summer eve are as starry as they look? Lo, Constance and Miranda. Did the bride herself realize what a hunger of loneliness was hers? Or Anna and Irby, with Madame between them. Could you, maybe, have guessed the veritable tempest beneath the maiden's serenity, or his inward gnashings against whatever it was that had blighted his hour with the elusive Flora?

Or can any one say, in these lives of a thousand concealments and restraints, *when* things *are* happening and when not, within us or without, or how near we are *now* to the unexpected—to fate? See, Flora and Hilary. He gave no outward show that he was burning to flee the spot and swing his fists and howl and tear the ground.

Yet Flora knew; knew by herself; by a cold rage in her own fair bosom, where every faculty stood gayly alert for each least turn of incident, to foil or use it, while they talked lightly of Virginia's great step, or of the night's loveliness, counting the stars. "How small they look," she said, "how calm how still."

"Yes, and then to think what they really are! so fearfully far from small—or cold—or still!"

"Like ourselves," she prompted.

"Yes!" cried the transparent soldier. "At our smallest the smallest thing in us is that we should feel small. And how deep down are we calm or cold? Miss Flora, I once knew a girl—fine outside, inside. Lovers

—she had to keep a turnstile. I knew a pair of them. To hear those two fellows separately tell what she was like, you couldn't have believed them speaking of the same person. The second one thought the first had —sort o'—charted her harbor for him; but when he came to sail in, 'pon my soul, if every shoal on the chart wasn't deep water, and every deep water a fortified shore—ha, ha, ha!"

Flora's smile was lambent. "Yes," she said, "that sweet Anna she's very intric-ate." Hilary flamed and caught his breath, but she met his eyes with the placidity of the sky above them.

Suddenly he laughed: "Now I know what I am! Miss Flora, I—I wish you'd be my pilot."

She gave one resenting sparkle, but then shook her averted head tenderly, murmured "Impossible," and smiled.

"You think there's no harbor there?"

"Listen," she said.

"Yes, I hear it, a horse."

"Captain Kincaid?"

"Miss Flora?"

"For dear Anna's sake *and* yours, shall I be that little bit your pilot, to say——?"

"What! to say, Don't see her to-night?"

Flora's brow sank.

"May I go with you, then, and learn why?" The words were hurried, for a horseman was in front and the others had so slackened pace that all were again in group. Anna caught Flora's reply:

"No, your cousin will be there. But to-morrow evening, bif-ore——"

The Cup of Tantalus

"Yes," he echoed, "before anything else. I'll come. Why!"—a whinny of recognition came from the road—"why, that's my horse!"

The horseman dragged in his rein. Constance gasped and Kincaid exclaimed, "Well! since when and from where, Steve Mandeville?"

The rider sprang clanking to the ground and whipped out a document. All pressed round him. He gave his bride two furious kisses, held her in one arm and handed the missive to Kincaid:

"With the compliment of Général Brodnax!"

Irby edged toward Flora, drawn by a look.

Hilary spoke: "Miss Anna, please hold this paper open for me while I—Thank you." He struck a match. The horse's neck was some shelter and the two pressed close to make more, yet the match flared. The others listened to Mandeville:

"And 'twas me dizcover' that tranzportation, juz' chanzing to arrive by the railroad——"

"Any one got a newspaper?" called Hilary. "Steve —yes, let's have a wisp o' that."

The paper burned and Hilary read. "Always the man of the moment, me!" said Mandeville. "And also 't is thangs to me you are the firs' inform', and if you are likewise the firs' to ripport——"

"Thank you!" cried Kincaid, letting out a stirrup leather. "Adolphe, will you take that despatch on to Bartleson?" He hurried to the other stirrup.

"*Tell him no!*" whispered Flora, but in vain, so quickly had Anna handed Irby the order.

"Good-night, all!" cried Hilary, mounting. He wheeled, swung his cap and galloped.

"Hear him!" laughed Miranda to Flora, and from up the dim way his song came back:

> "'I can't stand the wilderness
> But a few days, a few days.'"

Still swinging his cap he groaned to himself and dropped his head, then lifted it high, shook his locks like a swimmer, and with a soft word to his horse sped faster.

"Yo' pardon, sir," said Mandeville to Irby, declining the despatch, "I wou'n't touch it. For why he di'n' h-ask me? But my stable is juz yondeh. Go, borrow you a horse—all night 'f you like."

Thence Irby galloped to Bartleson's tent, returned to Callender House, dismounted and came up the steps. There stood Anna, flushed and eager, twining arms with the placid Flora. "Ah," said the latter, as he offered her his escort home, "but grandma and me, we——"

Anna broke in: "They're going to stay here all night so that you may ride at once to General Brodnax. Even we girls, Captain Irby, must do all we can to help your cousin get away with the battery, the one wish of his heart!" She listened, untwined and glided into the house.

Instantly Flora spoke: "Go, Adolphe Irby, go! Ah, *snatch* your luck, you lucky—man! Get him away to-night, cost what cost!" Her fingers pushed him. He kissed them. She murmured approvingly, but tore them away: "Go, go, go-o!"

Anna, pacing her chamber, with every gesture of self-arraignment and distress, heard him gallop. Then standing in her opened window she looked off across the veranda's balustrade and down into the camp, where at lines of mess-fires like strings of burning beads the boys were cooking three days' rations. A tap came on her door. She snatched up a toilet brush: "Come in?"

She was glad it was only Flora. "Chérie," tinkled the visitor, "they have permit' me!"

Anna beamed. "I was coming down," she recklessly replied, touching her temples at the mirror.

"Yes," said the messenger, "'cause Mandeville he was biggening to tell about Fort Sumter, and I asked them to wait—ah"—she took Anna's late pose in the window—"how plain the camp!"

"Yes," responded Anna with studied abstraction, "when the window happens to be up. It's so warm to-night, I——"

"Ah, Anna!"

"What, dear?" In secret panic Anna came and looked out at Flora's side caressingly.

"At last," playfully sighed the Creole, "'tis good-by, Kincaid's Battery. Good-by, you hun'red good fellows, with yo' hun'red horses and yo' hun'red wheels and yo' hun'red hurras."

"And hundred brave, true hearts!" said Anna.

"Yes, and good-by, Bartleson, good-by, Tracy, good-by ladies' man!—my dear, tell me once more! For him why always that name?" Both laughed.

"I don't know, unless it's because—well—isn't it—because every lady has a piece of his heart and—no one wants all of it?"

"Ah! no one?—when so many?——"

"Now, Flora, suppose some one did! What of it, if he can't, himself, get his whole heart together to give it to any one?" The arguer offered to laugh again, but Flora was sad:

"You bil-ieve he's that way—Hilary Kincaid?"

"There are men that way, Flora. It's hard for us women to realize, but it's true!"

"Ah, but for him! For him that's a dreadful!"

"Why, no, dear, I fancy he's happiest that way."

"But not best, no! And there's another thing—his uncle! You know ab-out that, I su'pose?"

"Yes, but he—come, they'll be sending——"

"No,—no! a moment! Anna! Ah, Anna, you are too wise for me! Anna, do you think"—the pair stood in the room with the inquirer's eyes on the floor—"you think his cousin is like that?"

Anna kissed her temples, one in pity, the other in joy: "No, dear, he's not—Adolphe Irby is not."

On the way downstairs Flora seized her hands: "Oh, Anna, like always—this is just bit-win us? Ah, yes. And, oh, I wish you'd try not to bil-ieve that way —ab-out *his* cousin! Me, I hope no! And yet——"

"Yet what, love?" (Another panic.)

"Nothing, but—ah, he's so ki-ind to my brother! And his cousin Adolphe," she whispered as they moved on down, "I don't know, but I fear perchanze he don't like his cousin Adolphe—his cousin Adolphe—on the outside, same as the General, rough—'t is a wondrous how his cousin Adolphe is fond of him!"

Poor Anna. She led the way into the family group actually wheedled into the belief that however she had blundered with her lover, with Flora she had been

"'Tis good-by, Kincaid's Battery"

clever. And now they heard the only true account of how Captain Beauregard and General Steve had taken Fort Sumter. At the same time every hearer kept one ear alert toward the great open windows. Yet nothing came to explain that Kincaid's detention up-town was his fond cousin's contriving, and Sumter's story was at its end when all started at once and then subsided with relief as first the drums and then the bugles sounded—no alarm, but only, drowsily, "taps," as if to say to Callender House as well as to the camp, "Go to slee-eep . . . Go to slee-eep . . . Go to bed, go to bed, go to slee-eep . . . Go to slee-eep, go to slee-eep . . . Go to slee-ee-eep."

XXIX

A CASTAWAY ROSE

GONE to sleep the camp except its sentinels, and all Callender House save one soul. Not Miranda, not the Mandevilles, nor Madame Valcour, nor any domestic. Flora knew, though it was not Flora. In her slumbers she knew.

Two of the morning. Had the leader, the idol of Kincaid's Battery, failed in his endeavor? Anna, on her bed, half disrobed, but sleepless yet, still prayed he might not succeed. Just this one time, oh, Lord! this one time! With Thee are not all things possible? Canst Thou not so order all things that a day or two's delay of Kincaid's Battery need work no evil to the Cause nor any such rending to any heart as must be hers if Kincaid's Battery should go to-night? Softly the stair clock boomed three. She lifted her head and for a full three minutes harkened toward the camp. Still no sound there, thank God! She turned upon her pillow.

But—what! Could that be the clock again, and had she slumbered? "Three, four," murmured the clock. She slipped from her bed and stole to the window. Just above the low, dim parapet, without a twinkle, the morning star shone large, its slender, mile-long radiance shimmering on the gliding river. In all the scented landscape was yet no first stir of dawn, but only clearness enough to show the outlines of the camp ground. She stared. She stared again! Not a tent was standing. Oh! and oh! through what bugling, what rolling of drums and noise of hoofs, wheels, and riders had she lain oblivious at last? None, really; by order of the commanding general—on a private suggestion of Irby's, please notice, that the practice would be of value—camp had been struck in silence. But to her the sole fact in reach was that all its life was gone!

Sole fact? Gone? All gone? What was this long band of darkness where the gray road should be, in the dull shadow of the levee? Oh, God of mercy, it was the column! the whole of Kincaid's Battery, in the saddle and on the chests, waiting for the word to march! Ah, thou ladies' man! Thus to steal away! Is this your profound—abiding—consuming love? The whisper was only in her heart, but it had almost reached her lips, when she caught her breath, her whole form in a tremor. She clenched the window-frame, she clasped her heaving side.

For as though in reply, approaching from behind the

house as if already the producer had nearly made its circuit, there sounded close under the balustrade the walking of a horse. God grant no other ear had noted it! Now just beneath the window it ceased. ' Hilary Kincaid! She could not see, but as sure as sight she knew. Her warrior, her knight, her emperor now at last, utterly and forever, she his, he hers, yet the last moment of opportunity flitting by and she here helpless to speak the one word of surrender and possession. Again she shrank and trembled. Something had dropped in at the window. There it lay, small and dark, on the floor. She snatched it up. Its scant tie of ribbon, her touch told her, was a bit of the one she had that other time thrown down to him, and the thing it tied and that looked so black in the dusk was a red, red rose.

She pressed it to her lips. With quaking fingers that only tangled the true-love knot and bled on the thorns, she stripped the ribbon off and lifted a hand high to cast it forth, but smote the sash and dropped the emblem at her own feet. In pain and fear she caught it up, straightened, and glanced to her door, the knot in one hand, the rose in the other, and her lips apart. For at some unknown moment the door had opened, and in it stood Flora Valcour.

Furtively into a corner fluttered rose and ribbon while the emptied hands extended a counterfeit welcome and beckoned the visitor's aid to close the window. As the broad sash came down, Anna's heart, in final despair, sunk like lead, or like the despairing heart of her disowned lover in the garden, Flora's heart the meantime rising like a recovered kite. They moved from the window with their four hands joined, the dejected girl dissembling elation, the elated one dejection.

"I don't see," twittered Anna, "how I should have closed it! How chilly it gets toward——"

"Ah!" tremulously assented the subtler one. "And such a dream! I was oblige' to escape to you!"

"And did just right!" whispered and beamed poor Anna. "What did you dream, dear?"

"I dremp the battery was going! and going to a battle! and with the res' my brother! And now——"

"Now it's but a dream!" said her comforter.

"Anna!" the dreamer flashed a joy that seemed almost fierce. She fondly pressed the hands she held and drew their owner toward the ill-used rose. "Dearest, behold me! a thief, yet innocent!"

Anna smiled fondly, but her heart had stopped, her feet moved haltingly. A mask of self-censure poorly veiled Flora's joy, yet such as it was it was needed. Up from the garden, barely audible to ears straining for it, yet surging through those two minds like a stifling smoke, sounded the tread of the departing horseman.

"Yes," murmured Anna, hoping to drown the footfall, and with a double meaning though with sincere tenderness, "you are stealing now, not meaning to."

"Now?" whispered the other, "how can that be?" though she knew. "Ah, if I could steal now your heart al-*so*! But I've stolen, I fear, only—your—confidenze!" Between the words she loosed one hand, stooped and lifted the flower. Each tried to press it to the other's bosom, but it was Anna who yielded.

"I'd make you take it," she protested as Flora pinned it on, "if I hadn't thrown it away."

A Castaway Rose

"Dearest," cooed the other, "that would make me a thief ag-ain, and this time guilty."

"Can't I give a castaway rose to whom I please?"

"Not this one. Ah, sweet, a thousand thousand pardon!"—the speaker bent to her hearer's ear—"I saw you when you kiss' it—and before."

Anna's face went into her hands, and face and hands to Flora's shoulder; but in the next breath she clutched the shoulder and threw up her head, while the far strain of a bugle faintly called, "Head of column to the right."

The cadence died. "Flora! your dream is true and that's the battery! It's going, Flora. It's gone! Your brother's gone! Your brother, Flora, your brother! Charlie! he's *gone*." So crying Anna sprang to the window and with unconscious ease threw it up.

The pair stood in it. With a bound like the girl's own, clear day had come. Palely the river purpled and silvered. No sound was anywhere, no human sign on vacant camp ground, levee, or highroad. "Ah!"— Flora made a well pretended gesture of discovery and distress—"'tis true! That bugl' muz' have meant us good-by."

"Oh, then it was cruel!" exclaimed Anna. "To you, dear, cruel to you to steal off in that way. Run! dress for the carriage!"

Flora played at hesitation: "Ah, love, if perchanze that bugl' was to call you?"

"My dear! how could even *he*—the 'ladies' man,' ha, ha!—*imagine* any true woman would come to the call of a bugle? Go! while I order the carriage."

They had left the window. The hostess lifted her

hand toward a bell-cord but the visitor stayed it, absently staring while letting herself be pressed toward the door, thrilled with a longing as wild as Anna's and for the same sight, yet cunningly pondering. Nay, waiting, rather, on instinct, which the next instant told her that Anna would inevitably go herself, no matter who stayed.

"You'll come al-long too?" she pleadingly asked.

"No, dear, I cannot! Your grandmother will, of course, and Miranda." The bell-cord was pulled.

"Anna, you must go, else me, I will not!"

"Ah, how can I? Dear, dear, you're wasting such *golden* moments! Well, I'll go with you! Only *make* haste while I call the others—stop!" Their arms fell lightly about each other's neck. "You'll never tell on me? . . . Not even to Miranda? . . . Nor h-his— his uncle? . . . Nor"—the petitioner pressed closer with brightening eyes—"nor his—cousin?"

Softly Flora's face went into her hands, and face and hands to Anna's shoulder, as neat a reduplication as ever was. But suddenly there were hoof-beats again. Yes, coming at an easy gallop. Now they trotted through the front gate. The eyes of the two stared. "A courier," whispered Anna, "to Captain Mandeville!" though all her soul hoped differently.

Only a courier it was. So said the maid who came in reply to the late ring, but received no command. The two girls, shut in together, Anna losing moments more golden than ever, heard the rider at the veranda steps accost the old coachman and so soon after greet Mandeville that it was plain the captain had already been up and dressing.

A Castaway Rose

"It's Charlie!" breathed Anna, and Flora nodded.

Now Charlie trotted off again, and now galloped beyond hearing, while Mandeville's booted tread re ascended to his wife's room. And now came Constance: "Nan, where on earth is Fl—? Oh, of course! News, Nan! Good news, Flora! The battery, you know——?"

"Yes," said Anna, with her dryest smile, "it's sneaked off in the dark."

"Nan, you're mean! It's marching up-town now, Flora. At least the guns and caissons are, so as to be got onto the train at once. And oh, girls, those poor, dear boys! the train—from end to end it's to be nothing but a freight train!"

"Hoh!" laughed the heartless Anna, "that's better than staying here."

The sister put out her chin and turned again to Flora. "But just now," she said, "the main command are to wait and rest in Congo Square, and about ten o'clock they're to be joined by all the companies of the Chasseurs that haven't gone to Pensacola and by the whole regiment of the Orleans Guards, as an escort of honor, and march in that way to the depot, led by General Brodnax and his staff—and Steve! And every one who wants to bid them good-by must do it there. Of course there'll be a perfect jam, and so Miranda's ordering breakfast at seven and the carriage at eight, and Steve —he didn't tell even me last night because—" Her words stuck in her throat, her tears glistened, she gnawed her lips. Anna laid tender hands on her.

"Why, what, Connie, dear?"

"St—Ste—Steve——"

"Is Steve going with them to Virginia?"

The face of Constance went into her hands, and face and hands to Anna's shoulder. Meditatively smiling, Flora slipped away to dress.

XXX

GOOD-BY, KINCAID'S BATTERY

AT one end of a St. Charles Hotel parlor a group of natty officers stood lightly chatting while they covertly listened. At the other end, with Irby and Mandeville at his two elbows, General Brodnax conversed with Kincaid and Bartleson, the weather-faded red and gray of whose uniforms showed in odd contrast to the smartness all about them.

Now he gave their words a frowning attention, and now answered abruptly: "Humph! That looks tremendously modest in you, gentlemen,—what? . . . Well, then, in your whole command if it's their notion. But it's vanity at last, sirs, pure vanity. Kincaid's Battery 'doesn't want to parade its dinginess till it's done something'—pure vanity! 'Shortest way'—nonsense! The shortest way to the train isn't the point! The point is to make so inspiring a show of you as to shame the damned stay-at-homes!"

"You'll par-ade," broke in the flaming Mandeville. "worse' dress than presently, when you rit-urn conqueror'!" But that wearied the General more.

"Oh, hell," he mumbled. "Captain Kincaid, eh—" He led that officer alone to a window and spoke low: "About my girl, Hilary,—and me. I'd like to decide that matter before you show your heels. You, eh,—default, I suppose?"

"No, uncle, she does that. I do only the hopeless loving."

"The wha–at? Great Lord! You don't tell me you——?"

"Yes, I caved in last night; told her I loved her. Oh, I didn't do it just in this ashes-of-roses tone of voice, but"—the nephew smiled—the General scowled —"you should have seen me, uncle. You'd have thought it was Mandeville. I made a gorgeous botch of it.

"You don't mean she——?"

"Yes, sir, adjourned me *sine die*. Oh, it's no use to look at me." He laughed. "The calf's run over me. My fat's in the fire."

The General softly swore and continued his gaze. "I believe," he slowly said, "that's why you wanted to slink out of town the back way."

"Oh, no, it's not. Or at least—well, anyhow, uncle, now you can decide in favor of Adolphe."

The uncle swore so audibly that the staff heard and exchanged smiles: "I neither can nor will decide— for either of you—yet! You understand? I *don't do it*. Go, bring your battery."

The city was taken by surprise. Congo Square was void of soldiers before half Canal street's new red-white-and-red bunting could be thrown to the air. In column of fours—escort leading and the giant in the bearskin hat leading it—they came up Rampart street. On their right hardly did time suffice for boys to climb the trees that in four rows shaded its noisome canal;

on their left not a second too many was there for the
people to crowd the doorsteps, fill windows and garden
gates, line the banquettes and silently gather breath and
ardor while the escort moved by, before the moment
was come in which to cheer and cheer and cheer, as
with a hundred flashing sabres at shoulder the dismounted, heavy-knapsacked, camp-worn battery, Kincaid's Battery—you could read the name on the flag—
Kincaid's Battery! came and came and passed. In
Canal street and in St. Charles there showed a fierce-
ness of pain in the cheers, and the march was by
platoons. At the hotel General Brodnax and staff
joined and led it—up St. Charles, around Tivoli Circle,
and so at last into Calliope street.

Meantime far away and sadly belated, with the Valcours cunningly to blame and their confiding hostesses
generously making light of it, up Love street hurried
the Callenders' carriage. Up the way of Love and
athwart the oddest tangle of streets in New Orleans,—
Frenchmen and Casacalvo, Greatmen, History, Victory,
Peace, Arts, Poet, Music, Bagatelle, Craps, and Mysterious—across Elysian Fields not too Elysian, past
the green, high-fenced gardens of Esplanade and
Rampart flecked red-white-and-red with the oleander,
the magnolia, and the rose, spun the wheels, spanked
the high-trotters. The sun was high and hot, shadows
were scant and sharp, here a fence and there a wall
were as blinding white as the towering fair-weather
clouds, gowns were gauze and the parasols were six,
for up beside the old coachman sat Victorine. She it
was who first saw that Congo Square was empty and
then that the crowds were gone from Canal street. It

was she who first suggested Dryads street for a short cut and at Triton Walk was first to hear, on before, the music,—ah, those horn-bursting Dutchmen! could they never, never hit it right?——

> "When other lips and other hearts
>   Their tale of love shall tell——"

and it was she who, as they crossed Calliope street, first espied the rear of the procession, in column of fours again, it was she who flashed tears of joy as they whirled into Erato street to overtake the van and she was first to alight at the station.

The General and his staff were just reaching it. Far down behind them shone the armed host. The march ceased, the music—"then you'll rememb'"—broke off short. The column rested. "Mon Dieu!" said even the Orleans Guards, "quel chaleur! Is it not a terrib', thad sun!" Hundreds of their blue képis, hundreds of gray shakos in the Confederate Guards, were lifted to wipe streaming necks and throats, while away down beyond our ladies' ken all the drummers of the double escort, forty by count, silently came back and moved in between the battery and its band to make the last music the very bravest. Was that Kincaid, the crowd asked, one of another; he of the thick black locks, tired cheek and brow, and eyes that danced now as he smiled and talked?. "Phew! me, I shou'n' love to be tall like that, going to be shot at, no! ha, ha! But thad's no wonder they are call' the ladies' man batt'rie!"

"Hah! they are not call' so because him, but because themse'v's! Every one he is that, and they did n' got the name in Circus street neither, ha, ha!—although—

Hello, Chahlie Valcour. Good-by, Chahlie. **Don't**
ged shoot in the back—ha, ha!——"

A command! How eternally different from the voice
of prattle. The crowd huddled back to either sidewalk, forced by the opening lines of the escort backed
against it, till the long, shelled wagon-way gleamed
white and bare. Oh, Heaven! oh, home! oh, love!
oh, war! For hundreds, hundreds—beat Anna's heart
—the awful hour had come, had come! She and her
five companions could see clear down both bayonet-
crested living walls—blue half the sun-tortured way,
gray the other half—to where in red képis and with
shimmering sabres, behind their tall captain, stretched
the dense platoons and came and came, to the crash of
horns, the boys, the boys, the dear, dear boys who with
him, with him must go, must go!

"Don't cry, Connie dear," she whispered, though
stubborn drops were salting her own lips, "it will make
it harder for Steve."

"Harder!" moaned the doting bride, "you don't
know him!"

"Oh, let any woman cry who can," laughed Flora,
"I wish I could!" and verily spoke the truth. Anna
meltingly pressed her hand but gave her no glance.
All eyes, dry or wet, were fixed on the nearing mass, all
ears drank the rising peal and roar of its horns and
drums. How superbly rigorous its single, two-hun-
dred-footed step. With what splendid rigidity the
escorts' burnished lines walled in its oncome.

But suddenly there was a change. Whether it
began in the music, which turned into a tune every
Tom, Dick, and Harry now had by heart, or whether

Good-by, Kincaid's Battery

a moment before among the blue-caps or gray-shakos,
neither Anna nor the crowd could tell. Some father
in those side ranks lawlessly cried out to his red-capped
boy as the passing lad brushed close against him,
"Good-by, my son!" and as the son gave him only a
sidelong glance he seized and shook the sabre arm,
and all that long, bristling lane of bayonets went out
of plumb, out of shape and order, and a thousand
brass-buttoned throats shouted good-by and hurrah.
Shakos waved, shoulders were snatched and hugged,
blue képis and red were knocked awry, beards were
kissed and mad tears let flow. And still, with a rigor
the superbest yet because the new tune was so perfect
to march by, fell the unshaken tread of the cannoneers, and every onlooker laughed and wept and
cheered as the brass rent out to the deafening drums,
and the drums roared back to the piercing brass,—

> De black-snake love' de blackbird' nes',
> De baby love' his mamy's bres',
> An' raggy-tag, aw spick-an'-span,
> De ladies loves de ladies' man.
> I loves to roll my eyes to de ladies!
> I loves to sympathize wid de ladies!
> As long as eveh I knows sugah f'om san'
> I's bound to be a ladies' man.

So the black-hatted giant with the silver staff strode
into the wide shed, the puffy-cheeked band reading
their music and feeling for foothold as they followed,
and just yonder behind them, in the middle of the
white way, untouched by all those fathers, unhailed by
any brother of his own, came Hilary Kincaid with all
the battery at his neat heels, its files tightly serried but

its platoons in open order, each flashing its sabres to a "present" on nearing the General and back to a "carry" when he was passed, and then lengthening into column of files to enter the blessed shade of the station.

In beside them surged a privileged throng of near kin, every one calling over every one's head, "Good-by!" "Good-by!" "Here's your mother, Johnnie!" and, "Here's your wife, Achille!" Midmost went the Callenders, the Valcours, and Victorine, willy-nilly, topsy-turvy, swept away, smothering, twisting, laughing, stumbling, staggering, yet saved alive by that man of the moment Mandeville, until half-way down the shed and the long box-car train they brought up on a pile of ordnance stores and clung like drift in a flood. And at every twist and stagger Anna said in her heart a speech she had been saying over and over ever since the start from Callender House; a poor commonplace speech that must be spoken though she perished for shame of it; that must be darted out just at the right last instant if such an instant Heaven would only send: "I take back what I said last night and I'm glad you spoke as you did!"

Here now the moment seemed at hand. For here was the officers' box-car and here with sword in sheath Kincaid also had stopped, in conference with the conductor, while his lieutenants marched the column on, now halted it along the train's full length, now faced it against the open cars and now gave final command to break ranks. In comic confusion the fellows clambered aboard stormed by their friends' fond laughter at the awkwardness of loaded knapsacks, and their retorting mirth drowned in a new flood of good-bys and adieus, fresh waving of hats and handkerchiefs, and made-over smiles from eyes that had wept themselves dry. The tear-dimmed Victorine called gay injunctions to her father, the undimmed Flora to her brother, and Anna laughed and laughed and waved in all directions save one. There Mandeville had joined Kincaid and the conductor and amid the wide downpour and swirl of words and cries was debating with them whether it were safer to leave the shed slowly or swiftly; and there every now and then Anna's glance flitted near enough for Hilary to have caught it as easily as did Bartleson, Tracy, every lieutenant and sergeant of the command, busy as they were warning the throng back from the cars; yet by him it was never caught.

The debate had ended. He gave the conductor a dismissing nod that sent him, with a signalling hand thrown high, smartly away toward the locomotive. The universal clatter and flutter redoubled. The bell was sounding and Mandeville was hotly shaking hands with Flora, Miranda, all. The train stirred, groaned, crept, faltered, crept on—on—one's brain tingled to the cheers, and women were crying again.

Kincaid's eyes ran far and near in final summing up. The reluctant train gave a dogged joggle and jerk, hung back, dragged on, moved a trifle quicker; and still the only proof that he knew she was here—here within three steps of him—was the careful failure of those eyes ever to light on her. Oh, heart, heart, heart! would it be so to the very end and vanishment of all?

"I take back—I take—" was there going to be no chance to begin it? Was he grief blind? or was he

scorn blind? No matter! what she had sown she
would reap if she had to do it under the very thunder-
cloud of his frown. All or any, the blame of estrange-
ment should be his, not hers! Oh, Connie, Connie!
Mandeville had clutched Constance and was kissing her
on lips and head and cheeks. He wheeled, caught a
hand from the nearest car, and sprang in. Kincaid
stood alone. The conductor made him an eager sign.
The wheels of the train clicked briskly. He glanced
up and down it, then sprang to Miranda, seized her
hand, cried "Good-by!" snatched Madame's, Flora's,
Victorine's, Connie's,—"Good-by—Good-by!"—and
came to Anna.

And did she instantly begin, "I take——?" Not at
all! She gave her hand, both hands, but her lips stood
helplessly apart. Flora, Madame, Victorine, Constance, Miranda, Charlie from a car's top, the three
lieutenants, the battery's whole hundred, saw Hilary's
gaze pour into hers, hers into his. Only the eyes of
the tumultuous crowd still followed the train and its
living freight. A woman darted to a car's open door
and gleaned one last wild kiss. Two, ten, twenty
others, while the conductor ran waving, ordering,
thrusting them away, repeated the splendid theft, and
who last of all and with a double booty but Constance!
Anna beheld the action, though with eyes still captive.
With captive eyes, and with lips now shut and now
apart again as she vainly strove for speech, she saw
still plainer his speech fail also. His hands tightened
on hers, hers in his.

"Good-by!" they cried together and were dumb
again; but in their mutual gaze—more vehement than

their voices joined—louder than all the din about them
—confession so answered worship that he snatched
her to his breast; yet when he dared bend to lay a kiss
upon her brow he failed once more, for she leaped and
caught it on her lips.

Dishevelled, liberated, and burning with blushes, she
watched the end of the train shrink away. On its last
iron ladder the conductor swung aside to make room
for Kincaid's stalwart spring. So! It gained one
handhold, one foothold. But the foot slipped, the
soldier's cap tumbled to the ground, and every onlooker drew a gasp. No, the conductor held him, and
erect and secure, with bare locks ruffling in the wind
of the train, he looked back, waved, and so passed from
sight.

Archly, in fond Spanish, "How do you feel now?"
asked Madame of her scintillant granddaughter as with
their friends and the dissolving throng they moved to
the carriage; and in the same tongue Flora, with a
caressing smile, rejoined, "I feel like swinging you
round by the hair."

Anna, inwardly frantic, chattered and laughed. "I
don't know what possessed me!" she cried.

But Constance was all earnestness: "Nan, you did
it for the Cause—the flag—the battery—anything but
him personally. *He* knows it. Everybody saw that.
Its very publicity——"

"Yes?" soothingly interposed Madame, "'t was a
so verrie pewblic that——"

"Why, Flora," continued the well-meaning sister,
"Steve says when he came back into Charleston from
Fort Sumter the ladies——"

"Of course!" said Flora, sparkling afresh. "Even Steve understands that, grandma." Her foot was on a step of the carriage. A child plucked her flowing sleeve:

"Misses! Mom-a say'"—he pressed into her grasp something made of broadcloth, very red and golden— "here yo' husband's cap."

XXXI

VIRGINIA GIRLS AND LOUISIANA BOYS

THANKS are due to Mr. Richard Thorndyke Smith for the loan of his copy of a slender and now extremely rare work which at this moment lies before me. "A History of Kincaid's Battery," it is called, "From Its Origin to the Present Day," although it runs only to February, '62, and was printed (so well printed, on such flimsy, coarse paper) just before the dreadful days of Shiloh and the fall of New Orleans.

Let us never paint war too fair; but this small volume tells of little beyond the gold-laced year of 'Sixty-one, nor of much beyond Virginia, even over whose later war-years the color effects of reminiscence show blue and green and sunlit despite all the scarlet of carnage, the black and crimson of burning, and the grim hues of sickness, squalor, and semi-starvation; show green and blue in the sunlight of victory, contrasted with those of the states west and south of her

It tells—this book compiled largely from correspondence of persons well known to you and me—of the

Virginia Girls and Louisiana Boys

first "eight-days' crawl" that conveyed the chaffing, chafing command up through Mississippi, across East Tennessee into south-east Virginia and so on through Lynchburg to lovely Richmond; tells how never a house was passed in town or country but handkerchiefs, neckerchiefs, snatched-off sunbonnets, and Confederate flags wafted them on. It tells of the uncounted railway stations where swarmed the girls in white muslin aprons and red-white-and-red bows, who waved them in as they came, and unconsciously squinted and made faces at them in the intense sunlight. It tells how the maidens gave them dainties and sweet glances, and boutonnières of tuberoses and violets, and bloodthirsty adjurations, and blarney for blarney; gave them seven wild well-believed rumors for as many impromptu canards, and in their soft plantation drawl asked which was the one paramount "ladies' man," and were assured by every lad of the hundred that it was himself. It tells how, having heard in advance that the more authentic one was black-haired, handsome, and overtowering, they singled out the drum-major, were set right only by the roaring laughter, and huddled backward like caged quails from Kincaid's brazen smile, yet waved again as the train finally jogged on with the band playing from the roof of the rear car,—

> "I'd offer thee this hand of mine
> If I could love thee less!"

To Anna that part seemed not so killingly funny or so very interesting, but she was not one of the book's editors.

Two or three pages told of a week in camp just out-

side the Virginian capital, where by day, by night, on its
rocky bed sang James river; of the business quarter
noisy with army wagons—"rattling o'er the stony
street," says the page; of colonels, generals, and states-
men by name—Hampton, Wigfall, the fiery Toombs,
the knightly Lee, the wise Lamar; of such and such
headquarters, of sentinelled warehouses, glowing iron-
works, galloping aides-de-camp and couriers and arriving and departing columns, some as trig (almost) as
Kincaid's Battery, with their black servants following
in grotesque herds along the sidewalks; and some
rudely accoutred, shaggy, staring, dust-begrimed, in
baggy butternut jeans, bearing flint-lock muskets and
trudging round-shouldered after fifes and drums that
squealed and boomed out the strains of their forgotten
ancestors: "The Campbells are coming," "Johnnie
was a piper's son," or—

> "My heart is ever turning back
> To the girl I left behind me."

"You should have seen the girls," laughs the book.
But there were girls not of the mountains or sand-
hills, whom also you should have seen, at battery
manœuvres or in the tulip-tree and maple shade of
proud Franklin street, or in its rose-embowered homes
by night; girls whom few could dance with, or even sit
long beside in the honeysuckle vines of their porticos,
without risk of acute heart trouble, testifies the callow
volume. They treated every lad in the battery like a
lieutenant, and the "ladies' man" like a king. You
should have seen him waltz them or in quadrille or
cotillon swing, balance, and change them, their eyes

brightening and feet quickening whenever the tune
became—

> "Ole mahs' love' wine, ole mis' love' silk,
>   De piggies, dey loves buttehmilk."

Great week! tarheel camp-sentries and sand-hill
street-patrols mistaking the boys for officers, saluting
as they passed and always getting an officer's salute in
return! Hilary seen every day with men high and
mighty, who were as quick as the girls to make merry
with him, yet always in their merriment seeming,
he and they alike, exceptionally upright, downright,
heartright, and busy. It kept the boys straight and
strong.

Close after came a month or so on the Yorktown
peninsula with that master of strategic ruse, Magruder,
but solely in the dreariest hardships of war, minus all
the grander sorts that yield glory; rains, bad food, ill-
chosen camps, freshets, terrible roads, horses sick and
raw-boned, chills, jaundice, emaciation, barely an occasional bang at the enemy on reconnoissances and picket-
ings, and marches and countermarches through blister-
ing noons and skyless nights, with men, teams, and
guns trying to see which could stagger the worst, along
with columns of infantry mutinously weary of forever
fortifying and never fighting. Which things the book
bravely makes light of, Hilary maintaining that the
battery boys had a spirit to bear them better than most
commands did, and the boys reporting—not to boast
the special kindness everywhere of ladies for ladies'
men—that Hilary himself, oftenest by sunny, but sometimes by cyclonic, treatment of commissaries, quarter-

masters, surgeons, and citizens, made their burdens trivial.

So we, too, lightly pass them. After all, the things most important here are matters not military of which the book does not tell. Of such Victorine, assistant editor to Miranda, learned richly from Anna—who merely lent letters—without Anna knowing it. Yet Flora drew little from Victorine, who was as Latin as Flora, truly loved Anna, and through Charlie was a better reader of Flora's Latin than he or Flora or any one suspected.

For a moment more, however, let us stay with the chronicle. At last, when all was suffered, the infuriated boys missed Ben Butler and Big Bethel! One day soon after that engagement, returning through Richmond in new uniforms—of a sort—with scoured faces, undusty locks, full ranks, fresh horses, new harness and shining pieces, and with every gun-carriage, limber, and caisson freshly painted, they told their wrath to Franklin street girls while drinking their dippers of water. Also—"Good-by!—

'I'd offer thee this hand of mine——'"

They were bound northward to join their own Creole Beauregard at a railway junction called ——.

XXXII

MANASSAS

FEMININELY enough, our little borrowed book, Miranda's and Victorine's compilation of letters from the front, gives no more than a few lines to the first great battle of the war.

Fred Greenleaf was one of its wounded prisoners. Hilary cared for him and sought his exchange; but owing to some invisible wire-pulling by Flora Valcour, done while with equal privacy she showed the captive much graciousness, he was still in the Parish Prison, New Orleans, in February, '62, when the book was about to be made, though recovered of wounds and prison ills and twice or thrice out on his parole, after dusk and in civilian's dress, at Callender House.

The Callenders had heard the combat's proud story often, of course, not only from battery lads bringing home dead comrades, or coming to get well of their own hurts, or never to get well of them, but also from gold-sleeved, gray-breasted new suitors of Anna (overstaying their furloughs), whom she kept from tenderer themes by sprightly queries that never tired and constantly brought forth what seemed totally unsought mentions of the battery. And she had gathered the tale from Greenleaf as well. Constance, to scandalized intimates, marvelled at her sister's tolerance of his outrageous version; but Miranda remembered how easy it is to bear with patience (on any matter but one) a rejected lover who has remained faithful, and Flora, to grandma, smiled contentedly.

Anna's own private version (sum of all), though never written even in her diary, was illustrated, mind-pictured. Into her reveries had gradually come a tableau of the great field. Inaccurate it may have been, incomplete, even grotesquely unfair; but to her it was at least clear. Here—through the middle of her blue-skied, pensive contemplation, so to speak—flowed Bull Run. High above it, circling in eagle majesty under still, white clouds, the hungry buzzard, vainly as yet, scanned the green acres of meadow and wood merry with the lark, the thrush, the cardinal. Here she discerned the untried gray brigades—atom-small on nature's face, but with Ewell, Early, Longstreet, and other such to lead them—holding the frequent fords, from Union Mills up to Lewis's. Here near Mitchell's, on a lonesome roadside, stood Kincaid's Battery, fated there to stay for hours yet, in hateful idleness and a fierce July sun, watching white smoke-lines of crackling infantry multiply in the landscape or bursting shells make white smoke-rings in the bright air, and to listen helplessly to the boom, hurtle and boom of other artilleries and the far away cheering and counter-cheering of friend and foe. Yonder in the far east glimmered Centerville, its hitherward roads, already in the sabbath sunrise, full of brave bluecoats choking with Virginia dust and throwing away their hot blankets as they came. Here she made out Stone Bridge, guarded by a brigade called Jackson's; here, crossing it east and west, the Warrenton turnpike, and yonder north of them that rise of dust above the trees which meant a flanking Federal column and crept westward as Evans watched it, toward Sudley Springs, ford, mill, and church, where already much blue infantry had stolen round by night from Centerville. Here, leading south from these, she descried the sunken Sudley road, that with a dip and a rise crossed the turnpike and Young's Branch. There eastward of it the branch turned north-east and then south-east between those sloping fields beyond which Evans and Wheat were presently fighting Burnside; through which Bee, among bursting shells, pressed to their aid against such as Keyes and Sherman, and back over which, after a long, hot struggle, she could see—could hear—the aiders and the aided swept in one torn, depleted tumult, shattered, confounded, and made the more impotent by their own clamor. Here was the many-ravined, tree-dotted, southward rise by which, in concave line, the Northern brigades and batteries, pressing across the bends of the branch, advanced to the famed Henry house plateau— that key of victory where by midday fell all the horrid weight of the battle; where the guns of Ricketts and Griffen for the North and of Walton and Imboden for the South crashed and mowed, and across and across which the opposing infantries volleyed and bled, screamed, groaned, swayed, and drove each other, staggered, panted, rallied, cheered, and fell or fought on among the fallen. Here cried Bee to the dazed crowd, "Look at Jackson's brigade standing like a stone wall." Here Beauregard and Johnson formed their new front of half a dozen states on Alabama's colours, and here a bit later the Creole general's horse was shot under him. Northward here, down the slope and over the branch, rolled the conflict, and there on the opposite rise, among his routed blues, was Greenleaf disabled and taken.

Kincaid's Battery

All these, I say, were in Anna's changing picture. Here from the left, out of the sunken road, came Howard, Heintzelman, and their like, and here in the oak wood that lay across it the blue and gray lines spent long terms of agony mangling each other. Here early n that part of the struggle—sent for at last by Beauregard himself, they say—came Kincaid's Battery, whirling, shouting, whip-cracking, sweating, with Hilary well ahead of them and Mandeville at his side, to the ground behind the Henry house when it had been lost and retaken and all but lost again. Here Hilary, spurring on away from his bounding guns to choose them a vantage ground, broke into a horrid mêlée alone and was for a moment made prisoner, but in the next had handed his captors over to fresh graycoats charging; and here, sweeping into action with all the grace and precision of the drill-ground at Camp Callender, came his battery, his and hers! Here rode Bartleson, here Villeneuve, Maxime with the colors, Tracy, Sam Gibbs; and here from the chests sprang Violett, Rareshide, Charlie and their scores of fellows, unlimbered, sighted, blazed, sponged, reloaded, pealed again, sent havoc into the enemy and got havoc from them. Here one and another groaned, and another and another dumbly fell. Here McStea, and St. Ange, Converse, Fusilier, Avendano, Ned Ferry and others limbered up for closer work, galloped, raced, plunged, reared, and stumbled, gained the new ground and made it a worse slaughter-pen than the first, yet held on and blazed, pealed, and smoked on, begrimed and gory. Here was Tracy borne away to field hospital leaving Avendano and McStea groveling in anguish under the wheels, and

Letters

brave Converse and young Willie Calder, hot-headed Fusilier and dear madcap Jules St. Ange lying near them out of pain forever. Yet here their fellows blazed on and on, black, shattered, decimated, short of horses, one caisson blown up, and finally dragged away to bivouac, proud holders of all their six Callender guns, their silken flag shot-torn but unsoiled and furled only when shells could no longer reach the flying foe.

XXXIII

LETTERS

HARDLY any part of this picture had come to Anna from Hilary himself.

Yes, they were in correspondence—after a fashion. That signified nothing, she would have had you understand; so were Charlie and Victorine, so were—oh!—every girl wrote to somebody at the front; one could not do less and be a patriot. Some girl patriots had a dozen on their list. Some lads had a dozen on theirs.

Ah, me! those swan-white, sky-blue, rose-pink maidens who in every town and on every plantation from Memphis to Charleston, from Richmond to New Orleans, despatched their billets by the forlornly precarious post only when they could not send them by the "urbanity" of such or such a one! Could you have contrasted with them the homeless, shelterless, pencil-borrowing, elbow-scratching, musty, fusty tatterde-malions who stretched out on the turfless ground beside their mess fires to extort or answer those cautious or incautious missives, or who for the fortieth time drew them from hiding to reread into their guarded or unguarded lines meanings never dreamed by their writers, you could not have laughed without a feeling of tears, or felt the tears without smiling. Many a chap's epistle was scrawled, many a one even rhymed, in a rifle-pit with the enemy's shells bursting over. Many a one was feebly dictated to some blessed, unskilled volunteer nurse in a barn or smoke-house or in some cannon-shattered church. From the like of that who with a woman's heart could withhold reply? Yes, Anna and Hilary were in correspondence.

So were Flora and Irby. So were Hilary and Flora. Was not Flora Anna's particular friend and Hilary's "pilot"? She had accepted the office on condition that, in his own heart's interest, their dear Anna should not know of it.

"The better part of life"—she wrote—"is it not made up of such loving concealments?"

And as he read the words in his tent he smilingly thought, "That looks true even if it isn't!"

Her letters were much more frequent than Anna's and always told of Anna fondly, often with sweet praises —not so sweet to him—of her impartial graciousness to her semicircle of brass-buttoned worshippers. Lately Flora had mentioned Greenleaf in a modified way especially disturbing.

If Anna could have made any one a full confidante such might have been Flora, but to do so was not in her nature. She could trust without stint. Distrust, as we know, was intolerable to her. She could not doubt her friends, but neither could she unveil her soul. Nevertheless, more than once, as the two exchanged—in a

Letters

purely academical way—their criticisms of life, some query raised by Anna showed just what had been passing between her and Hilary and enabled Flora to keep them steered apart.

No hard task, the times being so highly calculated to make the course of true love a "hard road to travel," as the singing soldier boys called "Jordan." Letters, at any time, are sufficiently promotive of misunderstandings, but in the Confederacy they drifted from camp to camp, from pocket to pocket, like letters in bottles committed to the sea. The times being such, I say, and Hilary and Anna as they were: he a winner of men, yes! but by nature, not art; to men and women equally, a grown up, barely grown up, boy. That is why women could afford to like him so frankly. The art of courtship—of men or women—was not in him. Otherwise the battery—every gun of which, they say, counted for two as long as he was by—must have lost him through promotion before that first year was half out. The moment he became a conscious suitor, to man or woman, even by proxy, his power went from him; from pen, from tongue, from countenance. And Anna—I may have shown the fact awkwardly, but certainly you see—Anna was incurably difficult.

Too much else awaits our telling to allow here a recital of their hearts' war while love—and love's foes—hid in winter quarters, as it were. That is to say, from the season of that mad kiss which she had never forgiven herself (much less repented), to the day of Beauregard's appeal, early in '62, to all the plantations and churches in Dixie's Land to give him their bells, bells, bells—every bit of bronze or brass they could rake up

171

or break off—to be cast into cannon; and to his own
Louisiana in particular to send him, hot speed, five
thousand more men to help him and Albert Sidney
Johnston drive Buel and Grant out of Tennessee.

Before the battery had got half way to Virginia Hilary
had written back to Anna his inevitable rhapsody over
that amazing performance of hers, taking it as patent
and seal of her final, utter, absolute self-bestowal. And
indeed this it might have turned out to be had he but
approached it by a discreet circuit through the simplest feminine essentials of negative make-believe. But
to spring out upon it in that straightforward manner—!
From May to February her answer to this was the only
prompt reply he ever received from her. It crowds our
story backward for a moment, for it came on one of
those early Peninsula days previous to Manassas, happening, oddly, to reach him—by the hand of Villeneuve
—as he stood, mounted, behind the battery, under a
smart skirmish fire. With a heart leaping in joyous
assurance he opened the small missive and bent his
eyes upon its first lines.

As he did so a hostile shell, first that had ever come
so near, burst just in front of his guns. A big lump of
metal struck one of them on the chase, glanced, clipped
off half the low top of his forage-cap and struck in the
trunk of an oak behind him, and as his good horse
flinched and quivered he looked unwillingly from the
page toward a puff of white smoke on a distant hill, and
with a broad smile said—a mere nonsense word; but
the humor of such things has an absurd valuation and
persistency in camps, and for months afterward, "Ah-r?
—indeed!" was the battery's gay response to every

startling sound. He had luck in catchwords, this Hilary. He fought the scrimmage through with those unread pages folded slim between a thumb and forefinger, often using them to point out things, and when after it he had reopened them and read them through —and through again—to their dizzying close, the battery surgeon came murmuring privately——

"Cap, what's wrong; bad news?"

"Oh!" said Hilary, looking up from a third reading, "what, this? No-o! nothing wrong in this. I was wrong. I'm all right now."

"No, you're not, Captain. You come along now and lie down. The windage of that chunk of iron has——"

"Why, Doc, I shouldn't wonder! If you'll just keep everybody away from me awhile, yourself included, I will lie down," said the unnerved commander, and presently, alone and supine, softly asked himself with grim humor, "Which chunk of iron?"

The actual text of Anna's chunk was never divulged, even to Flora. We do not need it. Neither did Flora. One of its later effects was to give the slender correspondence which crawled after it much more historical value to the battery and the battery's beloved home city than otherwise it might have had. From Virginia it told spiritedly of men, policies, and movements; sketched cabinet officers, the president, and the great leaders and subleaders in the field—Stuart, Gordon, Fitzhugh Lee. It gave droll, picturesque accounts of the artillerist's daily life; of the hard, scant fare and the lucky feast now and then on a rabbit or a squirrel, turtles' eggs, or wild strawberries. It depicted moonlight rides to dance with Shenandoah girls; the playing of camp charades; and the singing of war, home, and love songs around the late camp fire, timed to the antic banjo or the sentimental guitar. Drolly, yet with tenderness for others, it portrayed mountain storm, valley freshet, and heart-breaking night marches beside tottering guns in the straining, sucking, leaden-heavy, red clay, and then, raptly, the glories of sunrise and sunset over the contours of the Blue Ridge. And it explained the countless things which happily enable a commander to keep himself as busy as a mud-dauber, however idle the camp or however torn his own heart.

From Anna's side came such stories as that of a flag presentation to the *Sumter*, wherein she had taken some minor part; of seeing that slim terror glide down by Callender House for a safe escape through the blockading fleet to the high seas and a world-wide fame; of Flora's towboat privateer sending in one large but empty prize whose sale did not pay expenses, and then being itself captured by the blockaders; of "Hamlet" given by amateurs at the St. Charles Theatre; of great distress among the poor, all sorts of gayeties for their benefit, bad money, bad management, a grand concert for the army in Arkansas, women in mourning as numerous as men in uniform, and both men and women breaking down in body and mind under the universal strain.

Historically valuable, you see. Yet through all this impersonal interchange love shone out to love like lamplight through the blinds of two opposite closed windows, and every heart-hiding letter bore enough interlinear revealment of mind and character to keep mutual admiration glowing and growing. We might very justly

fancy either correspondent saying at any time in those
ten months to impatient or compassionate Cupid what
Hilary is reported to have said on one of the greatest
days between Manassas and Shiloh, in the midst of a
two-sided carnage: "Yes, General, hard hit, but please
don't put us out of action."

XXXIV

A FREE-GIFT BAZAAR

AGAIN it was February. The flag of Louisiana whose
lone star and red and yellow stripes still hovered
benignly over the Ionic marble porch of the city hall,
was a year old. A new general, young and active, was
in command of all the city's forces, which again on the
great Twenty-second paraded. Feebly, however; see
letters to Irby and Mandeville under Brodnax in Tennessee, or to Kincaid's Battery and its commander in
Virginia. For a third time the regimental standards
were of a new sort. They were the battle-flag now.
Its need had been learned at Manassas; eleven stars on
St. Andrew's Cross, a field blood red, and the cross span-
ning all the field!

Again marched Continentals, Chasseurs, and so on.
Yet not as before; all their ranks were of new men;
the too old, the too frail, the too young, they of helpless
families, and the "British subjects." Natives of France
made a whole separate "French Legion," in red képis,
blue frocks, and trousers shaped like inverted tenpins,
as though New Orleans were Paris itself. The whole
aspect of things was alert, anxious, spent.

But it was only now this spent look had come. Until lately you might have seen entire brigades of stout-hearted men in camps near by: Camps Benjamin, Walker, Pulaski and, up in the low pine hills of Tangi-pahoa, Camp Moore. From Camp Lewis alone, in November, on that plain where Kincaid's Battery had drilled before it was Kincaid's, the Bienville, Crescent City and many similar "Guards," Miles' Artillery, the Orleans Light Horse, the Orleans Howitzers, the Orleans Guards, the Tirailleurs d'Orleans, etc., had passed in front of Governor Moore and half a dozen generals, twenty-four thousand strong.

Now these were mostly gone—to Bragg—to Price— to Lee and Joe Johnston, or to Albert Sidney Johnston and Beauregard. For the foe swarmed there, refusing to stay "hurled back." True he was here also, and not merely by scores as battle captives, but alarmingly near, in arms and by thousands. Terrible Ship Island, occu-pied by the boys in gray and fortified, anathematized for its horrid isolation and torrid sands, had at length been evacuated, and on New Year's Day twenty-four of the enemy's ships were there disembarking blue-coats on its gleaming white dunes. Fair Carrollton was fortified (on those lines laid out by Hilary), and down at Camp Callender the siege-guns were manned by new cannoneers; persistently and indolently new and with-out field-pieces or brass music or carriage company.

The spent look was still gallant, but under it was a feeling of having awfully miscalculated: flour twelve dollars a barrel and soon to be twenty. With news in abundance the papers had ceased their evening issues, so scarce was paper, and morning editions told of

A Free-Gift Bazaar

Atlantic seaports lost, of Johnston's retreat from Kentucky, the fall of Fort Donelson with its fifteen thousand men, the evacuation of Columbus (one of the Mississippi River's "Gibraltars") and of Nashville, which had come so near being Dixie's capital. And yet the newspapers——

"'We see no cause for despondency,'" read Constance at the late breakfast table—"oh, Miranda, don't you see that with that spirit we can never be subjugated?" She flourished the brave pages, for which Anna vainly reached.

"Yes!" said Anna, "but find the report of the Bazaar!"—while Constance read on: "'Reverses, instead of disheartening, have aroused our people to the highest pitch of animation, and their resolution to conquer is invincible.'"

"Oh, how true! and ah, dearie!"—she pressed her sister's hand amid the silver and porcelain on the old mahogany—"that news (some item read earlier, about the battery), why, Miranda, just that is a sign of impending victory! Straws tell! and Kincaid's Battery is the——"

"Biggest straw in Dixie!" jeered Anna, grasping the paper, which Constance half yielded with her eye still skimming its columns.

"Here it is!" cried both, and rose together.

"'Final Figures of the St. Louis Hotel Free-Gift Lottery and Bazaar'!" called Constance, while Anna's eyes flew over the lines.

"What are they?" exclaimed Miranda.

"Oh, come and see! Just think, Nan: last May, in Odd-Fellows' Hall, how proud we were of barely thirteen thousand, and here are sixty-eight thousand dollars!"

Anna pointed Miranda to a line, and Miranda, with their cheeks together, read out: "'Is there no end to the liberality of the Crescent City?'"

"No-o!" cried gesturing Constance, "not while one house stands on another! Why, 'Randa, though every hall and hotel from here to Carrollton——"

Anna beamingly laid her fingers on the lips of the enthusiast: "Con!—Miranda!—*we* can have a bazaar right in this house! Every friend we've got, and every friend of the bat'— Oh, come in, Flora Valcour! you're just in the nick o' time—a second Kirby Smith at Manassas!"

Thus came the free-gift lottery and bazaar of Callender House. For her own worth as well as to enlist certain valuable folk from Mobile, Flora was, there and then—in caucus, as it were—nominated chairman of everything. "Oh, no, no, no!"—"Oh, yes, yes, yes!" —she "yielded at last to overpowering numbers."

But between this first rapturous inception and an all-forenoon argumentation on its when, who, how, what, and for what, other matters claimed notice. Further news from Charlie! How was his wound? What! a letter from his own hand—with full account of —what was this one? not a pitched battle, but——?"

"Anyhow a victory!" cried Constance.

"You know, Flora, don't you," asked Miranda, "that the battery's ordered away across to Tennessee?"

Flora was genuinely surprised.

"Yes," put in Constance, "to rejoin Beauregard— and Brodnax!"

A Free-Gift Bazaar

Flora turned to Anna: "You have that by letter?"

"No!" was the too eager reply, "It's here in the morning paper." They read the item. The visitor flashed as she dropped the sheet.

"Now I see!" she sorely cried, and tapped Charlie's folded letter. "My God! Anna, wounded like that, Hilary Kincaid is letting my brother go with them!"

"Oh-h-h!" exclaimed the other two, "but—my dear! if he's so much better that he can be allowed——"

"Allowed!—and in those box-car'!—and with that snow—rain—gangrene—lockjaw—my God! And when 'twas already *arrange'* to bring him home!"

Slow Callenders! not to notice the word "bring" in place of "send": "Ah, good, Flora! ah, fine! You'll see! The dear boy's coming that far with the battery only on his way home to us!"

"H-m-m!" Flora nodded in sore irony, but then smiled with recovered poise: "From Tennessee who will bring him—before they have firs' fight another battle?—and he—my brother?"—her smile grew droll.

"Your brother sure to be in it!" gasped Anna. The Callenders looked heart-wrung, but Flora smiled on as she thought what comfort it would be to give each of them some life-long disfigurement.

Suddenly Constance cheered up: "Flora, I've guessed something! Yes, I've guessed who was intending—and, maybe, still intends—to bring him!"

Flora turned prettily to Anna: "Have you?"

Quite as prettily Anna laughed. "Connie does the guessing for the family," she said.

Flora sparkled: "But don't you *know*—perchanze?"

179

Anna laughed again and blushed to the throat as she retorted, "What has that to do with our bazaar?"

It had much to do with it.

XXXV

THE "SISTERS OF KINCAID'S BATTERY"

A WEEK or two ran by, and now again it was March. Never an earlier twelvemonth had the women of New Orleans—nor of any town or time—the gentlewomen—spent in more unselfish or arduous toil.

At any rate so were flutteringly construed the crisp declarations of our pale friend of old, Doctor Sevier, as in Callender House he stood (with Anna seated half behind him as near as flounced crinoline would allow) beside a small table whose fragile beauty shared with hers the enthralled contemplation of every member of a numerous flock that nevertheless hung upon the Doctor's words; such a knack have women of giving their undivided attention to several things at once. Flora was getting her share.

This, he said, was a women's—a gentlewomen's—war.

"Ah!" A stir of assent ran through all the gathering. The long married, the newly wed, the affianced, the suspected, the débutantes, the post-marriageable, every one approved. Yes, a gentlewomen's war—for the salvation of society!

Hardly had this utterance thrilled round, however, when the speaker fell into an error which compelled Anna softly to interrupt, her amazed eyes and protesting smile causing a general hum of amusement and quickening of fans. "No-o!" she whispered to him, "she was not chairman of the L. S. C. A., but only one small secretary of that vast body, and chairman pro tem.—nothing more!—of this mere contingent of it, these "Sisters of Kincaid's Battery."

Pro tem., nothing more! But that is how—silly little Victorine leading the hue and cry which suddenly overwhelmed all counter-suggestion as a levee crevasse sweeps away sand-bags—that is how the permanent and combined chairmanship of Sisters and Bazaar came to be forcibly thrust upon Anna instead of Flora.

Experienced after Odd-Fellow' Hall and St. Louis Hotel, the ladies were able to take up this affair as experts. Especially they had learned how to use men; to make them as handy as—"as hairpins," prompted Miranda, to whom Anna had whispered it; and of men they needed all they could rally, to catch the first impact of the vast and chaotic miscellany of things which would be poured into their laps, so to speak, and upon their heads: bronzes, cutlery, blankets, watches, thousands of brick (orders on the brick-yards for them, that is), engravings, pianos, paintings, books, cosmetics, marbles, building lots (their titles), laces, porcelain, glass, alabaster, bales of cotton, big bank checks, hair flowers, barouches, bonds, shawls, carvings, shell-work boxes, jewellery, silks, ancestral relics, curios from half round the world, wax fruits, tapestries, and loose sapphires, diamonds, rubies, and pearls. The Callenders and Valcours could see, in fancy, all the first chaos of it and all the fair creation that was to arise from it.

What joy of planning! The grove should be ruddy with pine-knot flares perched high, and be full of luminous tents stocked with stuffs for sale at the most patriotic prices by Zingaras, Fatimas, and Scheherazades. All the walks of the garden would be canopied with bunting and gemmed with candles blinking like the fireflies round that bower of roses by Bendermere's stream. The verandas would be enclosed in canvas and be rich in wares, textiles, and works of art. Armed sentries from that splendid command, the Crescent Regiment, would be everywhere in the paved and latticed basement (gorged with wealth), and throughout the first and second floors. The centrepiece in the arrangement of the double drawing-rooms would be a great field-piece, one of Hilary's casting, on its carriage, bright as gold, and flanked with stacks of muskets. The leading item in the hall would be an allegorical painting—by a famous Creole artist of nearly sixty years earlier—Louisiana Refusing to Enter the Union. Glass cases borrowed of merchants, milliners and apothecaries would receive the carefully classified smaller gifts of rare value, and a committee of goldsmiths, art critics, and auctioneers, would set their prices. If one of those torrential hurricanes—however, there came none.

How much, now, could they hope to clear? Well, the women of Alabama, to build a gun-boat, had raised two hundred thousand dollars, and——

"They will 'ave to raise mo'," twittered Madame Valcour, "if New Orleans fall'."

"She will not fall," remarked Anna from the chair, and there was great applause, as great as lace mitts could make.

Thunder-Cloud and Sunburst

Speaking of that smaller stronghold, Flora had a capital suggestion: Let this enterprise be named "for the common defence." Then, in the barely conceivable event of the city's fall, should the proceeds still be in women's hands—and it might be best to keep them so —let them go to the defence of Mobile!

Another idea—Miranda's and Victorine's—quite as gladly accepted, and they two elected to carry it out— was, to compile, from everybody's letters, a history of the battery, to be sold at the bazaar. The large price per copy which that work commanded was small compared with what it would bring now.

XXXVI

THUNDER-CLOUD AND SUNBURST

COULD they have known half the toil, care, and trial the preparation of this Bazaar was to cost their friends, apologized the Callenders as it neared completion, they would never have dared propose it.

But the smiling reply was Spartan: "Oh! what are such trifles when we think how our own fathers, husbands, and brothers have suffered—even in victory!" The "Sisters" were still living on last summer's glory, and only by such indirections alluded to defeats.

Anna smiled as brightly as any, while through her mind flitted spectral visions of the secondary and so needless carnage in those awful field-hospitals behind the battles, and of the storms so likely to follow the fights, when the midnight rain came down in sheets on the wounded still lying among the dead. On all the teeming, bleeding front no father, husband, or brother was hers, but amid the multitudinous exploits and agonies her thoughts were ever on him who, by no tie but the heart's, had in the past year grown to be father, mother, sister, and brother to the superb hundred whom she so tenderly knew, who so worshipingly knew her, and still whose lives, at every chance, he was hurling at the foe as stones from a sling.

"After all, in these terrible time'," remarked Miss Valcour in committee of the whole—last session before the public opening—"any toil, even look' at selfishly, is better than to be idle."

"As if you ever looked at anything selfishly!" said a matron, and there was a patter of hands.

"Or as if she were ever in danger of being idle!" fondly put in a young battery sister.

As these two rattled and crashed homeward in a deafening omnibus they shouted further comments to each other on this same subject. It was strange, they agreed, to see Miss Valcour, right through the midst of these terrible times, grow daily handsomer. Concerning Anna, they were of two opinions. The matron thought that at moments Anna seemed to have aged three years in one, while to the girl it appeared that her beauty—Anna's—had actually increased; taken a deeper tone, "or something." This huge bazaar business, they screamed, was something a girl like Anna should never have been allowed to undertake.

"And yet," said the matron on second thought, "it may really have helped her to bear up."

"Against what?"

"Oh,—all our general disturbance and distress, but

the battery's in particular. You know its very guns are, as we may say, hers, and everything that happens around them, or to any one who belongs to them in field, camp, or hospital, happens, in her feeling, to her."

The girl interrupted with a knowing touch: "You realize there's something else, don't you?"

Her companion showed pain: "Yes, but—I hoped you hadn't heard of it. I can't bear to talk about it. I know how common it is for men and girls to trifle with each other, but for such as he—who had the faith of all of us, yes, and of all his men, that he wasn't as other men are—for Hilary Kincaid to dawdle with Anna— with Anna Callender——"

"Oh!" broke in the girl, a hot blush betraying her own heart, "I don't think you've got the thing right at all. Why, it's Anna who's making the trouble! The dawdling is all hers! Oh, I have it from the best authority, though I'm not at liberty——"

"My dear girl, you've been misled. The fault is all his. I know it from one who can't be mistaken."

The damsel blushed worse. "Well, at any rate," she said, "the case doesn't in any slightest way involve Miss Valcour."

"Oh, I know that!" was the cocksure reply as they alighted in Canal Street to take an uptown mule-car.

Could Madame and Flora have overheard, how they would have smiled to each other.

With now a wary forward step and now a long pause, and now another short step and another pause, Hilary, in his letters to Anna, despite Flora's often successful contrivings, had ventured back toward that understanding for which the souls of both were starving, until at length he had sent one which seemed, itself, to kneel, for him, at her feet—would have seemed, had it not miscarried. But, by no one's craft, merely through the "terribleness" of the times, it had gone forever astray. When, not knowing this, he despatched another, this latter had promptly arrived, but its unintelligible allusions to lines in the lost forerunner were unpardonable for lack of that forerunner's light, and it contained especially one remark—trivial enough—which, because written in the irrepressible facetiousness so inborn in him, but taken, alas! in the ineradicable earnest so natural to her, had compelled her to reply in words which made her as they went, and him as they smote him, seem truly to have "aged three years in one." Yet hardly had they left her before you would have said she had recovered the whole three years and a fraction over, on finding a postscript, till then most unaccountably overlooked, which said that its writer had at that moment been ordered (as soon as he could accomplish this and that and so and so) to hasten home to recruit the battery with men of his own choice, and incidentally to bring the wounded Charlie with him. Such godsends raise the spring-tides of praise and human kindness in us, and it was on the very next morning, after finding that postscript, that there had come to Anna her splendid first thought of the Bazaar.

And now behold it, a visible reality! Unlighted as yet, unpeopled, but gorgeous, multiform, sentinelled, and ready, it needed but the touch of the taper to set forth all the glories of art and wealth tenfolded by self-sacrifice for a hallowed cause. Here was the Bazaar,

Thunder-Cloud and Sunburst

and yonder, far away on the southern border of Tennessee, its wasted ranks still spruce in their tatters, the battery; iron-hearted Bartleson in command; its six yellow daughters of destruction a trifle black in the lips, but bright on the cheeks and virgins all; Charlie on the roster though not in sight, the silken-satin standard well in view, rent and pierced, but showing seven red days of valor legended on its folds, and with that white-moustached old centaur, Maxime, still upholding it in action and review.

Intermediate, there, yonder, and here, from the farthest Mississippi State line clear down to New Orleans, were the camps of instruction, emptying themselves northward, pouring forth infantry, cavalry, artillery by every train that could be put upon the worn-out rails and by every main-travelled wagon road. But homeward-bound Charlie and his captain, where were they? Irby knew.

Flora, we have seen, had been willing, eager, for them to come—to arrive; not because Charlie, but because his captain, was one of the two. But Irby, never sure of her, and forever jealous of the ladies' man, had contrived, in a dull way, to detain the home-comers in mid-journey, with telegraphic orders to see here a commandant and there a factory of arms and hurry men and munitions to the front. So he killed time and tortured hope for several hearts, and that was a comfort in itself.

However, here was the Bazaar. After all, its sentinels were not of the Crescent Regiment, for the same grave reason which postponed the opening until to-morrow; the fact that to-day that last flower of the city's young

high-life was leaving for the fields of war, as Kincaid's
Battery had left in the previous spring. Yet, oh, how
differently! Again up St. Charles Street and down
Calliope the bands played, the fifes squealed; once
more the old men marched ahead, opened ranks, let the
serried youngsters through and waved and hurrahed
and kissed and wept; but all in a new manner, far
more poignant than the earlier. God only knew what
was to happen now, to those who went or to those who
stayed, or where or how any two of them should ever
meet again. The Callenders, as before, were there.
Anna had come definitely resolved to give one particular beardless Dick Smith a rousing kiss, purely to nullify
that guilty one of last year. But when the time came
she could not, the older one had made it impossible;
and when the returning bands broke out—

"Charlie is my darling! my darling! my darling!"

and the tears came dripping from under Connie's veil
and Victorine's and Miranda's and presently her own,
she was glad of the failure.

As they were driving homeward across Canal Street,
she noted, out beyond the Free Market, a steamboat
softly picking its way in to the levee. Some coal-
barges were there, she remembered, lading with pitch-
pine and destined as fire-ships, by that naval lieutenant
of the despatch-boat whom we know, against the Federal fleet lying at the head of the passes.

The coachman named the steamer to Constance:
"Yass, 'm, de ole *Gen'al Quitman;* dass her."

"From Vicksburg and the Bends!" cried the inquirer. "Why, who knows but Charlie Val—?"

"I'm Come Hame, My Love"

With both hands she clutched Miranda and Victorine, and brightened upon Anna.

"And Flora not with us!" was the common lament.

XXXVII

"TILL HE SAID, 'I'M COME HAME, MY LOVE'"

How absurdly poor the chance! Yet they bade the old coachman turn that way, and indeed the facts were better than the hope of any one of them. Charlie, very gaunt and battered, but all the more enamored of himself therefor and for the new chevrons of a gun corporal on his dingy sleeve, was actually aboard that boat. In one of the small knots of passengers on her boiler deck he was modestly companioning with a captain of infantry and two of staff, while they now exchanged merry anecdotes of the awful retreat out of Tennessee into Mississippi, now grimly damned this or that bad strategy, futile destruction, or horrible suffering, now re-discussed the comical chances of a bet of General Brodnax's, still pending, and now, with the crowd, moved downstairs to the freight deck as the boat began to nose the wharf.

Meanwhile the Callenders' carriage had made easy speed. Emerging by the Free Market, it met an open hack carrying six men. At the moment every one was cringing in a squall of dust, but as well as could be seen these six were the driver, a colored servant at his side, an artillery corporal, and three officers. Some army wagons hauling pine-knots to the fire-fleet compelled both carriages to check up. Thereupon, the gust passing and Victorine getting a better glance at the men, she tossed both hands, gave a stifled cry and began to laugh aloud.

"Charlie!" cried Anna. "Steve!" cried Constance. "And Captain Irby!" remarked Miranda.

The infantry captain, a transient steamboat acquaintance, used often afterward to say that he never saw anything prettier than those four wildly gladdened ladies unveiling in the shade of their parasols. I doubt if he ever did. He talked with Anna, who gave him so sweet an attention that he never suspected she was ravenously taking in every word the others dropped behind her.

"But where he is, that Captain Kincaid?" asked Victorine of Charlie a second time.

"Well, really," stammered the boy at last, "we—we can't say, just now, where he is."

("He's taken prisoner!" wailed Anna's heart while she let the infantry captain tell her that hacks, in Nashville on the Sunday after Donelson, were twenty-five dollars an hour.)

"He means," she heard Mandeville put in, "he means—Charlie—only that we *muz* not tell. 'Tis a sicret."

"You've sent him into the enemy's lines!" cried Constance to Irby in one of her intuitions.

"We?" responded the grave Irby, "No, not we."

"Captain Mandeville," exclaimed Victorine, "us, you don't need to tell us some white lies."

The Creole shrugged: "We are telling you only the whitess we can!"

("Yes," the infantry captain said, "with Memphis

we should lose the largest factory of cartridges in the Confederacy.")

But this was no place for parleying. So while the man next the hack-driver, ordered by Mandeville and laden with travelling-bags, climbed to a seat by the Callenders' coachman the aide-de-camp crowded in between Constance and Victorine, the equipage turned from the remaining soldiers, and off the ladies spun for home, Anna and Miranda riding backward to have the returned warrior next his doting wife. Victorine was dropped on the way at the gate of her cottage. When the others reached the wide outer stair of their own veranda, and the coachman's companion had sprung down and opened the carriage, Mandeville was still telling of Mandeville, and no gentle hearer had found any chance to ask further about that missing one of whom the silentest was famishing to know whatever—good or evil—there was to tell. Was Steve avoiding their inquiries? wondered Anna.

Up the steps went first the married pair, the wife lost in the hero, the hero in himself. Was he, truly? thought Anna, or was he only trying, kindly, to appear so? The ever-smiling Miranda followed. A step within the house Mandeville, with eyes absurdly aflame, startled first his wife by clutching her arm, and then Miranda by beckoning them into a door at their right, past unheeded treasures of the Bazaar, and to a front window. Yet through its blinds they could discover only what they had just left; the carriage, with Anna still in it, the garden, the grove, an armed soldier on guard at the river gate, another at the foot of the steps, a third here at the top.

Kincaid's Battery

It was good to Anna to rest her head an instant on the cushioning behind it and close her eyes. With his rag of a hat on the ground and his head tightly wrapped in the familiar Madras kerchief of the slave deck-hand, the attendant at the carriage side reverently awaited the relifting of her lids. The old coachman glanced back on her.

"Missy?" he tenderly ventured. But the lids still drooped, though she rose.

"Watch out fo' de step," said the nearer man. His tone was even more musically gentle than the other's, yet her eyes instantly opened into his and she started so visibly that her foot half missed and she had to catch his saving hand.

"Stiddy! stiddy!" He slowly let the cold, slim fingers out of his as she started on, but she swayed again and he sprang and retook them. For half a breath she stared at him like a wild bird shot, glanced at the sentinels, below, above, and then pressed up the stair.

Constance, behind the shutters, wept. "Go away," she pleaded to her husband, "oh, go away!" but pushed him without effect and peered down again. "He's won!" she exclaimed in soft ecstasy, "he's won at last!"

"Yes, he's win!" hoarsely whispered the aide-de-camp. "He's win the bet!"

Constance flashed indignantly: "What has he bet?"

"Bet. 'He has bet three—ee général' he'll pazz down Canal Street and through the middl' of the city, un-reco'nize! And now he's done it, they'll let him do the rest!" From his Creole eyes the enthusiast blazed a complete argument, that an educated commander, so disguised and traversing an enemy's camp, can be worth a hundred of the common run who go by the hard name of spy, and may decide the fortunes of a whole campaign: "They'll let him! and he'll get the próm-otion!"

"Ho–oh!" breathed the two women, "he's getting all the promotion *he* wants, right now!" The three heard Anna pass into the front drawing-room across the hall, the carriage move off and the disguised man enter the hall and set down the travelling-bags. They stole away through the library and up a rear stair.

It was not yet late enough to set guards within the house. No soul was in the drawing-rooms. In the front one, on its big wheels between two stacks of bayoneted rifles, beneath a splendor of flags and surrounded by innumerable costly offerings, rested as mutely as a seated idol that superior engine of death and woe, the great brass gun. Anna stole to it, sunk on her knees, crossed her trembling arms about its neck and rested her brow on its face.

She heard the tread in the hall, quaked to rise and flee, and yet could not move. It came upon the threshold and paused. "Anna," said the voice that had set her heart on fire across the carriage step. She sprang up, faced round, clutched the great gun, and stood staring. Her follower was still in slave garb, but now for the first time he revealed his full stature. His black locks were free and the "Madras" dropped from his fingers to the floor. He advanced a pace or two.

"Anna," he said again, "Anna Callender,"—he came another step—"I've come back, Anna, to— to—" he drew a little nearer. She gripped the gun.

He lighted up drolly: "Don't you know what I've come for? I didn't know, myself, till just now, or I shouldn't have come in this rig, though many a better man's in worse these days. I didn't know—because—I couldn't hope. I've come—" he stole close—his arms began to lift—she straightened to her full height, but helplessly relaxed as he smiled down upon it.

"I've come not just to get your promise, Anna Callender, but to muster you in; to *marry* you."

She flinched behind the gun's muzzle in resentful affright. He lowered his palms in appeal to her wisdom. "It's the right thing, Anna, the only safe way! I've known it was, ever since Steve Mandeville's wedding. Oh! it takes a colossal assurance to talk to you so, Anna Callender, but I've got the *colossal assurance*. I've got that, beloved, and you've got all the rest—my heart—my soul—my life. Give me yours."

Anna had shrunk in against the farther wheel, but now rallied and moved a step forward. "Let me pass," she begged. "Give me a few moments to myself. You can wait here. I'll come back."

He made room. She moved by. But hardly had she passed when a soft word stopped her. She turned inquiringly and the next instant—Heaven only knows if first on his impulse or on hers—she was in his arms, half stifled on his breast, and hanging madly from his neck while his kisses fell upon her brow—temples— eyes—and rested on her lips.

Flora sat reading a note just come from that same "A. C." Her brother had gone to call on Victorine. Irby had just bade the reader good-by, to return soon

And the next instant she was in his arms

and go with her to Callender House to see the Bazaar. Madame Valcour turned from a window with a tart inquiry:

"And all you had to do was to say yes to him?"

"That would have been much," absently replied the reader, turning a page.

"'Twould have been little!—to make him rich!—and us also!"

"Not us," said the abstracted girl; "me." Something in the missive caused her brows to knit.

"And still you trifle!" nagged the grandam, "while I starve! And while at any instant may arrive—humph—that other fool."

Even this did not draw the reader's glance. "No." she responded. "He cannot. Irby and Charlie lied to us. He is already here." She was re-reading.

The grandmother stared, tossed a hand and moved across the floor. As she passed near the girl's slippered foot it darted out, tripped her and would have sent her headlong, but she caught by the lamp table. Flora smiled with a strange whiteness round the lips. Madame righted the shaken lamp, quietly asking, "Did you do that—h-m-m—for hate of the lady, or, eh, the ladies' man?"

"The latter," said the reabsorbed girl.

"Strange," sighed the other, "how we can have—at the same time—for the same one—both feelings."

But Flora's ears were closed. "Well," she audibly mused, "he'll get a recall."

"Even if it must be forged?" twittered the dame.

XXXVIII

ANNA'S OLD JEWELS

A REPORTERS' heaven, the Bazaar. So on its opening night Hilary named it to Flora.

"A faerye realm," the scribes themselves itemed it; "myriad lights—broad staircases gracef'y asc'd'g—ravish'g perfumes—met our gaze—garlandries of laurel and magn'a—prom'd'g from room to room—met our gaze—directed by masters of cerem'y in Conf'te G'd's unif'm—here turn'g to the right—fair women and brave men—carried thither by the dense throng—music with its volup's swell—met our gaze—again descend'g—arriv'g at din'g-hall—new scene of ench't bursts—refr't tables—enarched with ev'gr's and decked with labarums and burgees—thence your way lies through—costly volumes and shimm'g bijoutries—met our gaze!"

It was Kincaid who saw their laborious office in this flippant light, and so presented it to Anna that she laughed till she wept; laughing was now so easy. But when they saw one of the pencillers writing awkwardly with his left hand, aided by half a right arm in a pinned-up sleeve, her mirth had a sudden check. Yet presently it became a proud thrill, as the poor boy glowed with delight while Hilary stood and talked with him of the fearful Virginia day on which that ruin had befallen him at Hilary's own side in Kincaid's Battery, and then brought him to converse with her. This incident may account for the fervor with which a next morning's report extolled the wonders of the "fair

Anna's Old Jewels

chairman's" administrative skill and the matchless and most opportune executive supervision of Captain Hilary Kincaid. Flora read it with interest.

With interest of a different kind she read in a later issue another passage, handed her by the grandmother with the remark, "to warn you, my dear." The matter was a frothy bit of tragical romancing, purporting to have been gathered from two detectives out of their own experience of a year or so before, about a gift made to the Bazaar by Captain Kincaid, which had—"met our gaze jealously guarded under glass amid a brilliant collection of reliques, jewels, and bric-à-brac; a large, evil-looking knife still caked with the mud of the deadly affray, but bearing legibly in Italian on its blade the inscription, 'He who gets me in his body never need take a medicine,' and with a hilt and scabbard encrusted with gems."

Now, one of the things that made Madame Valcour good company among gentlewomen was her authoritative knowledge of precious stones. So when Flora finished reading and looked up, and the grandmother faintly smiled and shook her head, both understood.

"Paste?"

"Mostly."

"And the rest—not worth——?"

"Your stealing," simpered the connoisseur, and, reading, herself, added meditatively, "I should hate anyhow, for you to have that thing. The devil would be always at your ear."

"Whispering—what?"

The grandmother shrugged: "That depends. I look to see you rise, yet, to some crime of dignity; some-

thing really tragic and Italian. Whereas at present—"
she pursed her lips and shrugged again.

The girl blandly laughed: "You venerable in-
grate!"

At the Bazaar that evening, when Charlie and grandma and the crowd were gone, Flora handled the
unlovely curiosity. She and Irby had seen Hilary and
Anna and the Hyde & Goodrich man on guard just
there draw near the glass case where it lay "like a
snake on a log," as Charlie had said, take it in their
hands and talk of it. The jeweller was expressing confidentially a belief that it had once been set with real
stones, and Hilary was privately having a sudden
happy thought, when Flora and Adolphe came up
only in time to hear the goldsmith's statement of its
present poor value.

"But surely," said Kincaid, "this old jewellery lying
all about it here——"

"That? that's the costliest gift in the Bazaar!"

Irby inquired whose it was, Anna called it anony-
mous, and Flora, divining that the giver was Anna, felt
herself outrageously robbed. As the knife was being
laid back in place she recalled, with odd interest, her
grandmother's mention of the devil, and remembered a
time or two when for a moment she had keenly longed
for some such bit of steel; something much more
slender, maybe, and better fitting a dainty hand, but
quite as long and sharp. A wave from this thought
may have prompted Anna's request that the thing be
brought forth again and Flora allowed to finger it; but
while this was being done Flora's main concern was to
note how the jeweller worked the hidden spring by

which he opened the glass case. As she finally gave up the weapon: "Thank you," she sweetly said to both Anna and Hilary, but with a meaning reserved to herself.

You may remember how once she had gone feeling and prying along the fair woodwork of these rooms for any secret of construction it might hold. Lately, when the house began to fill with secretable things of large money value, she had done this again, and this time, in one side of a deep chimney-breast, had actually found a most innocent-looking panel which she fancied to be kept from sliding only by its paint. Now while she said her sweet thanks to Anna and Hilary she could almost believe in fairies, the panel was so near the store of old jewels. With the knife she might free the panel, and behind the panel hide the jewels till their scent grew cold, to make them her bank account when all the banks should be broken, let the city fall or stand. No one need ever notice, so many were parting with their gems perforce, so many buying them as a form of asset convenient for flight. So good-night, old dagger and jewels; see you again, but don't overdo your limited importance. Of the weapon Flora had further learned that it was given not to the Bazaar but to Anna, and of the jewels that they were not in that lottery of everything, with which the affair was to end and the proceeds of whose tickets were pouring in upon Anna, acting treasurer, the treasurer being ill.

Tormentingly in Hilary's way was this Lottery and Bazaar. Even from Anna, sometimes especially from Anna, he could not understand why certain things must not be told or certain things could not be done until this Bazaar—etc. Why, at any hour he might be recalled! Yes, Anna saw that—through very moist eyes. True, also, she admitted, Beauregard and Johnston *might* fail to hold off Buell and Grant; and true, as well, New Orleans *could* fall, and might be sacked. It was while confessing this that with eyes down and bosom heaving she accepted the old Italian knife. Certainly unless the pooh-poohing Mandeville was wrong, who declared the forts down the river impregnable and Beauregard, on the Tennessee, invincible, flight (into the Confederacy) was safest—but—the Bazaar first, flight afterward. "We women," she said, rising close before him with both hands in his, "must stand by *our* guns. We've no more right"—it was difficult to talk while he kissed her fingers and pressed her palms to his gray breast—"no more right—to be cowards—than you men."

Her touch brought back his lighter mood and he told the happy thought—project—which had come to him while they talked with the jeweller. He could himself "do the job," he said, "roughly but well enough." Anna smiled at the fanciful scheme. Yet—yes, its oddity was in its favor. So many such devices were succeeding, some of them to the vast advantage of the Southern cause.

When Flora the next evening stole a passing glance at the ugly trinket in its place she was pleased to note how well it retained its soilure of clay. For she had that day used it to free the panel, behind which she had found a small recess so fitted to her want that she had only to replace panel and tool and await some chance in the closing hours of the show. Pleased she was, too, to observe that the old jewels lay in a careless heap. Now to conceal all interest and to divert all eyes, even grandmama's! Thus, however, night after night an odd fact eluded her: That Anna and her hero, always singly, and themselves careful to lure others away, glimpsed that disordered look of the gems and unmolested air of the knife with a content as purposeful as her own. Which fact meant, when came the final evening, that at last every sham jewel in the knife's sheath had exchanged places with a real one from the loose heap, while, nestling between two layers of the sheath's material, reposed, payable to bearer, a check on London for thousands of pounds sterling. Very proud was Anna of her lover's tremendous versatility and craftsmanship.

XXXIX

TIGHT PINCH

From Camp Villeré, close below small Camp Callender, one more last regiment—Creoles—was to have gone that afternoon to the Jackson Railroad Station and take train to join their Creole Beauregard for the defence of their own New Orleans.

More than a day's and a night's journey away was "Corinth," the village around which he had gathered his forces, but every New Orleans man and boy among them knew, and every mother and sister here in New Orleans knew, that as much with those men and boys as with any one anywhere, lay the defence and deliverance of this dear Crescent City. With Grant swept back from the Tennessee, and the gunboats that threatened Island Ten and Memphis sunk, blown up, or driven back into the Ohio, New Orleans, they believed, could jeer at Farragut down at the Passes and at Butler out on horrid Ship Island. "And so can Mobile," said the Callenders to the Valcours.

"The fortunes of our two cities are one!" cried Constance, and the smiling Valcours were inwardly glad to assent, believing New Orleans doomed, and remembering their Mobile home burned for the defence of the two cities of one fortune.

However, the Camp Villeré regiment had not got off, but would move at midnight. On the train with them Hilary was sending recruits to the battery, younger brothers of those who had gone the year before. He had expected to conduct, not send, them, but important work justified—as Anna told Flora—his lingering until his uncle should bid him come. Which bidding Irby might easily have incited, by telegraph, had Flora let him. But Flora's heart was too hopelessly entangled to release Hilary even for the gain of separating him from Anna; and because it was so entangled (and with her power to plot caught in the tangle), she was learning to hate with a distemper of passion that awed even herself.

"But I *must* clear out mighty soon," said Hilary that evening to Greenleaf, whose exchange he had procured at last and, rather rashly, was taking him to Callender House to say good-by. They talked of Anna. Greenleaf knew the paramount secret; had bravely given his friend a hand on it the day he was told. Now Hilary said he had been begging her again for practical steps, and the manly loser commended.

Tight Pinch

"But think of that from me, Fred! who one year ago
—you know how I talked—about Steve, for instance.
Shame!—how reckless war's made us. Here we are, by
millions, in a perpetual crash of victory and calamity,
and yet—take me for an example—in spite of me my
one devouring anxiety—that wakes me up in the night
and gives me dreams in the day—is how to get *her*
before this next battle get's me. Yes, the instant I'm
ordered I go, and if I'm not ordered soon I go anyhow.
I wouldn't have my boys"—etc.

And still the prison-blanched Greenleaf approved.
But the next revelation reddened his brow: Anna,
Hilary said, had at last "come round—knuckled down!
Yes, sir-ee, cav-ed in!" and this evening, after the
Bazaar, to a few younger sisters of the battery whom
she would ask to linger for a last waltz with their young
heroes, she would announce her engagement and her
purpose to be wed in a thrillingly short time.

The two men found the Bazaar so amusingly col-
lapsed that, as Hilary said, you could spell it with a
small b. A stream of vehicles coming and going had
about emptied the house and grounds. No sentries
saluted, no music chimed. In the drawing-rooms the
brass gun valiantly held its ground, but one or two
domestics clearing litter from the floors seemed quite
alone there, and some gay visitors who still tarried in
the library across the hall were hardly enough to crowd
it. "Good," said Hilary beside the field-piece. "You
wait here and I'll bring the Callenders as they can
come."

But while he went for them whom should Greenleaf
light upon around a corner of the panelled chimney-

breast but that secret lover of the Union and all its defenders, Mademoiselle Valcour. Her furtive cordiality was charming as she hurriedly gave and withdrew a hand in joy for his liberation.

"Taking breath out of the social rapids?" he softly inquired.

"Ah, more! 'Tis from that deluge of——"

He understood her emotional gesture. It meant that deluge of disloyalty—rebellion—there across the hall, and all through this turbulent city and land. But it meant, too, that they must not be seen to parley alone, and he had turned away, when Miranda, to Flora's disgust, tripped in upon them with her nose in full wrinkle, archly surprised to see Flora here, and proposing to hale both into the general throng to applaud Anna's forthcoming "proclamation!"

Greenleaf de trop? Ah, nay! not if he could keep the old Greenleaf poise! and without words her merry nose added that his presence would only give happier point to what every one regarded as a great Confederate victory. At a subtle sign from Flora the hostess and he went, expecting her to follow.

But Flora was in a perilous strait. Surprised by Hilary's voice, with the panel open and the knife laid momentarily in the recess that both hands might bring the jewels from the case, she had just closed the opening with the dagger inside when Greenleaf confronted her. Now, in this last instant of opportunity at his and Miranda's back, should she only replace the weapon or still dare the theft? At any rate the panel must be re-opened. But when she would have slid it her dainty fingers failed, failed, failed until a cold damp came to

Tight Pinch

her brow and she trembled. Yet saunteringly she stepped to the show-case, glancing airily about. The servants had gone. She glided back, but turned to meet another footfall, possibly Kincaid's, and felt her anger rise against her will as she confronted only the inadequate Irby. A sudden purpose filled her, and before he could speak:

"Go!" she said, "telegraph your uncle! instantly!"

"I've done so."

Her anger mutinied again: "Without consult'—! And since when?"

"This morning."

She winced yet smiled: "And still—your cousin—he 's receive' no order?" Her fingers tingled to maim some one—this dolt—anybody! Her eyes sweetened.

Irby spoke: "The order has come, but——"

"What! you have not given it?"

"Flora, it includes me! Ah, for one more evening with you I am risking——"

Her look grew fond though she made a gesture of despair: "Oh, short-sighted! Go, give it him! Go!"

Across the hall a prolonged carol of acclamation, confabulation, laughter, and cries of "Ah-r, indeed!" told that Anna's word was out. "What difference," Irby lingered to ask, "can an hour or two between trains——?"

But the throng was upon them. "We don't know!" cried Flora. "Give it him! *We don't know!*" and barely had time herself to force a light laugh when here were Charlie and Victorine, Hilary, Anna, Miranda, Madame, Constance, Mandeville, and twenty others.

"Fred!" called Hilary. His roaming look found the gray detective: "Where's Captain Greenleaf?"

"Gone."

"With never a word of good-by? Oh, bless my soul, he *did* say good-by!" There was a general laugh. "But this won't do. It's not safe for him——"

The gray man gently explained that his younger associate was with Greenleaf as bodyguard. The music of harp and violins broke out and dancers swept round the brass gun and up and down the floors.

XL

THE LICENSE, THE DAGGER

HILARY had bent an arm around Anna when Flora called his name. Irby handed him the order. A glance made it clear. Its reader cast a wide look over the heads of the dancers and lifting the missive high beckoned with it to Mandeville. Then he looked for some one else: "Charlie!"

"Out on the veranda," said a passing dancer.

"Send him here!" The commander's eye came back to Irby: "Old man, how long have you had this?"

"About an hour."

"Oh, my stars, Adolphe, you should have told me!"

It was a fair sight, though maddening to Flora yonder by the glass case, to see the two cousins standing eye to eye, Hilary's brow dark with splendid concern while without a glance at Anna he passed her the despatch and she read it.

"Steve," he said, as the Mandeville pair pressed up,

The License, The Dagger

"look at that! boots-and-saddles! now! to-night! for you and Adolphe and me! Yes, Charlie, and you; go, get your things and put Jerry on the train with mine."

The boy's partner was Victorine. Before she could gasp he had kissed her. Amid a laugh that stopped half the dance he waved one farewell to sister, grandmother and all and sprang away. "Dance on, fellows," called Hilary, "this means only that I'm going with you." The lads cheered and the dance revived.

Their captain turned: "Miss Flora, I promised your brother he should go whenever——"

"But me al-*so* you promised!" she interrupted, and a fair sight also, grievous to Irby, startling to Anna, were this pair, standing eye to eye.

"Yes," replied Kincaid, "and I'll keep my word. In any extremity you shall come to him."

"As likewise my wive to me!" said the swelling Mandeville, openly caressing the tearful Constance. "Wive to 'usband," he declaimed, " sizter to brother——" But his audience was lost. Hilary was speaking softly to Anna. She was very pale. The throng drew away. You could see that he was asking if she only could in no extremity come to him. His words were inaudible, but any one who had ever loved could read them. And now evidently he proposed something. There was ardor in his eye—ardor and enterprise. She murmured a response. He snatched out his watch.

"*Just* time," he was heard to say, "time enough by soldier's measure!" His speech grew plainer: "The law's right for me to call and for you to come, that's all we want. What frightens you?"

"Nothing," she said, and smiled. "I only feared there wasn't time."

The lover faced his cousin so abruptly that all started and laughed, while Anna turned to her kindred, as red as a rose. "Adolphe," cried he, "I'm going for my marriage license. While I'm getting it, will you——?"

Irby went redder than Anna. "You can't get it at this hour!" he said. His eyes sought Flora, but she was hurriedly conferring with her grandmother.

Hilary laughed: "You'll see. I fixed all that a week ago. Will you get the minister?"

"Why, Hilary, this is——"

"Yass!" piped Madame, "he'll obtain him!"

The plaudits of the dancers, who once more had stopped, were loud. Flora's glance went over to Irby, and he said, "Why, yes, Hilary, if you—why, of course I will." There was more applause.

"Steve," said Hilary, "some one must go with me to the clerk's office to——"

"To vouch you!" broke in the aide-de-camp. "That will be Steve Mandeville!" Constance sublimely approved. As the three Callenders moved to leave the room one way and the three captains another, Anna seized the hands of Flora and her grandmother.

"You'll keep the dance going?" she solicited, and they said they would. Flora gave her a glowing embrace, and as Irby strode by murmured to him.

"Put your watch back half an hour."

In such disordered days social liberty was large. When the detective, after the Callenders were gone upstairs and the captains had galloped away, truthfully told Miss Valcour that his only object in tarrying here

The License, The Dagger

was to see the love-knot tied, she heard him affably, though inwardly in flames of yearning to see him depart. She burned to see him go because she believed him, and also because there in the show-case still lay the loosely heaped counterfeit of the booty whose reality she had already ignorantly taken and stowed away.

What should she do? Here was grandma, better aid than forty Irbys; but with both phases of her problem to deal with at once—how to trip headlong this wild matrimonial leap and how to seize this treasure by whose means she might leave Anna in a fallen city and follow Hilary to the war—she was at the end of her daintiest wits. She talked on with the gray man, for that kept him from the show-case. In an air full of harmonies and prattle, of fluttering draperies, gliding feet, undulating shoulders, twinkling lights, gallantry, fans, and perfume, she dazzled him with her approval when he enlarged on the merits of Kincaid and when he pledged all his powers of invention to speed the bridal. Frantic to think what better to do, she waltzed with him, while he described the colonel of the departing regiment as such a martinet that to ask him to delay his going would only hasten it; waltzed on when she saw her grandmother discover the knife's absence and telegraph her a look of contemptuous wonder. But ah, how time was flying! Even now Kincaid must be returning hitherward, licensed!

The rapturous music somewhat soothed her frenzy, even helped her thought, and in a thirst for all it could give she had her partner swing her into the wide hall whence it came and where also Hilary must first reappear. Twice through its length they had swept, when Anna, in altered dress, came swiftly down the stair with Constance protestingly at her side. The two were speaking anxiously together as if a choice of nuptial adornments (for Constance bore a box that might have held the old jewels) had suddenly brought to mind a forgotten responsibility. As they pressed into the drawing-rooms the two dancers floated after them by another door.

When presently Flora halted beside the gun and fanned while the dance throbbed on, the two sisters stood a few steps away behind the opened show-case, talking with her grandmother and furtively eyed by a few bystanders. They had missed the dagger. Strangely disregarded by Anna, but to Flora's secret dismay and rage, Constance, as she talked, was dropping from her doubled hands into the casket the last of the gems. Now she shut the box and laid it in Anna's careless arms.

Leaving the gray man by the gun, Flora sprang near. Anna was enduring, with distracted smiles, the eager reasonings of Madame and Constance that the vanished trinket was but borrowed; a thief would have taken the *jewels*, they argued; but as Flora would have joined in, every line of Anna's face suddenly confided to her a consternation whose cause the silenced Flora instantly mistook. "Ah, if you knew—!" Anna began, but ceased as if the lost relic stood for something incommunicable even to nearest and dearest.

"They've sworn their love on it!" was the thought of Flora and the detective in the same instant. It filled her veins with fury, yet her response was gentle and meditative. "To me," she said, "it seemed such a good-for-nothing that even if I saw it is gone, me, I think I would n' have take' notice." All at once she brightened: "Anna! without a doubt! without a doubt Captain Kincaid he has it!" About to add a caress, she was startled from it by a masculine voice that gayly echoed out in the hall:

"Without a doubt!"

The dance ceased and first the short, round body of Mandeville and then the tall form of Hilary Kincaid pushed into the room. "Without a doubt!" repeated Hilary, while Mandeville asked right, asked left, for Adolphe. "Without a doubt," persisted the lover, "Captain Kincaid he has it!" and proffered Anna the law's warrant for their marriage.

She pushed it away. Her words were so low that but few could hear. "The dagger!" she said. "Haven't you got the dagger? You haven't got it?"

XLI

FOR AN EMERGENCY

HILARY stared, reddened as she paled, and with a slow smile shook his head. She murmured again:

"It's lost! the dagger! with all——"

"Why,—why, Miss Anna,"—his smile grew playful, but his thought ran back to the exploded powder-mill, to the old inventor, to Flora in those days, the deported schoolmistress's gold still unpaid to him, the jeweller and the exchanged gems, the Sterling bill—"Why, Miss Anna! how do you mean, lost?"

"Taken! gone! and by my fault! I—*I forgot all about it.*"

He laughed aloud and around: "Pshaw! Now, ladies and gentlemen, this is some joke you're"—he glanced toward the show-case——

"No," insisted Anna, "it's taken! Here are the other things." She displayed the box.

Madame, very angry, smiled from it to Flora: "Oh, thou love's fool! not to steal *that* and leave the knife, with which, luckily! now that you have it, you dare not strike!"

All this the subtle girl read in the ancient lady's one small "ahem!" and for reply, in some even more unvoiced way, warned her against the eye of the gray man near the gun. To avoid whose scrutiny herself she returned sociably to his side.

"The other things!" scoffed meantime the gay Hilary, catching up Anna's word. "No! if you please, *here* is the only other thing!" and boyishly flaunted the license at Mandeville and all the Callenders, the throng merrily approving. His eye, falling upon the detective, kindled joyfully: "Oh, you godsend! *You* hunt up the lost frog-sticker, will you—while we—?" He flourished the document again and the gray man replied with a cordial nod. Kincaid waved thanks and glanced round. "Adolphe!" he called. "Steve, where in the dickens——?"

Whether he so designed it or not, the contrast between his levity and Anna's agitation convinced Flora, Madame, all, that the weapon's only value to the lovers was sentimental. "Or religious," thought the detective, whose adjectives could be as inaccurate as his divinations. While he conjectured, Anna spoke once more to Hilary. Her vehement words were too soft

For an Emergency

for any ear save his, but their tenor was so visible, her
distress so passionate and her firmness of resolve so
evident that every mere beholder fell back, letting the
Callender-Valcour group, with Steve and the gentle
detective, press closer. With none of them, nor yet
with Hilary, was there anything to argue; their plight
seemed to her hopeless. For them to marry, for her to
default, and for him to fly, all in one mad hour—one
whirlwind of incident—"It cannot be!" was all she
could say, to sister, to stepmother, to Flora, to Hilary
again: "We cannot do it! I will not!—till that lost
thing is found!"

With keen sympathy the detective, in the pack, enjoyed the play of Hilary's face, where martial animation
strove inspiringly against a torture of dashed hopes.
Glancing aside to Flora's as she turned from Anna,
he caught there no sign of the storm of joy which had
suddenly burst in her bosom; but for fear he might,
and to break across his insight and reckoning, she
addressed him.

"Anna she don't give any *reason*," she exclaimed.
"Ask her, you, the reason!"

"'Tain't reason at all," he softly responded, "it's
superstition. But hold on. Watch me." He gestured for the lover's attention and their eyes met. It
made a number laugh, to see Hilary's stare gradually
go senseless and then blaze with intelligence. Suddenly, joyfully, with every eye following his finger, he
pointed into the gray man's face:

"Smellemout, you've got it!"

The man shook his head for denial, and his kindly
twinkle commanded the belief of all. Not a glint in it

showed that his next response, however well-meant, was to be a lie.

"Then Ketchem has it!" cried Kincaid.

The silent man let his smile mean yes, and the alert company applauded. "Go h-on with the weddingg!" ordered the superior Mandeville.

"Where's Adolphe?" cried Kincaid, and "On with the wedding!" clamored the lads of the battery, while Anna stood gazing on the gray man and wondering why she had not guessed this very thing.

"Yes," he quietly said to her, "it's all right. You'll have it back to-morrow. 'Twon't cut love if you don't."

At that the gay din redoubled, but Flora, with the little grandmother vainly gripping her arms, flashed between the two.

"Anna!" she cried, "I don't bil-ieve!"

Whether it was true or false Mandeville cared nothing, but—"Yes, 't is true!" he cried in Flora's face, and then to the detective—"Doubtlezz to phot-ograph it that's all you want!"

The detective said little, but Anna assured Flora that was all. "He wants to show it at the trial!"

"Listen!" said Flora.

"Here's Captain Irby!" cried Mrs. Callender—Constance—half a dozen, but——

"Listen!" repeated Flora, and across the curtained veranda and in at the open windows, under the general clamor, came a soft palpitating rumble. Did Hilary hear it, too? He was calling:

"Adolphe, where's your man—the minister? Where in the—three parishes——?" and others were echoing, "The minister! where's the minister?"

For an Emergency

Had they also caught the sound?

"Isn't he here?" asked Irby. He drew his watch.

"Half-hour slow!" cried Mandeville, reading it.

"But have you heard noth——?"

"Nothingg!" roared Mandeville.

"Where'd you leave him?" sharply asked Kincaid.

His cousin put on great dignity: "At his door, my dear sir, waiting for the cab I sent him."

"Oh, sent!" cried half the group. "Steve," called Kincaid, "your horse is fresh——"

"But, alas, without wings!" wailed the Creole, caught Hilary's shoulder and struck a harkening pose.

"Too late!" moaned Flora to the detective, Madame to Constance and Miranda, and the battery lads to their girls, from whose hands they began to wring wild good-byes as a peal of fifes and drums heralded the oncome of the departing regiment.

Thus Charlie Valcour found the company as suddenly he reappeared in it, pushing in to the main group where his leader stood eagerly engaged with Anna.

"All right, Captain!" He saluted: "All done!" But a fierce anxiety was on his brow and he gave no heed to Hilary's dismissing thanks: "Captain, what's 'too late'?" He turned, scowling, to his sister: "What are we too late for, Flo? Good God! not the wedding? Not your wedding, Miss Anna? It's *not* too late. By Jove, it sha'n't be too late."

All the boyish lawlessness of his nature rose into his eyes, and a boy's tears with it. "The minister!" he retorted to Constance and his grandmother, "the minister be—Oh, Captain, don't wait for him! Have the thing without a minister!"

The whole room was laughing, Hilary loudest, but the youth's voice prevailed. "It'll hold good!" He turned upon the detective: "Won't it?"

A merry nod was the reply, with cries of "Yes," "Yes," from the battery boys, and he clamored on:

"Why, there's a kind of people——"

"Quakers!" sang out some one.

"Yes, the Quakers! Don't they do it all the time! Of course they do!" With a smile in his wet eyes the lad wheeled upon Victorine: "Oh, by S'n' Peter! if that was the only——"

But the small, compelling hand of the detective faced him round again and with a sudden swell of the general laugh he laughed too. "He's trying to behave like Captain Kincaid," one battery sister tried to tell another, whose attention was on a more interesting matter.

"Here!" the gray man was amiably saying to Charlie. "It's your advice that's too late. Look."

Before he had half spoken a hush so complete had fallen on the company that while every eye sought Hilary and Anna every ear was aware that out on the levee road the passing drums had ceased and the brass —as if purposely to taunt the theatrical spirit of Flora— had struck up The Ladies' Man. With military curtness Kincaid was addressing the score or so of new cannoneers:

"Corporal Valcour, this squad—no, keep your partners, but others please stand to the right and left— these men are under your command. When I presently send you from here you'll take them at a double-quick and close up with that regiment. I'll be at the train

For an Emergency

when you reach it. Captain Mandeville,"—he turned
to the married pair, who were hurriedly scanning the
license Miranda had just handed them,—"I adjure
you as a true and faithful citizen and soldier, and you,
madam, as well, to testify to us, all, whether that is or
is not the license of court for the marriage of Anna
Callender to Hilary Kincaid."

"It is!" eagerly proclaimed the pair.

"Hand it, please, to Charlie. Corporal, you and
your men look it over."

"And now—" His eyes swept the throng. Anna's
hand, trembling but ready, rose shoulder-high in his.
He noted the varied expressions of face among the
family servants hurriedly gathering in the doors, and
the beautiful amaze of Flora, so genuine yet so well
acted. Radiantly he met the flushed gaze of his
speechless cousin. "If any one alive," he cried,
"knows any cause why this thing should not be, let
him now speak or forever hereafter hold his peace."
He paused. Constance handed something to her husband.

"Oh, go on," murmured Charlie, and many smiled.

"Soldiers!" resumed the lover, "this fair godmother
of your flag agrees that for all we two want just now
Kincaid's Battery is minister enough. For all we want
is——" Cheers stopped him.

"The prayer-book!" put in Mandeville, pushing it
at him. The boys harkened again.

"No," said Kincaid, "time's too short. All we want
is to bind ourselves, before Heaven and all mankind,
in holy wedlock, for better, or worse, till death us do
part. And this we here do in sight of you all, and in

217

the name and sight and fear of God." He dropped his glance to Anna's: "Say Amen."

"Amen," said Anna. At the same moment in one of the doors stood a courier.

"All right!" called Hilary to him. "Tell your colonel we're coming! Just a second more, Captain Irby, if you please. Soldiers!—I, Hilary, take thee, Anna, to be my lawful wedded wife. And you——"

"I, Anna," she softly broke in, "take thee, Hilary, to be my——" She spoke the matter through, but he had not waited.

"Therefore!" he cried, "you men of Kincaid's Battery—and you, sir,—and you,"—nodding right and left to Mandeville and the detective,—"on this our solemn pledge to supply as soon as ever we can all form of law and social usage here omitted which can more fully solemnize this union—do now——"

Up went the detective's hand and then Mandeville's and all the boys', and all together said:

"Pronounce you man and wife."

"Go!" instantly rang Kincaid to Charlie, and in a sudden flutter of gauzes and clink of trappings, with wringing of soft fingers by hard ones, and in a tender clamor of bass and treble voices, away sprang every cannoneer to knapsacks and sabres in the hall, and down the outer stair into ranks and off under the stars at double-quick. Sisters of the battery, gliding out to the veranda rail, faintly saw and heard them a precious moment longer as they sped up the dusty road. Then Irby stepped quickly out, ran down the steps, mounted and galloped. A far rumble of wheels told the coming of two omnibuses chartered to bear the dancers all, with

For an Emergency

the Valcours and the detective, to their homes. Now out to the steps came Mandeville. His wife was with him and the maidens kindly went in. There the detective joined them. At a hall door Hilary was parting with Madame, Flora, Miranda. Anna was near him with Flora's arm about her in melting fondness. Now Constance rejoined the five, and now Hilary and Anna left the other four and passed slowly out to the garden stair alone.

Beneath them there, with welcoming notes, his lone horse trampled about the hitching-rail. Dropping his cap the master folded the bride's hands in his and pressed on them a long kiss. The pair looked deeply into each other's eyes. Her brow drooped and he laid a kiss on it also. "Now you must go," she murmured.

"My own beloved!" was his response. "My soul's mate!" He tried to draw her, but she held back.

"You must go," she repeated.

"Yes! kiss me and I fly." He tried once more to draw her close, but still in vain.

"No, dearest," she whispered, and trembled. Yet she clutched his imprisoning fingers and kissed them. He hugged her hands to his breast.

"Oh, Hilary," she added, "I wish I could! But—don't you know why I can't? Don't you see?"

"No, my treasure, not any more. Why, Anna, you're Anna Kincaid now. You're my wed'——"

Her start of distress stopped him short. "Don't call me that,—my—my own," she faltered.

"But if you are that——?"

"Oh, I am! thank God, I am! But don't name the name. It's too fearfully holy. We're married for an emergency, love, an awful crisis! which hasn't come to you yet, and may not come at all. When it does, so will I! in that name! and you shall call me by it!"

"Ah, if then you can come! But what do we know?"

"We know in whom we trust, Hilary; must, must, must trust, as we trust and must trust each other."

Still hanging to his hands she pushed them off at arm's-length: "Oh, my Hilary, my hero, my love, my life, my commander, go!" And yet she clung. She drew his fingers close down again and covered them with kisses, while twice, thrice, in solemn adoration, he laid his lips upon her heavy hair. Suddenly the two looked up. The omnibuses were here in the grove.

Here too was the old coachman, with the soldier's horse. The vehicles jogged near and halted. A troop of girls, with Flora, tripped out. And still, in their full view, with Flora closest, the bride's hands held the bridegroom's fast. He had neither the strength to pull free nor the wit to understand.

"What is it?" he softly asked, as the staring men waited and the girls about Flora hung back.

"Don't you know?" murmured Anna. "Don't you see—the—the difference?"

All at once he saw! Throwing away her hands he caught her head between his big palms. Her arms flew round his neck, her lips went to his, and for three heart-throbs they clung like bee and flower. Then he sprang down the stair, swung into the saddle, and fled after his men.

"Victory! I Heard it as Pl'—"

XLII

"VICTORY! I HEARD IT AS PL'—"

THE last few days of March and first three or four of April, since the battery boys and the three captains had gone, were as full of frightened and angry questions as the air is of bees around a shaken hive.

So Anna had foreboded, yet it was not so for the causes she had in mind; not one fierce hum asked another where the bazaar's money was. That earlier bazaar, in the St. Louis Hotel, had taken six weeks to report its results, and now, with everybody distracted by a swarm and buzz of far larger, livelier, hotter queries, the bazaar's sponsors might report or not, as they chose. Meanwhile, was the city really in dire and shameful jeopardy, or was it as safe as the giddiest boasted? Looking farther away, over across Georgia to Fort Pulaski, so tremendously walled and armed, was the "invader" merely wasting lives, trying to take it? On North Carolina's coast, where our priceless blockade-runners plied, had Newbern, as so stubbornly rumored, and had Beaufort, already fallen, or had they really not? Had the *Virginia not* sunk the *Monitor* and scattered the Northern fleets? Was it *not* by France, after all (asked the Creoles), but only by Paraguay that the Confederacy had been "reco'nize'"? Was there *no* truth in the joyous report that McClellan had vanished from Yorktown peninsula? *Was* the loss of Cumberland Gap a trivial matter, and did it in fact not cut in two our great strategic front? Up yonder at Corinth, our "new and far better" base, was Sidney

Johnston an "imbecile," a "coward," a "traitor"? or was he not rather an unparagoned strategist who, having at last "lured the presumptuous foe" into his toils, was now, with Beauregard, notwithstanding Beauregard's protracted illness, about to make the "one fell swoop" of our complete deliverance? And after the swoop and its joy and its glory, when Johnnie should come marching home, whose Johnnies, and how many, would never return? As to your past-and-gone bazaar, law, honey——!

So, as to that item, in all the wild-eyed city shaking with its ague of anxieties only Anna was troubled when day after day no detective came back with the old mud-caked dagger and now both were away on some quite alien matter, no one could say where. She alone was troubled, for she alone knew it was the bazaar's proceeds which had disappeared. Of what avail to tell even Miranda, Connie, or Flora if they must not tell others? It would only bind three more souls on the rack. "Vanished with the dagger!" That would be all they could gasp, first amazed, then scandalized, at a scheme of safe-keeping so fantastically reckless; reckless and fantastical as her so-called marriage. Yes, they would be as scandalized as they would have been charmed had the scheme prospered. And then they would blame not her but Hilary. Blame him in idle fear of a calamity that was not going to befall!

She might have told that sternest, kindest, wisest of friends, Doctor Sevier. As the family's trustee he might yet have to be told. But on that night of fantastical recklessness he had been away, himself at Corinth to show them there how to have vastly better hospitals,

" Victory ! I Heard it as Pl'—"

and to prescribe for his old friend Beauregard. He
had got back but yesterday. Or she might have told
the gray detective, just to make him more careful, as
Hilary, by letter, suggested. In part she had told him,
through Flora; told him that to save that old curio she
would risk her life. Surely, knowing that, he would safe-
guard it, in whatever hands, and return it the moment
he could. Who ever heard of a detective not returning
a thing the moment he could? Not Flora, *not* yet
Madame, they said. To be sure, thought Anna, those
professional masters of delay, the photographers, might
be more jewel-wise than trustworthy, but what photog-
rapher could ever be so insane as to rob a detective?
So, rather ashamed of one small solicitude in this day
of great ones, she urged her committees for final re-
ports—which never came—and felt very wifely in
writing her hero for his consent to things, and to assure
him that at the worst her own part of the family estate
would make everything good, the only harrowing question being how to keep Miranda and Connie from
sharing the loss.

On the first Sunday evening in April Doctor Sevier
took tea with the Callenders, self-invited, alone and
firmly oblivious of his own tardy wedding-gift to Anna
as it gleamed at him on the board. To any of a hundred hostesses he would have been a joy, to share with
as many friends as he would consent to meet; for in the
last week he had eaten " hog and hominy," and sipped
cornmeal coffee, in lofty colloquy with Sidney Johnston
and his "big generals"; had talked confidentially with
Polk, so lately his own bishop; had ridden through the
miry streets of Corinth with all the New Orleans com-

223

manders of division or brigade—Gibson, Trudeau, Ruggles, Brodnax; out on the parapets, between the guns, had chatted with Hilary and his loved lieutenants; down among the tents and mess-fires had given his pale hand, with Spartan injunctions and all the home news, to George Gregory, Ned Ferry, Dick Smith, and others of Harper's cavalry, and—circled round by Charlie Valcour, Sam Gibbs, Maxime, and scores of their comrades in Kincaid's Battery—had seen once more their silken flag, so faded! and touched its sacred stains and tatters. Now at the tea table something led him to remark that here at home the stubborn illness of this battery sister for whom Anna was acting as treasurer had compelled him to send her away.

Timely topic: How to go into the country, and whither. The Callenders were as eager for all the facts and counsel he could give on it as if they were the "big generals" and his facts and counsel were as to the creeks, swamps, ridges, tangled ravines, few small clearings, and many roads and by-roads in the vast, thinly settled, small-farmed, rain-drenched forests between Corinth and the clay bluffs of the Tennessee. For now the Callenders also were to leave the city, as soon as they could be ready.

"Don't wait till then," crisply said the Doctor.

"We must wait till Nan winds up the bazaar."

He thought not. In what bank had she its money?

When she said not in any he frowned. Whereupon she smilingly stammered that she was told the banks themselves were sending their treasure into the country, and that even ten days earlier, when some one wanted to turn a fund into its safest portable form, three banks

had declined to give foreign exchange for it at any price.

"Hmm!" he mused. "Was that your, eh,——?"

"My husband, yes," said Anna, so quietly that the sister and stepmother exulted in her. As quietly her eyes held the doctor's, and his hers, while the colour mounted to her brow. He spoke:

"Still he got it into some good shape for you, the fund, did he not?" Then suddenly he clapped a hand to a breast pocket and stared: "He gave me a letter for you. Did I——? Ah, yes, I have your written thanks. Anna, I thoroughly approve what you and he have done."

Constance and Miranda were overjoyed. He turned to them: "I told Hilary so up in camp. I told Steve. Yes, Anna, you were wise. You are wise. I've no doubt you're doing wisely about that fund."

It was hard for the wise one not to look guilty.

"Have you told anybody," he continued, "in what form you have it, or where?"

"No!" put in the aggrieved Constance, "not even her blood kin!"

"Wise again. Best for all of you. Now just hang to the lucre. It comes too late to be of use here; this brave town will have to stand or fall without it. But it's still good for Mobile, and Mobile saved may be New Orleans recovered.

On a hint from the other women, and urged by their visitor, Anna brought the letter and read him several closely written pages on the strategic meaning of things. The zest with which he discussed the lines made her newly proud of their source.

"They're so like his very word o' mouth," said he,

"they bring him right back here among us. Yes, and the whole theatre of action with him. They draw it about us so closely and relate it all to us so vitally that it——"

"Seems," broke in the delighted Constance, "as if we saw it all from the top of this house!"

The Doctor's jaw set. Who likes phrases stuffed into his mouth? Yet presently he allowed himself to resume. It confirmed, he said, Beauregard's word in his call for volunteers, that there, before Corinth, was the place to defend Louisiana. Soon he had regained his hueless ardor, and laid out the whole matter on the table for the inspiration of his three confiding auditors. Here at Chattanooga, so impregnably ours, issued Tennessee river and the Memphis and Charleston railroad from the mountain gateway between our eastern and western seats of war. Here they swept down into Alabama, passed from the state's north-east to its north-west corner and parted company. Here the railway continued westward, here it crossed the Mobile and Ohio railroad at Corinth, here the Mississippi Central at Grand Junction, and pressed on to Memphis, our back-gate key of the Mississippi.

"In war," said the Doctor, "rivers and railro'——"

"Are the veins and arteries of—oh, pardon!" The crime was Anna's this time.

"Are the lines fought for," resumed the speaker, "and wherever two or three of them join or cross you may look for a battle." His long finger dropped again to the table. Back here in Alabama the Tennessee turned north to seek the Ohio, and here, just over the Mississippi state line, in Tennessee, some twenty miles north of Corinth, it became navigable for the Ohio's steamboats—gunboats—transports—at a place called in the letter "Pittsburg Landing."

Yes, now, between Hilary's pages and the Doctor's logic, with Hilary almost as actually present as the physician, the ladies saw why this great Memphis-Chattanooga fighting line was, not alone pictorially, but practically, right at hand! barely beyond sight and hearing or the feel of its tremor; a veritable back garden wall to them and their beloved city; as close as forts Jackson and St. Philip, her front gate. Yes, and—Anna ventured to point out and the Doctor grudgingly admitted—if the brave gray hosts along that back wall should ever—could ever—be borne back so far southward, westward, the last line would have to run from one to another of the Crescent City's back doorsteps and doors; from Vicksburg, that is, eastward through Jackson, Mississippi's capital, cross the state's two north-and-south railways, and swing down through Alabama to Mobile on the Gulf. This, she silently perceived, was why the letter and the Doctor quite agreed that Connie, Miranda, and she ought to find their haven somewhere within the dim region between New Orleans and those three small satellite cities; not near any two railways, yet close enough to a single one for them to get news, public or personal, in time to act on it.

At leave-taking came the guest's general summing up of fears and faiths. All his hope for New Orleans, he said, was in the forts down at the Passes. Should they fall the city could not stand. But amid their illimitable sea marshes and their impenetrable swamp forests, chin-deep in the floods of broken levees, he truly believed, they would hold out. Let them do so only till the first hot breath of real Delta summer should bring typhoid, breakbone, yellow, and swamp fevers, the last by all odds the worst, and Butler's unacclimated troops would have to reëmbark for home pell-mell or die on Ship Island like poisoned fish. So much for the front gate. For the back gate, Corinth, which just now seemed—the speaker harkened.

"Seemed," he resumed, "so much more like the front—listen!" There came a far, childish call.

"An extra," laughed Constance. "Steve says we issue one every time he brushes his uniform."

"But, Con," argued Anna, "an extra on Sunday evening, brought away down here——" The call piped nearer.

"Victory!" echoed Constance. "I heard it as pl'——"

"Beauregard! Tennessee!" exclaimed both sisters. They flew to the veranda, the other two following. Down in the gate could be seen the old coachman, already waiting to buy the paper. Constance called to him their warm approval. "I thought," murmured Miranda, "that Beauregard was in Miss'——"

Anna touched her, and the cry came again: "Great victory——!" Yes, yes, but by whom, and where? Johnston? Corinth? "Great victory at——!" Where? Where, did he say? The word came again, and now again, but still it was tauntingly vague. Anna's ear seemed best, yet even she could say only, "I never heard of such a place—out of the bible. It sounds like—Shiloh."

Shiloh it was. At a table lamp indoors the Doctor

bent over the fresh print. "It's true," he affirmed.
"It's Beauregard's own despatch. 'A complete victory,' he says. 'Driving the enemy'——" The reader
ceased and stared at the page. "Why, good God!"
Slowly he lifted his eyes upon those three sweet women
until theirs ran full. And then he stared once more
into the page: "Oh, good God! Albert Sidney Johnston is dead."

XLIII

THAT SABBATH AT SHILOH

"WHOLE theatre of action."

The figure had sounded apt to Anna on that Sunday
evening when the Doctor employed it; apt enough—
until the outburst of that great and dreadful news
whose inseparable implications and forebodings robbed
her of all sleep that night and made her the first one
astir at daybreak. But thenceforward, and now for
half a week or more, the aptness seemed quite to have
passed. Strange was the theatre whose play was all and
only a frightful reality; whose swarming, thundering,
smoking stage had its audience, its New Orleans audience, wholly behind it, and whose curtain of distance,
however thin, mocked every bodily sense and compelled
all to be seen and heard by the soul's eye and ear, with
all the joy and woe of its actuality and all its suspense,
terror, triumph, heartbreak, and despair.

Yet here was that theatre, and the Doctor's metaphor
was still good enough for the unexacting taste of the
two Valcour ladies, to whom Anna had quoted it.
And here, sprinkled through the vast audience of that

theatre, with as keen a greed for its play as any, were all
the various non-combatants with whom we are here
concerned, though not easily to be singled out, such
mere units were they of the impassioned multitude
every mere unit of which, to loved and loving ones,
counted for more than we can tell.

However, our favourites might be glimpsed now and
then. On a certain mid-day of that awful half-week
the Callenders, driving, took up Victorine at her gate
and Flora at her door and sped up-town to the newspaper offices in Camp street to rein in against a countless surge of old men in fine dress, their precious dignity thrown to the dogs, each now but one of the common herd, and each against all, shouldering, sweating,
and brandishing wide hands to be the first purchaser
and reader of the list, the long, ever-lengthening list of
the killed and wounded. Much had been learned of
the great two-days' battle, and many an infantry sister,
and many a battery sister besides Anna, was second-
sighted enough to see, night and day, night and day,
the muddy labyrinth of roads and by-roads that braided
and traversed the wide, unbroken reaches of dense
timber—with their deep ravines, their long ridges, and
their creek-bottom marshes and sloughs—in the day's
journey from Corinth to the bluffs of the Tennessee.
They saw them, not empty, nor fearlessly crossed by the
quail, the wild turkey, the fox, or the unhunted deer,
nor travelled alone by the homespun "citizen" or by
scouts or foragers, but slowly overflowed by a great
gray, silent, tangled, armed host—cavalry, infantry,
ordnance trains, batteries, battery wagons and ambu-
ances: Saw Hilary Kincaid and all his heroes and

That Sabbath at Shiloh

their guns, and all the "big generals" and their smart escorts and busy staffs: Saw the various columns impeding each other, taking wrong ways and losing priceless hours while thousands of inexperienced boys, footsore, drenched and shivering yet keen for the fight, ate their five-days' food in one, or threw it away to lighten the march, and toiled on in hunger, mud, cold and rain, without the note of a horn or drum or the distant eye of one blue scout to tell of their oncoming.

They saw, did Anna and those sisters (and many and many a wife and mother from Callender House to Carrollton), the vast, stealthy, fireless bivouac at fall of night, in ear-shot of the enemy's tattoo, unsheltered from the midnight storm save by raked-up leaves: Saw, just in the bivouac's tortuous front, softly reddening the low wet sky, that huge, rude semicircle of camps in the dark ridged and gullied forests about Shiloh's log meeting-house, where the victorious Grant's ten-thousands—from Ohio, Kentucky, Indiana, Illinois, Missouri, Iowa, Wisconsin, Michigan, as new to arms as their foe, yet a band of lions in lair—lay dry-tented, full fed and fast asleep, safely flanked by swollen streams, their gunboats behind them and Buell coming, but without one mounted outpost, a scratch of entrenchment or a whisper of warning.

Amid the eager carriage talk, in which Anna kept her part, her mind's eye still saw the farther scene as it changed again and the gray dawn and gray host furtively rose together and together silently spread through the deep woods. She watched the day increase and noon soar up and sink away while the legions of Hardee, Bragg, Polk and Breckinridge slowly writhed out of their perplexed folds and set themselves, still undetected, in their three successive lines of battle. She beheld the sun set calm and clear, the two hosts lie down once more, one in its tents, the other on its arms, the leafy night hang over them resplendent with stars, its watches near by, the Southern lines reawaken in recovered strength, spring up and press forward exultantly to the awful issue, and the Sabbath dawn brighten into a faultless day with the boom of the opening gun.

As the ladies drew up behind the throng and across the throat of Commercial Alley the dire List began to flutter from the Picayune office in greedy palms and over and among dishevelled heads like a feeding swarm of white pigeons. News there was as well as names, but every eye devoured the names first and then—unless some name struck lightning in the heart, as Anna saw it do every here and there and for that poor old man over yonder—after the names the news.

"Nan, we needn't stay if you——"

"Oh, Miranda, isn't all this ours?"

The bulletin boards were already telling in outline, ahead of the list, thrilling things about the Orleans Guards, the whirlwind onset of whose maiden bayonets had captured double its share of the first camp taken from the amazed, unbreakfasted enemy, and who again and again, hour by hour, by the half-mile and mile, had splendidly helped to drive him—while he hammered back with a deadly stubbornness all but a match for their fury. Through forests, across clearings, over streams and bogs and into and out of ravines and thickets they had swept, seizing transiently a whole field battery, permanently hundreds of prisoners, and covering the

strife's broad wake with even more appalling numbers
of their own dead and wounded than of the foe's:
wailing wounded, ghastly, grimy dead, who but yesterday were brothers, cousins and playmates of these very
men snatching and searching the list. They told, those
boards, of the Washington Artillery (fifth company,
never before under fire) being thanked on the field by
one of the "big generals," their chests and wheels shot
half to splinters but no gun lost. They told of all
those Louisiana commands whose indomitable lines
charged and melted, charged and withered, over and
over the torn and bloody ground in that long, horrible
struggle that finally smoked out the "Hornets' Nest."
They told of the Crescent Regiment, known and loved
on all these sidewalks and away up to and beyond their
Bishop-General Polk's Trinity Church, whose desperate
gallantry had saved that same Washington Artillery
three of its pieces, and to whose thinned and bleeding
ranks swarms of the huddled Western farm boys, as
shattered and gory as their captors and as glorious, had
at last laid down their arms. And they told of Kincaid's
Battery, Captain Kincaid commanding; how, having
early lost in the dense oak woods and hickory brush the
brigade—Brodnax's—whose way they had shelled open
for a victorious charge, they had followed their galloping
leader, the boys running beside the wheels, from position to position, from ridge to ridge, in rampant obedi-
ence of an order to "go in wherever they heard the hottest firing"; how for a time they had fought hub to hub
beside the Washington Artillery; how two of their guns,
detached for a special hazard and sweeping into fresh
action on a flank of the "Hornets' Nest," had lost

every horse at a single volley of the ambushed foe, yet
had instantly replied with slaughterous vengeance; and
how, for an hour thereafter, so wrapped in their own
smoke that they could be pointed only by the wheel-ruts
of their recoil, they had been worked by their depleted
gunners on hands and knees with Kincaid and Villeneuve themselves at the trails and with fuses cut to
one second. So, in scant outline said the boards, or
more in detail read one man aloud to another as they
hurried by the carriage.

"But," said Anna, while Flora enjoyed her pallor,
"all that is about the first day's fight!"

"No," cried Constance, "it's the second day's, that
Beauregard calls 'a great and glorious victory!'"

"Yes," interposed Flora, "but writing from behind
his fortification' at Corinth, yes!"

XLIV

"THEY WERE ALL FOUR TOGETHER"

BOTH Constance and Victorine flashed to retort, but
saw the smiling critic as pale as Anna and recalled the
moment's truer business, the list still darting innumer-
ably around them always out of reach. The carriage
had to push into the very surge, and Victorine to stand
up and call down to this man and that, a fourth and
fifth, before one could be made to hear and asked to
buy for the helpless ladies. Yet in this gentlewomen's
war every gentlewoman's wish was a military command,
and when at length one man did hear, to hear was to
vanish in the turmoil on their errand. Now he was

back again, with the list, three copies! Oh, thank you, thank you and thank you!

Away trotted the handsome span while five pairs of beautiful eyes searched the three printed sheets, that bore —oh, marvellous fortune!—not one of the four names writ largest in those five hearts. Let joy be—ah, let joy be very meek while to so many there is unutterable loss. Yet let it meekly abound for the great loved cause so splendidly advanced. Miranda pointed Anna to a bit of editorial:

"Monday was a more glorious day than Sunday. We can scarcely forbear to speculate upon the great results that are to flow from this decisive victory. An instant pursuit of the flying enemy should——"

Why did the carriage halt at a Gravier Street crossing obliquely opposite the upper front corner of the St. Charles Hotel? Why did all the hotel's gold-braided guests and loungers so quietly press out against its upper balustrades? Why, under its arches, and between balcony posts along the curbstones clear down to Canal Street, was the pathetically idle crowd lining up so silently? From that point why, now, did the faint breeze begin to waft a low roar of drums of such grave unmartial sort? And why, gradually up the sidewalks' edges in the hot sun, did every one so solemnly uncover? Small Victorine stood up to see.

At first she made out only that most commonplace spectacle, home guards. They came marching in platoons, a mere company or two. In the red and blue of their dress was all the smartness yet of last year, but in their tread was none of it and even the bristle of their steel had vanished. Behind majestic brasses and muf-

fled drums grieving out the funeral march, they stepped
with slow precision and with arms reversed. But now
in abrupt contrast there appeared, moving as slowly
and precisely after them, widely apart on either side of
the stony way, two single attenuated files of but four
bronzed and shabby gray-jackets each, with four others
in one thin, open rank from file to file in their rear, and
in the midst a hearse and its palled burden. Rise,
Anna, Constance, Miranda—all. Ah, Albert Sidney
Johnston! Weep, daughters of a lion-hearted cause.
The eyes of its sons are wet. Yet in your gentle bosoms
keep great joy for whoever of your very own and
nearest the awful carnage has spared; but hither comes,
here passes slowly, and yonder fades at length from
view, to lie a day in state and so move on to burial, a
larger hope of final triumph than ever again you may
fix on one mortal man.

Hats on again, softly. Drift apart, aimless crowd.
Cross the two streets at once, diagonally, you, young man
from the St. Charles Hotel with purpose in your rapid
step, pencil unconsciously in hand and trouble on your
brow. Regather your reins, old coachman—nay, one
moment! The heavy-hearted youth passed so close
under the horses' front that only after he had gained
the banquette abreast the carriage did he notice its occupants and Anna's eager bow. It was the one-armed
Kincaid's Battery boy reporter. With a sudden pitying
gloom he returned the greeting, faltered as if to speak,
caught a breath and then hurried on and away. What
did that mean; more news; news bad for these five in
particular? Silently in each of them, without a glance
from one to another, the question asked itself.

"They Were all Four Together"

"The True Delta," remarked Anna to Miranda, "is right down here on the next square," and of his own motion the driver turned that way.

"Bitwin Common Strit and Can-al," added Victorine, needless words being just then the most needed.

Midway in front of the hotel Anna softly laid a hand on Flora, who respondingly murmured. For the reporter was back, moving their way along the sidewalk almost at a run. Now Constance was aware of him.

"When we cross Common Street," she observed to Miranda, "he'll want to stop us."

In fact, as soon as their intent to cross was plain, he sped out beside them and stood, his empty sleeve pinned up, his full one raised and grief evident in his courteous smile. Some fifty yards ahead, by the True Delta office, men were huddling around a fresh bulletin. Baring his brow to the sun, the young man came close to the wheels.

"Wouldn't you-all as soon—?" he began, but Constance interrupted:

"The news is as good as ever, isn't it?"

"Yes, but wouldn't you-all as soon drive round by Carondelet Street?" A gesture with his hat showed a piece of manifold writing in his fingers.

He looked to Miranda, but she faltered. Flora, in her own way, felt all the moment's rack and stress, but some natures are built for floods and rise on them like a boat. So thought she of herself and had parted her lips to speak for all, when, to her vexed surprise, Anna lifted a hand and in a clear, firm tone inquired, "Is there any bad news for us five?" The youth's tongue failed; he nodded.

"Brodnax's brigade?" she asked. "Our battery?"

"Yes, Monday, just at the last," he murmured.

"Not *taken?*"

"Not a gun!" replied the boy, with a flash. Anna reflected it, but her tone did not change:

"There are four men, you know, whom we five——"

"Yes."

"Which of them is the bad news about?"

"All four," murmured the youth. His eyes swam. His hat went under the stump of his lost arm and he proffered the bit of writing. Idlers were staring. "Take that with you," he said. "They were all four together and they're only——"

The carriage was turning, but the fair cluster bent keenly toward him. "Only what?" they cried.

"Missing."

XLV

STEVE—MAXIME—CHARLIE—

THERE was no real choice. Nothing seemed quite rational but the heaviest task of all—to wait, and to wait right here at home.

To this queenly city must come first and fullest all news of her own sons, and here the "five" would not themselves be "missing" should better tidings—or worse—come seeking them over the wires.

"At the front?" replied Doctor Sevier to Anna, "why, at the front you'll be kept in the rear, lost in a storm of false rumors."

General Brodnax, in a letter rife with fatherly romantic tenderness and with splendid praise of Hilary

as foremost in the glorious feat which had saved old
"Roaring Betsy" but lost (or mislaid) him and his
three comrades, also bade her wait. Everything, he
assured her, that human sympathy or the art of war
—or Beauregard's special orders—could effect was
being done to find the priceless heroes. In the retreat
of a great host—ah, me! retreat was his very word
and the host was Dixie's—retreating after its first
battle, and that an awful one, in deluging rains over
frightful roads and brimming streams, unsheltered,
ill fed, with sick and wounded men and reeling vehicles
hourly breaking down, a hovering foe to be fended off,
and every dwelling in the land a hospitable refuge,
even captains of artillery or staff might be most honor-
ably and alarmingly missing yet reappear safe and
sound. So, for a week and more it was sit and wait,
pace the floor and wait, wake in the night and wait;
so for Flora as well as for Anna (with a difference),
both of them anxious for Charlie—and Steve—and
Maxime, but in anguish for another.

Then tidings, sure enough! glad tidings! Mandeville and Maxime safe in camp again and back to duty,
whole, hale and in the saddle. Their letters came by
the wasted yellow hands of two or three of the home-
coming wounded, scores of whom were arriving by
every south-bound train. From the aide-de-camp
and the color-bearer came the first whole story of how
Kincaid, with his picked volunteers, barely a gun de-
tachment, and with Mandeville, who had brought the
General's consent, had stolen noiselessly over the
water-soaked leaves of a thickety oak wood in the
earliest glimmer of a rainy dawn and drawn off the

abandoned gun by hand to its waiting horses; also how, when threatened by a hostile patrol, Hilary, Mandeville, Maxime and Charlie had hurried back on foot into the wood and hotly checked the pursuit long enough for their fellows to mount the team, lay a shoulder to every miry wheel and flounder away with the prize. But beyond that keen moment when the four, after their one volley from ambush, had sprung this way and that shouting absurd orders to make-believe men, cheering and firing from behind trees, and (cut off from their horses) had made for a gully and swamp, the two returned ones could tell nothing of the two unreturned except that neither of them, dead or alive, was anywhere on the ground of the fight or flight as they knew it. For days, inside the enemy's advancing lines, they had prowled in ravines and lain in blackberry patches and sassafras fence-rows, fed and helped on of nights by the beggared yet still warm-hearted farm people and getting through at last, but with never a trace of Kincaid or Charlie, though after their own perilous search they had inquired, inquired, inquired.

So, wait, said every one and every dumb condition, even the miseries of the great gray army, of which Anna had mind pictures again, as it toiled through mire and lightning, rain, sleet and hail, and as its thousands of sick and shattered lay in Corinth dying fifty a day. And Flora and Anna waited, though with minds placid only to each other and the outer world.

"Yes," moaned Anna to Constance, when found at dead of night staring Corinthward from a chamber window. "Yes, friends advise! All our friends advise! What daring thing did any one ever do who waited for friends to advise it? Does your Steve wait for friends to advise? . . . Patience? Ah, lend me yours! You don't need it now. . . . Fortitude? Oh, I never had any! . . . What? command the courage to do nothing when nothing is the only hard thing to do? Who, I? Connie! I don't even want it. I'm a craven; I want the easy thing! I want to go nurse the box-carloads and mule-wagonloads of wounded at Corinth, at Okolona and strewed all the way down to Mobile— that's full of them. Hilary may be somewhere among them—unidentified! They say he wore no badge of rank that morning, you know, and carried the carbine of a wounded cavalryman to whom he had given his coat. Oh, he's mine, Con, and I'm his. We're not engaged, we're *married*, and I *must* go. It's only a step—except in miles—and I'm going! I'm going for your sake and Miranda's. You know you're staying on my account, not for me to settle this bazaar business but to wait for news that's never coming till I go and bring it!"

This tiny, puny, paltry business of the bazaar— the whereabouts of the dagger and its wealth, or of the detectives, gone for good into military secret service at the front—she drearily smiled away the whole trivial riddle as she lay of nights contriving new searches for that inestimable, living treasure, whose perpetual "missing," right yonder "almost in sight from the housetop," was a dagger in her heart.

And the Valcours? Yes, they, too, had their frantic impulses to rise and fly. For Madame, though her lean bosom bled for the lost boy, the fiercest pain of

waiting was that its iron coercion lay in their penury.
For Flora its sharpest pangs were in her own rage;
a rage not of the earlier, cold sort against Anna and
whoever belonged to Anna—that transport had always been more than half a joy—but a new, hot rage
against herself and the finical cheapness of her scheming,
a rage that stabbed her fair complacency with the
revelation that she had a heart, and a heart that could
ache after another. The knife of that rage turned
in her breast every time she cried to the grandam,
"We must go!" and that rapacious torment simpered,
"No funds," adding sidewise hints toward Anna's
jewels, still diligently manœuvred for, but still somewhere up-stairs in Callender House, sure to go with
Anna should Anna go while the manœuvrers were
away.

A long lane to any one, was such waiting, lighted,
for Anna, only by a faint reflection of that luster of
big generals' strategy and that invincibility of the
Southern heart which, to all New Orleans and even to
nations beyond seas, clad Dixie's every gain in light
and hid her gravest disasters in beguiling shadow.
But suddenly one day the long lane turned. The
secret had just leaked out that the forts down the river
were furiously engaged with the enemy's mortar-boats
a few miles below them and that in the past forty-
eight hours one huge bomb every minute, three thous-
and in all, had dropped into those forts or burst over
them, yet the forts were "proving themselves impregnable." The lane turned and there stood Charlie.

There he stood, in the stairway door of the front
room overlooking Jackson Square. The grandmother

and sister had been keenly debating the news and what to do about it, the elder bird fierce to stay, the younger bent on flight, and had just separated to different windows, when they heard, turned and beheld him there, a stranger in tattered gray and railway dirt, yet their own coxcomb boy from his curls to his ill-shod feet. Flora had hardly caught her breath or believed her eyes before the grandmother was on his neck patting and petting his cheeks and head and plying questions in three languages: When, where, how, why, how, where and when?

Dimly he reflected their fond demonstrations. No gladness was in his face. His speech, as hurried as theirs, answered no queries. He asked loftily for air, soap, water and the privacy of his own room, and when they had followed him there and seen him scour face, arms, neck, and head, rub dry and resume his jacket and belt, he had grown only more careworn and had not yet let his sister's eyes rest on his.

He had but a few hours to spend in the city, he said; had brought despatches and must carry others back by the next train. His story, he insisted, was too long to tell before he had delivered certain battery letters; one to Victorine, two to Constance Mandeville, and so on. Here was one to Flora, from Captain Irby; perhaps the story was in it. At any rate, its bearer must rush along now. He toppled his "grannie" into a rocking-chair and started away. He "would be back as soon as ever he——"

But Flora filled the doorway. He had to harden his glance to hers at last. In her breast were acutest emotions widely at war, yet in her eyes he saw only an unfeeling light, and it was the old woman behind him who alone noted how painfully the girl's fingers were pinched upon Irby's unopened letter. The boy's stare betrayed no less anger than suffering and as Flora spoke he flushed.

"Charlie," she melodiously began, but his outcry silenced her:

"Now, by the eternal great God Almighty, Flora Valcour, if you dare to ask me that—" He turned to the grandmother, dropped to his knees, buried his face in her lap and sobbed.

With genuine tenderness she stroked his locks. Yet while she did so she lifted to the sister a face lighted up with a mirth of deliverance. To nod, toss, and nod again, was poor show for her glee; she smirked and writhed to the disdaining girl like a child at a mirror, and, though sitting thus confined, gave all the effects of jigging over the floor. Hilary out of the way! Kincaid eliminated, and the whole question free of him, this inheritance question so small and mean to all but her and Irby, but to him and her so large, so paramount! Silently, but plainly to the girl, her mouth widely motioned, "Il est mort! grâce"—one hand stopped stroking long enough to make merrily the sign of cross—"grâce au ciel, il est mort!"

No moment of equal bitterness had Flora Valcour ever known. To tell half her distresses would lose us in their tangle, midmost in which was a choking fury against the man whom unwillingly she loved, for escaping her, even by a glorious death. One thought alone—that Anna, as truly as if stricken blind, would sit in darkness the rest of her days—lightened her torture, and with that thought she smiled a stony loathing on the mincing grandam and the boy's unlifted head. Suddenly, purpose gleamed from her. She could not break forth herself, but to escape suffocation she must and would procure an outburst somewhere. Measuredly, but with every nerve and tendon overstrung. she began to pace the room.

"Don't cry, Charlie," she smoothly said in a voice as cold as the crawl of a snake. The brother knew the tone, had known it from childhood, and the girl, glancing back on him, was pleased to see him stiffen. A few steps on she added pensively, "For a soldier to cry—and befo' ladies—a ladies' man—of that batt'rie —tha's hardly fair—to the ladies, eh, grandmama?"

But the boy only pressed his forehead harder down and clutched the aged knees under it till their owner put on, to the scintillant beauty, a look of alarm and warning. The girl, musingly retracing her calculated steps to where the kneeler seemed to clinch himself to his posture, halted, stroked with her slippered toe a sole of his rude shoes and spoke once more: "Do they oft-ten boohoo like that, grandma, those artillerie?"

The boy whirled up with the old woman clinging. A stream of oaths and curses appallingly original poured from him, not as through the lips alone but from his very eyes and nostrils. That the girl was first of all a fool and damned was but a trivial part of the cry—of the explosion of his whole year's mistaken or half-mistaken inferences and smothered indignation. With equal flatness and blindness he accused her of rejoicing in the death of Kincaid: the noblest captain (he ramped on) that ever led a battery;

kindest friend that ever ruled a camp; gayest, hottest, daringest fighter of Shiloh's field; fiercest for man's purity that ever loved the touch of women's fingers; sternest that ever wept on the field of death with the dying in his arms; and the scornfullest of promotion that ever was cheated of it at headquarters.

All these extravagances he cursed out, too witless to see that this same hero of his was the one human being, himself barely excepted, for whose life his sister cared. He charged her of never having forgiven Hilary for making Anna godmother of their flag, and of being in some dark league against him—"hell only knew what"—along with that snail of a cousin whom everybody but Kincaid himself and the silly old uncle knew to be the fallen man's most venomous foe. Throughout the storm the grandmother's fingers pattered soothing caresses, while Flora stood as unruffled by his true surmises as by any, a look of cold interest in her narrowed eyes, and her whole bodily and spiritual frame drinking relief from his transport. Now, while he still raged, she tenderly smiled on their trembling ancestress.

"Really, *you* know grandmama, sometimes me also I feel like that, when to smazh the furniture 't would be a delightful—or to wring somebody the neck, yes. But for us, and to-day, even to get a li'l' mad, how is that a possibl'?" She turned again, archly, to the brother, but flashed in alarm and sprang toward him.

His arm stiffly held her off. With failing eyes bent on the whimpering grandmother he sighed a disheartened oath and threshed into a chair gasping—

"My wound—opened again."

The School of Suspense

XLVI

THE SCHOOL OF SUSPENSE

THUS it fell to Flora to be letter-bearer and news-bearer in her brother's stead. Yet he had first to be cared for by her and the grandmother in a day long before "first aid" had become common knowledge. The surgeon they had hailed in had taken liberal time to show them how, night and morning, to unbandage, cleanse and rebind, and to tell them (smiling into the lad's mutinous eyes) that the only other imperative need was to keep him flat on his back for ten days. Those same weeks of downpour which had given the Shiloh campaign two-thirds of its horrors had so overfed the monstrous Mississippi that it was running four miles an hour, overlapping its levees and heaving up through the wharves all along the city's front, until down about the Convent and Barracks and Camp Callender there were streets as miry as Corinth. And because each and all of these hindrances were welcome to Flora as giving leisure to read and reread Irby's long letter about his cousin and uncle, and to plan what to say and do in order to reap all the fell moment's advantages, the shadows were long in the Callender's grove when she finally ascended their veranda steps.

She had come round by way of Victorine's small, tight-fenced garden of crape-myrtles, oleanders and pomegranates—where also the water was in the streets, backwater from the overflowed swamp-forests between city and lake—and had sent her to Charlie's bed-side. Pleasant it would be for us to turn back with the

247

damsel and see her, with heart as open as her arms, kiss the painted grandam, and at once proceed to make herself practically invaluable; or to observe her every now and then dazzle her adored patient with a tear-gem of joy or pity, or of gratitude that she lived in a time when heroic things could happen right at home and to the lowliest, even to her; sweet woes like this, that let down, for virtuous love, the barriers of hum-drum convention. But Flora draws us on, she and Anna. As she touched the bell-knob Constance sprang out to welcome her, though not to ask her in—till she could have a word with her alone, the young wife explained.

"I saw you coming," she said, drawing her out to the balustrade. "You didn't get Anna's note of last night—too bad! I've just found out—her maid forgot it! What do you reckon we've been doing all day long? Packing! We're going we don't know where! Vicksburg, Jackson, Meridian, Mobile, wherever Anna can best hunt Hilary from—and Charlie too, of course."

"Yes," said Flora, one way to the speaker and quite another way to herself.

"Yes, she wants to do it, and Doctor Sevier says it's the only thing for her. Ah, Flora, how well *you* can understand that!"

"Indeed, yes," sighed the listener, both ways again.

"We know how absolutely you believe the city's our best base, else we'd have asked you to go with us." The ever genuine Constance felt a mortifying specious-ness in her words and so piled them on. "*We* know the city is best—unless it should fall, and it won't— oh, it won't, God's not going to let so many prayers

The School of Suspense

go unanswered, Flora! But we've tossed reason aside and are going by instinct, the way I always feel safest in, dear. Ah, poor Anna! Oh, Flora, she's so sweet about it!"

"Yes? Ab-out what?"

"You, dear, and whoever is suffering the same——"

Flora softly winced and Constance blamed herself so to have pained another sister's love. "And she's so quiet," added the speaker, "but, oh, so pale—and so hard either to comfort or encourage, or even to discourage. There's nothing you can say that she isn't already heart-sick of saying herself, to herself, and I beg you, dear, in your longing to comfort her, please don't bring up a single maybe-this or maybe-that; any hope, I mean, founded on a mere doubt."

"Ah, but sometime' the doubt—it is the hope!"

"Yes, sometimes; but not to her, any more. Oh, Flora, if it's just as true of you, you won't be—begrudge my saying it of my sister—that no saint ever went to her matyrdom better prepared than she is, right now, for the very worst that can be told. There's only one thing to which she never can and never will resign herself, and that is doubt. She can't breathe its air, Flora. As she says herself, she isn't so built; she hasn't that gift."

The musing Flora nodded compassionately, but inwardly she said that, gift or no gift, Anna should serve her time in Doubting Castle, with her, Flora, for turnkey. Suddenly she put away her abstraction and with a summarizing gesture and chastened twinkle spoke out: "In short, you want to know for w'at am I come."

"Flora!"

"Ah, but, my dear, you are ri-ight. That is 'all correct,' as they say, and one thing I'm come for—'t is—" She handed out Mandeville's two letters.

The wife caught them to her bosom, sprang to her tiptoes, beamed on the packet a second time and read aloud, "Urbanity of Corporal Valcour!" She heaved an ecstatic breath to speak on, but failed. Anna and Miranda had joined them and Flora had risen from her seat on the balustrade, aware at once that the rôle she had counted on was not to be hers, the rôle of comforter to an undone rival.

Pale indeed was the rival, pale as rivalry could wish. Yet instantly Flora saw, with a fiery inward sting, how beautiful pallor may be. And more she saw: with the chagrin then growing so common on every armed front—the chagrin of finding one's foe entrenched—she saw how utterly despair had failed to crush a gentle soul. Under cover of affliction's night and storm Anna, this whole Anna Callender, had been reinforced, had fortified and was a new problem.

She greeted Flora with a welcoming beam, but before speaking she caught her sister's arm and glanced herself, at the superscription.

"Flora!" she softly cried, "oh, Flora Valcour! has your brother—your Charlie!—come home alive and well?—What; no?—No, he has not?"

The visitor was shaking her head: "No. Ah, no! home, yes, and al-ive; but——"

"Oh, Flora, Flora! alive and at home! home and alive!" While the words came their speaker slowly folded her arms about the bearer of tidings, and with

From the Burial Squad

a wholly unwonted strength pressed her again to the rail and drew bosom to bosom, still exclaiming, "Alive! alive! Oh, whatever his plight, be thankful, Flora, for so much! Alive enough to *come* home!"

XLVII

FROM THE BURIAL SQUAD

THE pinioned girl tried to throw back her head and bring their eyes together, but Anna, through some unconscious advantage, held it to her shoulder, her own face looking out over the garden.

"Ah, let me be glad for you, Flora, let me be glad for you! Oh, think of it! You *have* him! have him at home, to look upon, to touch, to call by name! and to be looked upon by *him* and touched and called by name! Oh, God in heaven! God in heaven!"

Miranda's fond protests were too timorous to check her, and Flora's ceased in the delight of hearing that last wail confess the thought of Hilary. Constance strove with tender energy for place and voice: "Nan, dearie, Nan! But listen to Flora, Nan. See, Nan, I haven't opened Steve's letter yet. Wounded and what, Flora, something worse? Ah, if worse you couldn't have left him."

"I know," sighed Anna, relaxing her arms to a caress and turning her gaze to Flora. "I see. Your brother, our dear Charlie, has come back to life, but wounded and alone. Alone. Hilary is still missing. Isn't that it? That's all, isn't it?"

Constance, in a sudden thought of what her letters

might tell, began to open one, though with her eyes at every alternate moment on Flora as eagerly as Miranda's or Anna's. Flora stood hiddenly revelling in that complexity of her own spirit which enabled her to pour upon her questioner a look, even a real sentiment, of ravishing pity, while nevertheless in the depths of her being she thrilled and burned and danced and sang with joy for the very misery she thus compassionated. By a designed motion she showed her grandmother's reticule on her arm. But only Anna saw it; Constance, with her gaze in the letter, was drawing Miranda aside while both bent their heads over a clause in it which had got blurred, and looked at each other aghast as they made it out to read, "'—from the burial squad.'" The grandmother's silken bag saved them from Anna's notice.

"Oh, Flora!" said Anna again, "is there really something worse?" Abruptly, she spread a hand under the bag and with her eyes still in the eyes of its possessor slid it gently from the yielding wrist. Dropping her fingers into it she brought forth a tobacco-pouch, of her own embroidering, and from it, while the reticule fell unheeded to the floor, drew two or three small things which she laid on it in her doubled hands and regarded with a smile. Vacantly the smile increased as she raised it to Flora, then waned while she looked once more on the relics, and grew again as she began to handle them. Her slow voice took the tone of a child alone at play.

"Why, that's *my* photograph," she said. "And this—this is his watch—watch and chain." She dangled them. A light frown came and went between her smiles.

From the Burial Squad

With soft eagerness Flora called Constance, and the sister and Miranda stood dumb.

"See, Connie," the words went on, "see, 'Randa, this is my own photograph, and this is his own watch and chain. I must go and put them away—with my old gems." Constance would have followed her as she moved but she waved a limp forbiddal, prattling on: "This doesn't mean he's dead, you know. Oh, not at all! It means just the contrary! Why, I saw him alive last night, in a dream, and I can't believe anything else, and I won't! No, no, not yet!" At that word she made a misstep and as she started sharply to recover it the things she carried fell breaking and jingling at her feet.

"Oh-h!" she sighed in childish surprise and feebly dropped to her knees. Flora, closest by, sprang crouching to the rescue, but recoiled as the kneeling girl leaned hoveringly over the mementos and with distended eyes and an arm thrust forward cried aloud, "No! No! No-o!"

At once, however, her voice was tender again. "Mustn't anybody touch them but me, ever any more," she said, regathering the stuff, regained her feet and moved on. Close after her wavering steps anxiously pressed the others, yet not close enough. At the open door, smiling back in rejection of their aid, she tripped, and before they could save her, tumbled headlong within. From up-stairs, from down-stairs came servants running, and by the front door entered a stranger, a private soldier in swamp boots and bespattered with the mire of the river road from his spurs to his ragged hat.

"No, bring her out," he said to a slave woman

who bore Anna in her arms, "out to the air!" But the burden slipped free and with a cleared mind stood facing him.

"Ladies," he exclaimed, his look wandering, his uncovered hair matted, "if a half-starved soldier can have a morsel of food just to take in his hands and ride on with—" and before he could finish servants had sprung to supply him.

"Are you from down the river?" asked Anna, quietly putting away her sister's pleading touch and Flora's offer of support.

"I am!" spouted the renegade, for renegade he was, "I'm from the very thick of the massacre! from day turned into night, night into day, and heaven and earth into—into——"

"Hell," placidly prompted Flora.

"Yes! nothing short of it! Our defenses become death-traps and slaughter-pens—oh, how foully, foully has Richmond betrayed her sister city!"

Flora felt a new tumult of joy. "That Yankee fleet—it has pazz' those fort'?" she cried.

"My dear young lady! By this time there ain't no forts for it to pass! When I left Fort St. Philip there wa'n't a spot over in Fort Jackson as wide as my blanket where a bumbshell hadn't buried itself and blown up, and every minute we were lookin' for the magazine to go! Those *awful* shells! they'd torn both levees, the forts were flooded, men who'd lost their grit were weeping like children——"

"Oh!" interrupted Constance, "why not leave the forts? We don't need them now; those old wooden ships can never withstand our terrible ironclads!"

"No! not under this roof—nor in sight of *these things*"

From the Burial Squad

"Well, they're mighty soon going to try it! Last night, right in the blaze of all our batteries, they cut the huge chain we had stretched across the river——"

"Ah, but when they see— oh, they'll never dare face even the *Manassas*—the 'little turtle,' ha-ha!— much less the great *Louisiana!*"

"Alas! madam, the *Louisiana* ain't ready for 'em. There she lies tied to the levee, with engines that can't turn a wheel, a mere floating battery, while our gunboats—" Eagerly the speaker broke off to receive upon one hand and arm the bounty of the larder and with a pomp of gratitude to extend his other hand to Anna; but she sadly shook her head and showed on her palms Hilary's shattered tokens:

"These poor things belong to one, sir, who, like you, is among the missing. But, oh, thank God! *he* is missing at the front, *in* the front."

The abashed craven turned his hand to Flora, but with a gentle promptness Anna stepped between: "No, Flora dear, see; he hasn't a red scratch on him. Oh, sir, go—eat! If hunger stifles courage, eat! But eat as you ride, and ride like mad back to duty and honor! No! not under this roof—nor in sight of *these things*—can any man be a ladies' man, who is missing *from* the front, at the rear."

He wheeled and vanished. Anna turned: "Connie, what do your letters say?"

The sister's eyes told enough. The inquirer gazed a moment, then murmured to herself, "I—don't— believe it—yet," grew very white, swayed, and sank with a long sigh into out-thrown arms.

XLVIII

FARRAGUT

The cathedral clock struck ten of the night. Yonder its dial shone, just across that quarter of Jackson Square nearest the Valcours' windows, getting no response this time except the watchman's three taps of his iron-shod club on corner curbstones.

An hour earlier its toll had been answered from near and far, up and down the long, low-roofed, curving and recurving city—"seven, eight, nine"—"eight, nine"—the law's warning to all slaves to be indoors or go to jail. Not Flora nor Anna nor Victorine nor Doctor Sevier nor Dick Smith's lone mother nor any one else among all those thousands of masters, mistresses and man- and maid-servants, or these thousands of home-guards at home under their mosquito-bars, with uniforms on bedside chairs and with muskets and cartridge-belts close by—not one of all these was aware, I say, that however else this awful war might pay its cost, it was the knell of slavery they heard, and which they, themselves, in effect, were sounding.

Lacking wilder excitement Madame sat by a lamp knitting a nubia. Victorine had flown home at sundown. Charlié lay sleeping as a soldier lad can. His sister had not yet returned from Callender House, but had been fully accounted for some time before by messenger. Now the knitter heard horses and wheels. Why should they come at a walk? It was like stealth. They halted under the balcony. She slipped out and peered down. Yes, there was Flora. Constance was with

her. Also two trim fellows whom she rightly guessed
to be Camp Callender lads, and a piece of luggage—
was it not?—which, as they lifted it down, revealed a
size and weight hard even for those siege-gunners to
handle with care. Unseen, silently, they came in and up
with it, led by Flora. (Camp Callender was now only
a small hither end of the "Chalmette Batteries," which
on both sides of the river mounted a whole score of big
black guns. No wonder the Callenders were leaving.)

Presently here were the merry burden-bearers behind their radiant guide, whispered ah's and oh's
and wary laughter abounding.

"'Such a getting up-stairs I never did see!'"

A thousand thanks to the boys as they set down their
load; their thanks back for seats declined; no time
even to stand; a moment, only, for new vows of secrecy.
"Oui!—Ah, non!—Assurément!" (They were Creoles.) "Yes, mum 't is the word! And such a so
quiet getting down-stair'!"—to Mrs. Mandeville again
—and trundling away!

When the church clock gently mentioned the half-
hour the newly gleeful grandam and hiddenly tortured
girl had been long enough together and alone for the
elder to have nothing more to ask as to this chest of
plate which the Callenders had fondly accepted Flora's
offer to keep for them while they should be away.
Not for weeks and weeks had the old lady felt such ease
of mind on the money—and bread—question. Now
the two set about to get the booty well hid before
Charlie should awake. This required the box to be
emptied, set in place and reladen, during which proc-
ess Flora spoke only when stung.

"Ah!" thinly piped she of the mosquito voice, "what a fine day tha's been, to-day!" but won no reply. Soon she cheerily whined again:

"All day nothing but good luck, and at the end— this!" (the treasure chest).

But Flora kept silence.

"So, now, said the aged one, "they will not make such a differenze, those old jewel'."

"I will get them yet," murmured the girl.

"You think? Me, I think no, you will never."

No response.

The tease pricked once more: "Ah! all that day I am thinking of that Irbee. I am glad for Irbee. He is 'the man that waits,' that Irbee!"

The silent one winced; fiercely a piece of the shining ware was lifted high, but it sank again. The painted elder cringed. There may have been genuine peril, but the one hot sport in her fag end of a life was to play with this beautiful fire. She held the girl's eye with a look of frightened admiration, murmuring, "You are a *merveilleuse!*"

"Possible?"

"Yes, to feel that way and same time to be ab'e to smile like that!"

"Ah? how is that I'm feeling?"

"You are filling that all this, and all those jewel' of Anna, and the life of me, and of that boy in yond', you would give them all, juz' to be ab'e to bil-ieve that foolishness of Anna—that he's yet al-live, that Kin——"

The piece of plate half rose again, but—in part because the fair threatener could not help enjoying

258

the subtlety of the case—the smile persisted as she rejoined, "Ah! when juz' for the fun, all I can get the chance, I'm making her to bil-ieve that way!"

"Yes," laughed the old woman, "but why? Only biccause that way you, you cannot bil-ieve."

The lithe maiden arose to resume their task, the heavy silver still in her hand. The next moment the kneeling grandam crouched and the glittering metal swept around just high enough to miss her head. A tinkle of mirth came from its wielder as she moved on with it, sighing, "Ah! ho! what a pity—that so seldom the aged commit suicide."

"Yes," came the soft retort, "but for yo' young grandmama tha'z not yet the time, she is still a so indispensib'."

"Very true, ma chère," sang Flora, "and in heaven you would be so uzeless."

Out in the hazy, dark, heavily becalmed night the clock tolled eleven. Eleven—one—three—and all the hours, halves and quarters between and beyond, it tolled; and Flora, near, and Anna, far, sometimes each by her own open window, heard and counted. A thin old moon was dimly rising down the river when each began to think she caught another and very different sound that seemed to arrive faint from a long journey out of the southeast, if really from anywhere, and to pulse in dim persistency as soft as breathing, but as constant. Likely enough it was only the rumble of a remote storm and might have seemed to come out of the north or west had their windows looked that way, for still the tempestuous rains were frequent and everywhere, and it was easy and

common for man to mistake God's thunderings for
his own.

Yet, whether those two wakeful maidens truly
heard or merely fancied, in fact just then some seventy
miles straight away under that gaunt old moon, there
was rising to heaven the most terrific uproar this
delta land had ever heard since man first moved upon
its shores and waters. Six to the minute bellowed
and soared Porter's awful bombs and arched and
howled and fell and scattered death and conflagration.
While they roared, three hundred and forty great guns
beside, on river and land, flashed and crashed, the
breezeless night by turns went groping-black and clear-
as-day red with smoke and flame of vomiting funnels,
of burning boats and fire-rafts, of belching cannon, of
screaming grape and canister and of exploding maga-
zines. And through the middle of it all, in single file—
their topmasts, yards, and cordage showing above the
murk as pale and dumb as skeletons at every flare of
the havoc, a white light twinkling at each masthead, a
red light at the peak and the stars and stripes there with
it—Farragut and his wooden ships came by the forts.

"Boys, our cake's all dough!" said a commander in
one of the forts.

When day returned and Anna and Flora slept, the
murmur they had heard may after all have been only
God's thunder and really not from the southeast; but
just down there under the landscape's flat rim both
forts, though with colors still gallantly flying, were smoking ruins, all Dixie's brave gunboats and rams lay along
the river's two shores, sunken or burned, and the whole
victorious Northern fleet, save one boat rammed and

gone to the bottom, was on its cautious, unpiloted way, snail-slow but fate-sure, up the tawny four-mile current and round the gentle green bends of the Mississippi with New Orleans for its goal and prey.

XLIX

A CITY IN TERROR

BEFORE the smart-stepping lamplighters were half done turning off the street lights, before the noisy market-houses all over the town, from Camp Callender to Carrollton, with their basket-bearing thousands of jesting and dickering customers, had quenched their gaslights and candles to dicker and jest by day, or the devotees of early mass had emerged from the churches, Rumor was on the run. With a sort of muffled speed and whisper she came and went, crossed her course and reaffirmed herself, returned to her starting-point and stole forth again, bearing ever the same horrid burden, brief, persistent, unexaggerated: The Foe! The Foe! In five great ships and twice as many lesser ones—counted at Quarantine Station just before the wires were cut—the Foe was hardly twenty leagues away, while barely that many guns of ours crouched between his eight times twenty and our hundred thousand women and children.

Yet, for a brief spell, so deep are the ruts of habit, the city kept to its daily routine, limp and unmeaning though much of it had come to be. The milkman, of course, held to his furious round in his comical two-wheeled cart, whirling up to alley gates, shouting and ringing his big hand-bell. In all his tracks followed the hooded bread-cart, with its light-weight loaves for worthless money and with only the staggering news for lagnappe. Families ate breakfast, one hour and another, wherever there was food. Day cabmen and draymen trotted off to their curbstones; women turned to the dish-pan, the dust-pan, the beds, the broom; porters, clerks and merchants—the war-mill's wasteful refuse and residuum, some as good as the gray army's best, some poor enough—went to their idle counters, desks and sidewalks; the children to the public schools, the beggar to the church doorstep, physicians to their sick, the barkeeper to his mirrors and mint, and the pot-fisher to his catfish lines in the swollen, sweeping, empty harbor.

But besides the momentum of habit there was the official pledge to the people—Mayor Monroe's and Commanding-General Lovell's—that if they would but keep up this tread-mill gait, the moment the city was really in danger the wires of the new fire-alarm should strike the tidings from all her steeples. So the school teachers read Scripture and prayers and the children sang the "Bonnie Blue Flag," while outside the omnibuses trundled, the one-mule street-cars tinkled and jogged and the bells hung mute.

Nevertheless a change was coming. Invisibly it worked in the general mind as that mind gradually took in the meanings of the case; but visibly it showed as, from some outpost down the river, General Lovell, (a sight to behold for the mud on him), came spurring at full speed by Callender House, up through the Creole Quarter and across wide Canal Street to the St. Charles.

A City in Terror

Now even more visibly it betrayed itself, where all through the heart of the town began aides, couriers and frowning adjutants to gallop from one significant point to another. Before long not a cab anywhere waited at its stand. Every one held an officer or two, if only an un-uniformed bank-officer or captain of police, and rattled up or down this street and that, taking corners at breakneck risks. That later the drays began to move was not so noticeable, for a dray was but a dray and they went off empty except for their drivers and sometimes a soldier with a musket and did not return. Moreover, as they went there began to be seen from the middle of almost any cross-street, in the sky out over the river front, here one, there another, yonder a third and fourth, upheaval of dense, unusual smoke, first on the hither side of the harbor, then on the far side, yet no fire-engines, hand or steam, rushed that way, nor any alarm sounded.

From the Valcours' balcony Madame, gasping for good air after she and Flora had dressed Charlie's wound, was startled to see one of those black columns soar aloft. But it was across the river, and she had barely turned within to mention it, when up the stair and in upon the three rushed Victorine, all tears, saying it was from the great dry-dock at Slaughter-House Point, which our own authorities had set afire.

The enfeebled Charlie half started from his rocking-chair laughing angrily. "Incredible!" he cried, but sat mute as the girl's swift tongue told the half-dozen other dreadful things she had just beheld on either side the water. The sister and grandmother sprang into the balcony and stood astounded. Out of the narrow streets beneath them—Chartres, Condé, St. Peter, St. Ann, Cathedral Alley—scores and scores of rapidly walking men and women and scampering boys and girls streamed round and through the old Square by every practicable way and out upon the levee.

"Incredib'!" retorted meanwhile the pouting daughter of Maxime, pressing into the balcony after Flora. "Hah! and look yondah another incredib'!" She pointed riverward across the Square.

"Charlie, you must not!" cried Flora, returning half into the room.

"Bah!" retorted the staggering boy, pushed out among them and with profane mutterings stood agaze.

Out across the Square and the ever-multiplying flow of people through and about it, and over the roof of the French Market close beyond, the rigging of a moored ship stood pencilled on the sky. It had long been a daily exasperation to his grandmother's vision, being (unknown to Charlie or Victorine), the solitary winnings of Flora's privateering venture, early sold, you will remember, but, by default of a buyer, still in some share unnegotiably hers and—in her own and the grandmother's hungry faith—sure to command triple its present value the moment the fall of the city should open the port. Suddenly the old lady wheeled upon Flora with a frantic look, but was checked by the granddaughter's gleaming eyes and one inaudible, visible word: "Hush!"

The gazing boy saw only the ship. "Oh, great Lord!" he loathingly drawled, "is it Damned Fools' Day again?" Her web of cordage began to grow dim in a rising smoke, and presently a gold beading

A City in Terror

of fire ran up and along every rope and spar and clung quivering. Soon the masts commenced, it seemed, to steal nearer to each other, and the vessel swung out from her berth and started down the wide, swift river, a mass of flames.

"Oh, Mother of God," cried Victorine with a new gush of tears! "'ave mercy upon uz women!" and in the midst of her appeal the promised alarum began to toll—here, yonder, and far away—here, yonder, and far away—and did not stop until right in the middle of the morning it had struck twelve.

"Good-by! poor betrayed New Orleans!" exclaimed Charlie, turning back into the room. "Good-by, sweetheart, I'm off! Good-by, grannie—Flo'!"

The three followed in with cries of amazement, distress, indignation, command, reproach, entreaty, all alike vain. As if the long-roll of his own brigade were roaring to him, he strode about the apartment preparing to fly.

His sister tried to lay preventing hands on him, saying, "Your life! your life! you are throwing it away!"

"Well, what am I in Kincaid's Battery for?" he retorted, with a sweep of his arm that sent her staggering. He caught the younger girl by the shoulders: "Jularkie, if you want to go, too, with or without grannie and Flo', by Jove, come along! I'll take care of you!"

The girl's eyes melted with yearning, but the response was Flora's: "Simpleton! When you have n' the sense enough to take care of yourself!"

"Ah, shame!" ventured the sweetheart. "He's the lover of his blidding country, going ag-ain to fighd

265

for her—and uz—whiles he can!—to-day!—al-lone!
—now!" Her fingers clutched his wrists, that still
held her shoulders, and all her veins surged in the
rapture of his grasp.

But Charlie stared at his sister. It could not enter
his mind that her desires were with the foe, yet his voice
went deep in scorn: "And have you too turned coward?"

The taunt stung. Its victim flashed, but in the
next breath her smile was clemency itself as she drew
Victorine from him and shot her neat reply, well knowing he would never guess the motives behind it—the
bow whence flew the shaft: the revenge she owed the
cause that had burned their home; her malice against
Anna; the agony of losing him they now called dead
and buried; the new, acute loathing that issued from
that agony upon the dismal Irby; her baffled hunger
for the jewels; her plans for the chest of plate; hopes
vanishing in smoke with yonder burning ship; thought
of Greenleaf's probable return with the blue army,
of the riddles that return might make, and of the ruin, the
burning and sinking riot and ruin, these things were
making in her own soul as if it, too, were a city lost.

"Charlie," she said, "you 'ave yo' fight. Me, I
'ave mine. Here is grandma. Ask her—if my fight
—of every day—for you and her—and not yet finish'
—would not eat the last red speck of courage out of
yo' blood."

She turned to Victorine: "Oh, he's brave! He 'as
all that courage to go, in that condition! Well, we
three women, we 'ave the courage to let him go and
ourselve' to stay. But—Charlie! take with you the
Callender'! Yes! You, you can protec' them, same

time they can take care of you. Stop!—Grandma!—
yo' bonnet and gaiter'! All three, Victorine, we will
help them, all four, get away!"

On the road to Callender House, while Charlie and
Victorine palavered together—"I cannot quite make
out," minced the French-speaking grandmother to
Flora, "the real reason why you are doing this."

"'T is with me the same!" eagerly responded the
beauty, in the English she preferred. "I thing maybe
't is juz inspiration. What you thing?"

"I? I am afraid it is only your great love for Anna
—making you a trifle blind."

The eyes of each rested in the other's after the
manner we know and the thought passed between
them, that if further news was yet to come of the lost
artillerist, any soul-reviving news, it would almost
certainly come first to New Orleans and from the
men in blue.

"No," chanted the granddaughter, "I can't tell
what is making me do that unlezz my guardian angel!"

L

ANNA AMAZES HERSELF

ONCE more the Carrollton Gardens.

Again the afternoon hour, the white shell-paved
court, its two playing fountains, the roses, lilies, jas-
mines and violets, their perfume spicing all the air,
and the oriole and mocking-bird enrapturing it with
their songs, although it was that same dire twenty-
fourth of April of which we have been telling. Town-

ward across the wide plain the distant smoke of suicidal
conflagration studded the whole great double crescent
of the harbor. Again the slim railway, its frequent
small trains from the city clanging round the flowery
miles of its half-circle, again the highway on either
side the track, and again on the highway, just reaching the gardens, whose dashing coach and span, but
the Callenders'?

Dashing was the look of it, not its speed. Sedately it
came. Behind it followed a team of four giant mules,
a joy to any quartermaster's vision, drawing a plantation wagon filled with luggage. On the old coachman's box sat beside him a slave maid, and in the
carriage the three Callenders and Charlie. Anna and
Miranda were on the rear seat and for the wounded boy's
better ease his six-shooter lay in Anna's lap. A brave
animation in the ladies was only the more prettily set
off by a pinkness of earlier dejection about their eyes.
Abreast the gate they halted to ask an armed sentry
whether the open way up the river coast was through
the gardens or——

He said there was no longer any open way without
a pass from General Lovell, and when they affably
commended the precaution and showed a pass he
handed it to an officer, a heated, bustling, road-soiled
young Creole, who had ridden up at the head of a
mounted detail. This youth, as he read it, shrugged.
"Under those present condition'," he said, with a wide
gesture toward the remote miles of blazing harbor,
"he could not honor a pazz two weeks ole. They
would 'ave to rit-urn and get it renew'."

"Oh! how? How hope to do so in all yonder chaos?

Anna Amazes Herself

And how! oh, how! could an army—in full retreat—
leaving women and wounded soldiers to the mercy of
a ravening foe—compel them to remain in the city it
was itself evacuating?" A sweet and melodious
dignity was in all the questions, but eyes shone, brows
arched, lips hung apart and bonnet-feathers and hat-
feathers, capes and flounces, seemed to ruffle wider,
with consternation and hurt esteem.

The officer could not explain a single how. He
could do no more than stubbornly regret that the ques-
tioners must even return by train, the dread exigencies
of the hour compelling him to impress these horses for
one of his guns and those mules for his battery-wagon.

Anna's three companions would have sprung to
their feet but in some way her extended hand stayed
them. A year earlier Charlie would have made sad
mistakes here, but now he knew the private soldier's
helplessness before the gold bars of commission, and
his rage was white and dumb, as, with bursting eyes,
he watched the officer pencil a blank.

"Don't write that, sir," said a clear voice, and the
writer, glancing up, saw Anna standing among the
seated three. Her face was drawn with distress and
as pale as Charlie's, but Charlie's revolver was in her
hand, close to her shoulder, pointed straight upward at
full cock, and the hand was steady. "Those mules
first," she spoke on, "and then we, sir, are going to
turn round and go home. Whatever our country needs
of us we will give, not sell; but we will not, in her
name, be robbed on the highway, sir, and I will put a
ball through the head of the first horse or mule you
lay a hand on. Isaac, turn your team."

Unhindered, the teamster, and then the coachman, turned and drove. Back toward, and by and by, into the vast woe-stricken town they returned in the scented airs and athwart the long shadows of that same declining sun which fourteen years before—or was it actually but fourteen months?—had first gilded the splendid maneuverings of Kincaid's Battery. The tragi-comic rencounter just ended had left the three ladies limp, gay, and tremulous, with Anna aghast at herself and really wondering between spells of shame and fits of laughter what had happened to her reason.

With his pistol buckled on again, Charlie had only a wordy wrath for the vanished officer, and grim worship of Anna, while Constance and Miranda, behind a veil of mirthful recapitulations, tenderly rejoiced in the relief of mind and heart which the moment had brought to her who had made it amazing. And now the conditions around them in streets, homes, and marts awoke sympathies in all the four, which further eased their own distresses.

The universal delirium of fright and horror had passed. Through all the city's fevered length and breadth, in the belief that the victorious ships, repairing the lacerations of battle as they came, were coming so slowly that they could not arrive for a day or two, and that they were bringing no land forces with them, thousands had become rationally, desperately busy for flight. Everywhere hacks, private carriages, cabs, wagons, light and heavy, and carts, frail or strong, carts for bread or meat, for bricks or milk, were bearing fugitives—old men, young mothers, grandmothers, maidens and children—with their trunks, bales, bundles, slaves

Anna Amazes Herself

and provisions—toward the Jackson Railroad to board the first non-military train they could squeeze into, and toward the New and Old Basins to sleep on schooner decks under the open stars in the all-night din of building deckhouses. Many of them were familiar acquaintances and chirruped good-by to the Callenders. Passes? No trouble whatever! Charlie need only do this and that and so and so, and there you were!

But Charlie was by this time so nervously spent and in such pain that the first thing must be to get him into bed again—at Callender House, since nothing could induce him to let sister, sweetheart or grandmother know he had not got away. To hurt his pride the more, in every direction military squads with bayonets fixed were smartly fussing from one small domicile to another, hustling out the laggards and marching them to encampments on the public squares. Other squads—of the Foreign Legion, appointed to remain behind in "armed neutrality"—patroled the sidewalks strenuously, preserving order with a high hand. Down this street drums roared, fifes squealed and here passed yet another stately regiment on toward and now into and down, Calliope Street, silent as the rabble it marched through, to take train for Camp Moore in the Mississippi hills.

"Good Lord!" gasped Charlie, "if that isn't the Confederate Guards! Oh, what good under heaven can those old chaps do at the front?"—the very thing the old chaps were asking themselves.

LI

THE CALLENDER HORSES ENLIST

MERE mind should ever be a most reverent servant
to the soul. But in fact, and particularly in hours
stately with momentous things, what a sacrilegious
trick it has of nagging its holy mistress with triflet
light as air—small as gnats yet as pertinacious.

To this effect, though written with a daintier pen,
were certain lines but a few hours old, that twenty-
fourth of April, in a diary which through many months
had received many entries since the one that has already
told us of its writer paired at Doctor Sevier's dinner-
party with a guest now missing, and of her hearing,
in the starlight with that guest, the newsboys' cry that
his and her own city's own Beauregard had opened fire
on Fort Sumter and begun this war—which now behold!

Of this droll impishness of the mind, even in this
carriage to-day, with these animated companions, and
in all this tribulation, ruin, and flight, here was a harry-
ing instance: that every minute or two, whatever the
soul's outer preoccupation or inner anguish, there
would, would, would return, return and return the
doggerel words and swaggering old tune of that song
abhorred by the gruff General, but which had first
awakened the love of so many hundreds of brave men
for its brave, gay singer now counted forever lost:

"Ole mahs' love' wine, ole mis' love' silk——"

Generally she could stop it there, but at times it
contrived to steal unobserved through the second line

and then no power could keep it from marching on to
the citadel, the end of the refrain. Base, antic awak-
ener of her heart's dumb cry of infinite loss! For
every time the tormenting inanity won its way, that
other note, that unvoiced agony, hurled itself against
the bars of its throbbing prison.

"Ole mahs' love' wine, ole mis' love'——"

"Oh, Hilary, my Hilary!"
From the Creole Quarter both carriage and wagon
turned to the water front. Charlie's warning that even
more trying scenes would be found there was in vain.
Anna insisted, the fevered youth's own evident wish
was to see the worst, and Constance and Miranda,
dutifully mirthful, reminded him that through Anna
they also had now tasted blood. As the equipage
came out upon the Levee and paused to choose a way,
the sisters sprang up and gazed abroad, sustaining
each other by their twined arms.

To right, to left, near and far—only not just here
where the Coast steamboats landed—the panorama
was appalling. All day Anna had hungered for some
incident or spectacle whose majesty or terror would
suffice to distract her from her own desolation; but
here it was made plain to her that a distress before
which hand and speech are helpless only drives the
soul in upon its own supreme devotion and woe. One
wide look over those far flat expanses of smoke and
flame answered the wonder of many hours, as to where
all the drays and floats of the town had gone and
what they could be doing. Along the entire sinuous
riverside the whole great blockaded seaport's choked-in

stores of tobacco and cotton, thousands of hogsheads, ten thousands of bales—lest they enrich the enemy— were being hauled to the wharves and landings and were just now beginning to receive the torch, the wharves also burning, and boats and ships on either side of the river being fired and turned adrift.

Yet all the more because of the scene, a scene that quelled even the haunting strain of song, that other note, that wail which, the long day through, had writhed unreleased in her bosom, rose, silent still, yet only the stronger and more importunate——

"Oh, Hilary, my soldier, my flag's, my country's defender, come back to me—here!—now!—my yet living hero, my Hilary Kincaid!"

Reluctantly, she let Constance draw her down, and presently, in a voice rich with loyal pride, as the carriage moved on, bade Charlie and Miranda observe that only things made contraband by the Richmond Congress were burning, while all the Coast Landing's wealth of Louisiana foodstuffs, in barrels and hogsheads, bags and tierces, lay unharmed. Yet not long could their course hold that way, and——

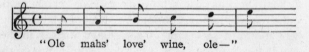

"Ole mahs' love' wine, ole—"

it was Anna who first proposed retreat. The very havoc was fascinating and the courage of Constance and Miranda, though stripped of its mirth, remained undaunted; but the eye-torture of the cotton smoke was enough alone to drive them back to the inner streets.

The Callender Horses Enlist

Here the direction of their caravan, away from all avenues of escape, no less than their fair faces, drew the notice of every one, while to the four themselves every busy vehicle—where none was idle,—every sound remote or near, every dog in search of his master, and every man—how few the men had become!—every man, woman or child, alone or companioned, overladen or empty-handed, hurrying out of gates or into doors, standing to stare or pressing intently or distractedly on, calling, jesting, scolding or weeping—and how many wept!—bore a new, strange interest of fellowship. So Callender House came again to view, oh, how freshly, dearly, appealingly beautiful! As the Callender train drew into its gate and grove, the carriage was surrounded, before it could reach the veranda steps, by a full dozen of household slaves, male and female, grown, half-grown, clad and half-clad, some grinning, some tittering, all overjoyed, yet some in tears. There had been no such gathering at the departure. To spare the feelings of the mistresses the dominating "mammy" of the kitchen had forbidden it. But now that they were back, Glory! Hallelujah!

"And had it really," the three home-returning fair ones asked, "seemed so desolate and deadly perilous just for want of them? What!—had seemed so even to stalwart Tom?—and Scipio?—and Habakkuk? And were Hettie and Dilsie actually so in terror of the Yankees?"

"Oh, if we'd known that we'd never have started!" exclaimed Constance, with tears, which she stoutly quenched, while from all around came sighs and moans of love and gratitude.

And were the three verily back to stay?

Ah! that was the question. While Charlie, well attended, went on up and in they paused on the wide stair and in mingled distress and drollery asked each other, "*Are* we back to stay, or not?"

A new stir among the domestics turned their eyes down into the garden. Beyond the lingering vehicles a lieutenant from Camp Callender rode up the drive. Two or three private soldiers hung back at the gate.

"It's horses and mules again, Nan," gravely remarked Constance, and the three, facing toward him, with Miranda foremost, held soft debate. Whether the decision they reached was to submit or resist, the wide ears of the servants could not be sure, but by the time the soldier was dismounting the ladies had summoned the nerve to jest.

"Be a man, Miranda!" murmured Constance.

"But not the kind I was!" prompted Anna.

"No," said her sister, "for this one coming is already scared to death."

"So's Miranda," breathed Anna as he came up the steps uncovering and plainly uncomfortable. A pang lanced through her as she caught herself senselessly recalling the flag presentation. And then——

"—oh! *oh!*"

"Mrs. Callender?" asked the stranger.

"Yes, sir," said that lady.

"My business"—he glanced back in nervous protest

The Callender Horses Enlist

as the drivers beneath gathered their reins—"will you kindly detain——?"

"If you wish, sir," she replied, visibly trembling. "Isaac——"

From the rear of the group came the voice of Anna: "Miranda, dear, I wouldn't stop them." The men regathered the lines. She moved half a step down and stayed herself on her sister's shoulder. Miranda wrinkled back at her in an ecstasy of relief:

"Oh, Anna, do speak for all of us!"

The teams started away. A distress came into the soldier's face, but Anna met it with a sober smile: "Don't be troubled, sir, you shall have them. Drive round into the basement, Ben, and unload." The drivers went. "You shall have them, sir, on your simple word of honor as——"

"Of course you will be reimbursed. I pledge——"

"No, sir," tearfully put in Constance, "we've given our men, we can't sell our beasts."

"They are not ours to sell," said Anna.

"Why, Nan!"

"They belong to Kincaid's Battery," said Anna, and Constance, Miranda, and the servants smiled a proud approval. Even the officer flushed with a fine ardor:

"You have with you a member of that command?"

"We have."

"Then, on my honor as a Southern soldier, if he will stay by them and us as far as Camp Moore, to Kincaid's Battery they shall go. But, ladies——"

"Yes," knowingly spoke Miranda. "Hettie, Scipio,

Dilsie, you-all can go 'long back to your work now."
She wrinkled confidentially to the officer.

"Yes," he replied, "we shall certainly engage the
enemy's ships to-morrow, and you ladies must——"

"Must not desert our home, sir," said Anna.

"Nor our faithful servants," added the other two.

"Ah, ladies, but if we should have to make this
house a field hospital, with all the dreadful——"

"Oh, that settles it," cried the three, "we stay!"

LII

HERE THEY COME!

WHAT a night! Yet the great city slept. Like its
soldiers at their bivouac fires it lay and slumbered
beside its burning harbor. Sleep was duty.

Callender House kept no vigil. Lighted by the far
devastation, its roof shone gray, its cornice white, its
tree-tops green above the darkness of grove and garden.
From its upper windows you might have seen the townward bends of the river gleam red, yellow, and bronze,
or the luminous smoke of destruction (slantingly over
its flood and farther shore) roll, thin out, and vanish
in a moonless sky. But from those windows no one
looked forth. After the long, strenuous, open-air day,
sleep, even to Anna, had come swiftly.

Waking late and springing to her elbow she presently knew that every one else was up and about. Her
maid came and she hastened to dress. Were the
hostile ships in sight? Not yet. Was the city still
undestroyed? Yes, though the cotton brought out

Here They Come!

to the harbor-side was now fifteen thousand bales and with its blazing made a show as if all the town were afire. She was furiously hungry; was not breakfast ready? Yes, Constance and Miranda—"done had breakfuss and gone oveh to de cottage fo' to fix it up fo' de surgeon . . . No, 'm, not dis house; he done change' his mine." Carriage horses—mules? "Yass, 'm, done gone. Mahs' Chahlie gone wid 'm. He gone to be boss o' de big gun what show' f'om dese windehs." Oh, but that was an awful risk, wounded as he was! "Yass, 'm, but he make his promise to Miss Flo'a he won't tech de gun hisseff." What! Miss Flora—? "Oh, she be'n, but she gone ag'in. Law'! she a brave un! It e'en a'most make me brave, dess to see de high sperits she in!" The narrator departed.

How incredible was the hour. Looking out on the soft gray sky and river and down into the camp, that still kept such quiet show of routine, or passing down the broad hall stair, through the library and into the flowery breakfast room, how keenly real everything that met the eye, how unreal whatever was beyond sight. How vividly actual this lovely home in the sweet ease and kind grace of its lines and adornments. How hard to move with reference to things unseen, when heart and mind and all power of realizing unseen things were far away in the ravaged fields, mangled roads and haunted woods and ravines between Corinth and Shiloh.

But out in the garden, so fair and odorous as one glided through it to the Mandeville cottage, things boldly in view made sight itself hard to believe. Was that bespattered gray horseman no phantom, who came galloping up the river road and called to a servant at the gate that the enemy's fleet was in sight from English Turn? Was that truly New Orleans, back yonder, wrapped in smoke, like fallen Carthage or Jerusalem? Or here! this black-and-crimson thing drifting round the bend in mid-current and without a sign of life aboard or about it, was this not a toy or sham, but one more veritable ship in veritable flames? And beyond and following it, helpless as a drift-log, was that lifeless white-and-crimson thing a burning passenger steamer—and that behind it another? Here in the cottage, plainly these were Constance and Miranda, and, on second view, verily here were a surgeon and his attendants. But were these startling preparations neither child's play nor dream?

Child's play persistently seemed, at any rate, the small bit of yellow stuff produced as a hospital flag. Oh, surely! would not a much larger be far safer? It would. Well, at the house there was some yellow curtaining packed in one of the boxes, Isaac could tell which——

"I think I know right where it is!" said Anna, and hurried away to find and send it. The others, widow and wife, would stay where they were and Anna would take command at the big house, where the domestics would soon need to be emboldened, cheered, calmed, controlled. Time flies when opening boxes that have been stoutly nailed and hooped over the nails. When the goods proved not to be in the one where Anna "knew" they were she remembered better, of course, and in the second they were found. Just as the stuff had been drawn forth and was being hurried away by the hand of Dilsie, a sergeant and private from the camp, one with a field glass, the other with a signal flag, came asking leave to use them from the belvedere on the roof. Anna led them up to it.

How suddenly authentic became everything, up here. Flat as a map lay river, city, and plain. Almost under them and amusingly clear in detail, they looked down into Camp Callender and the Chalmette fortifications. When they wigwagged, "Nothing in sight," to what seemed a very real toy soldier with a very real toy flag, on a green toy mound in the midst of the work (the magazine), he wigwagged in reply, and across the river a mere speck of real humanity did the same from a barely definable parapet.

With her maid beside her Anna lingered a bit. She loved to be as near any of the dear South's defenders as modesty would allow, but these two had once been in Kincaid's Battery, her Hilary's own boys. As lookouts they were not yet skilled. In this familiar scene she knew things by the eye alone, which the sergeant, unused even to his glass, could hardly be sure of through it.

Her maid looked up and around. "Gwine to rain ag'in," she murmured, and the mistress assented with her gaze in the southeast. In this humid air and level country a waterside row of live-oaks hardly four miles off seemed at the world's edge and hid all the river beyond it.

"There's where the tips of masts always show first," she ventured to the sergeant. "We can't expect any but the one kind now, can we?"

"'Fraid not, moving up-stream."

"Then yonder they come. See? two or three tiny, needle-like—h-m-m!—just over that farth'——?"

He lowered the glass and saw better without it.

The maid burst out: "Oh, Lawd, *I* does! Oh, good Gawd A'mighty!" She sprang to descend, but with a show of wonder Anna spoke and she halted.

"If you want to leave me," continued the mistress, "you need only ask."

"Law', Miss Nannie! Me leave you? I——"

"If you do—now—to-day—for one minute, I'll never take you back. I'll have Hettie or Dilsie."

"Missie,"—tears shone—"d' ain't nothin' in Gawd's worl' kin eveh make me a runaway niggeh f'om you! But ef you tell me now fo' to go fetch ev'y dahky we owns up to you——"

"Yes! on the upper front veranda! Go, do it!"

"Yass, 'm! 'caze ef us kin keep 'em anywahs it'll be in de bes' place fo' to see de mos' sights!" She vanished and Anna turned to the soldiers. Their flagging had paused while they watched the far-away top-gallants grow in height and numbers. Down in the works the long-roll was sounding and from every direction men were answering it at a run. Across the river came bugle notes. Sighingly the sergeant lowered his glass:

"Lordy, it's the whole kit and b'ilin'! Wag, John. When they swing up round this end of the trees I'll count 'em. Here they come! One, . . . two, . . . why, what small—oh, see this big fellow! Look at the width of those yards! And look at all their hulls, painted the color of the river! And see that pink

Here They Come!

flutter—look!" he said to Anna, "do you get it? high up among the black ropes? that pink——"

"Yes," said Anna solemnly, "I see it——"

"That's the old——"

"Yes. Must we fire on that? and fire first?"

"We'd better!" laughed the soldier, "if we fire at all. Those chaps have got their answer ready and there won't be much to say after it." The three hurried down, the men to camp, Anna to the upper front veranda. There, save two or three with Constance and Miranda, came all the servants, shepherded by Isaac and Ben with vigilant eyes and smothered vows to "kill de fuss he aw she niggeh dat try to skedaddle"; came and stood to gaze with her over and between the grove trees. Down in the fortification every man seemed to have sprung to his post. On its outer crest, with his adjutant, stood the gilded commander peering through his glass.

"Missie," sighed Anna's maid, "see Mahs' Chahlie dah? stan'in' on de woodworks o' dat big gun?"

"Yes," said Anna carelessly, but mutely praying that some one would make him get down. Her brain teemed with speculations: Where, how occupied and in what state of things, what frame of mind, was Victorine, were Flora and Madame? Here at Steve's cottage with what details were 'Randa and Connie busy? But except when she smiled round on the slaves, her gaze, like theirs, abode on the river and the shore defenses, from whose high staffs floated brightly the Confederate flag. How many a time in this last fearful year had her own Hilary, her somewhere still living, laughing, loving Hilary, stood like yon commander, about to deal havoc from, and to draw it upon, Kincaid's Battery. Who would say that even now he might not be so standing, with her in every throb of his invincible heart?

Something out in the view disturbed the servants.

"Oh, Lawd 'a' massy!" moaned a woman.

"Trus' Him, Aun' Jinnie!" prompted Anna's maid. "Y' always is trus' Him!"

"Whoeveh don't trus' Him, I'll bus' him!" confidentially growled Isaac to those around him.

"We all of us must and will!" said Anna elatedly, though with shameful inward sinkings and with no sustaining word from any of the flock, while out under the far gray sky, emerging from a slight angle of the shore well down the water's long reach the battle line began to issue, each ship in its turn debouching into full relief from main-truck to water-line.

LIII

SHIPS, SHELLS, AND LETTERS

STRANGE! how little sense of calamity came with them—at first. So graceful they were. So fitted—like waterfowl—to every mood of air and tide; their wings all furled, their neat bodies breasting the angry flood by the quiet power of their own steam and silent submerged wheels. So like to the numberless crafts which in kinder days, under friendly tow, had come up this same green and tawny reach and passed on to the queenly city, laden with gifts, on the peaceful embassies of the world.

Ships, Shells, and Letters

But, ah! how swiftly, threateningly they grew: the smaller, two-masted fore-and-afts, each seemingly unarmed but for one monster gun pivoted amidships, and the towering, wide-armed three-masters, the low and the tall consorting like dog and hunter. Now, as they came on, a nice eye could make out, down on their hulls, light patches of new repair where our sunken fleet had so lately shot and rammed them, and, hanging over the middle of each ship's side in a broad, dark square to protect her vitals, a mass of anchor chains. Their boarding-netting, too, one saw, drawn high round all their sides, and now more guns—and more!—and more! the huger frowning over the bulwarks, the lesser in unbroken rows, scowling each from its own port-hole, while every masthead revealed itself a little fort bristling with arms and men. Yes, and there, high in the clouds of rigging, no longer a vague pink flutter now, but brightly red-white-and-blue and smilingly angry—what a strange home-coming for it! ah, what a strange home-coming after a scant year-and-a-half of banishment!—the flag of the Union, rippling from every peak.

"Ain' dey neveh gwine shoot?" asked a negro lad.

"Not till they're out of line with us," said Anna so confidently as to draw a skeptical grunt from his mother, and for better heart let a tune float silently in and out on her breath:

> "I loves to be a beau to de ladies.
> I loves to shake a toe wid de ladies——"

She felt her maid's touch. Charlie was aiming his

great gun, and on either side of her Isaac and Ben were repeating their injunctions. She spoke out:

"If they all shoot true we're safe enough now."

"An' ef de ships don't," put in Isaac, "dey'll mighty soon——"

The prophecy was lost. All the shore guns blazed and crashed. The white smoke belched and spread. Broken window-panes jingled. Wails and moans from the slave women were silenced by imperious outcries from Isaac and Ben. There followed a mid-air scream and roar as of fifty railway trains passing each other on fifty bridges, and the next instant a storm of the enemy's shells burst over and in the batteries. But the house stood fast and half a dozen misquotations of David and Paul were spouted from the braver ones of Anna's flock. In a moment a veil of smoke hid ships and shore, yet fearfully true persisted the enemy's aim. To home-guards, rightly hopeless of their case and never before in action, every hostile shot was like a volcano's eruption, and their own fire rapidly fell off. But on the veranda, amid a weeping, prattling, squealing and gesturing of women and children, Anna could not distinguish the bursting of the foe's shells from the answering thunder of Confederate guns, and when in a bare ten minutes unarmed soldiers began to come out of the smoke and to hurry through the grove, while riders of harnessed horses and mules—harnessed to nothing—lashed up the levee road at full run, and Isaac and Ben proudly cried that one was Mahs' Chahlie and that the animals were theirs of Callender House, she still asked over the balustrade how the fight had gone.

For reply despairing hands pointed her back toward

the river, and there, as she and her groaning servants gazed, the great black masts and yards, with headway resumed and every ensign floating, loomed silently forth and began to pass the veranda. Down in the intervening garden, brightly self-contained among the pale stragglers there, appeared the one-armed reporter, with a younger brother in the weather-worn gray and red of Kincaid's Battery. They waved a pocket-soiled letter and asked how to get in and up to her; but before she could do more than toss them a key there came, not from the ships but from close overhead under a blackening sky, one last, hideous roar and ear-splitting howl. The beautiful treasure-laden home heaved, quivered, lurched and settled again, the women shrieked and crouched or fell ·prone with covered heads, and a huge shell, sent by some pain-crazed fugitive from a gun across the river, and which had entered at the roof, exploded in the basement with a harrowing peal and filled every corner of the dwelling with blinding smoke and stifling dust.

Constance and Miranda met Anna groping and staggering out of the chaos. Unharmed, herself, and no one badly hurt? Ah, hear the sudden wail of that battery boy as he finds his one-armed brother! Anna kneels with him over the writhing form while women fly for the surgeon, and men, at her cry, hasten to improvise a litter. No idle song haunts her now, yet a clamoring whisper times itself with every pulsation of her bosom: "The letter? the letter?"

Pity kept it from her lips, even from her weeping eyes; yet somehow the fallen boy heard, but when he tried to answer she hushed him. "Oh, never mind that," she said, wiping away the sweat of his agony, "it isn't important at all."

"Dropped it," he gasped, and had dropped it where the shell had buried it forever.

Each for the other's sake the lads rejected the hospital, with its risk of capture. The younger had the stricken one hurried off toward the railway and a refugee mother in the hills, Constance tenderly protesting until the surgeon murmured the truth:

"It'll be all one to him by to-morrow."

As the rearmost ship was passing the house Anna, her comeliness restored, half rose from her bed, where Miranda stood trying to keep her. From all the far side of the house remotely sounded the smart tramp and shuffle of servants clearing away wreckage, and the din of their makeshift repairs. She was "all right again," she said as she sat, but the abstraction of her eyes and the harkening droop of her head showed that inwardly she still saw and heard the death-struck boy.

Suddenly she stood. "Dear, brave Connie!" she exclaimed, "we must go help her, 'Randa." And as they went she added, pausing at the head of a stair, "Ah, dear! if we, poor sinners all, could in our dull minds only multiply the awful numbers of war's victims by the woes that gather round any one of them, don't you think, 'Randa——?"

Yes, Miranda agreed, certainly if man—yes, and woman—had that gift wars would soon be no more.

On a high roof above their apartment stood our Valcour ladies. About them babbling feminine groups looked down upon the harbor landings black with male

Ships, Shells, and Letters

vagabonds and witlings smashing the precious food freight (so sacred yesterday), while women and girls scooped the spoils from mire and gutter into buckets, aprons or baskets, and ran home with it through Jackson Square and scurried back again with grain-sacks and pillow-slips, and while the cotton burned on and the ships, so broadly dark aloft, so pale in their war-paint below and so alive with silent, motionless men, came through the smoking havoc.

"No uze to hope," cooed the grandmother to Flora, whose gaze clung to the tree-veiled top of Callender House. "It riffuse' to burn. 'T is not a so inflammab' like that rope and tar." The rope and tar meant their own burnt ship.

"Ah, well," was the light reply, "all shall be for the bes'! Those who watch the game close and play it with courage——"

"And cheat with prudence——?"

"Yes! to them God is good. How well you know that! And Anna, too, she's learning it—or she shall —dear Anna! Same time me, I am well content."

"Oh, you are joyful! But not because God is good, neither juz' biccause those Yankee' they arrive. Ah, that muz' bring some splendid news, that lett'r of Irbee, what you riscieve to-day and think I don't know it. 'T is maybe ab-out Kincaid's Batt'rie, eh?" At Flora's touch the speaker flinched back from the roof's edge, the maiden aiding the recoil.

"Don't stand so near, like that," she said. "It temp' me to shove you over."

They looked once more to the fleet. Slowly it came on. Near its line's center the flag-ship hovered

just opposite Canal Street. The rear was far down
by the Mint. Up in the van the leading vessel was
halting abreast St. Mary's Market, a few hundred
yards behind which, under black clouds and on an
east wind, the lone-star flag of seceded Louisiana
floated in helpless defiance from the city hall. All
at once heaven's own thunders pealed. From a warning sprinkle the women near about fled down a roofed
hatchway. One led Madame. But on such a scene
Flora craved a better curtain-fall and she lingered alone.

It came. As if all its millions of big drops raced
for one prize the deluge fell on city, harbor, and fleet
and on the woe-smitten land from horizon to horizon,
while in the same moment the line of battle dropped
anchor in mid-stream. With a swirling mist wetting
her fair head she waved in dainty welcome Irby's
letter and then pressed it to her lips; not for his sake
—hah!—but for his rueful word, that once more his
loathed cousin, Anna's Hilary! was riding at the head
of Kincaid's Battery.

LIV

SAME APRIL DAY TWICE

BLACK was that Friday for the daughters of Dixie.
Farragut demanded surrender, Lovell declined. The
mayor, the council, the Committee of Public Safety
declined.

On Saturday the two sides parleyed while Lovell
withdrew his forces. On Sunday the Foreign Legion
preserved order of a sort highly displeasing to "a

plain sailor," as Farragut, on the *Hartford*, called himself, and to all the plain sailors of his fleet—who by that time may have been hard to please. On Monday the "plain sailor" bade the mayor, who had once been a plain stevedore, remove the city's women and children within forty-eight hours. But on Tuesday, in wiser mood, he sent his own blue-jackets, cutlasses, muskets and hand-dragged howitzers, lowered the red-and-yellow-striped flag of one star and on mint and custom-house ran up the stars and stripes. Constance and Miranda, from their distant roof, saw the emblem soar to the breeze, and persuaded Anna to an act which cost her as many hours as it need have taken minutes—the destruction of the diary. That was on the twenty-ninth of April.

Let us not get dates confused. "On the twenty-ninth of April," says Grant, "the troops were at Hard Times (Arkansas), and the fleet (another fleet), under Admiral Porter, made an attack upon Grand Gulf (Mississippi), while I reconnoitered." But that twenty-ninth was a year later, when New Orleans for three hundred and sixty-five separate soul-torturing days had been sitting in the twilight of her captivity, often writhing and raving in it, starved to madness for news of Lee's and Stonewall's victories and of her boys, her ragged, gaunt, superb, bleeding, dying, onpressing boys, and getting only such dubious crumbs of rumor as could be smuggled in, or such tainted bad news as her captors delighted to offer her through the bars of a confiscated press. No? did the treatment she was getting merely—as Irby, with much truth, on that twenty-ninth remarked in a group about a headquarters camp-fire near Grand Gulf—did it merely seem so bad to poor New Orleans?

Oh, but!—as the dingy, lean-faced Hilary cried, springing from the ground where he lay and jerking his pipe from his teeth—was it not enough for a world's pity that to her it seemed so? How it seemed to the Callenders in particular was a point no one dared raise where he was. To them had come conditions so peculiarly distressing and isolating that they were not sharers of the common lot around them, but of one strangely, incalculably worse. Rarely and only in guarded tones were they spoken of now in Kincaid's Battery, lately arrived here, covered with the glory of their part in Bragg's autumn and winter campaign through Tennessee and Kentucky, and with Perryville, Murfreesboro' and Stone River added to the long list on their standard. Lately arrived, yes; but bringing with them as well as meeting here a word apparently so authentic and certainly so crushing, (as to those sweet Callenders), that no one ever let himself hint toward it in the hearing even of Charlie Valcour, much less of their battle-scarred, prison-wasted, march-worn, grief-torn, yet still bright-eyed, brave-stepping, brave-riding Major. Major of Kincaid's Battalion he was now, whose whole twelve brass pieces had that morning helped the big iron batteries fight Porter's gunboats.

"Finding Grand Gulf too strong," says Grant, "I moved the army below, running the batteries there as we had done at Vicksburg. Learning here that there was a good road from Bruinsburg up to Port Gibson" (both in Mississippi), "I determined to cross——"

Same April Day Twice

How pleasantly familiar were those names in New Orleans. Alike commercially and socially they meant parterres, walks, bowers in her great back-garden. From the homes of the rich planters around the towns and landings so entitled, and from others all up and down the river from Natchez to Vicksburg and the Bends, hailed many a Carondelet Street nabob and came yearly those towering steamboat-loads—those floating cliffs—of cotton-bales that filled presses, ships and bank-boxes and bought her imports—plows, shoes, bagging, spices, silks and wines: came also their dashing sons and daughters, to share and heighten the splendors of her carnivals and lure away her beaux and belles to summer outings and their logical results. In all the region there was hardly a family with which some half-dozen of the battery were not acquainted, or even related.

"Home again, home again from a foreign shore,"

sang the whole eighty-odd, every ladies' man of them, around out-of-tune pianos with girls whose brothers were all away in Georgia and Virginia, some forever at rest, some about to fight Chancellorsville. Such a chorus was singing that night within earshot of the headquarters group when Ned Ferry, once of the battery, but transferred to Harper's cavalry, rode up and was led by Hilary to the commanding general to say that Grant had crossed the river. Piano and song hushed as the bugles rang, and by daybreak all camps had vanished and the gray columns were hurrying, horse, foot, and wheels, down every southerly road to crush the invader.

Kincaid's Battery

At the head of one rode General Brodnax. Hearing Hilary among his staff he sent for him and began to speak of Mandeville, long gone to Richmond on some official matter and daily expected back; and then he mentioned "this fellow Grant," saying he had known him in Mexico. "And now," he concluded, "he's the toughest old he one they've got."

On the face of either kinsman there came a fine smile that really made them look alike. "We'll try our jaw-teeth on him to-morrow," laughed the nephew.

"Hilary, you weren't one of those singers last evening, were you?"

"Why, no, uncle, for once you'll be pleased——"

"Not by a dam-site!" The smile was gone. "You know, my boy, that in such a time as this if a leader —and above all such a capering, high-kicking colt as you—begins to mope and droop like a cab-horse in the rain, his men will soon not be worth a—what? . . . Oh, blast the others, when *you* do so you're moping, and whether your men can stand it or not, I can't!— what? . . . Well, then, for God's sake don't! For there's another point, Hilary: as long as you were every night a 'ladies' man' and every day a laugher at death you could take those boys through hell-fire at any call; but if they once get the notion—which you came mighty near giving them yesterday—that you hold their lives cheap merely because you're tired of your own, they'll soon make you wish you'd never set eyes on a certain friend of ours, worse than you or they or I have ever wished it yet."

"I've never wished it yet, uncle. I can't. I've never believed one breath of all we've heard. It's not true. It can't be, simply because it can't be."

"Then why do you behave as if it were?"

"I won't, uncle. Honor bright! You watch me."

And next day, in front of Port Gibson, through all the patter, smoke, and crash, through all the charging, cheering and volleying, while the ever-thinning, shortening gray lines were being crowded back from rise to rise —back, back through field, grove, hedge, worm-fence and farmyard, clear back to Grindstone Ford, Bayou Pierre, and with the cavalry, Harper's, cut off and driven up eastward through the town—the enraged old brigadier watched and saw. He saw far, saw close, with blasphemous exultation, how Hilary and his guns, called here, sent there, flashed, thundered, galloped, blazed, howled and held on with furious valor and bleeding tenacity yet always with a quick-sightedness which just avoided folly and ruin, and at length stood rock fast, honor bright, at North Fork and held it till, except the cavalry, the last gray column was over and the bridges safely burning.

That night Ned Ferry—of the cavalry withdrawn to the eastward uplands to protect that great source of supplies and its New Orleans and Jackson Railroad— was made a lieutenant, and a certain brave Charlotte, whom later he loved and won, bringing New Orleans letters to camp, brought also such news of the foe that before dawn, led by her, Ferry's Scouts rode their first ride. All day they rode, while the main armies lay with North Fork between them, the grays entrenching, the blues rebridging. When at sundown she and Ned Ferry parted, and at night he bivouacked his men for a brief rest in a black solitude from which the camp-fires of both hosts were in full sight and the enemy's bridge-building easily heard, he sought, uncompanioned, Kincaid's Battery and found Hilary Kincaid. War is what Sherman called it, who two or three days later, at Grand Gulf (evacuated), crossed into this very strife. Yet peace (so-called) and riches rarely bind men in such loving pairs as do cruel toil, deadly perils, common griefs, exile from woman and daily experience of one another's sweetness, valor, and strength, and it was for such things that this pair, loving so many besides, particularly loved each other.

With glad eyes Kincaid rose from a log.

"Major," began the handsome scout, dapper from képi to spurs in contrast to the worn visage and dress of his senior, but Hilary was already speaking.

"My gentle Ned!" he cried. "*Lieutenant*—Ferry!"

Amid kind greetings from Captain Bartleson and others the eyes of the two—Hilary's so mettlesome, Ferry's so placid—exchanged meanings, and the pair went and sat alone on the trail of a gun; on Roaring Betsy's knee, as it were. There Hilary heard of the strange fair guide and of news told by her which brought him to his feet with a cry of joy that drew the glad eyes of half the battery.

"The little mother saint of your flag, boys!" he explained to a knot of them later, "the little godmother of your guns!" The Callenders were out of New Orleans, banished as "registered enemies."

In Darkest Dixie and Out

LV

IN DARKEST DIXIE AND OUT

UNHAPPY Callender House! Whether "oppressors" or "oppressed" had earliest or oftenest in that first year of the captivity lifted against it the accusing finger it would be hard to tell.

When the Ship Island transports bore their blue thousands up the river, and the streets roared a new drum-thunder, before the dark columns had settled down in the cotton-yards, public squares, Carrollton suburb and Jackson Barracks, Callender House—you may guess by whose indirection—had come to the notice of a once criminal lawyer, now the plumed and emblazoned general-in-chief, to whom, said his victims (possibly biased), no offense or offender was too small for his hectoring or chastisement.

The women in that house, that nest of sedition, he had been told, at second-hand, had in the very dawn of secession completely armed the famous "Kincaid's Battery" which had early made it hot for him about Yorktown. Later in that house they had raised a large war-fund—still somewhere hidden. The day the fleet came up they had sent their carriage-horses to Beauregard, helped signal the Chalmette fortifications, locked ten slaves in the dwelling under shell fire and threatened death to any who should stir to escape. So for these twelve months, with only Isaac, Ben, and their wives as protectors and the splendid freedom to lock themselves in, they had suffered the duress of a guard camped in the grove, their every townward step openly watched and their front door draped with the stars and stripes, under which no feminine acquaintance could be enticed except the dear, faithful Valcours.

But where were old friends and battery sisters? All estranged. Could not the Callenders go to them and explain? Explain! A certain man of not one-fifth their public significance or "secesh" record, being lightly asked on the street if he had not yet "taken the oath" and as lightly explaining that he "wasn't going to," had, fame said, for that alone, been sent to Ship Island—where Anna "already belonged," as the commanding general told the three gentle refusers of the oath, while in black letters on the whited wall above his judgment seat in the custom-house they read, "No distinction made here between he and she adders."

But could not the Valcours, those strangely immune, yet unquestioned true-lovers of poor Dixie, whose marvelous tact won priceless favors for so many distressed Dixie-ites, have explained for the Callenders? Flora had explained!—to both sides, in opposite ways, eagerly, tenderly, over and over, with moist eyes, yet ever with a cunning lameness that kept convincement misled and without foothold. Had the Callenders dwelt up-town the truth might have won out; but where they were, as they were, they might as well have been in unspeakable Boston. And so by her own sweet excusings she kept alive against them beliefs or phantoms of beliefs, which would not have lived a day in saner times.

Calumny had taken two forms: the monstrous black

In Darkest Dixie and Out

smoke of a vulgar version and the superior divinings of the socially elect; a fine, hidden flame fed from the smoke. According to the vulgate the three ladies, incensed at a perfectly lawful effort to use their horses for the Confederate evacuation and actually defying it with cocked revolver, had openly abjured Dixie, renounced all purpose to fly to it and, denying shelter to their own wounded, had with signal flags themselves guided the conquering fleet past the town's inmost defenses until compelled to desist by a Confederate shell in their roof. Unable to face an odium so well earned they had clung to their hiding, glad of the blue camp in their grove, living fatly on the bazaar's proceeds and having high times with such noted staff-officers as Major Greenleaf, their kindness to whom in the days of his modest lieutenancy and first flight and of his later parole and exchange was not so hard now to see through.

Greenleaf had come back with General Banks when Banks had succeeded Butler. Oppressed with military cares, he had barely time to be, without scrutiny, a full believer in the Valcours' loyalty to the Union. Had they not avowed it to him when to breathe it was peril, on that early day when Irby's command became Kincaid's Battery, and in his days of Parish Prison and bazaar? How well those words fitly spoken had turned out! "Like apples of gold," sang Flora to the timorous grandmother, "in wrappers of greenbacks."

All the more a believer was he because while other faithfuls were making their loyalty earn big money off the government this genteel pair, reminding him

that they might yet have to risk themselves inside the
gray lines again to extricate Charlie, had kept their
loyalty as gracefully hidden as of old except from a
general or two. Preoccupied Greenleaf, amiable
generals, not to see that a loyalist in New Orleans
stood socially at absolute zero, whereas to stand at the
social ebullition point was more to the Valcours than
fifty Unions, a hundred Dixies and heaven beside.
It was that fact, more than any other, save one, which
lent intrepidity to Flora's perpetual, ever quickening
dance on the tight-rope of intrigue; a performance
in which her bonny face had begun to betray her discovery that she could neither slow down nor dance
backward. However, every face had come to betray
some cruel strain; Constance's, Anna's, even Victorine's
almond eyes and Miranda's baby wrinkles. Yes, the
Valcours, too, had, nevertheless, their monetary gains,
but these were quiet and exclusively from their ever
dear, however guilty, "rebel" friends, who could not
help making presents to Madame when brave Flora,
spurning all rewards but their love, got for them, by
some spell they could not work, Federal indulgences;
got them through those one or two generals, who—
odd coincidence!—always knew the "rebel" city's
latest "rebel" news and often made stern use of it.

Full believer likewise, and true sorrower, was Greenleaf, in Hilary's death, having its seeming proof from
Constance and Miranda as well as from Flora. For
in all that twelvemonth the Callenders had got no glad
tidings, even from Mandeville. Battle, march and devastation, march, battle and devastation had made letters
as scarce as good dreams, in brightest Dixie. But dark-

In Darkest Dixie and Out

est Dixie was New Orleans. There no three "damned secesh" might stop on a corner in broadest sunlight and pass the time of day. There the "rebel" printing-presses stood cold in dust and rust. There churches were shut and bayonet-guarded because their ministers would not read the prayers ordered by the "oppressor," and there, for being on the street after nine at night, ladies of society, diners-out, had been taken to the lock-up and the police-court. In New Orleans all news but bad news was contraband to any "he or she adder," but four-fold contraband to the Callenders, the fairest member of whose trio, every time a blue-and-gold cavalier forced her conversation, stung him to silence with some word as mild as a Cordelia's. And yet, (you demur,) in the course of a whole year, by some kind luck, surely the blessed truth— Ah, the damsel on the tight-rope took care against that! It was part of her dance to drop from that perch as daintily as a bee-martin way-laying a hive, devour each home-coming word as he devours bees, and flit back and twitter and flutter as a part of all nature's harmony, though in chills of dismay at her peril and yet burning to go to Hilary, from whom this task alone forever held her away.

So throughout that year Anna had been to Green-leaf the veiled widow of his lost friend, not often or long, and never blithely met; loved more ardently than ever, more reverently; his devotion holding itself in a fancied concealment transparent to all; he defending and befriending her, yet only as he could without her knowledge, and incurring a certain stigma from his associates and superiors, if not an actual distrust. A whole history of itself would be the daily, nightly, monthly war of passions between him, her, Flora, and those around them, but time flies.

One day Greenleaf, returning from a week-long circuit of outposts, found awaiting him a letter bearing Northern imprints of mailing and forwarding, from Hilary Kincaid, written long before in prison and telling another whole history, of a kind so common in war that we have already gone by it; a story of being left for dead in the long stupor of a brain hurt; of a hairbreadth escape from living burial; of weeks in hospital unidentified, all sense of identity lost; and of a daring feat of surgery, with swift mental, not so swift bodily, recovery. Inside the letter was one to Anna. But Anna was gone. Two days earlier, without warning, the Callenders —as much to Flora's affright as to their relief, and "as much for Fred's good as for anything," said his obdurate general when Flora in feigned pity pleaded for their stay—had been deported into the Confederacy.

"Let me carry it to her," cried Flora to Greenleaf, rapturously clasping the letter and smiling heroically. "We can overtague them, me and my gran'mama! And then, thanks be to God! my brother we can bring him back! Maybe also—ah! maybee! I can obtain yo' generals some uzeful news!"

After some delay the pair were allowed to go. At the nearest gray outpost, in a sudden shower of the first true news for a week—the Mississippi crossed, Grant victorious at Port Gibson and joined by Sherman at Grand Gulf—Flora learned, to her further joy, that the Callenders, misled by report that Brodnax's brigade was at Mobile, had gone eastward, as straight away from Brodnax and the battery as Gulf-shore roads could take them, across a hundred-mile stretch of townless pine-barrens with neither railway nor telegraph.

Northward, therefore, with Madame on her arm, sprang Flora, staggeringly, by the decrepit Jackson Railroad, along the quiet eastern bound of a region out of which, at every halt, came gloomy mention of Tallahala River and the Big Black; of Big Sandy, Five Mile and Fourteen Mile creeks; of Logan, Sherman and Grant; of Bowen, Gregg, Brodnax and Harper, and of daily battle rolling northward barely three hours' canter away. So they reached Jackson, capital of the state and base of General Joe Johnston's army. They found it in high ferment and full of stragglers from a battle lost that day at Raymond scarcely twenty miles down the Port Gibson road, and on the day following chanced upon Mandeville returning at last from Richmond. With him they turned west, again by rail, and about sundown, at Big Black Bridge, ten miles east of Vicksburg, found themselves clasping hands in open air with General Brodnax, Irby and Kincaid, close before the torn brigade and the wasted, cheering battery. Angels dropped down they seemed, tenderly begging off from all talk of the Callenders, who, Flora distressfully said, had been "grozzly exaggerated," while, nevertheless, she declared herself, with starting tears, utterly unable to explain why on earth they had gone to Mobile—"unlezz the bazaar." No doubt, however, they would soon telegraph by way of Jackson. But next day, while she, as mistress of a field hospital, was winning adoration on every side,

Jackson, only thirty miles off but with every wire cut, fell, clad in the flames of its military factories, mills, foundries and supplies and of its eastern, Pearl River, bridge.

LVI

BETWEEN THE MILLSTONES

TELEGRAPH! They had been telegraphing for days, but their telegrams have not yet been delivered.

On the evening when the camps of Johnston and Grant with burning Jackson between them put out half the stars a covered carriage, under the unsolicited escort of three or four gray-jacketed cavalrymen and driven by an infantry lad seeking his command after an illness at home, crossed Pearl River in a scow at Ratcliff's ferry just above the day's battle-field.

"When things are this bad," said the boy to the person seated beside him and to two others at their back, his allusion being to their self-appointed guard, "any man you find straggling to the *front* is the kind a lady can trust."

This equipage had come a three hours' drive, from the pretty town of Brandon, nearest point to which a railway train from the East would venture, and a glimpse into the vehicle would have shown you, behind Constance and beside Miranda, Anna, pale, ill, yet meeting every inquiry with a smiling request to push on. They were attempting a circuit of both armies to reach a third, Pemberton's, on the Big Black and in and around Vicksburg.

Thus incited they drove on in the starlight over the

gentle hills of Madison county and did not accept repose until they had put Grant ten miles behind and crossed to the south side of the Vicksburg and Jackson Railroad at Clinton village with only twenty miles more between them and Big Black Bridge. The springs of Anna's illness were more in spirit than body. Else she need not have lain sleepless that night at Clinton's many cross-roads, still confronting a dilemma she had encountered in Mobile.

In Mobile the exiles had learned the true whereabouts of the brigade, and of a battery then called Bartleson's as often as Kincaid's by a public which had half forgotten the seemingly well-established fact of Hilary's death. Therein was no new shock. The new shock had come when, as the three waited for telegrams, they stood before a vast ironclad still on the ways but offering splendid protection from Farragut's wooden terrors if only it could be completed, yet on which work had ceased for lack of funds though a greater part of the needed amount, already put up, lay idle solely because it could not be dragged up to a total that would justify its outlay.

"How much does it fall short?" asked Anna with a heart at full stop, and the pounding shock came when the shortage proved less than the missing proceeds of the bazaar. For there heaved up the problem, whether to pass on in the blind hope of finding her heart's own, or to turn instead and seek the two detectives and the salvation of a city. This was the dilemma which in the last few days had torn half the life out of her and, more gravely than she knew, was threatening the remnant.

Constance and Miranda yearned, yet did not dare,
to urge the latter choice. They talked it over covertly
on the back seat of the carriage, Anna sitting bravely
in front with the young "web-foot," as their wheels
next day plodded dustily westward out of Clinton.
Hilary would never be found, of course; and *if* found
how would he explain why he, coming through whatever vicissitudes, he the ever ready, resourceful and
daring, he the men's and ladies' man in one, whom to
look upon drew into his service whoever looked, had
for twelve months failed to get so much as one spoken
or written word to Anna Callender; to their heart-
broken Nan, the daily sight of whose sufferings had
sharpened their wits and strung their hearts to blame
whoever, on any theory, could be blamed. Undoubtedly he might have some dazzling explanation ready,
but that explanation they two must first get of him
before she should know that her dead was risen.

Our travellers were minus their outriders now. At
dawn the squad, leaving tender apologies in the night's
stopping-place, had left the ladies also, not foreseeing
that demoralized servants would keep them there with
torturing delays long into the forenoon. When at
length the three followed they found highways in
ruin, hoof-deep in dust and no longer safe from blue
scouts, while their infantry boy proved as innocent of
road wisdom as they, and on lonely by-ways led them
astray for hours. We may picture their bodily and
mental distress to hear, at a plantation house whose
hospitality they craved when the day was near its end,
that they were still but nine miles from Clinton with
eleven yet between them and Big Black Bridge.

Between the Millstones

Yet they could have wept for thanks as readily as for chagrin or fatigue, so kindly were they taken in, so stirring was the next word of news.

"Why, you po' city child'en!" laughed two sweet unprotected women. "Let these girls bresh you off. You sho'ly got the hafe o' Hinds County on you. . . . Pemberton's men? Law, no; they *wuz* on Big Black but they right out here, now, on Champion's Hill, in sight f'om our gin-house. . . . Brodnax' bri'—now, how funny! We jess heard o' them about a' hour ago, f'om a bran' new critter company name' Ferry's Scouts. Why, Ferry's f'om yo' city! Wish you could 'a' seen him—oh, all of 'em, they was that slick! But, oh, slick aw shabby, when our men ah fine they ah fine, now, ain't they! There was a man ridin' with him —dressed diff'ent—he *wuz* the batteredest-lookin', gayest, grandest—he might 'a' been a gen'al! when in fact he was only a majo', an' it was him we heard say that Brodnax was some'uz on the south side o' the railroad and couldn't come up befo' night. . . . What, us? no, we on the nawth side. You didn't notice when you recrossed the track back yondeh? Well, you *must* 'a' been ti-ud!"

Anna dropped a fervid word to Miranda that set their hostesses agape. "Now, good Lawd, child, ain't you in hahdship and dangeh enough? Not one o' you ain't goin' one step fu'ther this day. Do you want to git shot? Grant's men are a-marchin' into Bolton's Depot right now. Why, honey, you might as well go huntin' a needle in a haystack as to go lookin' fo' Brodnax's brigade to-night. Gen'al Pemberton him-self—why, he'd jest send you to his rear, and that's

Vicksburg, where they a-bein' shelled by the boats day
and night, and the women and child'en a-livin' in caves.
You don't want to go there?"

"We don't know," drolly replied Anna.

"Well, you stay hyuh. That's what that majo' told
us. Says 'e, 'Ladies, we got to fight a battle here to-
morrow, but yo'-all's quickest way out of it'll be to stay
right hyuh. There'll be no place like home to-morrow,
not even this place,' says 'e, with a sort o' twinkle that
made us laugh without seein' anything to laugh at!"

LVII

GATES OF HELL AND GLORY

THE next sun rose fair over the green, rolling, open
land, rich in half-grown crops of cotton and corn between fence-rows of persimmon and sassafras. Before
it was high the eager Callenders were out on a main
road. Their Mobile boy had left them and given the
reins to an old man, a disabled and paroled soldier
bound homeward into Vicksburg. Delays plagued
them on every turn. At a cross-road they were compelled to wait for a large body of infantry, followed
by its ordnance wagons, to sweep across their path with
the long, swift stride of men who had marched for two
years and which changed to a double-quick as they
went over a hill-top. Or next they had to draw wildly
aside into the zigzags of a worm-fence for a column
of galloping cavalry and shroud their heads from its
stifling dust while their driver hung to his mules'
heads by the bits. More than once they caught from

some gentle rise a backward glimpse of long thin lines puffing and crackling at each other; oftener and more and more they heard the far resound of artillery, the shuffling, clattering flight of shell, and their final peal as they reported back to the guns that had sent them; and once, when the ladies asked if a certain human note, rarefied by distance, was not the hurrahing of boys on a school-ground, the old man said no, it was "the Yanks charging." But never, moving or standing from aides or couriers spurring to front or flank, or from hobbling wounded men or unhurt stragglers footing to the rear, could they gather a word as to Brodnax's brigade or Kincaid's Battery.

"Kincaid's Battery hell! You get those ladies out o' this as fast as them mules can skedaddle."

By and by ambulances and then open wagons began to jolt and tilt past them full of ragged, grimy, bloody men wailing and groaning, no one heeding the entreaties of the three ladies to be taken in as nurses. Near a cross-road before them they saw on a fair farmhouse the yellow flag, and a vehicle or two at its door, yet no load of wounded turned that way. Out of it, instead, excited men were hurrying, some lamely, feebly, afoot, others at better speed on rude litters, but all rearward across the plowed land. Two women stepped out into a light trap and vanished behind a lane hedge before Constance could call the attention of her companions.

"Why, Nan, if we didn't *know* she was in New Orleans I'd stand the world down that that was Flora!"

There was no time for debate. All at once, in plain sight, right at hand, along a mask of young willows in the near left angle of the two roads, from a double line of gray infantry whose sudden apparition had startled Anna and Miranda, rang a long volley. From a fringe of woods on the far opposite border the foe's artillery pealed, and while the Callenders' mules went into agonies of fright the Federal shells began to stream and scream across the space and to burst before and over the gray line lying flat in the furrows and darting back fire and death. With their quaking equipage hugging the farther side of the way the veiled ladies leaned out to see, but drew in as a six-mule wagon coming from the front at wild speed jounced and tottered by them. It had nearly passed when with just a touch of hubs it tossed them clear off the road, smashing one of their wheels for good and all. Some one sprang and held their terrified mules and they alighted on a roadside bank counting themselves already captured.

"Look out, everybody," cried a voice, "here come our own guns, six of 'em, like hell to split!" and in a moment the way was cleared.

A minute before this, down the cross-road, southward a quarter of a mile or so, barely out of sight behind fence-rows, the half of a battalion of artillery had halted in column, awaiting orders. With two or three lesser officers a general, galloping by it from behind, had drawn up on a slight rise at the southwest corner of the fire-swept field, taken one glance across it and said, "Hilary, can your ladies' men waltz into action in the face of those guns?"

"They can dance the figure, General."

"Take them in."

Bartleson, watching, had mounted drivers and cannoneers before Kincaid could spur near enough to call,

Gates of Hell and Glory

"Column, forward!" and turn again toward the General and the uproar beyond. The column had barely stretched out when, looking back on it as he quickened pace, Hilary's cry was, "Battery, trot, march!" So the six guns had come by the general: first Hilary, sword out, pistols in belt; then his adjutant; then bugler and guidon, and then Bartleson and the boys; horses striding out—ah, there were the Callenders' own span! —whips cracking, carriages thumping and rumbling, guns powder-blackened and brown, their wheels, trails, and limbers chipped and bitten, and their own bronze pock-pitted by the flying iron and lead of other fights, and the heroes in saddle and on chests—with faces as war-worn as the wood and metal and brute life under them—cheering as they passed. Six clouds of dust in one was all the limping straggler had seen when he called his glad warning, for a tall hedge lined half the cross-road up which the whirlwind came; but a hundred yards or so short of the main way the whole battery, still shunning the field because of spongy ground, swept into full view at a furious gallop. Yet only as a single mass was it observed, and despite all its thunder of wheels was seen only, not heard. Around the Callenders was a blindfold of dust and vehicles, of shouting and smoke, and out in the field the roar of musketry and howling and bursting of shell. Even Flora, in her ambulance close beyond both roads, watching for the return of a galloping messenger and seeing Hilary swing round into the highway, low bent over his charger at full run, knew him only as he vanished down it hidden by the tempest of hoofs, wheels, and bronze that whirled after him.

Kincaid's Battery

At Anna's side among the rearing, trembling teams a mounted officer, a surgeon, Flora's messenger, was commanding and imploring her to follow Constance and Miranda into the wagon which had wrecked their conveyance. And so, alas! all but trampling her down, yet unseeing and unseen though with her in every leap of his heart, he who despite her own prayers was more to her than a country's cause or a city's deliverance flashed by, while in the dust and thunder of the human avalanche that followed she stood asking whose battery was this and with drowned voice crying, as she stared spell-bound, "Oh, God! is it only Bartleson's? Oh, God of mercy! where is Hilary Kincaid?" A storm of shell burst directly overhead. Men and beasts in the whirling battery, and men and beasts close about her wailed, groaned, fell. Anna was tossed into the wagon, the plunging guns, dragging their stricken horses, swept out across the field, the riot of teams, many with traces cut, whipped madly away, and still, thrown about furiously in the flying wagon, she gazed from her knees and mutely prayed, but saw no Hilary because while she looked for a rider his horse lay fallen.

Never again came there to that band of New Orleans boys such an hour of glory as this at Champion's Hill. For two years more, by the waning light of a doomed cause, they fought on, won fame and honor; but for blazing splendor—of daring, skill, fortitude, loss and achievement which this purblind world still sees plainest in fraternal slaughter—that was the mightiest hour, the mightiest ten minutes, ever spent, from 'Sixty-one to 'Sixty-five, by Kincaid's Battery.

Gates of Hell and Glory

Right into the face of death's hurricane sprang the ladies' man, swept the ladies' men. "Battery, trot, walk. Forward into battery! Action front!" It was at that word that Kincaid's horse went down; but while the pieces trotted round and unlimbered and the Federal guns vomited their fire point-blank and blue skirmishers crackled and the gray line crackled back, and while lead and iron whined and whistled, and chips, sand and splinters flew, and a dozen boys dropped, the steady voice of Bartleson gave directions to each piece by number, for "solid shot," or "case" or "double canister." Only one great blast the foe's artillery got in while their opponents loaded, and then, with roar and smoke as if the earth had burst, Kincaid's Battery answered like the sweep of a scythe. Ah, what a harvest! Instantly the guns were wrapped in their own white cloud, but, as at Shiloh, they were pointed again, again and again by the ruts of their recoil, Kincaid and Bartleson each pointing one as its nine men dwindled to five and to four, and in ten minutes nothing more was to be done but let the gray line through with fixed bayonets while Charlie, using one of Hilary's worn-out quips, stood on Roaring Betsy's trunnion-plates and cursed out to the shattered foe, "Bricks, lime and sand always on hand! —, —, —!"

Yet this was but a small part of the day's fight, and Champion's Hill was a lost battle. Next day the carnage was on Baker's Creek and at Big Black Bridge, and on the next Vicksburg was invested.

LVIII

ARACHNE

BEHOLD, "Vicksburg and the Bends."

In one of those damp June-hot caves galleried into the sheer yellow-clay sides of her deep-sunken streets, desolate streets where Porter's great soaring, howling, burrowing "lamp-posts" blew up like steamboats and flew forty ways in search of women and children, dwelt the Callenders. Out among Pemberton's trenches and redans, where the woods were dense on the crowns and faces of the landside bluffs, and the undergrowth was thick in the dark ravines, the minie-ball forever buzzed and pattered, and every now and then dabbed mortally into some head or breast. There ever closer and closer the blue boys dug and crept while they and the gray tossed back and forth the hellish hand-grenade, the heavenly hard-tack and tobacco, gay jokes and lighted bombs. There, mining and countermining, they blew one another to atoms, or under shrieking shells that tore limbs from the trees and made missiles of them hurled themselves to the assault and were hurled back. There, in a ruined villa whose shrubberies Kincaid named "Carrollton Gardens," quartered old Brodnax, dining on the fare we promised him from the first, and there the nephew sang an ancient song from which, to please his listeners, he had dropped "old Ireland" and made it run:

"O, my heart's in New Orleans wherever I go——"

meaning, for himself, that wherever roamed a certain

Arachne

maiden whose whereabouts in Dixie he could only conjecture, there was the New Orleans of his heart.

One day in the last week of the siege a young mother in the Callenders' cave darted out into the sunshine to rescue her straying babe and was killed by a lump of iron. Bombardments rarely pause for slips like that, yet the Callenders ventured to her burial in a graveyard not far from "Carrollton Gardens." As sympathy yet takes chances with contagions it took them then with shells.

Flora Valcour daily took both risks—with contagions in a field hospital hard by the cemetery, and with shells and stray balls when she fled at moments from the stinking wards to find good air and to commune with her heart's desires and designs. There was one hazard beside which foul air and stray shots were negligible, a siege within this siege. To be insured against the mere mathematical risk that those designs, thus far so fortunate, might by any least mishap, in the snap of a finger, come to naught she would have taken chances with the hugest shell Grant or Porter could send. For six weeks Anna and Hilary—Anna not knowing if he was alive, he thinking her fifty leagues away—had been right here, hardly an hour's walk asunder. With what tempest of heart did the severed pair rise at each dawn, lie down each night; but Flora suffered no less. Let either of the two get but one glimpse, hear but one word, of the other, and—better a shell, slay whom it might.

On her granddaughter's brow Madame Valcour saw the murk of the storm. "The lightning must strike some time, you are thinking, eh?" she simpered.

"No, not necessarily—thanks to your aid!"

Thanks far more to Flora's subtlety and diligence. It refreshed Madame to see how well the fair strategist kept her purposes hid. Not even Irby called them—those he discerned—hers. In any case, at any time, any possessive but my or mine, or my or mine on any lip but his, angered him. Wise Flora, whenever she alluded to their holding of the plighted ones apart, named the scheme his till that cloyed, and then "ours" in a way that made it more richly his, even when—clearly to Madame, dimly to him, exasperatingly to both—her wiles for its success—woven around his cousin—became purely feminine blandishments for purely feminine ends. In her own mind she accorded Irby only the same partnership of aims which she contemptuously shared with the grandam, who, like Irby, still harped on assets, on that estate over in Louisiana which every one else, save his uncle, had all but forgotten. The plantation and its slaves were still Irby's objective, and though Flora was no less so, any chance that for jealousy of her and Hilary he might throw Anna into Hilary's arms, was offset by his evident conviction that the estate would in that moment be lost to him and that no estate meant no Flora. Madame kept that before him and he thanked and loathed her accordingly.

Flora's subtlety and diligence, yes, indeed. By skill in phrases and silences, by truth misshapen, by flatteries daintily fitted, artfully distributed, never overdone; by a certain slow, basal co-operation from Irby (his getting Mandeville sent out by Pemberton with secret despatches to Johnston, for example), by a deft

touch now and then from Madame, by this fine perti-
nacity of luck, and by a sweet new charity of speech
and her kindness of ministration on every side, the pretty schemer had everybody blundering into her hand,
even to the extent of keeping the three Callenders convinced that Kincaid's Battery had been cut off at Big
Black Bridge and had gone, after all, to Mobile. No
wonder she inwardly trembled.

And there was yet another reason: since coming
into Vicksburg, all unaware yet why Anna so inordi-
nately prized the old dagger, she had told her where
it still lay hid in Callender House. To a battery lad
who had been there on the night of the weapon's dis-
appearance and who had died in her arms at Champion's Hill, she had imputed a confession that, having
found the moving panel, a soldier boy's pure wanton-
ness had prompted him to the act which, in fact, only
she had committed. So she had set Anna's whole
soul upon getting back to New Orleans to regain the
trinket-treasure and somehow get out with it to Mobile,
imperiled Mobile, where now, if on earth anywhere,
her hope was to find Hilary Kincaid.

Does it not tax all patience, that no better intuition
of heart, no frenzy of true love in either Hilary or
Anna—suffering the frenzies they did—should have
taught them to rend the poor web that held them separate almost within the sound of each other's cry? No,
not when we consider other sounds, surrounding conditions: miles and miles of riflemen and gunners in
so constant a whirlwind of destruction and anguish
that men like Maxime Lafontaine and Sam Gibbs
went into open hysterics at their guns, and even while

sleeping on their arms, under humming bullets and crashing shells and over mines ready to be sprung, sobbed and shivered like babes, aware in their slumbers that they might "die before they waked." In the town unearthly howlings and volcanic thunders, close overhead, cried havoc in every street, at every cave door. There Anna, in low daily fevers, with her "heart in New Orleans," had to be "kept quiet" by Miranda and Constance, the latter as widowed as Anna, wondering whether "Steve was alive or not."

This is a history of hearts. Yet, time flying as it does, the wild fightings even in those hearts, the famishing, down-breaking sieges in them, must largely be left untold—Hilary's, Anna's, Flora's, all. Kincaid was in greater temptation than he knew. Many a battery boy, sick, sound or wounded—Charlie for one—saw it more plainly than he. Anna, supposed to be far away and away by choice, was still under the whole command's impeachment, while Flora, amid conditions that gave every week the passional value of a peace-time year, was here at hand, an ever-ministering angel to them and to their hero; yet they never included him and Flora in one thought together but to banish it, though with tender reverence. Behind a labored disguise of inattention they jealously watched lest the faintest blight or languor should mar, in him, the perfect bloom of that invincible faith to, and faith in, the faithless Anna, which alone could satisfy their worship of him. Care for these watchers brought the two much together, and in every private moment they talked of the third one; Flora still fine in the rôle of

Arachne

Anna's devotee and Hilary's "pilot," rich in long-thought-out fabrications, but giving forth only what was wrung from her and parting with each word as if it cost her a pang. Starving and sickening, fighting and falling, the haggard boys watched; yet so faultless was the maiden's art that when in a fury of affright at the risks of time she one day forced their commander to see her heart's starvation for him the battery saw nothing, and even to him she yet appeared faultless in modesty and utterly, marvelously, splendidly ignorant of what she had done.

"Guide right!" he mused alone. "At last, H. K., your nickname's got a meaning worth living up to!"

While he mused, Flora, enraged both for him and against him, and with the rage burning in her eye and on her brow, stood before her seated grandmother, mutely giving gaze for gaze until the elder knew.

The old woman resumed her needle. "And all you have for it," was the first word, "is his pity, eh?"

"Wait!" murmured the girl. "I will win yet, if I have to lose——"

"Yes?" skeptically simpered the grandam, "—have to lose yourself to do it?"

The two gazed again until the maiden quietly nodded and her senior sprang half up:

"No, no! ah, no-no-no! There's a crime awaiting you, but not that! Oh, no, you are no such fool!"

"No?" The girl came near, bent low and with dancing eyes said, "I'll be fool enough to lead him on till his sense of honor——"

"Sense of—oh, ho, ho!"

"Sense of his honor and *mine*—will make him my

319

prisoner. Or else—!" The speaker's eyes burned.
Her bosom rose and fell.

"Yes," said the seated one—to her needle—"or
else his sense that Charlie—My God! don't pinch my
ear off!"

"Happy thought," laughed Flora, letting go, "but
a very poor guess."

LIX

IN A LABYRINTH

FOR ladies' funerals, we say, mortars and siege-
guns, as a rule, do not pause. But here at Vicksburg
there was an hour near the end of each day when the
foe, for some mercy to themselves, ceased to bombard,
and in one of these respites that procession ventured
forth in which rode the fevered Anna: a farm wagon,
a battered family coach, a carryall or two.

Yet in the midst of the graveyard rites there broke
out on the unseen lines near by, northward, an uproar
of attack, and one or two shells burst in plain view,
frightening the teams. The company leaped into the
vehicles any way they could and started townward
over a miserable road with the contest resounding on
their right. As they jostled along the edge of a wood
that lay between them and the firing some mishap to the
front team caused all to alight, whereupon a shell,
faultily timed, came tearing through the tree-tops and
exploded in the remains of a fence close beyond them.
Amid thunder, smoke, and brute and human terror
the remounting groups whirled away and had en-

In a Labyrinth

tirely left the scene before that was asked which none
could tell: Where was Anna?

Anna herself did not know, could not inquire of
her own mind. With a consciousness wholly disem-
bodied she was mainly aware of a great pain that
seemed to fill all the region and atmosphere, an atmosphere charged with mysterious dim green light and
full of great boomings amid a crackle of smaller ones;
of shouts and cheers and of a placid quaking of myriad
leaves; all of which things might be things or only
divers manifestations of her undefinable self.

By and by through the pain came a dream of some
one like her living in a certain heaven of comfort and
beauty, peace, joy, and love named "Callender House";
but the pain persisted and the dream passed into a
horrible daytime darkness that brought a sense of
vast changes near and far; a sense of many having
gone from that house, and of many having most for-
biddenly come to it; a sense of herself spending years
and years, and passing from world to world, in quest of
one Hilary, Hilary Kincaid, whom all others believed
to be dead or false, or both, but who would and should
and must be found, and when found would be alive
and hale and true; a sense of having, with companions,
been all at once frightfully close to a rending of the
sky, and of having tripped as she fled, of having fallen
and lain in a thunderous storm of invisible hail, and
of having after a time risen again and staggered on, an
incalculable distance, among countless growing things,
fleeing down-hill, too weak to turn up-hill, till suddenly the whole world seemed to strike hard against
something that sent it reeling backward.

And now her senses began feebly to regather within truer limits and to tell her she was lying on the rooty ground of a thicket. Dimly she thought to be up and gone once more, but could get no farther than the thought although behind her closed lids glimmered a memory of deadly combat. Its din had passed, but there still sounded, just beyond this covert, fierce commands of new preparation, and hurried movements in response—a sending and bringing, dismissing, and summoning of men and things to rear or front, left or right, in a fury of supply and demand.

Ah, what! water? in her face? Her eyes opened wildly. A man was kneeling beside her. He held a canteen; an armed officer in the foe's blue. With lips parting to cry out she strove to rise and fly, but his silent beseechings showed him too badly hurt below the knees to offer aid or hindrance, and as she gained her feet she let him plead with stifled eagerness for her succor from risks of a captivity which, in starving Vicksburg and in such plight, would be death.

He was a stranger and an enemy, whose hurried speech was stealthy and whose eyes went spying here and there, but so might it be just then somewhere with him for whom she yet clung to life. For that one's sake, and more than half in dream, she gave the sufferer her support, and with a brow knit in anguish, but with the fire of battle still in his wasting blood, he rose, fitfully explaining the conditions of the place and hour. To cover a withdrawal of artillery from an outer to an inner work a gray line had unexpectedly charged, and as it fell back with its guns, hotly pressed, a part of the fight had swung down into and half across this ra-

In a Labyrinth

vine, for which another struggle was furiousiy preparing on both sides, but which, for him, in the interval, was an open way of deliverance if she would be his crutch.

In equal bewilderment of thought and of outer sense, pleadingly assured that she would at once be sent back under flag of truce, with compassion deepening to compulsion and with a vague inkling that, failing the white flag, this might be heaven's leading back to Callender House and the jewel treasure, to Mobile and to Hilary, she gave her aid. Beyond the thicket the way continued tangled, rough and dim. Twice and again the stricken man paused for breath and ease from torture, though the sounds of array, now on two sides, threatened at every step to become the cry of onset. Presently he stopped once more, heaved, swayed and, despite her clutch, sank heavily to the ground.

"Water!" he gasped, but before she could touch the canteen to his lips he had fainted. She sprinkled his face, but he did not stir. She gazed, striving for clear thought, and then sprang up and called. What word? Ah, what in all speech should she call but a name, the name of him whose warrant of marriage lay at that moment in her bosom, the name of him who before God and the world had sworn her his mated, life-. long protection?

"Hilary!" she wailed, and as the echoes of the green wood died, "Hilary!" again. On one side there was more light in the verdure than elsewhere and that way she called. That way she moved stumblingly and near the edge of a small clear space cried once more, "Hilary! . . . Hilary!"

Kincaid's Battery

LX

HILARY'S GHOST

FAINTLY the bearer of that name heard the call; heard it rise from a quarter fearfully nearer the foe's line than to his; caught it with his trained ear as, just beyond sight of Irby, Miranda, and others, he stood in amazed converse with Flora Valcour. Fortune, smiling on Flora yet, had brought first to her the terrified funeral group and so had enabled her to bear to Hilary the news of the strange estrayal, skilfully blended with that revelation of Anna's Vicksburg sojourn which she, Flora, had kept from him so cleverly and so long.

With mingled rapture and distress, with a heart standing as still as his feet, as still as his lifted head and shining eyes, he listened and heard again. Swiftly, though not with the speed he would have chosen, he sprang toward the call; sped softly through the brush, softly and without voice, lest he draw the enemy's fire; softly and mutely, with futile backward wavings and frowning and imploring whispers to Flora as in a dishevelled glow that doubled her beauty she glided after him.

Strangely, amid a swarm of keen perceptions that plagued him like a cloud of arrows as he ran, that beauty smote his conscience; her beauty and the worship and protection it deserved from all manhood and most of all from him, whose unhappy, unwitting fortune it was to have ensnared her young heart and brought it to the desperation of an unnatural self-revealment;

Hilary's Ghost

her uncoveted beauty, uncourted love, unwelcome presence, and hideous peril! Was he not to all these in simplest honor peculiarly accountable? They lanced him through with arraignment as, still waving her beseechingly, commandingly back, with weapons undrawn the more swiftly to part the way before him, his frenzy for Anna drew him on, as full of introspection as a drowning man, thinking a year's thoughts at every step. Oh, mad joy in pitiful employment! Here while the millions of a continent waged heroic war for great wrongs and rights, here on the fighting-line of a beleaguered and starving city, here when at any instant the peal of his own guns might sound a fresh onset, behold him in a lover's part, loving "not honor more," setting the seal upon his painful alias, filching time out of the jaws of death to pursue one maiden while clung to by another. Oh, Anna! Anna Callender! my life for my country, but this moment for thy life and thee! God stay the onslaught this one moment!

As he reached the edge of that narrow opening from whose farther side Anna had called he halted, glanced furtively about, and harkened forward, backward, through leafy distances grown ominously still. Oh, why did the call not come again? Hardly in a burning house could time be half so priceless. Not a breath could promise that in the next the lightnings, thunders, and long human yell of assault would not rend the air. Flora's soft tread ceased at his side.

"Stay back!" he fiercely breathed, and pointed just ahead: "'The enemy's skirmishers!'"

"Come away!" she piteously whispered, trembling with terror. For, by a glimpse as brief as the catch

of her breath, yonder a mere rod or so within the farther
foliage, down a vista hardly wider than a man's shoulders, an armed man's blue shoulders she had seen,
under his black hat and peering countenance. Joy
filled the depth of her heart in the belief that a thin
line of such black hats had already put Anna behind
them, yet she quaked in terror, terror of death, of
instant, shot-torn death that might leave Hilary Kincaid alive.

With smiting pity he saw her affright. "Go back!"
he once more gasped: "In God's name, go back!"
while recklessly he stepped forward out of cover.
But in splendid desperation, with all her soul's battle
in her eyes—horror, love, defiance, and rending chagrin
striving and smiting, she sprang after him into the
open, and clutched and twined his arms. The blue
skirmish-line, without hearing, saw him; saw, and
withheld their fire, fiercely glad that tactics and mercy
should for once agree. And Anna saw.

"Come with me back!" whispered Flora, dragging
on him with bending knees. "She's lost! She's gone
back to those Yankee, and to Fred Greenleaf! And
you"—the whisper rose to a murmur whose pathos
grew with her Creole accent—"you, another step
and you are a deserter! Yes! to your country—to
Kincaid' Batt'ree—to me-me-me!" The soft torrent
of speech grew audible beyond them: "Oh, my God!
Hilary Kincaid, listen-to-me-listen! You 'ave no
right; no ri-ight to leave me! *Ah, you shall not!* No
right—ri-ight to leave yo' Flora—sinze she's tol' you
—sinze she's tol' you—w'at she's tol' you!"

In this long history of a moment the blue skirmish-

" You 'ave no ri-ight to leave me! *Ah, you shall not!*"

Hilary's Ghost

ers had not yet found Anna, but it was their advance, their soft stir at her back as they came upon their fallen leader, that had hushed her cries. At the rift in the wood she had leaned on a huge oak and as body and mind again failed had sunk to its base in leafy hiding. Vaguely thence she presently perceived, lit from behind her by sunset beams, the farther edge of the green opening, and on that border, while she feebly looked, came suddenly a ghost!

Ah, Heaven! the ghost of Hilary Kincaid! It looked about for her! It listened for her call! By the tree's rough bark she drew up half her height, clung and, with reeling brain, gazed. How tall! how gaunt! how dingy gray! How unlike her whilom "ladies' man," whom, doubtless truly, they now called dead and buried. But what—what—was troubling the poor ghost? What did it so wildly avoid? what wave away with such loving, tender pain? Flora Valcour! Oh, see, see! Ah, death in life! what does she see? As by the glare of a bursting midnight shell all the empty gossip of two years justified—made real—in one flash of staring view. With a long moan the beholder cast her arms aloft and sank in a heap, not knowing that the act had caught Hilary's eye, but willingly aware that her voice had perished in a roar of artillery from the farther brink of the ravine, in a crackle and fall of tree-tops, and in the "rebel yell" and charge.

Next morning, in a fog, the blue holders of a new line of rifle-pits close under the top of a bluff talked up to the grays in a trench on its crest. Gross was the banter, but at mention of "ladies" it purified.

"Johnnie!" cried "Yank," "who is she, the one we've

got?" and when told to ask her, said she was too ill to ask. By and by to "Johnnie's" inquiries the blues replied:

"He? the giant? Hurt? No-o, not half bad enough, when we count what he cost us. If we'd known he was only stunned we"—and so on, not very interestingly, while back in the rear of the gray line tearful Constance praised, to her face, the haggard Flora and, in his absence, the wounded Irby, Flora's splendid rescuer in the evening onslaught.

"A lifetime debt," Miranda thought Flora owed him, and Flora's meditative yes, as she lifted her eyes to her grandmother's, was—peculiar.

A few days later Anna, waking in the bliss of a restored mind, and feeling beneath her a tremor of paddle-wheels, gazed on the nurse at her side.

"Am I a—prisoner?" she asked.

The woman bent kindly without reply.

"Anyhow," said Anna, with a one-sided smile, "they can't call me a spy." Her words quickened: "I'm a rebel, but I'm no spy. I was lost. And he's no spy. He was in uniform. Is he—on this boat?"

Yes, she was told, he was, with a few others like him, taken too soon for the general parole of the surrender. Parole? she pondered. Surrender? What surrender? "Where are we going?" she softly inquired; "not to New Orleans?"

The nurse nodded brightly.

"But how can we get—by?"

"By Vicksburg? We're already by there."

"Has Vicks—? . . . Has Vicksburg—fallen?"

The confirming nod was tender. Anna turned

The Flag-of-Truce Boat

away. Presently—"But not Mobile? Mobile has-
n't——?

"No, not yet. But it must, don't you think?"

"No!" cried Anna. "It must not! Oh, it must
not! I—if I—Oh, if I——"

The nurse soothed her smilingly: "My poor child,"
she said, "*you* can't save Mobile."

LXI

THE FLAG-OF-TRUCE BOAT

SEPTEMBER was in its first week. The news of
Vicksburg—and Port Hudson—ah, yes, and Gettys-
burg!—was sixty days old.

From Southern Mississippi and East Louisiana
all the grays who marched under the slanting bayonet
or beside the cannon's wheel were gone. Left were
only the "citizen" with his family and slaves, the post
quartermaster and commissary, the conscript-officer,
the trading Jew, the tax-in-kind collector, the hiding
deserter, the jayhawker, a few wounded boys on fur-
lough, and Harper's cavalry. Throughout the Delta
and widely about its grief-broken, discrowned, beggared,
shame-crazed, brow-beaten Crescent City the giddying
heat quaked visibly over the high corn, cotton, and cane,
up and down the broken levees and ruined highways,
empty byways, and grass-grown railways, on charred
bridges, felled groves, and long burnt fence lines. The
deep, moss-draped, vine-tangled swamps were dry.

So quivered the same heat in the city's empty thoroughfares. Flowers rioted in the unkept gardens. The

cicada's frying note fried hotter than ever. Dazzling thunder-heads towered in the upper blue and stood like snow mountains of a vaster world. The very snake coiled in the shade. The spiced air gathered no freshness from the furious, infrequent showers, the pavements burned the feet, and the blue "Yank" (whom there no one dared call so by word or look), so stoutly clad, so uncouthly misfitted, slept at noon face downward in the high grass under the trees of the public squares preëmpted by his tents, or with piece loaded and bayonet fixed slowly paced to and fro in the scant shade of some confiscated office-building, from whose upper windows gray captives looked down, one of them being "the ladies' man."

Not known of his keepers by that name, though as the famous Major Kincaid of Kincaid's Battery (the latter at Mobile with new guns), all July and August he had been of those who looked down from such windows; looked down often and long, yet never descried one rippling fold of one gossamer flounce of a single specimen of those far-compassionated "ladies of New Orleans," one of whom, all that same time, was Anna Callender. No proved spy, she, no incarcerated prisoner, yet the most gravely warned, though gentlest, suspect in all the recalcitrant city.

Neither in those sixty days had Anna seen him. The blue sentries let no one pass in sight of that sort of windows. "Permit?" She had not sought it. Some one in gold lace called her "blamed lucky" to enjoy the ordinary permissions accorded Tom, Dick, and Harry. Indeed Tom, Dick, and Harry were freer than she. By reason of hints caught from her in wanderings of her mind on the boat, in dreams of a great service to be done for Dixie, the one spot where she most yearned to go and to be was forbidden her, and not yet had she been allowed to rest her hungry eyes on Callender House. Worse than idle, therefore, perilous for both of them and for any dream of great service, would it have been even to name the name of Hilary Kincaid.

What torture the double ban, the two interlocked privations! Yonder a city, little sister of New Orleans, still mutely hoping to be saved, here Hilary alive again, though Anna still unwitting whether she should love and live or doubt and die. Yet what would they say when they should meet? How could either explain? Surely, we think, love would have found a way; but while beyond each other's sight and hearing, no way could Hilary, at least, descry.

To him it seemed impossible to speak to her—even to Fred Greenleaf had Fred been there!—without betraying another maiden, one who had sealed his lips forever by confessing a heart which had as much— had more right to love than he to live. True, Anna, above all, had right to live, to love, to know; but in simplest honor to commonest manhood, in simplest manhood's honor to all womankind, to Flora, to Anna herself, this knowledge should come from any other human tongue rather than from his. From Anna he needed no explanation. That most mysteriously she should twice have defaulted as keeper of sacred treasure; that she stood long accused, by those who would most gladly have scouted the charge, of leanings to another suitor, a suitor in the blue, and of sympathies, nay,

services, treasonous to the ragged standards of the
gray; that he had himself found her in the enemy's
lines, carried there by her own steps, and accepting
captivity without a murmur, ah, what were such light-
as-air trials of true love's faith while she was still Anna
Callender, that Anna from whom one breath saying,
"I am true," would outweigh all a world could show
or surmise in accusation?

And Anna: What could she say after what she had
seen? Could she tell him—with Flora, as it were,
still in his arms—could she *explain* that she had been
seeking him to cast herself there? Or if she stood
mute until he should speak, what could he say to count
one heart-throb against what she had seen? Oh, before God! before God! it was not *jealousy* that could
make her dumb or deaf to either of them. She confessed its pangs. Yes! yes! against both of them,
when she remembered certain things or forgot this
and that, it raged in her heart, tingled in the farthest
reach of her starved and fever-dried veins. Yet to
God himself, to whom alone she told it, to God himself she protested on her knees it did not, should not,
could not rule her. What right had she to give it
room? Had she not discerned from the beginning
that those two were each other's by natural destiny?
Was it not well, was it not God-sent to all three, that
in due time, before too late, he and she—that other,
resplendent she—should be tried upon each other alone
—together? Always hitherto she, Anna, had in some
way, some degree, intervened, by some chance been
thrust and held between them; but at length nature,
destiny, had all but prevailed, when once more she—

stubbornly astray from that far mission of a city's rescue so plainly hers—had crashed in between to the shame and woe of all, to the gain of no cause, no soul, no sweet influence in all love's universe. Now, meeting Hilary, what might she do or say?

One thing! Bid him, on exchange or escape—if Heaven should grant the latter—find again Flora, and in her companionship, at last unhindered, choose! Yes, that would be justice and wisdom, mercy and true love, all in one. But could she do it, say it? She sprang up in bed to answer, "No-o-o! no, she was no bloodless fool, she was a woman! Oh, God of mercy and true love, no! For reasons invincible, no! but most of all for one reason, one doubt, vile jealousy's cure and despair's antidote, slow to take form but growing as her strength revived, clear at last and all-sufficing; a doubt infinitely easier, simpler, kinder, and more blessed than to doubt true love. Nay, no doubt, but a belief! the rational, life-restoring belief, that in that awful hour of twilight between the hosts, of twilight and delirium, what she had seemed to see she had but seemed to see. Not all, ah, no, not all! Hilary alive again and grappling with death to come at her call had been real, proved real; the rest a spectre of her fevered brain! Meeting him now—and, oh, to meet him now!—there should be no questionings or explainings, but while he poured forth a love unsullied and unshaken she, scarce harkening, would with battle haste tell him, her life's commander, the one thing of value, outvaluing all mere lovers' love: The fact that behind a chimney-panel of Callender House, in its old trivial disguise, lay yet that long-lost fund pledged to

Kincaid's Battery

Mobile's defense—by themselves as lovers, by poor war-wasted Kincaid's Battery, and by all its scattered sisters; the fund which must, as nearly on the instant as his and her daring could contrive, be recovered and borne thither for the unlocking of larger, fate-compelling resources of deliverance.

One day Victorine came to Anna with ecstasy in her almond eyes and much news on her lips. "To bigin small," she said, Flora and her grandmother had "arrive' back ag-ain" at dawn that morning! Oddly, while Anna forced a smile, her visitor's eyes narrowed and her lips tightened. So they sat, Anna's smile fading out while her soul's troubles inwardly burned afresh, Victorine's look growing into clearer English than her Creole tongue could have spoken. "I trust her no more," it said. "Long have I doubted her, and should have told you sooner but for—Charlie; but now, dead in love as you know me still to be, you have my conviction. That is all for the present. There is better news."

The ecstasy gleamed again and she gave her second item. These weeks she had been seeking, for herself and a guardian aunt, a passport into the Confederacy and lo! here it lay in her pretty hand.

"Deztitution!" she joyfully confessed to be the plea on which it had been procured—by Doctor Sevier through Colonel—guess!—"Grinleaf!—juz' riturn'" from service in the field.

And how were the destitute pair to go?

Ah! did Anna "rim-emb'r" a despatch-boat of unrivalled speed whose engines Hilary Kin——?

Yes, ah, yes!

The Flag-of-Truce Boat

On which she and others had once——?

Yes, yes!

And which had been captured when the city fell? That boat was now lying off Callender House! Did Anna *not* know that her shattered home, so long merely the headquarters of a blue brigade, had lately become of large, though very quiet, importance as a rendezvous of big generals who by starlight paced its overgrown garden alleys debating and planning something of great moment? Doctor Sevier had found that out and had charged Victorine to tell it with all secrecy to the biggest general in Mobile the instant she should reach there. For she was to go by that despatch-boat.

"Aw-dinner-illy," she said, a flag-of-truce craft might be any old tub and would go the short way, from behind the city and across the lakes, not all round by the river and the Chandeleur Islands. But this time—that very morning—a score or so of Confederate prisoners (officers, for exchange) had been put aboard that boat, bound for Mobile. Plainly the whole affair was but a mask for reconnaissance, the boat, swiftest in all the Gulf, to report back at top speed by way of the lakes. But!—the aunt would not go at all! Never having been a mile from her door, she was begging off in a palsy of fright, and here was the niece with a deep plot—ample source of her ecstasy —a plot for Anna, duly disguised, to go in the aunt's place, back to freedom, Dixie, and the arms of Constance and Miranda.

Anna trembled. She could lovingly call the fond schemer, over and over, a brave, rash, generous little heroine and lay caresses on her twice and again, but to know whether this was Heaven's leading was beyond her. She paced the room. She clasped her brow. A full half of her own great purpose (great to her at least) seemed all at once as good as achieved, yet it was but the second half, as useless without the first as half a bridge on the far side of the flood. "I cannot go!" she moaned. For the first half was Hilary, and he—she saw it without asking—was on this cartel of exchange.

Gently she came and took her rescuer's hands: "Dear child! If—if while there was yet time—I had only got a certain word to—*him*—you know? But, ah, me! I keep it idle yet; a secret, Victorine, a secret worth our three lives! oh, three times three hundred lives! Even now——"

"Give it me, Anna! Give it! Give it me, that sick-rate! I'll take it him!"

Anna shook her head: "Ah, if you could—in time! Or even—even without him, letting him go, if just you and I—Come!" They walked to and fro in embrace: "Dear, our front drawing-room, so ruined, you know, by that shell, last year——"

"Ah, the front? no! The behine, yes, with those two hole' of the shell and with thad *beegue* hole in the floor where it cadge fiah."

"Victorine, I could go—with you—in that boat, if only I could be for one minute in that old empty front room alone."

Victorine halted and sadly tossed a hand: "Ah! h-amptee, yes, both the front and the back—till yes-teh-day! This morning, the front, no! Juz' sinze laz' week they 'ave brick' up bitwin them cloze by

that burned hole, to make of the front an office, and
now the front 't is o'cupy!"

"Oh, not as an office, I hope?"

"Worse! The worse that can be! They 'ave
stop' five prisoner' from the boat and put them yondeh.
Since an hour Col-on-el Grinleaf he tol' me that—
and she's ad the bottom, that Flora! Bicause—"
The speaker gazed. Anna was all joy.

"Because what?" demanded Anna, "because
Hil——?"

"Yaas! bicause he's one of them! Ringgleadeh!
I dunno, me, what is that, but tha'z what he's accuse'
—ringg-leadingg!"

Still the oblivious Anna was glad. "It *is* Flora's
doing," she gratefully cried. "She's done it! done
it for us and our cause!"

"Ah-h! not if she know herseff!"

Anna laughed the discussion down: "Come, dear,
come! the whole thing opens to me clear and
wide!"

Not so clear or wide as she thought. True, the
suffering Flora was doing this, in desperate haste;
but not for Anna, if she knew herself. Yet when
Anna, in equal haste, made a certain minute, lengthy
writing and, assisted by that unshaken devotee,
her maid, and by Victorine, baked five small cakes
most laughably alike (with the writing in one)
and laid them beside some plainer food in a pretty
basket, the way still seemed wide enough for patriotism.

Now if some one would but grant Victorine leave
to bestow this basket! As she left Anna she gave her

pledge to seek this favor of any one else rather than of
Greenleaf; which pledge she promptly broke, with a
success that fully reassured her cheerful conscience.

LXII

FAREWELL, JANE!

"Happiest man in New Orleans!"

So called himself, to Colonel Greenleaf, the large,
dingy-gray, lively-eyed Major Kincaid, at the sentinelled
door of the room where he and his four wan fellows,
snatched back from liberty on the eve of release, were
prisoners in plain view of the vessel on which they were
to have gone free.

With kind dignity Greenleaf predicted their un-
doubted return to the craft next morning. Strange
was the difference between this scene and the one in
which, eighteen months before, these two had last
been together in this room. The sentry there knew
the story and enjoyed it. In fact, most of the blue
occupants of the despoiled place had a romantic feeling,
however restrained, for each actor in that earlier epi-
sode. Yet there was resentment, too, against Greenleaf's clemencies.

"Wants?" said the bedless captive to his old chum,
"no, thank you, not a want!" implying, with his eyes,
that the cloud overhanging Greenleaf for favors shown
to—hmm!—certain others was already dark enough.
"We've *parlor* furniture galore," he laughed, pointing
out a number of discolored and broken articles that
had been beautiful. One was the screen behind
which the crouching Flora had heard him tell the ruin

Farewell, Jane!

of her Mobile home and had sworn revenge on this home and on its fairest inmate.

During the evening the prisoners grew a bit noisy, in song; yet even when their ditties were helped out by a rhythmic clatter of boot-heels and chair-legs the too indulgent Greenleaf did not stop them. The voices were good and the lines amusing not merely to the guards here and there but to most of their epauleted superiors who, with lights out for coolness, sat in tilted chairs on a far corner of the front veranda to catch the river breeze. One lay was so antique as to be as good as new:

"Our duck swallowed a snail,
And her eyes stood out with wonder.
Our duck swallowed a snail,
And her eyes stood out with wonder
Till the horns grew out of her tail, tail, tail,

Tail,	Tail,
Tail,	Tail,
Tail,	Tail,
And tore it	All asunder.

Farewell, Jane!

Our old horse fell into the well
Around behind the stable.
Our old horse fell into the well
Around behind the stable.
He couldn't fall all the way but he fell,

Fell,
Fell,
Fell,
Fell,
Fell,
Fell,
As far as he was able.
Farewell, Jane!"

339

Kincaid's Battery

It is here we may safest be brief. The literature of prison escapes is already full enough. Working in the soft mortar of so new a wall and worked by one with a foundryman's knowledge of bricklaying, the murdered Italian's stout old knife made effective speed as it kept neat time with the racket maintained for it. When the happiest man in New Orleans warily put head and shoulders through the low gap he had opened, withdrew them again and reported to his fellows, the droll excess of their good fortune moved the five to livelier song, and as one by one the other four heads went in to view the glad sight the five gave a yet more tragic stanza from the farewell to Jane. The source of their delight was not the great ragged hole just over the intruding heads, in the ceiling's lath and plaster, nor was it a whole corner torn off the grand-piano by the somersaulting shell as it leaped from the rent above to the cleaner one it had left at the baseboard in the room's farther end. It was that third hole, burned in the floor; for there it opened, shoulder wide, almost under their startled faces, free to the basement's floor and actually with the rough ladder yet standing in it which had been used in putting out the fire. That such luck could last a night was too much to hope.

Yet it lasted. The songs were hushed. The room whence they had come was without an audible stir. Sleep stole through all the house, through the small camp of the guard in the darkened grove, the farther tents of the brigade, the anchored ships, the wide city, the starlit landscape. Out in that rear garden-path where Madame Valcour had once been taken to see the head-high wealth of roses two generals, who had been there

340

through all the singing, still paced to and fro and talked, like old Brodnax at Carrollton in that brighter time, "not nearly as much alone as they seemed." One by one five men in gray, each, for all his crouching and gliding, as true and gallant a gentleman as either of those commanders, stole from the house's basement and slipped in and out among the roses. Along a back fence a guard walked up and down. Two by two, when his back was turned, went four of the gliding men, as still as bats, over the fence into a city of ten thousand welcome hiding-places. The fifth, their "ringg-leadeh," for whom they must wait concealed until he should rejoin them, lingered in the roses; hovered so close to the path that he might have touched its occupants as they moved back and forth; almost— to quote his uncle——

"Sat in the roses and heard the birds sing"—

heard blue birds, in soft notes not twittered, muttered as by owls, revealing things priceless for Mobile to know.

Bragg's gray army, he heard, was in far Chattanooga facing Rosecrans, and all the slim remnants of Johnston's were hurrying to its reinforcement. Mobile was merely garrisoned. Little was there save artillery. Here in New Orleans lay thousands of veterans flushed with their up-river victories, whose best and quickest aid to Rosecrans would be so to move as to turn Bragg's reinforcements back southward. A cavalry dash across the pine-barrens of East Louisiana to cut the railroad along the Mississippi-Alabama line, a quick joint movement of land and naval forces by way of the lakes, sound, and gulf, and Mobile would fall.

341

These things and others, smaller yet more startling, the listener learned of, not as pastime talk, but as a vivid scheme already laid, a mine ready to be sprung if its secret could be kept three days longer; and now he hurried after his four compatriots, his own brain teeming with a counterplot to convey this secret through the dried-up swamps to the nearest Confederate telegraph station while Anna should bear it (and the recovered treasure) by boat to Mobile, two messengers being so many times surer than one.

Early next morning Madame Valcour, entering an outer room from an inner one, found Flora writing a note. The girl kept on, conscious that her irksome critic was taking keen note of a subtle, cruel decay of her beauty, a spiritual corrosion that, without other fault to the eye, had at last reached the surface in a faint hardening of lines and staleness of bloom. Now she rose, went out, despatched her note and returned. Her manner, as the two sat down to bread and coffee, was bright though tense.

"From Greenleaf?" inquired her senior, "and to the same?"

The girl shook her fair head and named one of his fellow-officers at Callender House: "No, Colonel Greenleaf is much too busy. Hilary Kincaid has——"

"Esca-aped?" cried the aged one, flashed hotly, laughed, flashed again and smiled. "That Victorine kitten—with her cakes! And you—and Greenleaf—hah! you three catspaws—of one little—Anna!"

Flora jauntily wagged a hand, then suddenly rose and pointed with a big bread knife: "Go, dress! We'll save the kitten—if only for Charlie! Go! *she must*

The Iron-clad Oath

leave town at once. Go! But, ah, grannie dear,"
—she turned to a window—"for Anna, spite of all
we can do, I am af-raid—Ship Island! Poor *Anna!*"
At the name her beautiful arm, in one swift motion,
soared, swung, drove the bright steel deep into the
window-frame and left it quivering.

"Really," said a courteous staff-officer as he and
Doctor Sevier alighted at the garden stair of Callender
House and helped Anna and her maid from a public
carriage, "only two or three of us will know you're"—
His smile was awkward. The pale doctor set his jaw.
Anna musingly supplied the term:

"A prisoner." She looked fondly over the house's
hard-used front as they mounted the steps. "If they'd
keep me here, Doctor," she said at the top, "I'd
be almost happy. But"—she faced the aide-de-camp
—"they won't, you know. By this time to-morrow I
shall be"—she waved playfully—"far away."

"Mainland, or island?" grimly asked the Doctor.

She did not know. "But I know, now, how a rabbit feels with the hounds after her. Honestly," she
said again to the officer, "I wish I might have her
cunning." And the soldier murmured, "Amen."

LXIII

THE IRON-CLAD OATH

UNDER Anna's passive air lay a vivid alertness to
every fact in range of eye or ear.

Any least thing now might tip the scale for life or
death, and while at the head of the veranda steps she

spoke of happiness her distressed thought was of Hilary's madcap audacity, how near at hand he might be even then, under what fearful risk of recognition and capture. She was keenly glad to hear two men complain that the guard about the house and grounds was to-day a new one awkward to the task. Of less weight now it seemed that out on the river the despatch-boat had shifted her berth down-stream and with steam up lay where the first few wheel turns would put her out of sight. Indoors, where there was much official activity, it relieved her to see that neither Hilary's absence nor her coming counted large in the common regard. The brace of big generals were in the library across the hall, busy on some affair much larger than this of "ourn."

The word was the old coachman Israel's. What a tender joy it was to find him in the wretched drawing-room trying to make it decent for her and dropping his tears as openly as the maid. With what a grace, yet how boldly, he shut the door between them and blue authority. While the girl arranged on a table, for Anna's use, a basket of needlework brought with them he honestly confessed his Union loyalty, yet hurriedly, under his breath, bade Anna not despair, and avowed a devotion to the safety and comfort of "ole mahs's and mis's sweet baby" as then and for-ever his higher law. He was still autocrat of the base-ment, dropsied with the favor of colonels and generals, deferential to "folks," but a past-master in taking liberties with things. As he talked he so corrected the maid's arrangement of the screen that the ugly hole in the wall was shut from the view of visitors,

The Iron-clad Oath

though left in range of Anna's work-table, and as Anna rose at a tap on the door, with the gentle ceremony of the old home he let in Doctor Sevier and Colonel Greenleaf and shut himself out.

"Anna," began the Doctor, "There's very little belief here that you're involved in this thing."

"Why, then," archly said Anna, "who is?"

"Ah, that's the riddle. But they say if you'll just take the oath of allegiance——"

Anna started so abruptly as to imperil her table. Her color came and her voice dropped to its lowest note as she said between long breaths: "No!—no!—no!".

But the Doctor spoke on:

"They believe that if *you* take it you'll keep it, and they say that the moment you take it you may go free, here or anywhere—to Mobile if you wish."

Again Anna flinched: "Mobile!" she murmured, and then lifting her eyes to Greenleaf's, repeated, "No! No, not for my life. Better Ship Island."

Greenleaf reddened. "Anna," put in the Doctor, but she lifted a hand:——

"They've never offered it to you, Doctor? H-oh! They'd as soon think of asking one of our generals. They'd *almost* as soon"—the corners of her lips hinted a smile—"ask Hilary Kincaid."

"I've never advised any one against it, Anna."

"Well, I do!—every God-fearing Southern man and woman. A woman is all I am and I may be shortsighted, narrow, and foolish, but—Oh, Colonel Greenleaf, you shouldn't have let Doctor Sevier take this burden for you. It's hard enough——"

345

Kincaid's Battery

The Doctor intervened: "Anna, dear, this old friend of yours"—laying a finger on Greenleaf—"is in a tight place. Both you and Hilary——"

"Yes, I know, and I know it's not fair to him. Lieutenant—Colonel, I mean, pardon me!—you sha'n't be under odium for my sake or his. As far as I stand accused I must stand alone. The one who must go free is that mere child Victorine, on her pass, to-day, this morning. When I hear the parting gun of that boat down yonder I want to know by it that Victorine is safely on her way to Mobile, as she would be had she not been my messenger yesterday."

"She carried nothing but a message?"

"Nothing but a piece of writing—mine! Colonel, I tell you faithfully, whatever Major Kincaid broke prison with was not brought here yesterday by any one and was never in Victorine's hands."

"Nor in yours, either?" kindly asked Greenleaf.

Anna caught her breath and went redder than ever. Doctor Sevier stirred to speak, but Anna's maid gave her a soft thrust, pointed behind the screen, and covered a bashful smile with her apron. Anna's blush became one of mirth. Her eyes went now to the Doctor and again to the broken wall.

"Israel!" she laughed, "why do you enter——?"

"On'y fitten' way, missie. House so full o' comin' and goin', and me havin' dis cullud man wid me."

Out on the basement ladder, at the ragged gap of Israel's "on'y fittin' way," was visible, to prove his word, another man's head, white-turbaned like his own, and two dark limy hands passing in a pail of mortar. Welcome distraction. True, Greenleaf's luck-

346

less question still stood unanswered, but just then an orderly summoned him to the busy generals and spoke aside to Doctor Sevier.

"Miss Valcour," explained the Doctor to Anna.

"Oh, Doctor," she pleaded, "I want to see her! Beg them, won't you, to let her in?"

LXIV

"NOW, MR. BRICK-MASON,—"

AMID the much coming and going that troubled Israel—tramp of spurred boots, clank of sabres, seeking, meeting and parting of couriers and aides— Madame Valcour, outwardly placid, inwardly terrified, found opportunity to warn her granddaughter, softly, that unless she, the granddaughter, could get that look of done-for agony out of her eyes, the sooner and farther they fled this whole issue, this fearful entanglement, the better for them.

But brave Flora, knowing the look was no longer in the eyes alone but had for days eaten into her visage as age had for decades into the grandam's, made no vain effort to paint it out with smiles but accepted and wore it in show of a desperate solicitude for Anna. Yet this, too, was futile, and before Doctor Sevier had exchanged five words with her she saw that to him the make-up was palpable and would be so to Greenleaf. Poor Flora! She had wrestled her victims to the edge of a precipice, yet it was she who at this moment, this dazzling September morning, seemed doomed to go first over the brink. Had not both Hilary and Anna met again this Greenleaf and through him found answer for all their burning questions? She could not doubt her web of deceptions had been torn to shreds, cast to the winds. Not one of the three could she now hope to confront successfully, much less any two of them together. To name no earlier reason—having reached town just as Kincaid was being sent out of it, she had got him detained on a charge so frivolous that how to sustain it now before Greenleaf and his generals she was tortured to contrive.

Yet something must be done. The fugitive must be retaken and retained, the rival deported, and, oh, Hilary Kincaid! as she recalled her last moment with you on that firing-line behind Vicksburg, shame and rage outgrew despair, and her heart beat hot in a passion of chagrin and then hotter, heart and brain, in a frenzy of ownership, as if by spending herself she had bought you, soul and body, and if only for self-vindication would have you from all the universe.

"The last wager and the last card," she smilingly remarked to her kinswoman, "they sometimes win out," and as the smile passed added, "I wish I had that bread-knife."

To Doctor Sevier her cry was, "Oh, yes, yes! Dear Anna! Poor Anna! Yes, before I have to see any one else, even Colonel Greenleave! Ah, please, Doctor, beg him he'll do me that prizelezz favor, and that for the good God's sake he'll keep uz, poor Anna and me, not long waiting!"

Yet long were the Valcours kept. It was the common fate those days. But Flora felt no title to the common fate, and while the bustle of the place went

on about them she hiddenly suffered and, mainly for
the torment it would give her avaricious companion,
told a new reason for the look in her eyes. Only a
few nights before she had started wildly out of sleep
to find that she had *dreamed* the cause of Anna's ir-
reconcilable distress for the loss of the old dagger.
The dream was true on its face, a belated perception
awakened by bitterness of soul, and Madame, as she
sat dumbly marvelling at its tardiness, chafed the more
against each minute's present delay, seeing that now
to know if Kincaid, or if Anna, held the treasure was
her liveliest hankering.

Meantime the captive Anna was less debarred than
they. As Greenleaf and the Doctor, withdrawing,
shut her door, and until their steps died away, she had
stood by her table, her wide thought burning to know
the whereabouts, doings, and plight of him, once more
missing, with whom a scant year-and-a-half earlier—
if any war-time can be called scant—she had stood
on that very spot and sworn the vows of marriage: to
know his hazards now, right now! with man; police,
informer, patrol, picket, scout; and with nature; the
deadly reptiles, insects, and maladies of thicketed swamp
and sun-beaten, tide-swept marsh; and how far he
had got on the splendid mission which her note, with
its words of love and faith and of patriotic abnegation,
had laid upon him.

Now eagerly she took her first quick survey of the
room she knew so well. Her preoccupied maid was
childishly questioning the busy Israel as he and the
man out on the basement ladder removed bricks from
the edges of the ragged opening between them.

"Can't build solid ef you don't staht solid," she heard the old coachman say. She glided to the chimney-breast, searching it swiftly with her eyes and now with her hands. Soilure and scars had kept the secret of the hidden niche all these months, and neither stain, scar, nor any sign left by Hilary or Flora betrayed it now. Surely *this* was the very panel Flora had named. Yet dumbly, rigidly it denied the truth, for Hilary, having reaped its spoil, had, to baffle his jailors, cunningly made it fast. And time was flying! Tremblingly the searcher glanced again to the door, to the screen, to the veranda windows—though these Israel had rudely curtained—and then tried another square, keenly harkening the while to all sounds and especially to the old negro's incessant speech:

"Now, Mr. Brick-mason, ef you'll climb in hyuh I'll step out whah you is and fetch a bucket o' warteh. Gal, move one side a step, will you?"

While several feet stirred lightly Anna persisted in her trembling quest—not to find the treasure, dear Heaven, but only to find it gone. Would that little be denied? So ardent was the mute question that she seemed to have spoken it aloud, and in alarm looked once more at the windows, the door, the screen—the screen! A silence had settled there and as her eye fell on it the stooping mason came from behind it, glancing as furtively as she at windows and door and then exaltedly to her. She stiffened for outcry and flight, but in the same instant he straightened up and she knew him; knew him as right here she had known him once before in that same disguise, which the sad fortunes of their cause had prevented his further use of till now. He started forward, but with beseeching signs and whispers, blind to everything between them but love and faith, she ran to him. He caught her to his heart and drew her behind the screen under the enraptured eyes of her paralyzed maid. For one long breath of ecstasy the rest of the universe was nothing. But then——

"The treasure?" she gasped. "The dagger?"

He showed the weapon in its precious scabbard and sought to lay it in her hands, but—"Oh, why! why!" she demanded, though with a gaze that ravished his,— "Why are you not on your way——?"

"Am!" he softly laughed. "Here, leave me the dirk, but take the sheath. Everything's there that we put there long ago, beloved, and also a cypher report of what I heard last night in the garden—never mind what!—*take it*, you will save Mobile! Now both of you slip through this hole and down the ladder and quietly skedaddle—quick—come!"

"But the guards?"

"Just brass it out and walk by them. Victorine's waiting out behind with all her aunt's things at a house that old Israel will tell you of—listen!" From just outside the basement, near the cisterns, a single line of song rose drowsily and ceased:

"Heap mo' dan worteh-million juice——"

"That's he. It means come on. Go!" He gathered a brick and trowel and rang them together as if at work. The song answered:

"Aw 'possum pie aw roasted goose——"

The trowel rang on. Without command from her

mistress the maid was crouching into the hole. In the noise Anna was trying to press an anxious query upon Hilary, but he dropped brick and tool and snatched her again into his embrace.

"Aw soppin's o' de gravy pan——"

called the song. The maid was through!

"But you, Hilary, my life?" gasped Anna as he forced her to the opening.

"The swamp for me!" he said, again sounding the trowel. "I take this"—the trowel—"and walk out through the hall. Go, my soul's treasure, go!"

Anna, with that art of the day which remains a wonder yet, gathered her crinoline about her feet and twisted through and out upon the ladder. Hilary seized a vanishing hand, kissed it madly, and would have loosed it, but it clung till his limy knuckles went out and down and her lips sealed on them the distant song's fourth line as just then it came:

"De ladies loves de ladies' man!"

As mistress and maid passed in sight of the dark singer he hurried to them, wearing the bucket of water on his turban as lightly as a hat. "Is you got to go so soon?" he asked, and walked beside them. Swiftly, under his voice, he directed them to Victorine and then spoke out again in hearing of two or three blue troopers. "You mus' come ag'in, whensomeveh you like."

They drew near a guard: "Dese is ole folks o' mine, Mr. Gyuard, ef you please, suh, dess a-lookin' at de ole home, suh."

352

" Now, Mr. Brick-Mason—"

"We were admitted by Colonel Greenleaf," said Anna, with a soft brightness that meant more than the soldier guessed, and he let them out, feeling as sweet, himself, as he tried to look sour.

"Well, good-by, Miss Nannie," said the old man, "I mus' recapitulate back to de house; dey needs me pow'ful all de time. Good luck to you! Gawd bless you! . . . Dass ow ba-aby, Mr. Gyuard—Oh, Lawd, Lawd, de days I's held dat chile out on one o' dese ole han's!" He had Flora's feeling for stage effects.

Toiling or resting, the Southern slaves were singers. With the pail on his head and with every wearer of shoulder-straps busy giving or obeying some order, it was as normal as cock-crowing that he should raise yet another line of his song and that from the house the diligent bricklayer should reply.

Sang the water-carrier:

> "I's natch-i-ully gallant wid de ladies,——"

and along with the trowel's tinkle came softly back,

> "I uz bawn wid a talent fo' de ladies."

For a signal the indoor singer need not have gone beyond that line, but the spirit that always grew merry as the peril grew, the spirit which had made Kincaid's Battery the fearfulest its enemies ever faced, insisted:

> "You fine it on de map o' de contrac' plan,
> I's boun' to be a ladies' man!"

Kincaid's Battery

LXV

FLORA'S LAST THROW

NORMAL as cock-crowing seemed the antiphony to the common ear, which scarcely noticed the rareness of the indoor voice. But Greenleaf's was not the common ear, nor was Flora Valcour's.

To her that closing strain made the torture of inaction finally unbearable. Had Anna heard? Leaving Madame she moved to a hall door of the room where they sat. Was Anna's blood surging like her own? It could not! Under what a tempest of conjectures she looked down and across the great hall to the closed and sentinelled door of that front drawing-room so rife with poignant recollections. There, she thought, was Anna. From within it, more faintly now, came those sounds of a mason at work which had seemed to ring with the song. But the song had ceased. About the hall highly gilded officers conferred alertly in pairs or threes, more or less in the way of younger ones who smartly crossed from room to room. Here came Greenleaf! Seeking her? No, he would have passed unaware, but her lips ventured his name.

Never had she seen such a look in his face as that with which he confronted her. Grief, consternation, discovery and wrath were all as one save that only the discovery and wrath meant her. She saw how for two days and nights he had been putting this and that and this and that and this and that together until he had guessed her out. Sternly in his eyes she perceived contumely withholding itself, yet even while she felt the

354

Flora's Last Throw

done-for cry heave through her bosom, and the floor fail like a sinking deck, she clung to her stage part, babbled impromptu lines.

"Doctor Sevier—?" she began——

"He had to go."

Again she read the soldier's eyes. God! he was comparing her changed countenance—a fool could see he was!—with Anna's! both smitten with affliction, but the abiding peace of truth in one, the abiding war of falsehood in the other. So would Kincaid do if he were here! But the stage waited: "Ah, Colonel, Anna! poor Anna!" Might not the compassion-wilted supplicant see the dear, dear prisoner? She rallied all her war-worn fairness with all her feminine art, and to her amazement, with a gleam of purpose yet without the softening of a lineament, he said yes, waved permission across to the guard and left her.

She passed the guard and knocked. Quietly in the room clinked the brick-mason's work. He strongly hummed his tune. Now he spoke, as if to his helper, who seemed to be leaving him. Again she knocked, and bent her ear. The mason sang aloud:

"Some day dis worl' come to an en',
    I don't know how, I don't know when——"

She turned the door-knob and murmured, "Anna!"

The bricklaying clinked, tapped and scraped on. The workman hummed again his last two lines.

"Who is it?" asked a feigned voice which she knew so instantly to be Kincaid's that every beat of her heart jarred her frame.

"'Tis I, Anna, dear. 'Tis Flora." She was mindful

of the sentry, but all his attention was in the busy hall.

There came a touch on the inner door-knob. "Go away!" murmured the manly voice, no longer disguised. "In God's name! for your own sake as well as hers, go instantly!"

"No," melodiously replied Flora, in full voice for the sentry's ear, but with resolute pressure on the door, "no, not at all. . . . No, I muz' not, cannot."

"Then wait one moment till you hear me at work!"

She waited. Presently the trowel sounded again and its wielder, in a lowered tone, sang with it:

> "Dat neveh trouble Dandy Dan
> Whilst de ladies loves de ladies' man."

At the first note she entered with some idle speech, closed the door, darted her glance around, saw no one, heard only the work and the song and sprang to the chimney-breast. She tried the panel—it would not yield! Yet there, as if the mason's powerful hands had within that minute reopened and reclosed it, were the wet marks of his fingers. A flash of her instinct for concealment bade her wipe them off and she had barely done so when he stepped from the screen, fresh from Israel's water-bucket, drying his face on his hands, his hands on his face and un-turbaned locks, prison-worn from top to toe, but in Dixie's full gray and luminous with the unsmiling joy of danger.

"It's not there," he loudly whispered, showing the bare dagger. "Here it is. She has the rest, scabbard and all."

Flora clasped her hands as in ecstasy: "And is free? surely free?"

Flora's Last Throw

"Almost! Surely when that despatch-boat fires!" In a few rapid words Hilary told the scheme of Anna's flight, at the same time setting the screen aside so as to show the hole in the wall nearly closed, humming his tune and ringing the trowel on the brickwork.

Flora made new show of rapture. Nor was it all mere show. Anna escaping, the treasure would escape with her, and Flora be thrown into the dungeon of penury. Yet let them both go, both rival and treasure! Love's ransom! All speed to them since they left her Hilary Kincaid and left him at her mercy. But the plight was complex and suddenly her exultation changed to affright. "My God! Hilary Kincaid," she panted, "you 'ave save' her to deztroy yo'seff! You are——"

Proudly, gaily he shook his head: "No! No! against her will I've sent her, to save——" He hushed. He had begun to say a city, Flora's city. Once more a captive, he would gladly send by Flora also, could she contrive to carry it, the priceless knowledge which Anna, after all, might fail to convey. But something—it may have been that same outdone and done-for look which Greenleaf had just noted—silenced him, and the maiden resumed where she had broken off:

"My God, Hilary Kincaid, you are in denger to be hanged a spy! Thiz minute you 'ave hide yo' dizguise in that panel!"

"You would come in," said Hilary, with a playful wave of the trowel, and turned to his work, singing:

"When I hands in my checks——"

Flora ran and clung tenderly to his arm, but with a distressed smile he clasped her wrists in one hand

357

and gently forced her back again while she asked in burning undertone, "And you 'ave run that h-awful risk for me? for me? But, why? why? why?"

"Oh!" he laughingly said, and at the wall once more waved the ringing trowel, "instinct, I reckon; ordinary manhood—to womanhood. If you had recognized me in that rig——"

"And I would! In any rigue thiz heart would reco'-nize you!"

"Then you would have had to betray me or else go, yourself, to Ship Island."

"H-o-oh! I would have gone!"

"That's what I feared," said Hilary, though while he spoke she fiercely felt that she certainly would have betrayed him; not for horror of Ship Island but because now, *after this*, no Anna Callender nor all the world conspired should have him from her alive.

He lifted his tool for silence, and fresh anger wrung her soul to see joy mount in his eyes as from somewhere below the old coachman sang:

"When I hands in my checks, O, my ladies!"

Yet she showed elation: "That means Anna and Victorine they have pazz' to the boat?"

With merry nods and airy wavings of affirmation he sang back, rang back:

"Mighty little I espec's, O, my ladies!
But whaheveh——"

Suddenly he darkened imperiously and motioned Flora away. "Now! now's your time! go! now! this instant go!" he exclaimed, and sang on:

"—I is sent——"

358

Flora's Last Throw

"Ah!" she cried, "they'll h-ask me ab-out her!"

"I don't believe it!" cried he, and sang again:

"—dey mus' un-deh-stan'——"

"Yes," she insisted, "—muz' undehstan', and they will surely h-ask me!"

"Well, let them ask their heads off! Go! at once! before you're further implicated!"

"And leave you to——?"

"Oh, doggon *me*. The moment that boat's gun sounds —if only you're out o' the way—I'll make a try. Go! for Heaven's sake, go!"

Instead, with an agony of fondness, she glided to him. Distress held him as fast and mute as at the flag presentation. But when she would have knelt he caught her elbows and held her up by force.

"No," he moaned, "you sha'n't do that."

She crimsoned and dropped her face between their contending arms while for pure anguish he impetuously added, "Maybe in God's eyes a woman has this right, I'm not big enough to know; but *as I'm made* it can't be done. I'm a man, no more, no less!"

Her eyes flashed into his: "You are Hilary Kincaid. I will stan'!"

"No,"—he loosed his hold,—"I'm *only* Hilary Kincaid and you'll go—in mercy to both of us—in simple good faith to every one we love—Oh, leave me!" He swung his head in torture: "I'd sooner be shot for a spy or a coward than be the imbecile this makes me." Then all at once he was fierce: "Go!"

Almost below her breath she instantly replied, "I will not!" She stood at her full, beautiful height. "To-

359

gether we go or together stay. List-en!—no-no, not
for *that*." (Meaning the gun.) In open anger she
crimsoned again: "'Twill shoot, all right, and Anna,
she'll go. Yes, she will *leave* you. She can do that.
And you, you can sen' her away!"

He broke in with a laugh of superior knowledge and
began to draw back, but she caught his jacket in both
hands, still pouring forth,—"She *has* leave you—to
me! me to you! My God! Hilary Kincaid, could she
do that if she love' you? She don't! She knows not
how—and neither you! But you, ah, you shall learn.
She, she never can!" Through his jacket her knuckles
felt the bare knife. Her heart leapt.

"Let go," he growled, backing away and vainly dis-
engaging now one of her hands and now the other.
"My trowel's too silent."

But she clung and dragged, speaking on wildly:
"You know, Hilary, you know? *You love me.* Oh,
no-no-no, don' look like that, I'm not crazee." Her
deft hands had got the knife, but she tossed it into the
work-basket: "Ah, Hilary Kincaid, oft-en we love where
we thing we do not, and oft-en thing we love where we
do not——"

He would not hear: "Oh, Flora Valcour! You
smother me in my own loathing—oh, God send that
gun!" The four hands still strove.

"Hilary, list-en me yet a moment. See me. Flora
Valcour. Could Flora Valcour do like this—*ag-ains'
the whole nature of a woman*—if she——?"

"Stop! stop! you shall not——"

"If she di'n' know, di'n' feel, di'n' see, thad you are
loving her?"

Flora's Last Throw

"Yet God knows I've never given cause, except as——"

"A ladies' man?" prompted the girl and laughed.

The blood surged to his brow. A wilder agony was on hers as he held her from him, rigid; "Enough!" he cried; "We're caged and doomed. Yet you still have this one moment to save us, *all of us*, from lifelong shame and sorrow."

She shook her head.

"Yes, yes," he cried. "You can. I cannot. I'm helpless now and forever. What man or woman, if I could ever be so vile as to tell it, could believe the truth of this from me? In God's name, then, go!" He tenderly thrust her off: "Go, live to honor, happiness and true love, and let me——"

"Ezcape, perchanze, to Anna?"

"Yes, if I—" He ceased in fresh surprise. Not because she toyed with the dagger lying on Anna's needlework, for she seemed not to know she did it; but because of a strange brightness of assent as she nodded twice and again.

"I will go," she said. Behind the brightness was the done-for look, plainer than ever, and with it yet another, a look of keen purpose, which the grandam would have understood. He saw her take the dirk, so grasping it as to hide it behind wrist and sleeve; but he said only, beseechingly,—"Go!"

"Stay," said another voice, and at the small opening still left in the wall, lo! the face of Greenleaf and the upper line of his blue and gilt shoulders. His gaze was on Flora. She could do nothing but gaze again. "I know, now," he continued, "your whole two-years' business. Stay just as you are till I can come round and in. Every guard is doubled and has special orders."

She dropped into a seat, staring like one demented, now at door and windows, now from one man to the other, now to the floor, while Kincaid sternly said, "Colonel Greenleaf, the reverence due from any soldier to any lady—" and Greenleaf interrupted——

"The lady may be sure of."

"And about this, Fred, you'll be—dumb?"

"Save only to one, Hilary."

"Where is she, Fred?"

"On that boat, fancying herself disguised. Having you, we're only too glad not to have her."

The retaken prisoner shone with elation: "And those fellows of last night?—got them back?"

Greenleaf darkened, and shook his head.

"Hurrah," quietly remarked the smiling Hilary.

"Wait a moment," said the blue commander, and vanished.

LXVI

"WHEN I HANDS IN MY CHECKS"

KINCAID glanced joyfully to Flora, but her horrified gaze held him speechless.

"Now," she softly asked, "who is the helplezz—the cage'—the doom'? You 'ave kill' me."

"I'll save you! There's good fighting yet, if——"

"H-oh! already, egcep' inside me, I'm dead."

"Not by half! There's time for a last shot and I've

She dropped into a seat, staring like one demented

seen it win!" He caught up the trowel, turned to his work and began to sing once more:

"When I hands in my checks, O, my ladies,
Mighty little I espec's, O, my ladies——"

He ceased and listened. Certainly, somewhere, some one had moaned. Sounds throughout the house were growing, as if final orders had set many in motion at once. For some cause unrelated to him or to Anna, to Flora or the silent boat, bugles and drums were assembling the encamped brigade. Suddenly, not knowing why, he flashed round. Flora was within half a step of him with her right arm upthrown. He seized it, but vain was the sparring skill that had won at the willow pond. Her brow was on his breast, the knife was in her left hand, she struck with thrice her natural power, an evil chance favored her, and, hot as lightning, deep, deep, the steel plunged in. He gulped a great breath, his eyes flamed, but no cry came from him or her. With his big right hand crushing her slim fingers as they clung to the hilt, he dragged the weapon forth and hurled her off.

Before he could find speech she had regained her balance and amazed him yet again with a smile. The next instant she had lifted the dagger against herself, but he sprang and snatched it, exclaiming as he drew back:—

"No, you sha'n't do that, either."

She strove after it. He held her off by an arm, but already his strength was failing. "My God!" he groaned, "it's you, Flora Valcour, who've killed me. Oh, how did—how did you—was it accid'—wasn't it accident? Fly!" He flung her loose. "For your life, fly! Oh, that gun! Oh, God send it! Fly! Oh, Anna, Anna Callender! Oh, your city, Flora Valcour, your own city! Fly, poor child! I'll keep up the sham for you!"

Starting now here, now there, Flora wavered as he reeled to the broken wall and seized the trowel. The knife dropped to the floor but he set foot on it, brandished the tool and began to sing:

"When I hands in my checks, O, my ladies——"

A cry for help rang from Flora. She darted for the door but was met by Greenleaf. "Stay!" he repeated, and tone, hand, eye told her she was a prisoner. He halted aghast at the crimson on her hands and brow, on Hilary's, on Hilary's lips and on the floor, and himself called, "Help here! a surgeon! help!" while Kincaid faced him gaily, still singing:

"Mighty little I espec's, O, my ladies——"

Stooping to re-exchange the tool for the weapon, the singer went limp, swayed, and as Greenleaf sprang to him, toppled over, lengthened out and relaxed on the arm of his foe and friend. Wild-eyed, Flora swept to her knees beside him, her face and form all horror and affright, crying in a voice fervid and genuine as only truth can make it in the common run of us, "He di'n' mean! Oh, he di'n' mean! 'Twas all accident! He di'n' mean!"

"Yes, Fred," said Hilary. "She—she—mere accident, old man. Keep it mum." He turned a suffering brow to Flora: "You'll explain for me—when"—he gathered his strength—"when the—boat's gone."

Mobile

The room had filled with officers asking "who, how, what?" "Did it himself, to cheat the gallows," Madame heard one answer another as by some fortune she was let in. She found Greenleaf chief in a group busy over the fallen man, who lay in Flora's arms, deadly pale, yet with a strong man's will in every lineament.

"Listen, Fred," he was gasping. "It'll sound. It's got to! Oh, it will! One minute, Doctor, please. My love and a city—Fred, can't some one look and see if——?"

From a lifted window curtain the young aide who had brought Anna to the house said, "Boat's off."

"Thank God!" panted Hilary. "Oh, Fred, Fred, my girl and *all!* Just a minute, Doctor,—*there!*"

A soft, heavy boom had rolled over the land. The pain-racked listener flamed for joy and half left the arms that held him: "Oh, Fred, wasn't that heaven's own music?" He tried to finish his song:

"But whaheveh I is sent, dey mus' undehstan'—"

and swooned.

LXVII

MOBILE

ABOUT a green spot crowning one of the low fortified hills on a northern edge of Mobile sat Bartleson, Mandeville, Irby, Villeneuve and two or three lieutenants, on ammunition-boxes, fire-logs and the sod, giving their whole minds to the retention of Anna and Miranda Callender, who sat on camp-stools. The absent Constance was down in the town, just then bestowing favors not possible for any one else to offer so acceptably to a certain duplicate and very self-centered Steve aged eighty days—sh-sh-sh!

The camp group's soft discourse was on the character of one whom this earliest afternoon in August they had followed behind muffled drums to his final rest. Beginning at Carrollton Gardens, they said, then in the flowery precincts of Callender House, later in that death-swept garden on Vicksburg's inland bluffs, and now in this one, of Flora's, a garden yet, peaceful and fragrant, though no part of its burnt house save the chimneys had stood in air these three years and a half, the old hero——

"Yes," chimed Miranda to whoever was saying it——

The old hero, despite the swarm of mortal perils and woes he and his brigade and its battery had come through in that period, had with a pleasing frequency—to use the worn-out line just this time more—

"Sat in the roses and heard the birds' song."

The old soldier, they all agreed, had had a feeling for roses and song, which had gilded the edges and angles of his austere spirit and betrayed a tenderness too deep hid for casual discovery, yet so vital a part of him that but for its lacerations—with every new public disaster —he never need have sunk under these year-old Vicksburg wounds which had dragged him down at last.

Miranda retold the splendid antic he had cut in St. Charles Street the day Virginia seceded. Steve recounted how the aged warrior had regained strength from Chickamauga's triumph and lost it again after Chattanooga. Two or three recalled how he had suf-

Mobile

fered when Banks' Red River Expedition desolated his fair estate and "forever lured away" his half-a-thousand "deluded people." He must have succumbed then, they said, had not the whole "invasion" come to grief and been driven back into New Orleans. New Orleans! younger sister of little Mobile, yet toward which Mobile now looked in a daily torture of apprehension. And then Hilary's beloved Bartleson put in what Anna sat wishing some one would say.

"With what a passion of disowned anxiety," he remarked, "had the General, to the last, watched every step, slip and turn in what Steve had once called 'the multifurieuse carreer' of Hilary Kincaid."

So turned the talk upon the long-time absentee, and instances were cited of those outbreaks of utter nonsense which were wont to come from him in awful moments: gibes with which no one reporting them to the uncle could ever make the "old man" smile. The youngest lieutenant (a gun-corporal that day the Battery left New Orleans) told how once amid a fearful havoc, when his piece was so short of men that Kincaid was himself down on the ground sighting and firing it, and an aide-de-camp galloped up asking hotly, "Who's in command here!" the powder-blackened Hilary had risen his tallest and replied,—

"I! . . . b, e, x, bex, Ibex!"

A gentle speculation followed as to which of all Hilary's utterances had taken finest effect on the boys, and it was agreed that most potent for good was the brief talk away back at Camp Callender, in which he had told them that, being artillery, they must know how to wait unmurmuring through months of "rotting idleness" from one deadly "tea-party" to another. For a year, now, they had done that, and done it the better because he had all that same time been forced to do likewise in New Orleans, a prisoner in hospital, long at death's door, and only now getting well.

Anna remained silent. While there was praise of him what more could she want for sweet calm?

"True," said somebody, "in these forty-odd months between March, 'Sixty-one, and August, 'Sixty-four, all hands had got their fill of war; laurels gained were softer to rest on than laurels unsprouted, and it ought to be as easy as rolling off a log for him to lie on his prison-hospital cot in "rotting idleness," lulled in the proud assurance that he had saved Mobile, or at least postponed for a year——"

"Hilary?" frowningly asked Adolphe.

"Yes," with a firm quietness said Anna.

Villeneuve gallantly amended that somebody else owned an undivided half in the glory of that salvation and would own more as soon as the Union fleet (daily growing in numbers) should try to enter the bay: a hint at Anna, of course, and at the great ram *Tennessee*, which the Confederate admiral, Buchanan, had made his flag-ship, and whose completion, while nothing else was ready but three small wooden gunboats, was due—they had made even Anna believe—to the safe delivery of the Bazaar fund.

So then she, forced to talk, presently found herself explaining how such full news of Hilary had so often come in these awful months; to wit, by the long, kind letters of a Federal nurse—and Federal officer's wife—but for whose special devotion the captive must have perished, and who, Anna revealed, was the schoolmistress banished North in 'Sixty-one. What she kept untold was that, by favor of Greenleaf, Hilary had been enabled to auction off the poor remains of his home belongings and thus to restore the returned exile her gold. The speaker let her eyes wander to an approaching orderly, and a lieutenant took the chance to mention that early drill near Carrollton, which the General had viewed from the Callenders' equipage. Their two horses, surviving the shells and famine of Vicksburg, had been among the mere half-dozen of good beasts retained at the surrender by some ruse, and——

The orderly brought Bartleson a document and Mandeville a newspaper——

And it was touching, to-day, the lieutenant persisted, to see that once so beautiful span, handsome yet, leading in the team of six that drew the draped caisson which—

"Ah, yes!" assented all.

Mandeville hurried to read out the news from Virginia, which could still reach them through besieged Atlanta. It was of the Petersburg mine and its slaughter, and thrilled every one. Yet Anna watched Bartleson open his yellow official envelope.

"Marching orders?" asked Miranda, and while his affirming smile startled every one, Steve, for some reason in the newspaper itself, put it up.

"Are the enemy's ships—?" began Anna——

"We're ordered down the bay," replied Bartleson.

"Then so are we," she dryly responded, at which all laughed, though the two women had spent much time of late on a small boat which daily made the round of the bay's defenses. In a dingy borrowed rig they hastened away toward their lodgings.

As they drove, Anna pressed Miranda's hand and murmured, "Oh, for Hilary Kincaid!"

"Ah, dear! not to be in this—'tea-party'?"

"Yes! Yes! His boys were in so many without him, from Shiloh to Port Gibson, and now, with all their first guns lost forever—theirs and ours—lost *for* them, not by them—and after all this year of idleness, and the whole battery hanging to his name as it does—oh, 'Randy, it would do more to cure his hurts than ten hospitals, there or here."

"But the new risks, Nan, as he takes them!"

"He'll take them wherever he is. I can't rest a moment for fear he's trying once more to escape."

(In fact, that is what, unknown to her, he had just been doing.)

"But, 'Randa?"

"Yes, dear?"

"Whether he's here or there, Kincaid's Battery, his other self, will be in whatever goes on, and so, of course, will the *Tennessee*."

"Yes," said Miranda, at their door.

"Yes, and it's not just all our bazaar money that's in her, nor all our toil——"

"Nor all your sufferings," interrupted Miranda, as Constance wonderingly let them in.

"Oh, nor yours! nor Connie's! nor all—his; nor our whole past of the last two interminable years; but this whole poor terrified city's fate, and, for all we know, the war's final issue! And so I—Here, Con," (handing a newspaper), "from Steve, husband."

370

By the Dawns' Early Light

(Behind the speaker Miranda, to Constance, made eager hand and lip motions not to open it there.)

"And so, 'Ran, I wish we could go ashore to-morrow, as far down the bay as we can make our usefulness an excuse, and stay!—day and night!—till—!" She waved both hands.

Constance stared: "Why, Nan Callender!"

"Now, Con, hush. You and Steve Second are non-combatants! Oh, 'Randa, let's do it! For if those ships—some of them the same we knew so well and so terribly at home—if they come I—whatever happens—I want to see it!"

LXVIII

BY THE DAWN'S EARLY LIGHT

LUCK loves to go in mask. It turned out quite as well, after all, that for two days, by kind conspiracy of Constance and Miranda, the boat trip was delayed. In that time no fleet came.

Here at the head of her lovely bay tremblingly waited Mobile, never before so empty of men, so full of women and children. Southward, from two to four leagues apart, ran the sun-beaten, breezy margins of snow-white sand-hills evergreen with weird starveling pines, dotted with pretty summer homes and light steamer-piers. Here on the Eastern Shore were the hotels: "How-ard's," "Short's," "Montrose," "Battle's Wharf" and Point Clear, where summer society had been wont to resort all the way from beloved New Orleans. Here, from Point Clear, the bay, broadening south-westward, doubled its width, and here, by and by, this eastern shore-line suddenly became its southern by returning straight westward in a long slim stretch of dazzling green-and-white dunes, and shut its waters from the Gulf of Mexico except for a short "pass" of a few hundred yards width and for some three miles of shoal water between the pass and Dauphin Island; and there on that wild sea-wall's end—Mobile Point—a dozen leagues due south from the town—sat Fort Morgan, keeping this gate, the port's main ship-channel. Here, north-west from Morgan, beyond this main entrance and the league of impassable shoals, Fort Gaines guarded Pelican Channel, while a mile further townward Fort Powell held Grant's Pass into and out of Mississippi Sound, and here along the west side, out from Mobile, down the magnolia-shaded Bay Shell Road and the bark road below it, Kincaid's Battery and the last thousand "reserves" the town's fighting blood could drip—whole platoons of them mere boys—had marched, these two days, to Forts Powell and Gaines.

All this the Callenders took in with the mind's eye as they bent over a candle-lighted map, while aware by telegraph that behind Gaines, westward on Dauphin Island, blue troops from New Orleans had landed and were then night-marching upon the fort in a black rain-storm. Furthest down yonder, under Morgan's hundred and fifteen great guns, as Anna pointed out, in a hidden east-and-west double row athwart the main channel, leaving room only for blockade-runners, were the torpedoes, nearly seventy of them. And, lastly, just under Morgan's north side, close on the channel's eastern edge, rode, with her three small gunboats, the *Tennessee*, ugly to look at but worse to meet, waiting, watching, as up here in Fort Powell, smiling at the scurviness of their assignment, watched and waited Kincaid's Battery.

Upstairs the new Steve gently wailed.

"Let me!" cried Anna, and ran.

Constance drew out Mandeville's newspaper. Miranda smiled despairingly.

"I wish, now," sighed the sister, "we'd shown it when we got it. I've had enough of keeping things from Nan Callender. Of course, even among our heroes in prison, there still may be a 'Harry Rénard'; but it's far more likely that some one's telegraphed or printed 'Hilary Kincaid' that way; for there *was* a Harry Rénard, Steve says, a captain, in Harper's cavalry, who months ago quietly died in one of our own hospitals—at Lauderdale. Now, at headquarters, Steve says, they're all agreed that the name isn't a mite more suggestive than the pure daring of the deed, and that if they had to guess who did it they'd every one guess Hilary Kincaid."

She spread the story out on her knee: Exchange of prisoners having virtually ceased, a number of captive Confederate officers had been started up the Mississippi from New Orleans, under a heavy but unwary guard, on a "tin-clad" steamer, to wear out the rest of the war in a Northern prison. Forbidden to gather even in pairs, they had yet moved freely about, often passing each other closely enough to exchange piecemeal counsels unnoticed, and all at once, at a tap of the boat's bell, had sprung, man for man, upon their keepers and instantly were masters of them, of their arms stacked on the boiler-deck and of the steamboat, which they had promptly run ashore on the East Louisiana side and burned. So ran the tale, and so broke off. Ought Anna to be told it, or not?

"No," said the sister. "After all, why should we put her again through all those sufferings that so nearly killed her after Shiloh?"

"If he would only——"

"Telegraph? How do we know he hasn't?"

Next morning the two unencumbered Callend rs went down the bay. But they found no need to leave the boat. A series of mishaps delayed her, the tide hindered, rain fell, and at length she was told to wait for orders and so lay all night at anchor just off Fort Gaines, but out of the prospective line of fire from the foe newly entrenched behind it. The rain ceased and, as one of Hilary's songs ran—

"The stars shed forth their light serene."

The ladies had the captain's room, under the pilot-house. Once Anna woke, and from the small windows that opened to every quarter except up the bay townward looked forth across the still waters and low shores. Right at hand loomed Fort Gaines. A league away northwest rose small Fort Powell, just enough from the water to show dimly its unfinished parapets. In her heart's vision she saw within it her own Kincaid's Battery, *his* and hers. South-eastward, an opposite league away, she could make out Fort Morgan, but not the *Tennessee*. The cool, briny air hung still, the wide waters barely lifted and fell. She returned and slept again until some one ran along the narrow deck under her reclosed windows, and a male voice said—

By the Dawn's Early Light

"The Yankee fleet! It's coming in!"

Miranda was dressing. Out on the small deck voices were quietly audible and the clink of a ratchet told that the boat was weighing anchor. She rang three-bells. The captain's small clock showed half-past five. Now the swiftly dressed pair opened their windows. The rising sun made a golden path across the tranquil bay and lighted up the three forts and the starry battle-cross softly stirring over each. Dauphin Island and Mobile Point were moss-green and pearly white. The long, low, velvety pulsations of the bay were blue, lilac, pink, green, bronze. But angry smoke poured from the funnels of the *Tennessee* and her three dwarf consorts, they four also showing the battle-flag, and some seven miles away, out in the Gulf, just beyond the gleaming eastern point of Sand Island, was one other sign of unrest.

"You see they're under way?" asked Anna.

Yes, Miranda saw, and sighed with the questioner. For there, once more—low crouched, war-painted and gliding like the red savages so many of them were named for, the tall ones stripped of all their upper spars, but with the pink spot of wrath flickering at every masthead —came the ships of Farragut.

The two women could not count them, so straight on were they headed, but a man near the window said there were seven large and seven less, lashed small to large in pairs. Yet other counting they did, for now out of Sand Island Channel, just west of the ships, came a shorter line—one, two, three, four strange barely discernible things, submerged like crocodiles, a hump on each of the first two, two humps on each of the others,

375

crossed the fleet's course and led the van on the sunward side to bring themselves first and nearest to Morgan, its water-battery, and the *Tennessee*.

Anna sighed while to Miranda the man overflowed with information. Ah, ah! in Hampton Roads the *Virginia* had barely coped with one of those horrors, of one hump, two guns; while here came four, whose humps were six and their giant rifles twelve.

"Twenty-two guns in our whole flotilla," the man was saying to Miranda, "and they've got nearly two hundred." The anchor was up. Gently the boat's engines held her against the flood-tide. The man had turned to add some word, when from the land side of Gaines a single columbiad roared and a huge shell screamed off into the investing entrenchments. Then some lighter guns, thirty-twos, twenty-fours, cracked and rang, and the foe replied. His shells burst over and in the fort, and a cloud of white and brown smoke rolled eastward, veiling both this scene and the remoter, sea-ward, silent, but far more momentous one of Fort Morgan, the fleet, and the *Tennessee*.

The boat crept southward into the cloud, where only Gaines was dimly visible, flashing and howling land-ward. Irby was in that flashing. Steve was back yonder in Powell with Kincaid's Battery. Through Steve, present at the reading of a will made at Vicksburg the day after Hilary's capture there, Irby had just noti-fied Anna, for Hilary, that their uncle had left everything to him, Adolphe. She hoped it was true, but for once in her life had doubts without discomfort. How idly the mind can drift in fateful moments. The bell tapped for six. As it did so the two watchers descried through a rift in the smoke the *Tennessee* signaling her grim litter, and the four crawling forward to meet the ships. Again the smoke closed in, but the small boat stole through it and hovered at its edge while the minutes passed and the foe came on. How plain to be seen was each pair, how familiar some of those taller shapes!

"The *Brooklyn*, 'Randa, right in front. And there again is the admiral's flag, on the *Hartford*. And there, with her topmasts down, is the *Richmond*—oh, 'Ran', it's the same bad dream once more!"

Not quite. There were ships new to them, great and less, whose savage names, told by the man near the window, chilled the blood with reminder of old wars and massacres: the *Winnebago, Chickasaw, Octorora, Ossipee, Metacomet, Seminole.* "Look!" said the man, pointing, "the *Tecumseh*——"

LXIX

SOUTHERN CROSS AND NORTHERN STAR

A RED streak and white sun-lit puff sprang from the leading monitor's turret, and the jarring boom of a vast gun came over the water, wholly unlike the ringing peals of Gaines's lighter armament. Now its opposite cranny puffed and thundered. The man smiled an instant. "Spitting on her hands," he said, but then murmured to himself, "Lord! look at that wind!"

"Is it bad?" asked Anna.

"It'll blow every bit of smoke into our men's eyes," he sighed.

The two white puffs melted into the perfect blue of

sea and sky unanswered. Fort Gaines and its besiegers even ceased to fire. Their fate was not in their own guns. More and more weird waxed the grisly dumbness of five-sided Morgan and the spectral silence of the oncoming league-long fleet. The light wind freshened. By the bell's six taps it was seven o'clock. The boat drifting in on the tide made Fort Gaines seem to move seaward. Miranda looked back to Fort Powell and then out to sea again.

"The worst," said Anna, reading her thought, "will be down there with the *Tennessee*."

Miranda answered low: "Suppose, Nan, that, after all, he should——?"

Anna turned sharply: "Get here? I expect it! Oh, you may gaze! I don't forget how often I've flouted Con's intuitions. But I've got one now, a big one!"

"That he's coming?"

"Been coming these two days—pure presentiment!"

"Nan, whether he is or not, if you'll tell us what Colonel Greenleaf wrote you I'll tell you——"

For a second Anna stared, Miranda wrinkling; but then, with her eyes on the fleet, she shook her head: "You're mighty good, 'Randa, you and Con, never to have asked me in all these months; but neither he nor Hilary nor I will ever tell that. I wish none of us knew it. For one thing, we don't, any of us, know clearly enough what really happened. Dear Fred Greenleaf! —if he *does* wear the blue, and *is* right now over there behind Fort Gaines!"

She stood a moment pondering a fact not in the Union soldier's letter at all; that only through his masterful, self-sacrificing intercession in military court had Hilary escaped the death of a spy. But then her thought came back to Miranda's request: "I can't tell you, for I can't tell Con. Flora's her cousin, through Steve, and if she ever marries Captain Irby she'll be Hilary's cousin, and——"

There, suddenly and once for all, the theme was dropped. Some man's quick word broke in. Fort.Morgan had veiled itself in the smoke of its own broadside. Now came its thunder and the answering flame and roar of the *Brooklyn's* bow-chaser. The battle had begun. The ship, still half a mile from its mark, was coming on as straight as her gun could blaze, her redskin ally at her side, and all the others, large and less, bounding after by twos. And now in lurid flash and steady roar the lightning and thunder darted and rolled from Morgan, its water-battery, and the Mobile squadron, and from the bow guns of the *Brooklyn* and *Hartford.*

How marvelously fire, din and smoke shriveled up the time, which the captain's small clock so mincingly ticked off. A cabin-boy brought a fragrant tray of breakfast, but the grateful ladies could only laugh at it. There was no moment to observe even the few pretty sail-boats which the fearful import and majesty of the strife lured down about them on the light side-wind.

"Has the *Tennessee* not fired yet?" anxiously asked Anna, but no one was sure. Across the breeze, that kept the near side of the picture uncurtained, she perfectly saw the *Tecumseh* close abreast of the flashing, smoke-shrouded fort, the *Brooklyn* to windward abreast of both, and the *Hartford* at the *Brooklyn's* heels with her signal fluttering to all behind, "Close order."

"Why don't the ships—?" Anna had it on her lips

to cry, when the whole sunward side of the *Brooklyn*, and then of the *Hartford*, vomited fire, iron and blinding, strangling smoke into the water-battery and the fort, where the light air held it. God's mercy! you could see the cheering of the fleet's crews, which the ear could barely gather out of the far uproar, and just as it floated to the gazers they beheld the *Tecumseh* turn square toward them and head straight across the double line of torpedoes for the *Tennessee*.

We never catch all of "whatever happens," and neither Callender saw the brave men in gray who for one moment of horror fled from their own guns in water-battery and fort; but all at once they beheld the *Tecumseh* heave, stagger, and lurch like a drunkard, men spring from her turret into the sea, the *Brooklyn* falter, slacken fire and draw back, the *Hartford* and the whole huddled fleet come to a stand, and the rallied fort cheer and belch havoc into the ships while the *Tecumseh* sunk her head, lifted her screw into air and vanished beneath the wave. They saw Mobile Point a semicircle of darting fire, and the *Brooklyn* "athwart the *Hartford's* hawse"; but they did not see, atom-small, perched high in the rigging of the flag-ship and demanding from the decks below, "why this?" and "why that?" a certain "plain sailor" well known to New Orleans and the wide world; did not see the torpedoes lying in watery ambush for him, nor hear the dread tale of them called to him from the *Brooklyn* while his ship passed astern of her, nor him command "full speed ahead" as he retorted, "Damn the torpedoes!"

They saw his ship and her small consort sweep undestroyed over the dead-line, the Brooklyn follow with hers, the Mobile gunboats rake the four with a fire they could not return, and behind them Fort Morgan and the other ships rend and shatter each other, shroud the air with smoke and thresh the waters white with shot and shell, shrapnel, canister and grape. And then they saw their own *Tennessee* ignore the monitors and charge the *Hartford*. But they beheld, too, the *Hartford's* better speed avoid the fearful blow and press on up the channel and the bay, though torn and bleeding from her foe's broadside, while her own futilely glanced or rebounded from his impenetrable mail.

Wisely, rightly their boat turned and slowly drew away toward Fort Powell and Cedar Point. Yet as from her after deck they saw the same exploit, at the same murderous cost, repeated by the *Brooklyn* and another and another great ship and their consorts, while not a torpedo did its work, they tearfully called the hour "glorious" and "victorious" for the *Tennessee* and her weak squadron, that still fought on. So it seemed to them even when more dimly, as distance and confusion grew and rain-clouds gathered, they saw a wooden ship ram the *Tennessee*, but glance off, and the slow *Tennessee* drop astern, allow a sixth tall ship and small consort to pass, but turn in the wake of the seventh and all but disembowel her with the fire of her great bow gun.

Ah, Anna! Even so, the shattered, steam-scalded thing came on and the last of the fleet was in. Yonder, a mere league eastward, it moved up the bay. Yet proudly hope throbbed on while still Mobile, behind other defenses, lay thirty miles away, while her gunboats still raked the ships, while on Powell, Gaines and Morgan still floated the Southern cross, and while, down in the pass, still unharmed, paused only for breath the *Tennessee*.

"Prisoners! they are all our prisoners!" tearfully exulted the fond Callenders. But on the word they saw the scene dissolve into a new one. Through a squall of wind and rain, out from the line of ships, four of their consorts glided away eastward, flashing and howling, in chase of the overmatched gunboats, that flashed and howled in retort as they fled. On the west a Federal flotilla in Mississippi Sound, steaming up athwart Grant's Pass, opened on Fort Powell and awoke its thunders. Ah, ah! Kincaid's Battery at last! Red, white and red they sent buffet for buffet, and Anna's heart was longing anew for their tall hero and hers, when a voice hard by said, "She's coming back, sir, the *Tennessee*."

Out in the bay the fleet, about to anchor, turned and awaited the new onset. By the time it was at hand the Mobile gunboats, one burning, one fled, one captured, counted for nothing, yet on crept the *Tennessee*, still singling out the *Hartford*, and here the two Callenders, their boat hovering as near Powell and Gaines as it dared, looked on the titanic melée that fell round her. Like hounds and hunters on a bear robbed of her whelps, seventeen to one, they set upon her so thickly that their trouble was not to destroy one another. Near the beginning one cut her own flag-ship almost to the water-line. The first that smote the quarry—at ten knots speed—glanced and her broadside rolled harmless into the bay, while two guns of her monster adversary let daylight through and through the wooden ship. From the turret of a close-creeping monitor came the four-

THEY kissed
It looks stran
see how to hold
matter of cours
randa, and whe
An ambulanc
brought him ar
Side. A sail-bo
beach. Here it
as she gathered
not so weak or
with his crutch
while with reco
master and thes
He said thin
here to be secr
would yet be fo
day was lost; as
if not shrewdly
Her captain n
the junior offic
say 'the day,''
"Both," he n
one hand direct
way off Morgan
gunboats on M
the Gulf, behin
land force entre

hundred-and-forty-pound bolt of her fifteen-inch gun, crushing the lone foe terribly yet not quite piercing through. Another wooden ship charged, hit squarely a tearing blow, yet slid off, lay for a moment touching sides with the ironclad, while they lacerated each other like lion and tiger, and then dropped away. The hunted *Hartford* gave a staggering thrust and futile broadside.

So for an hour went the fight; ships charging, the *Tennessee* crawling ever after her one picked antagonist, the monitors' awful guns forever pounding her iron back and sides. But at length her mail began to yield, her best guns went silent, her smokestack was down, her steering-chains were gone, Buchanan lay heavily wounded. Of Farragut's twenty-seven hundred men more than a seventh had fallen, victims mainly of the bear and her cubs, yet there she weltered, helpless. From her grim disjointed casemate her valorous captain let down the Southern cross, the white flag rose, and instantly, everywhere, God's thunder and man's alike ceased, and the merciful heavens smiled white and blue again. But their smile was on the flag of the Union, and mutely standing in each other's embrace, with hearts as nearly right as they could know, Anna and Miranda gazed on the victorious stars-and-stripes and wept.

What caused Anna to start and glance behind she did not know; but doing so she stared an instant breathless and then, as she clutched Miranda for support, moaned to the tall, wasted, sadly smiling, crutched figure that moved closer—

"Oh, Hilary! Are you Hilary Kincaid?"

Kincaid's Battery

LXX

GAINS AND LOSSES

THEY kissed.

It looks strange written and printed, but she did not see how to hold off when he made it so tenderly manful a matter of course after his frank hand-shake with Miranda, and when there seemed so little time for words.

An ambulance drawn by the Callenders' horses had brought him and two or three others down the West Side. A sail-boat had conveyed them from the nearest beach. Here it was, now, in tow beside the steamboat as she gathered headway toward Fort Powell. He was not so weak or broken but he could point rapidly about with his crutches, the old light of command in his eyes, while with recognized authority he spoke to the boat's master and these companions.

He said things freely. There was not much down here to be secret about. Mobile had not fallen. She would yet be fought for on land, furiously. But the day was lost; as, incidentally, might be, at any moment, if not shrewdly handled, this lonesome little boat.

Her captain moved to the pilot-house. Miranda and the junior officers left Hilary with Anna. "Did you say 'the day,'" she softly asked, "or 'the bay'?"

"Both," he murmured, and with his two crutches in one hand directed her eyes: to the fleet anchored midway off Morgan, Gaines, and Powell; to the half-dozen gunboats on Mississippi Sound; to others still out in the Gulf, behind Morgan, off Mobile Point; to the blue land force entrenched behind Gaines, and to the dunes east of Morgan, where similar besiegers would undoubtedly soon be landed.

"Yes . . . Yes," she said to his few explanations. It was all so sadly clear.

"A grand fort yet," he musingly called Morgan, "but it ought to be left and blown to fare-you-well tonight, before it's surroun—— I wish my cousin were there instead of in Gaines. 'Dolphe fights well, but he knows when not to fight and that we've come, now, to where every man we've got, and every gun, counts bigger than to knock out any two of the enemy's. You know Fred's over yonder, don't you? and that Kincaid's Battery, without their field-pieces, are just here in Powell behind her heavy guns? . . . Yes, Victorine said you did; I saw her this morning, with Constance." He paused, and then spoke lower:

"Beloved?"

She smiled up to him.

"Our love's not through all the fire, yet," he said, but her smile only showed more glow.

"My soul's-mate, war-mate soldier-girl," he murmured on.

"Well?"

"If you stand true in what's before us now, before just you and me, now and for weeks to come, I want your word for it right here that your standing true shall not be for the sake of any vow you've ever made to me, or for me, or with me, in the past, the blessed, blessed past. You promise?"

"I promise," she breathed. "What is it?"

"A thing that takes more courage than I've got."

"Then how will you do it?" she lightly asked.

385

Kincaid's Battery

"By borrowing all yours. May I?"

"You may. Is it to save—our battery?"

"Our battery, yes, against their will, with others, if I can persuade the fort's commander. At low tide to-night, when the shoals can be forded to Cedar Point, I shall be"—his words grew hurried—the steamer was touching the fort's pier—the sail-boat, which was to take Anna and Miranda to where the ambulance and their own horses awaited them had cast off her painter— "I shall be the last man out of Powell and shall blow it up. Come, it may be we sha'n't meet again until I've"—he smiled—"been court-martialed and degraded. If I am, we——"

"If you are," she murmured, "you may take me to the nearest church—or the biggest—that day."

"No, no!" he called as she moved away, and again, with a darkening brow, "no, no!"

"But, "Yes, yes," she brightly insisted as she rejoined Miranda. "Yes!"

For the horses' sake the ladies went that afternoon only to "Frascati," lower limit of the Shell Road, where, in a small hour of the night Anna heard the sudden boom and long rumble that told the end of Fort Powell and salvation of its garrison.

That Gaines held out a few days, Morgan a few weeks, are heroic facts of history, which, with a much too academic shrug, it calls "magnifique, mais—!" Their splendid armament and all their priceless men fell into their besiegers' hands. Irby, haughtily declining the strictly formal courtesies of Fred Greenleaf, went to prison in New Orleans. What a New Orleans! The mailed clutch on her throat (to speak as she felt) had

Gains and Losses

grown less ferocious, but everywhere the Unionist civilian—the once browbeaten and still loathed "Northern sympathizer," with grudges to pay and losses to recoup and re-recoup—was in petty authority. Confiscation was swallowing up not industrial and commercial properties merely, but private homes; espionage peeped round every street corner and into every back window, and "A. Ward's" ante-bellum jest, that "a white man was as good as a nigger as long as he behaved himself," was a jest no more. Miss Flora Valcour, that ever faithful and daring Southerner, was believed by all the city's socially best to be living—barely living—under "the infamous Greenleaf's" year-long threat of Ship Island for having helped Anna Callender to escape to Mobile. Hence her haunted look and pathetic loss of bloom. Now, however, with him away and with General Canby ruling in place of Banks, she and her dear fragile old grandmother could breathe a little.

They breathed much. We need not repeat that the younger was a gifted borrower. She did other things equally well; resumed a sagacious activity, a two-sided tact, and got Irby paroled. On the anniversary of the day Hilary had played brick-mason a city paper (Unionist) joyfully proclaimed the long-delayed confiscation of Kincaid's Foundry and of Callender House, and announced that "the infamous Kincaid" himself had been stripped of his commission by a "rebel" court-martial. Irby promptly brought the sheet to the Valcours' lodgings, but Flora was out. When she came in, before she could lay off her pretty hat:——

"You've heard it!" cried the excited grandam. "But why so dead-alive? Once more the luck is yours!

387

Play your knave! play Irby! He's just been here! He
will return! He will propose this evening if you allow
him! Let him do it! Let him! Mobile may fall any
day! If you dilly-dally till those accursed Callenders
get back, asking, for instance, for their—ha, ha!—their
totally evaporated chest of plate—gr-r-r! Take him!
He has just shown me his uncle's will—as he calls it:
a staring forgery, but you, h-you won't mind *that*, and
the 'ladies' man'—ah, the 'ladies' man,' once you are
his cousin, he'll never let on. Take Irby! he is, as you
say, a nincompoop"—she had dropped into English—
"and seldom sober, *mais* take him! 't is the las' call of
the auctioneer, yo' fav-oreet auctioneer—with the
pointed ears and the forked black tail."

Flora replied from a mirror with her back turned:
"I'll thing ab-out it. And maybee—yes! Ezpecially
if you would do uz that one favor, lazd thing when you
are going to bed the night we are married. Yez, if you
would—ahem!—juz' blow yo' gas without turning it?"

That evening, when the accepted Irby, more nearly
happy than ever before in his life, said good-night
to his love they did not kiss. At the first stir of proffer
Flora drew back with a shudder that reddened his brow.
But when he demanded, "Why not?" her radiant shake
of the head was purely bewitching as she replied, "No,
I have n' fall' that low yet."

When after a day or so he pressed for immediate
marriage and was coyly referred to Madame, the old lady
affectionately—though reluctantly—consented. With
a condition: If the North should win the war his inheritance would be "confiz-*cate*'" and there would be
nothing to begin life on but the poor child's burned-

Gains and Losses

down home behind Mobile, unless, for mutual protection, nothing else,—except "one dollar and other valuable considerations,"—he should preconvey the Brodnax estate to the poor child, who, at least, had never been "foun' out" to have done anything to subject property of hers to confiscation.

This transfer Irby, with silent reservations, quietly executed, and the day, hour and place, the cathedral, were named   A keen social flutter ensued and presently the wedding came off—stop! That is not all. Instantly upon the close of the ceremony the bride had to be more lifted than led to her carriage and so to her room and couch, whence she sent loving messages to the bridegroom that she would surely be well enough to see him next day.   But he had no such fortune, and here claims record a fact even more wonderful than Anna's presentiment as to Hilary that morning in Mobile Bay. The day after his wedding Irby found his parole revoked and himself, with others, back in prison and invited to take the oath and go free—stand up in the war-worn gray and forswear it—or stay where they were to the war's end.   Every man of them took it—when the war was over; but until then? not one.   Not even the bridegroom robbed of his bride.   Every week or so she came and saw him, among his fellows, and bade him hold out! stand fast!   It roused their great admiration, but not their wonder.   The wonder was in a fact of which they knew nothing: That the night before her marriage Flora had specifically, minutely prophesied this whole matter to her grandmother, whose only response was that same marveling note of nearly four years earlier—

"You are a genius!"

Kincaid's Battery

LXXI

SOLDIERS OF PEACE

In March, 'Sixty-five, the Confederacy lay dying. While yet in Virginia and the Carolinas, at Mobile and elsewhere her armies daily, nightly strove on, bled on, a stricken quiet and great languor had come over her, a quiet with which the quiet ending of this tale is only in reverent keeping.

On Mobile's eastern side Spanish Fort and Fort Blakely, her last defenses, were fighting forty thousand besiegers. Kincaid's Battery was there, and there was heavy artillery, of course, but this time the "ladies' men" —still so called—had field-guns, though but three. They could barely man that number. One was a unit of the original six lost "for them, not by them," at Vicksburg, and lately recovered.

Would there were time for its story! The boys had been sent up the state to reinforce Forrest. Having one evening silenced an opposing battery, and stealing over in the night and bringing off its best gun, they had slept about "her" till dawn, but then had laughed, hurrahed, danced, and wept round her and fallen upon her black neck and kissed her big lips on finding her no other than their own old "Roaring Betsy." She might have had a gentler welcome had not her lads just learned that while they slept *the* "ladies' man" had arrived from Mobile with a bit of news glorious alike for him and them.

The same word reached New Orleans about the same date. Flora, returning from a call on Irby, brought

Soldiers of Peace

it to her grandmother. In the middle of their sitting-room, with the worst done-for look yet, standing behind a frail chair whose back she gripped with both hands, she meditatively said——

"All privieuse statement' ab-out that court-martial on the 'vacuation of Ford Powell are prim-ature. It has, with highez' approval, *acquit'* every one concern' in it." She raised the light chair to the limit of her reach and brought it down on another with a force that shivered both. Madame rushed for a door, but—"Stay!" amiably said the maiden. "Pick up the pieces—for me—eh? I'll have to pick up the pieces of you some day—soon—I hope—mm?"

She took a book to a window seat, adding as she went, "Victorine. You've not heard ab-out that, neither? She's biccome an orphan. Hmm! Also—the little beggar!—she's—married. Yes. To Charles Valcour. My God! I wish I was a man.

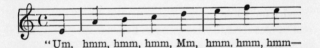

"Um, hmm, hmm, hmm, Mm, hmm, hmm, hmm—

"Leave the room!"

But these were closed incidents when those befell which two or three final pages linger to recount. The siege of Spanish Fort was the war's last great battle. From March twenty-sixth to April the eighth it was deadly, implacable; the defense hot, defiant, audacious. On the night of the eighth the fort's few hundred cannoneers spiked their heavy guns and, taking their light ones along, left it. They had fought fully

391

aware that Richmond was already lost, and on the
next day, a Sabbath, as Kincaid's Battery trundled
through the town while forty thousand women and
children—with the Callenders and little Steve—wept,
its boys knew their own going meant Mobile had
fallen, though they knew not that in that very hour
the obscure name of Appomattox was being made forever great in history.

"I reached Meridian," writes their general, "refitted
the . . . field batteries and made ready to march
across (country) and join General Joseph E. Johnston
in Carolina. The tidings of Lee's surrender soon came.
. . . But . . . the little army of Mobile remained
steadfastly together, and in perfect order and discipline
awaited the final issue of events."

It was while they so waited that Kincaid's Battery
learned of the destruction, by fire, of Callender House,
but took comfort in agreeing that now, at last, come or
fail what might, the three sweetest women that ever
lived would live up-town.

One lovely May morning a Federal despatch-boat—
yes, the one we know—sped down Mobile Bay with
many gray-uniformed men aboard, mostly of the ranks
and unaccoutred, but some of them officers still belted
for their unsurrendered swords. Many lads showed the
red artillery trim and wore jauntily on their battered
caps K. B. separated by crossed cannon. "Roaring
Betsy" had howled her last forever. Her sergeant,
Valcour, was there, with his small fond bride, both
equally unruffled by any misgiving that they would not
pull through this still inviting world happily.

Mandeville was present, his gilt braid a trifle more

gilt than any one else's. Constance and little Steve—
who later became president of the Cotton Exchange—
were with him. Also Miranda. Out forward yonder on
the upper deck, beside tall Hilary Kincaid, stood Anna.
Greenleaf eyed them from the pilot-house, where he
had retired to withhold the awkward reminder inseparable from his blue livery. In Hilary's fingers was
a writing which he and Anna had just read together.
In reference to it he was saying that while the South
had fallen to the bottom depths of poverty the North
had been growing rich, and that New Orleans, for instance, was chock full of Yankees—oh, yes, I'm afraid
that's what he called them—Yankees, with greenbacks
in every pocket, eager to set up any gray soldier who
knew how to make, be or do anything mutually profit-
able. Moved by Fred Greenleaf, who could furnish
funds but preferred, himself, never to be anything but
a soldier, the enterprising husband of the once deported but now ever so happily married schoolmistress
who——

"Yes, I know," said Anna——

Well, for a trifle, at its confiscation sale, this man
had bought Kincaid's Foundry, which now stood
waiting for Hilary to manage, control and in the end
recover to his exclusive ownership on the way to larger
things. What gave the subject an intense tenderness of
unsordid interest was that it meant for the pair—what
so many thousands of paroled heroes and the women
they loved and who loved them were hourly finding out
—that they were not such beggars, after all, but they
might even there and then name their wedding day,
which then and there they named.

Kincaid's Battery

"Let Adolphe and Flora keep the old estate and be as happy on it, and in it, as Heaven will let them; they've got each other to be happy with. The world still wants cotton, and if they'll stand for the old South's cotton we'll stand for a new South and iron; iron and a new South, Nan, my Nannie; a new and better South and even a new and better New Orl—see where we are! Right yonder the *Tennessee*——"

"Yes," interrupted Anna, "let's put that behind us —henceforth, as the boat is doing now."

The steamer turned westward into Grant's Pass. To southward lay Morgan and Gaines, floating the ensign of a saved Union. Close here on the right lay the ruins of Fort Powell. From the lower deck the boys, pressing to the starboard guards to see, singly or in pairs smiled up to Hilary's smile. Among them was Sam Gibbs, secretly bearing home the battery's colors wrapped round him next his scarred and cross-scarred body. And so, farewell Mobile. Hour by hour through the beautiful blue day, island after island, darkling green or glistering white, rose into view, drifted by between the steamer and the blue Gulf and sunk into the deep; Petit Bois, Horn Island, Ship Island, Cat Island. Now past Round Island, up Lake Borgne and through the Rigolets they swept into Pontchartrain, and near the day's close saw the tide-low, sombre but blessed shore beyond which a scant half-hour's railway ride lay the city they called home.

Across the waters westward, where the lake's margin, black-rimmed with cypresses, lapsed into a watery horizon, and the sun was going down in melancholy splendor, ran unseen that northbound railway by which

Soldiers of Peace

four years earlier they had set off for the war with ranks full and stately, with music in the air and with thousands waving them on. Now not a note, not a drumtap, not a boast nor a jest illumined their return. In the last quarter-hour aboard, when every one was on the lower deck about the forward gangway, Hilary and Anna, having chanced to step up upon a coil of rope, found it easier, in the unconscious press, to stay there than to move on, and in keeping with his long habit as a leader he fell into a lively talk with those nearest him, —Sam and Charlie close in front, Bartleson and Mandeville just at his back,—to lighten the general heaviness. At every word his listeners multiplied, and presently, in a quiet but insistent tone, came calls for a "speech" and the "ladies' man."

"No," he gaily replied, "oh, no, boys!" But his words went on and became something much like what they craved. As he ceased came the silent, ungreeted landing. Promptly followed the dingy train's short run up the shore of the New Canal, and then its stop athwart St. Charles Street, under no roof, amid no throng, without one huzza or cry of welcome, and the prompt dispersal of the outwardly burdenless wanderers, in small knots afoot, up-town, down-town, many of them trying to say over again those last words from the chief hero of their four years' trial by fire. The effort was but effort, no full text has come down; but their drift seems to have been that, though disarmed, unliveried, and disbanded, they could remain true soldiers: That the perfect soldier loves peace, loathes war: That no man can be such who cannot, whether alone or among thousands of his fellows, strive, suffer and wait with magnanimous patience, stake life and fortune, and, in extremity, fight like a whirlwind, for the victories of peace: That every setting sun will rise again *if it is a true sun:* That good-night was not good-by: and that, as for their old nickname, no one can ever be a whole true ladies' man whose *aim* is not at some title far above and beyond it—which last he said not of himself, but in behalf and by request of the mother of the guns they had gone out with and of the furled but unsullied banner they had brought home.

THE END.